Loving Luther

Center Point
Large Print

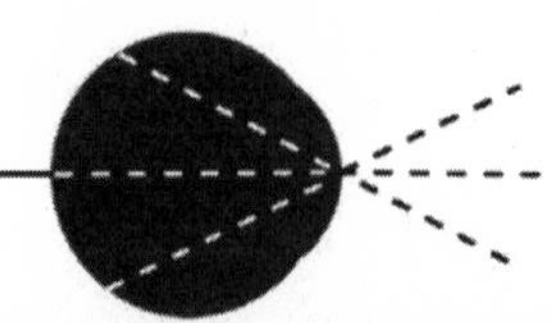

This Large Print Book carries the Seal of Approval of N.A.V.H.

Loving Luther

ALLISON PITTMAN

CENTER POINT LARGE PRINT
THORNDIKE, MAINE

This Center Point Large Print edition
is published in the year 2018 by arrangement with
Tyndale House Publishers, Inc.

Loving Luther is a work of fiction. Where real people,
events, establishments, organizations, or locales appear,
they are used fictitiously. All other elements of
the novel are drawn from the author's imagination.

The text of this Large Print edition is unabridged.
In other aspects, this book may vary
from the original edition.
Printed in the United States of America
on permanent paper.
Set in 16-point Times New Roman type.

ISBN: 978-1-68324-683-1

Library of Congress Cataloging-in-Publication Data

Names: Pittman, Allison, author.
Title: Loving Luther / Allison Pittman.
Description: Center Point Large Print edition. | Thorndike, Maine :
Center Point Large Print, 2018.
Identifiers: LCCN 2017051153 | ISBN 9781683246831
(hardcover : alk. paper)
Subjects: LCSH: Large type books. | GSAFD: Christian fiction.
Classification: LCC PS3616.I885 L68 2018 | DDC 813/.6—dc23
LC record available at https://lccn.loc.gov/2017051153

Acknowledgments

In the summer of 2014, my agent, Bill Jensen, leaned over and whispered, "I have a fabulous idea for your next book." We were having dinner at the Christy Awards, and while our table-mates discussed all things Book Industry, he told me about Martin Luther and Katharina von Bora. Literally—just the names. And I, a life-long Southern Baptist who was nominated for a book about a party-girl flapper, thought to myself, *No way.* But then, as the evening wore on, and I had no award to accept, I read a Wikipedia page on my smartphone, and by the time Bill brought me my conciliatory drink, Katharina von Bora was alive in my head. For the rest of that summer, while I wondered if the smart people at Tyndale would ever entrust an Americana girl with a Renaissance woman, the entire story unfolded. Therese and Girt. Jerome. Martin. And Katharina, Käthe, Kat, Katie, and Kate.

So thank you, Bill Jensen, for knowing everything about everything and sharing your brilliant ideas with me.

And thank you, Jan Stob and the entire Tyndale

team, for trusting me with this tale and being willing to keep it a secret for so long.

I am so blessed to be part of such an awesome community of writers. I love you, my Monday night group, for always being so encouraging, and refreshing, and energizing, and brutally honest! You are my prayer warriors and my family in Christ. Also, my ACFW chapter—how I love my Saturdays at La Madeleine, that dark wooden room. What strength we draw from each other. You all inspire me to work on and on, even when discouragement looms.

This book would not have happened without the daily (hourly?) messaging with Rachel McMillan. With you, my friend, the word *Luther* brings its own life, and you have held me up in some pretty dark moments of doubt. You are the best, though I have not saved you for last.

My last bit of gratitude extends to the women who live their lives—today, and in all generations stretching back to the birth of the church—in sacrifice to our Savior, Jesus Christ. I admit to falling a bit in love with the life of a nun: the sorority, the simplicity, the silence. There's a beautiful serenity at the heart of service. Then I think about the glorious freedom I have in Christ. Freedom to know that my eternity is secure, even when my days don't seem to be. How I am loved, despite my flaws. How I am held when the world seems shaky. How he has given me the perfect family for my moods and messes.

Finally, thank you, all my readers, for being so patient in waiting for this story to make its way to you. I've been waiting too. So for Beth Armstrong, who has been asking me almost every day for three years, "How is Mrs. Luther coming along?" Well, here she is.

I think she was worth the wait.

A soul rises up, restless with tremendous desire for God's honor and the salvation of souls. She has for some time exercised herself in virtue and has become accustomed to dwelling in the cell of self-knowledge in order to know better God's goodness toward her, since upon knowledge follows love. And loving, she seeks to pursue truth and clothe herself in it.

It is true, then, that the soul is united to God through love's affection.

From *The Dialogue* by Catherine of Siena, 1378

Part I

Benedictine Monastery, Brehna

1505 — 1509

Chapter 1

My father always told me if I never took a sip of wine, I'd never shed a single tear. One begat the other, and only the common cup in the hands of a priest, the blessed wine of the sacrament, could offer peace. Only the blood of Christ could offer life. Any other was nothing more than ruin, a sinner's way of washing sin.

And yet he drank. Every night, the flames of our small fire danced in the cut glass of his goblet.

It seemed a silly warning, but for all of my brief childhood at home, I had only two sips of wine. The first over a year ago when, at the age of five, I begged for a taste at the grand table. The other just months ago, in the feast following Mother's funeral. Then, true to my father's prophecy, tears streamed down my face.

So, too, as I stood in his embrace, the cold wind of November whipping all around us. Ice like pinpricks upon my cheeks. Perhaps I'd taken in a sufficient amount from the constant scent of wine on his breath, and from the traces left on his lips when he kissed me.

"My Katharina." He stretched my name, and I

imagined it pouring out in a stream mixed with tears and wine. He knelt before me, the patched fabric of his breeches touching the last bit of unsanctified ground.

"Papa? Where are we?"

To answer, he took me by my shoulders and turned me to look at the foreboding stone structure on the other side of the iron gate. "A church, kitten. A house of God."

That much I assumed from the tall, arched windows and the lingering echo of the bell that had been tolling upon our approach. Six rings, and the sun nearly set. A new sound emerged in the wake of the bells. Footsteps, strident and rhythmic, displacing the tiny stones on the path beyond the gate. They carried what looked like a shadow—tall and black and fluttering.

Frightened, I twisted back in my father's embrace. "Papa?"

"Be strong, my girl."

Before I could say another word, I heard the screech of metal and a voice that matched its tone in every way. "Katharina von Bora?"

"Papa?" I clung to him, even as he stood tall and away.

"*Ja*. This is my daughter."

A heavy hand fell on my shoulder. "Say good-bye to your papa, little one."

Good-bye?

Two days before, when Papa told me to pack

a few things—extra stockings and my sleeping cap—into a small drawstring bag, he'd said nothing about leaving me at a church to say *good-bye.* In all our travel, the miles riding in the back of farm carts, the night spent among strangers at the small, damp inn, he answered my questions with platitudes about what a fine, strong girl I was, and how it was good to get away, just the two of us.

"Is it because of the new mama?" The woman loomed large, even with two days' distance between us. Her stern commands, her wooden spoon ever at the ready to correct a sullen temper, her furrowed brow as she counted the meager coins in the little wooden box above the stove. "I can be good, Papa. I will work harder and speak to her more sweetly. I'll be a good girl. I promise. Papa—*please!*"

I grasped his hand, repeating my promises, feeling victorious when he scooped me up off the ground. I tried to bury my face in his neck, but he jostled me and gripped my chin in his fingers.

"*Ruhig sein.*" His voice and eyes were stern. "Hush, I say. You are Katharina von Bora. Do you know what that means?"

"*Ja*, Papa." I touched my hand against his grizzled whiskers. "Bearer of a great and proper name."

"Very old, and very great." He was whispering now, his back turned to the shadowy figure.

From this height, looking down over Papa's shoulder, I could clearly see that it was only a nun. A soft, pale face peered from behind a veil, while long black sleeves fluttered around clasped hands. A tunic over a plain black dress bore an embroidered cross, and in many ways she was not unlike the nuns I knew from our church back home. So why had Papa brought me here, so far away?

"But I don't want to stay here, Papa." I had to look down into his face, and it made him seem so much smaller.

"Be a good girl." He set me back on my feet and bowed down to meet me eye to eye. "Grow up to be a strong, smart young lady. And do not cry."

"But—"

His admonishing finger, nail bitten to the quick and grimy from travel, staved off the prick of new tears. "Strong, I tell you."

"Are you coming back for me? After a time, after I've grown up a little? When I'm a lady?"

A weak smile played across his lips, and he cast a quick, nervous glace up to the nun. "Child," he said, gripping my shoulders, "I am delivering you into the hands of God, the same God who once gave you to me. Could you ask for anything better than to be in his loving care?"

I knew, instantly, how I should answer. Thinking back to our small, dark home, with rooms shut away to ward off the chill. My three older brothers crowded around the table, squabbling for the last bowl of stew, and taking mine when there wasn't enough. Now, with me gone, there would be more for everybody else. Not enough, but more. Maybe the new mama would smile a bit and not stomp through the kitchen rattling pots like a thunderstorm. Maybe my brothers would stop stealing bread and making their papa lie to the red-faced baker when he came pounding on the door. There would be one less body to soak up the heat from the fire, and more space in the crowded bed.

I stood up straight and wiped my nose on my sleeve. "I'm ready now, Papa."

"That's my good girl." He kissed my forehead, my cheeks, then briefly, my lips. One kiss, he said, for each of my brothers, and one final from Mother watching from heaven. The nun kept her own silent watch until the end, when Papa handed me the small bundle he'd been carrying over his shoulder for the last mile of our walk.

"No." The sister's sturdy hand stretched from within the long black sleeve. "She comes with nothing."

"Please, Sister—"

"Sister Odile, reverend mother of the convent of Brehna."

"It's just a nightcap," Papa said, not mentioning that it was the cap Mama—my mama—had stitched with small purple flowers. "And clean stockings and an apron."

"Nothing." Sister Odile tightened her grip and dragged me to her side.

Head low, Papa shouldered the bag once again, saying, "As it should be, I suppose."

I noticed the quiver in his chin and knew it was one of those times when I would have to be strong in his place. I needed to stand straighter, fix my eyes above, and set my mind in obedience. A pinpoint of cold pierced my shoulder where the gold band on Sister Odile's finger touched my flesh. Ignoring the growing grayness of the sky and the imminent demise of Papa's resolve, I took a deep, cleansing breath.

"You should start for home, Papa. It will be dark soon."

"Yes," he said. And that was all. In the next instant, I was turned toward the gate, then marched through it. Sister Odile's robes flapped against her, an irregular rhythm in the growing wind. For all I knew, Papa remained behind the iron bars, watching every step. Counting them, maybe, as I did. I listened for his voice, waiting for him to call me back, but if he did, the words were lost to the crunching of the stones beneath Sister Odile's bearlike feet. I myself felt each one through the thin, patched leather of my shoes. When we came to a turn in the path, one sharp enough to afford a glance out of the corner of my eye, I saw the gate, with Papa nowhere to be found.

Then came the rush of tears.

"Stop that, now."

To emphasize her command, Sister Odile stopped in the middle of the path, leaving me no choice but to do the same. I scrunched my face, calculating the distance between the looming church and the empty gate. Both were within a few easy, running steps. And I was fast—faster than any other girl on my street, and some of the boys, too. I could outrun my brothers when I needed to avoid one of their senseless poundings, and I could cover the distance from our front door to the top of the street before Papa could finish calling out my name in the evenings when he came home before dark. In an instant I could be free, back at the gate, squeezed through, and in Papa's arms before the nun would even realize I'd escaped. Or I could fly, straight and fast, right up the path to the looming church. Surely Sister Odile's cloddish feet and flapping sleeves would make her lag in pursuit. The height and breadth of the outer stone walls promised a labyrinth of dark corridors and twisting halls within. I could run away, hide away, lose myself in the shadows until morning, when the clouds might disperse and reveal a shining sun to direct me home.

Labyrinth. It was a word Papa taught me, reading from a big book of ancient stories. A monster lived in its midst—half man, half bull. *Minotaur*. I mouthed the word, feeling the dryness of my chapped lips at the silent *m,* and reached a tentative hand out to Sister Odile's skirt, wondering if the voluminous fabric might not be hiding such a creature within.

"*Hör auf.*" Sister Odile slapped my hand away and resumed our journey, doing nothing to allay my fear that I might well be in the custody of a monster. The size of the feet alone promised supernatural proportions, and now the woman's breath came in snorts and puffs like some great-chested beast.

"You want to run, don't you, girl?"

"No." The lie didn't bother me one bit.

Sister Odile let out a laugh deep enough to lift the cross off her frock. "Back out the gate, wouldn't you? And what if I told you to go ahead? You're little enough to squeeze right through, aren't you? You want to chase down your papa? Do you even know which way he went? Up the road or down?"

Every word in every question climbed a scale, ending in a high, gasping wheeze.

"If I did run, you'd never catch me. I'd disappear like a shadow." It's what I did at home, on nights when Papa wasn't there. I'd fold myself into the corners, away from the reach of the new mama's spoon.

"Not even a shadow can escape the wolves,"

Sister Odile said, her grip softening a little. "And hear me when I tell you this, my girl. That is all that waits for you outside these walls. Wolves ready to tear little girls into scraps for their pups."

This, I knew, held some truth, as Papa had often said the same thing. Still, my trust faltered. "And what is inside the walls?"

Sister Odile laughed again, but this time the sound rumbled in her throat, like the comfort of long-off thunder. "Great mysteries and secrets. The kind that most little girls will never learn."

"Like in books?"

"In the greatest book of all. And sacred language."

Our steps fell into a common pace, with mine trotting two to every one of Sister Odile's.

"I can read a little already," I said, my words warm with pride. "Papa taught me. I can read better than my brother, and he's eleven."

"Then your father has done a very good and unselfish thing, allowing you to come here. Let your *Dummkopf* brother fend for himself."

I stopped my laughter with the back of my hand. Fabian was an idiot, by all measures. Cruel and thick and lazy. He was the closest to me in age, and therefore the most likely to deliver abuse. Clemens was thirteen, and Hans a full-grown man, almost, and I wondered if they would even notice my absence. Our sister, Maria, had been gone for nearly a year, married to a solicitor's clerk, and had rarely been mentioned since.

"You can find peace here," Sister Odile was saying, "because we work to keep the darkness of the world away."

We'd come to a heavy wooden door with an iron ring fastened so high, Sister Odile had to stretch up on her toes to reach it.

Thud. Thud. Thud.

"There is another door on the other side of the building," Sister Odile said, "open to all who seek sanctuary. This one is just for us."

Us. I repeated the word.

"The sisters. And the girls. Other little girls, just like you. And bigger, too. We don't lock the door until after supper, and then don't open it at all after dark. You got here just in time."

The mention of the word *supper* brought my stomach rumbling to life, as loud as the sound of the sliding bolt and creaking hinges. Whatever hunger I felt, however, knotted itself into pure fear at the image in the open doorway. No amount of black fabric could shroud the twisted figure of the old woman who stood, leaning heavily on a thick walking stick, on the other side. A stub of candle illuminated a face the likes of which I had never seen before. One eye clouded with blindness, thin lips mismatched to each other, and a cascade of fleshy pink-tinged boils dripping like wax down one side. In stature, she was not much taller than I, and I stood silent and still as a post under the woman's studious gaze. Then the single squinted eye was aimed up at Sister Odile, and a voice squawked, "She's too late."

"Sister Gerda." Sister Odile spoke soothingly as both greeting and introduction. "This is our newest charge, Katharina."

"Supper's over and cleaned up." Her lips moved like waves, producing a spittle that dripped unchecked down her chin. "Thought you made it clear to have her here by three o'clock."

"So are we to stay out here until morning?" Sister Odile brought me close to her side. "Or will you kindly allow us to come in?"

Sister Gerda muttered as she scuttled backward, opening the door wide enough for a full view of the entry, where another door—equally impressive—dominated the facing wall. The long, narrow room was lined with two wooden benches. Above each hung a tapestry, but the light was too dim to make out the images.

"Go and fetch her a cup of water," Sister Odile said, leading me to sit on one of the benches. "And some bread, too. I'm sure you're hungry, aren't you?"

I nodded, then said, "Yes, ma'am," in case it was too dark for a silent response. An invisible prod from Papa prompted me to add, "Thank you, ma'am."

"Kitchen's closed up," Sister Gerda said with a sniff. "Cleaned up, too. It's nearly seven."

"This wouldn't be the first time somebody crept into the kitchen for a slice of bread after dark. Would our Lord not bid us to share what we have? Does our obedience to him snuff out with the sun? You're a quick, silent little one, Sister Gerda. No doubt you can be there and back before the hour tolls. And should anyone comment, tell them you are there on my errand. *Schnell*! Before the poor girl collapses from hunger."

I listened, fascinated by the rise and fall of Sister Odile's tone. Demanding at first, then affectionate, authoritative, and almost playful at the end. Almost as if four different women spoke from within the habit, each spinning to show her face from behind the veil. This, I knew, was a woman to be respected, maybe even feared. While her size brought on a certain intimidation, a level of comfort came with it too. Stooping, she took the candle stub from Sister Gerda, touched it to a sconce on the wall, and handed it back with a sweetly whispered reminder to hurry. Then she went to one of the benches and settled her weight upon it, bringing out a creaking protest from the wood.

"*Komm her*." She held out her hands, gold band winking in the candlelight. It was impossible to distinguish sleeves from shadow, but the face floating in the midst of the darkness was wide and smiling.

Without another thought, I took the few steps to cross the room and climbed up into the softness of Sister Odile. Arms wrapped around me, and I was absorbed in the deepest embrace I could remember since before Mama fell ill. I pressed my face into the warm, worn wool and felt the rumbling of the sister's breath. Humming, now, a tune I did not recognize, but somehow knew to be ancient. Sacred. I closed my eyes, knowing it would be safe to cry now. The tears could flow into the wool, and as long as I did not sniffle, I could pour my fear and sadness into this woman. Instead, with each breath, I felt the block of fatigue from the journey begin to crumble, turning to little pebbles like those on the walkway, and finally to dust. I felt heavy, too heavy to cry. Too heavy to lift my head and ask where I might go to sleep. Too heavy to close my lips when I felt its pull.

The last thing I remembered was the coarseness of the cross on Sister Odile's breast pressed into my cheek, each stitch wrapped around the lullaby.

Chapter 2

Voices whispered at the edge of sleep.

"Should we wake her?"

"We have to, or Sister Gerda won't let her have any breakfast."

My stomach gurgled at the mention of it. I hadn't eaten since breakfast the previous day, and I'd fallen fast asleep, forgetting about the half of a sausage in my pocket, let alone the meal the monstrous sister was sent to fetch for me.

"Poke her shoulder, Girt."

"*You* poke her shoulder. You're the brave one."

"How brave do you have to be to poke a little girl's shoulder? It's the perfect opportunity for you to grow your courage."

"What if she bites?"

"She won't bite."

"But what if—"

At that moment I wished I *could* bite, imagining a snap of my teeth around their pointing fingers. They'd howl in pain and I'd jump up and run away. Back home, even, if I could remember the path. Instead, I clamped my eyelids down tighter and could feel them vibrating with the pressure.

"Wait a minute." The first voice again, and

close enough that I could feel warm breath on my cheek. “I think she’s awake. Hey, girl. Are you awake?”

Then came a none-too-gentle push—almost a shove, really—to my shoulder, and I brought my arms up protectively.

“Not so rough, Therese. She’s little.”

“Well, she’s never going to get any bigger if she sleeps through breakfast. I’m going to go tell Sister Gerda she wouldn’t wake up. In fact—” the voice was so close now, I tried to push my head deeper into the wooden bench to escape the words—“I’ll tell her that the little thing just died in the night. And we can drag her out to the rubbish heap and have her portions for ourselves.”

“Stop that.” There was a sound of a scuffle, the girl Therese being yanked away, and feeling as though a protector had been established, I opened my eyes.

“Well, it’s about time.”

I knew from the voice that this was Therese—the same girl who had been speaking so menacingly close, but who proved herself too beautiful to inspire further fear. She looked like she’d been assembled from new, fresh snow. White-blonde hair framed a porcelain face; ice-blue eyes held a steady gaze above a pointed nose. Her mouth hid behind a pretty hand, one finger touched to her lips, warning me to silence.

"Good morning, sleepyhead." This from the other voice, Girt, and I pulled my gaze away from Therese to see a vision of pure, warm joy. Both girls wore plain dresses of homespun wool, with stiff aprons, thick black socks, and sturdy wooden shoes. While Therese somehow managed to look like a fairy princess trapped in a peasant's dress, Girt looked like a sturdy, milk-fed farmer's daughter, complete with full cheeks and wide brown eyes. Just looking at her made me think of gingerbread, my mother's gingerbread, straight from the oven. Sweet and peppery. I fought an overwhelming urge to reach out to take a pinch of Girt's freckled flesh.

"Your name's Katharina," Therese said, as if making a proclamation. "And you're six years old, but you're small. I would have said you were four, but they don't like to take in girls that little. Sometimes they wet the bed, and then everything smells awful for days. You don't wet the bed, do you?"

"No," I said, though I would have lied in the moment and refused sleep for the rest of my life if I did.

"Good. Because we haven't time for babies here. You'll start lessons with the rest of us and just have to keep up. Can you read at all?"

"A little." This was not so much a lie as an exaggeration. I knew my letters and could write my name and the names of everyone in my family. I'd been working a sampler with Mama and had covered the hearth with charcoal renderings of my practice until the new mama made me wash it all away.

"We're learning Latin," Girt said, beaming with pride. "And if we practice and study very hard, someday we'll be able to read the Scriptures as easily as the priests can."

"That's Sister Odile's doing," Therese said, her nose wrinkled. "I think it's a giant waste of time."

I regarded Therese closely, trying to guess the girl's age. She had the stature and features of a child, but everything else about her seemed like a grown-up stuffed into a little girl's body. Her eyes held both wisdom and sadness, and her words came out with a snap of authority. Like at this moment, when she pointed directly at me and said, "What is that? Give it to me."

My hand went to my throat and touched the familiar gold chain. "It's my mother's." I drew out the locket attached to the chain, but would not open it. Not in front of these girls, because inside were tiny, braided strands of hair. Mine and my mother's, intertwined, no thicker than the width of embroidery silk. I would cry if I looked at them right now, and in just these few moments, I knew I never wanted to cry in front of Therese. Girt, maybe. She seemed softer, like a mother in training, but Therese would have no patience for tears.

“Give it,” Therese said, reaching, but I took the necklace off, wadded it in my fist, and hid it behind my back. I knew it was a losing battle, the two of them against me, each outmatching me in size and strength, but I’d put up a fight if I had to. Growing up with three older brothers had taught me to use my size to an advantage. I could kick hard and low and bite into the soft flesh above the wrist. I bared my teeth in preparation and sat back on the bench, feet straight out in defense.

“It’s all right.” Girt moved to sit beside me and positioned herself as a barrier. “You can trust her with it, or give it to me if you’d rather. We’ll keep it safe, I promise. The sisters will take it away, and you won’t see it again. We’re not allowed to keep anything personal.”

“Or valuable,” Therese interjected. “Not if they can swap it for a few more coins in the coffer.”

“Here.” Girt held out her hand, and the softness of the gesture beckoned mine. I remembered Sister Odile’s admonition. *Nothing.* Tightening my fingers around the chain, I offered a silent thanks to God for the darkness that had kept this treasure hidden. Until now, of course, when the glint of gold had caught Therese’s eye. Better Therese than one of the sisters, though? According to these girls, yes, and Girt at least seemed deserving of my trust. With the last bit of hesitation, I loosened my grip and watched the chain and locket fall into Girt’s waiting hand.

"Don't open it," I said, wishing I sounded strong enough to carry out some punishment should they disobey.

"We won't."

Girt immediately handed the locket over to Therese, who flipped up the hem of her skirt and secreted the necklace into a pocket on the underside. "Once you get your new dress," she said, smoothing her pinafore, "you need to tear it. Trip and fall, or step on the hem when you're on the stairs, or catch it on a nail—"

"Wait a few days," Girt chimed in, "so it doesn't look suspicious."

"And when you mend it, put in a pocket. We're not allowed to have pockets, but some of us do."

"But not everyone." Girt again, a voice of caution. "So don't tell any of the other girls. You'll ask Sister Gerda for a scrap to mend your dress. She'll want you to do it right in front of her. Can you sew?"

"Yes, I sew all the time at home."

"Well, forget you can," Therese said. "Make a mess of it, and ask Sister Gerda to help you."

"She won't, of course," Girt said, "because she can hardly see. She'll send you off to find an *older girl* to help."

"And we'll be the older girl." Therese finished the plot with a note of such finality, I couldn't imagine not complying.

"When will I get a new dress?"

Girt took a pinch of my sleeve. “This is in good shape. They could get a few pennies for it, and you’re small enough to get something handed down to you. I’d say even today.”

“So if you have anything else,” Therese said, “hand it over. Because if you’re caught with it, you’ll get stripes.”

“What are stripes?”

“Never mind.” Girt turned to Therese. “Why are you being so mean? Trying to scare her on the first day. Still—” she leaned in close—“do you have anything else you want us to hold for you?”

There was something else, deep in the pocket—the *real* pocket—of my dress, wrapped in a bit of coarse napkin taken from the inn where Papa and I had spent the night. The sausage. Rather, half of a sausage, a little more than half, as I’d been too nervous to eat it for breakfast. It had traveled the course of a day’s walk in my pocket and had remained as I slept. I reached for it now, bringing out the grease-soaked napkin to the utter delight of the two girls. Girt, in particular, appeared to be restraining herself from snatching it away.

“It’s sausage, isn’t it?” She inhaled, scrunching her whole face up in the process. “Sage and pepper. I can smell it.”

Therese practiced no such control and grabbed it. “So will everyone else. It’s Friday, stupid girl. Were you thinking you were going to carry it around until the resurrection?”

"Blasphemy!" Girt cried, hands clasped to her mouth in horror only to be beset by her own giggle.

"I forgot about it," I said weakly. "And I lost track of the days. Papa didn't say anything. I should have—"

I was interrupted by an echoing screech.

"Girt! Therese! You naughty girls!"

The halls outside this small room must have been cavernous. Therese pulled us into a circle.

"Sister Gerda," Girt whispered. "We were supposed to fetch you straight to the dining hall for breakfast." She turned to Therese. "What should we do?"

"Go to breakfast, of course."

"But what about—?" Girt pointed to the greasy bundle. "We'll get stripes for sure."

"Better than having our immortal souls condemned to hell." Again our names were called, this time with greater impatience, and the first hint of fear crept into Therese's face. "All right," she hissed. Then, to me, "Have you had your first Holy Communion yet?"

"N-no," I stammered, too caught up in fear to consider whether or not this was an enviable state.

"Then it's not such a sin for you." Therese tore the sausage into three pieces and handed each of us our portion. "And, Girt, we have a week before confession, and I'll take half portions of every meal until then as penance. Now hurry."

Not until the morsel passed my lips did I realize how truly hungry I'd been. Never mind that it had gone cold and crumbly, the sage and spices had a dizzying effect, and I grasped the arm of the wooden bench to keep myself steady as I ate. From the expressions on their faces, Girt and Therese were equally enraptured, so much so that when the heavy wooden door flew open, they turned their backs and continued to chew, steadily, offering a guttural "G'morning, Sister Gerda," to the nun's chastising greeting.

The woman was no less frightening in the fullness of morning, especially given the grayish quality of the light coming through the narrow windows, and the sight of her was enough to make the bit of sausage stick in my throat. I covered my mouth, hoping to disguise the choking as nothing more than a cough, as Girt and Therese gathered around me, hiding their discretion behind the goodwill act of petting the new girl.

"Don't tell me she's sick," Sister Gerda said, making no move to offer comfort. "Got enough of that with the last one, bringing half you girls into the infirmary before she died."

I hazarded a peek under Therese's arm and noticed not only the density of the cloud over one of Sister Gerda's eyes, but that the other was nearly hidden by the rise of tumorous flesh. She was looking not so much *at* us but *toward* us, making me wonder why we should bother to hide mortal sin, until Sister Gerda's nose wrinkled with authoritative scrutiny.

"What's that?"

Girt's whole body shuddered in a swallow. "What's what, Sister Gerda?"

"I smell—"

"It's the girl," Therese said, and that's when I noticed she was not only patting my back in the guise of relieving my cough, she was rubbing the greasy napkin over every inch of my dress. "I think they must have spent the night next to a smokehouse or a butcher's shop. She reeks of sausage."

"That's it," Sister Gerda confirmed. "That's the smell. Sausage." She said it with a wistfulness that testified to the rareness of the treat. "She's going to have all our mouths watering, this one will."

I gulped and was about to speak when Therese elbowed me, hard.

"She needs a bath. And she's been riding in carts with all kinds of animals. Personally, I think it would make me sick to sit next to her and try to eat. The other girls too." She leaned in close, nearly nose-to-nose. "Are you really very hungry, Katharina? Or do you think you can wait until dinner? That's at noon, just a few hours from now."

Of course I was hungry. The nibble of sausage had only served to awaken my appetite, but I couldn't attribute the sudden weakness of my knees to day-old emptiness or newborn fear. I'd sinned, caused others to follow, and now was part of a complex lie to cover it up. At home I paid little attention to such things, what with the constant barrage of my brothers' fists, my father's tears, and my mother's slow, lingering death. Now it seemed I'd carried all of that darkness into this holy place and divided it among these innocents who had been nothing but helpful. Perhaps not entirely kind, but I was after all a stranger, and they had offered me a camaraderie forged in secrets. In Girt, I might have a friend, but Therese was more than that. She was a protector. What I would bring to the trio, I didn't know. I was little, weak, and not even a real Catholic yet, but I felt pure strength coming through Therese's direct gaze and Girt's lingering grip on my arm.

"No," I said softly at first, then louder, "no, I'm not hungry at all."

Chapter 3

My introduction to Brehna came with a cold, hard scrubbing, the likes of which I had never before experienced. My skin was left pink and raw, with droplets of blood in places where the scrapes and scratches of a farm cart voyage were torn open with the friction of the cloth. As I learned was the custom with all new girls, my hair had been chopped to little more than fuzz and a foul-smelling oil rubbed into my scalp, intended to kill any vermin that might be lurking. Bald and freshly scrubbed, I stepped into my new dress, identical to those worn by Girt, Therese, and every one of the dozens of girls at Brehna. Black coarsely spun wool, it was the simplest dress I'd ever worn, nothing more than a single seam up the back and a ribbon-tie closure at the neck. No matter the decline of my family's fortune, my dresses always had some form of adornment. The one Sister Gerda took away had brightly painted wooden buttons, and I wished I'd thought to rip them off, to hide them in Therese's secret pocket. But I hadn't, and now the only comfort was to think that some poor little girl—poorer than me—had been given such a treasure.

This new dress, at least, was clean and warm enough as long as I never stayed too still to notice. My new stockings were well knit and without a single hole, my pinafore and cap crisp, and my shoes sturdy, with wooden soles that made a delightful *clack* when I walked.

"It's so we don't wander off," Therese told me. "Only Jesus hears our thoughts, but the sisters hear our steps."

It seemed a pity to follow through on Therese's instructions to rip my new dress, and for the first week, I made no attempt to do so. There hadn't been much of an opportunity, as none of the girls would play with the girl who had such stinky hair. And because I was unfamiliar with the hallways, I went everywhere in careful, slow, echoing steps. Still, I desperately wanted my locket returned to my possession and begged Therese on several secret occasions to reassure me of its well-being.

"Just a peek," Therese would say before opening her slim, pretty fingers to reveal the filigree gold within.

"Can't I have it, please? I'll keep it safe. Under my pillow, or inside my shoe."

"It won't last a week under your pillow, and you'll wear a bruise into your foot if it's in your shoe."

And so I began in earnest to prepare a place for its return. I wandered near the thistle bushes in the play yard, hoping to snag the fabric, but the tiny branches were too often soft and wet with snow, and the dress escaped unscathed. I walked along the edge of the walls, but the bricks and stones were worn smooth. In prayer, I knelt upon the hem, then stretched myself up, feeling the fabric taut beneath my chin. But it would not rip. Once, I launched myself into a game of catch, whispering to Girt and Therese to hold my skirt as I ran away.

"And get in trouble for ripping your dress?" Girt said. "We'll get stripes for sure."

Therese also refused. "And you needn't be so obvious about it. If they think you're being careless or wasteful, you'll get stripes too."

By now I knew full well what they meant by stripes. Naughty girls—those who whispered during chapel or complained about their food or daydreamed during class—were brought to the front of the room, where Sister Odile waited with a thin black reed. The offending girl would hold out her hand, and Sister Odile would bring it down—*whack!*—upon the flesh. The sound was sharp, and all the girls winced as if they, too, felt its sting. Afterward, angry red welts rose from the skin. Stripes. One, or three, or five, depending on the offense and Sister Odile's mercy.

"The wounds of Christ absolve you from your sin," Sister Odile would say before and after each administration of the reed. "May these stripes remind you to sin no more."

Back home, I had more than once felt the crack of the new mama's wooden ladle between my shoulders, or just above my ears, or anywhere the crazed woman could find for it to land. Still, it did not bring the lingering pain and humiliation of the stripes. Girls with stripes could not properly hold their spoons and dribbled soup down the front of their aprons. They would have to rely on other girls to comb and plait their hair. Sometimes, after fresh discipline, their chalk pieces would be stained with blood and the numbers tinted pink when they worked their sums on their slates.

I determined early on that stripes were given to silly girls, weak girls, and I vowed never to merit my own. So when I spotted a weevil tunneling in my porridge, I said nothing, only fished it out with my finger and wiped it under the bench. When Ilse, a fat, mean older girl who always smelled of sweet onions, poked me in the side repeatedly during Vespers, I remained stoic and still, even though the girl's prodding left a blue mark between my ribs. More than anything, I paid rapt attention during all of my classes, though I rarely understood what the sister at the front of the room imparted. But I quickly latched on to what I *did* understand—the simple bits of addition during arithmetic, the phonetic familiarity of letters in reading—and found my mind building itself up. I mimicked the other girls in my answers and begged Girt and Therese to tutor me during the quiet moments before sleep.

Sunday morning Mass meant two long hours listening to Father Johann drone from behind the massive pulpit. The tone with which he spoke of God's love and mercy was equal to that which he used to warn us of God's judgment and condemnation, making me wonder if he were truly an authority on either. Only the language—German or Latin—separated his words from those read from the Holy Scriptures, and because my Latin was still so rudimentary, I spent the entirety of the service swinging between boredom and confusion. Sometimes I would let my feet swing too, as they came nowhere near to touching the floor, but on those occasions I would get a warning jab to my ribs from Girt or Therese, and I would bring them to a stop, envying their eventual sleep.

Months had passed since my arrival, how many I didn't know because I had little reason to measure time. I only knew that my hair had grown to be its own cap of short, soft curls beneath the now-dingy white one. Father Johann read from the Holy Gospel of John, and I tried with all my might to picture the words on the page. But too many distractions hindered my efforts, not the least of which was Father Johann's wobbling jowls, carrying each syllable with flapping imprecision. I closed my eyes to shut out the sight, and in the darkness saw the letters forming. Scrambled, unscrambled, finally matching the phonetic cadence of the priest.

"Kt." It was a singular sound, ticked from Girt beside me, meant to capture the essence of my name and draw my attention from the darkness. I opened my eyes to Sister Odile launching herself from the high-backed chair beside the altar and descending upon me—not stopping until her face was nose-to-nose with mine.

"Katharina von Bora. Do I need to find a nursery so you can take a proper nap?"

I didn't know what to do, as it was strictly forbidden to speak during Mass, but I could hardly choose not to answer Sister Odile. Quickly, I calculated the severity of the two sins, deciding that the nun, by proximity alone, posed the greater threat. I hoped to mitigate my offense by keeping my voice to a slip of a whisper, something Sister Odile hadn't bothered to do.

"No, Sister."

"Come with me."

The command sounded nothing like the invitation of that first night, when Sister Odile folded me into the abundance of her lap. Still, I obeyed, standing, then taking one wooden footstep after another. Clearly she meant to lead me out of the sanctuary, to administer my stripes without further disruption of worship, but Father Johann bade us to stop, and we stood at the altar for all to see.

Humiliation burned my cheeks, as the congregation consisted of not only the other girls, who would clearly understand my plight, but people from the surrounding village as well, who would think me a simple, wicked girl. Perhaps I overestimated the empathy of the other girls because I heard them snickering, stopping only under the combined threat of Sister Odile from the front of the room and Therese's glance over her shoulder. Soon I was standing with nothing but a wall of black in front of me, shielding me from the glare of the priest behind it. I looked straight up, noting briefly that Sister Odile's nostrils curled toward each other like two cavernous kidney beans.

"Do you find the words of our Lord to be boring, Katharina von Bora?" She posed the question with as much kindness as I'm sure she dared.

"No, Sister."

"Has our Lord not provided you with a comfortable bed to sleep on at night?"

"He has, Sister."

"Then why were you sleeping just now?"

I wiggled my toes in the tips of my shoes,

hoping to distract my knees from knocking. “I wasn’t sleeping, Sister. I was listening.”

“Listening, were you?” The nostrils flared before she hazarded a glance over her shoulder at Father Johann. “And why were your eyes closed?”

How to explain to this woman who knew everything? I pictured the inside of Sister Odile’s mind, all the words hiding behind her eyes. Perfectly spelled, long sentences folding over on themselves, hopping from language to language, with ciphering and history and catechism in between. How would she ever understand the jumbled-up nest of thoughts in a little girl’s head?

“I want to see the letters,” I said at last, speaking as the thought formed. Another trickling of laughter cut short. “We don’t get to look. Only listen. But someday, if I can, I want to open the Scriptures for myself and read. And understand. I want to remember what the words sound like, so I can help the image on the page and the memory of the sound find each other.”

Now there would be no stemming the tide of the girls’ amusement, and I heard laughter coming from the pews at the back of the room.

“Girls!” Sister Odile shouted. *“Girls!”*

Her authority extended beyond her pupils, for not only did they finally stifle themselves to silence after she clapped her hands three times, so did the rest of the congregation. The girls, I knew, had been reminded of the sharpness of the striping reed. In fact, Sister Odile's palms were similarly pink from effort and warm when she touched my cheek, yet that gesture hinted of mercy in front of all those watchful eyes.

"That is a noble explanation for a silly idea."

"It is nonsense," Father Johann intoned, dashing all hope for grace.

If I was going to get stripes, it would be for a worthwhile offense. My spine straightened into something stronger than the reed that surely awaited, and I looked beyond the mountain of Sister Odile to the man who stood behind her, holding the tome of Scripture as a shield.

"It isn't nonsense."

Behind me, at least eleven girls responded in a single gasp. Behind them, the people of the town echoed their shock.

"Sister Odile." Father Johann's face flapped in indignation. "Do you sanction this manner of impudence?"

"We do not, Father."

"Then I insist the girl be chastised. Immediately, before her rebellious spirit takes root."

"Here?" Sister Odile said, taken aback. "In the sanctuary?"

"Where better to practice a lesson of obedience than in the house of the Lord?"

Sister Odile appeared to be shrinking before

my very eyes. "I don't have—what I mean to say is, I'm not prepared."

Father Johann laid the Bible on the rough-hewn podium and clambered down the steps. "You sisters and your silly sticks." He shouldered Sister Odile out of his path and grabbed my arm, turning it and pushing up the sleeve, exposing the soft white flesh above my wrist. "Were you sleeping during the reading of the Holy Word?"

"No."

"You were listening then, eh? Paying close attention?"

"Yes." I took no comfort in the truth, especially once I caught the malevolent glint in his eye.

"Then prove it to me."

I looked up, then over to Sister Odile, searching for help, but the nun was glaring at the priest who held me.

"Say it!" He jerked my arm, making me fear it would be pulled off at the elbow. "Say *the word.* Say *the sounds,* as you remember them." His lips, thick and twisted into a sneer, gathered bits of spittle. "Can you?"

Too frightened to respond, I could no more speak than fly. Father Johann's grip tightened once again before—in a gesture that inspired a curious new fear—he brought his hand to his mouth, extended his tongue, and raked it along the first two fingers of his right hand. Then, with the gold of his ring flashing like lightning, he brought the fingers, whiplike, to my exposed flesh. Immediate, red-hot pain rose to life on my skin, tinging it pink. This was nothing like the slaps and spoons of the new mama. This turned me into something raw.

"Say it!"

When I didn't, the sting came again. Pain layered upon pain, and I winced in Father Johann's grip.

"I'll ask you yet again." His tongue extended, the tips of his fingers near to touching it, and something broke loose within me.

"*Ego sum . . .*" The words formed an unfamiliar shadow in my mouth, and I knew if I looked at Father Johann, they would disappear entirely. I fixed my eyes on the cloudlike pink wound above my pulse. "*Ego sum,*" I repeated, "*via, et ver—veri—*"

"*Veritas,*" Sister Odile prompted.

"*Ego sum via, et veritas—*" I wanted so badly to remember, not only to stay the hand of Father Johann, but because each word lessened the sting of my flesh.

Sister Odile prompted, "*Et veritas et—*"

"*Ruhig, Schwester.*"

Father Johann's admonition could not hold back the flood of memory, and my lips spilled it forth.

"*Ego sum via et veritas et vita.*"

I felt his grip go slack, my wrist a mere twig

within, but I dared not pull away. Only when he released me did I take a single step back, stopping when I felt the wide, welcoming robes of Sister Odile.

Father Johann resumed his place behind the pulpit and opened the Bible, his face wiped clean of any expression that could be construed as malice or mercy. He opened to the page marked with the length of silk ribbon and unceremoniously read: "*Ego sum via et veritas et vita. Nemo venit ad Patrem nisi per me.*"

He closed the book, the collision of pages echoing in the sanctuary now stunned into silence, and stared me down once again. "Tell me," he said, smirking, "do you know what that means?"

I shook my head. I already knew the consequences of truth. "No, Father."

"Well then, my child," he said, looking down at me as if I were a stray dog in the kitchen, "you would have done just as well to have slept."

After the service, those from the village spilled out to their homes while we girls filed silently into the dining room to sit at the long table and be served a simple dinner of flavored broth and bread. As the bread was the last of the week's baking, it would need to be soaked in the broth in order to eat it. At Girt's wordless instruction, I broke my bread into chunks and allowed them to float and bob on the surface of the broth, scooping them up with my spoon once they'd been soaked through. I pretended they were dumplings and that somewhere beneath them, morsels of meat awaited a similar fate. Besides the cool water in the pewter cup, nothing else was offered.

"It's to keep us weak," Therese had whispered the first Sunday. "So we won't have enough energy to want to play."

"And to keep us hungry," Girt added, "so we won't be lulled to sleep."

The initial sting of Father Johann's punishment had all but dissipated, leaving behind a curious ache like nothing I had ever felt before. I longed to push up my sleeve to see the condition of my skin, but not here. Not at the table, where the other girls who had snickered could see.

The only sound came from the occasional bump of a pewter spoon against a wooden bowl and the sniffs from those with constantly running noses. We stood in one accord when the sisters came in to join us and didn't sit again until instructed to do so by one soft syllable muttered by Sister Odile.

When I sat, my feet dangled in the open air above the floor. On any other day, Sister Gerda would snap, "Stop swinging those feet, Katharina von Bora! Or you're likely to walk yourself down an invisible path to the devil."

Sister Gerda would be proud today. My feet

hung still as a stopped clock, and I ate my bread and broth only to be spared further chastisement for the day. When the last drop trickled down my throat, I rested my spoon upright in the empty bowl, drank my water, and sat with my hands folded in my lap, head bowed.

Thank you, Father in heaven, for this food.

When all the girls were finished, Sister Odile's quiet instruction that we should go to the common room dismissed us. Almost noiselessly, we vacated the long benches that ran the length of the table and took small, shuffling steps down the corridor, muffling the usual clatter of our shoes. Giggling and lighthearted playfulness had no home on the holy afternoon. The undercurrent of *silly on Sunday, stripes on Monday* tugged at the edge of every girl's mind. Now there was a new revelation: that stripes could happen on Sunday, too. Or something like them. Maybe something worse.

The discomfort of silence was somewhat softened by the pleasance of privilege in being allowed to spend the afternoon in the sitting room. Unlike the dark classroom or the ever-dank dining hall, the common room had an entire wall with four windows stretching nearly from the floor to the ceiling. Upholstered sofas and chairs were grouped throughout, giving the impression that, were it not a Sunday afternoon, the room might be buzzing with conversations. Instead, it swelled with the sound of little girls shifting and sighing. The only acceptable activities were needlework or copying psalms onto the blank pages of a prayer book.

That day, I climbed up into what had quickly become my favorite chair, one with a faded floral upholstery over the arms. It faced the windows and kept one side of my face turned toward the brown stone fireplace. Once settled, I inched the sleeve of my dress up to my elbow, revealing an arm that had turned into a calico of bruising with multiple shades of blue and purple. In the center, a clear imprint left by Father Johann. Gingerly, I placed my own fingers in the imprint, trying to imagine what it would feel like to strike anything with such force. It didn't hurt anymore—not much, anyway. What pain remained found its home in my mind and memory, lingering long after I pulled the sleeve back down to my wrist.

My friends' now-familiar *psst!* caught my attention, and I craned my neck around the back of the chair to see Therese and Girt straddling a bench, passing a forbidden game of cat's cradle between them. Wordlessly, they communicated, *Are you all right?*

Yes.

Did it hurt?

Yes.

Does it still?

Knowing I couldn't disguise the half truth of

the answer, I turned my attention to watch the big, fat snowflakes—a final protest of spring—floating in their own lazy silence. Later, when I said my evening prayers, I would remember to thank God for the shelter of this warm room, where one or another of the older girls took charge to poke or refuel the fire whenever a new chill threatened. Outside, the bell chimed another hour gone by. Three o'clock. There would be two more hours, at the very least, until we girls would be permitted to get up, stretch, and splash our hands and faces with water before the evening meal. In the meantime, one side of my face glowed warm, my legs turned numb with listlessness, and my eyelids grew heavy with the effort of watching the perfect, dancing snow.

"Look." Therese's voice exploded into the silence. "She's sleeping again. I guess some girls just never learn their lesson."

A smattering of snickers undercut the silence, until someone had the good sense to whisper, *"Hush."*

Now fully awake, I sat straight up and shot my friend my best withering stare.

Shut up!

Therese, however, refused to heed my silent plea and engaged a confused Girt in her stunt.

"Tell you what," she said to the poor girl who stared, slack-jawed, the forgotten cat's cradle limp and dangling from her fingers. "You be

Käthe and I'll be Father Johann. That's right, just like that. You just sit there and stare up at me looking stupid."

"Stop it," Girt whispered, her eyes darting around the room as if the sisters might jump out from between the wood paneling. "You're going to get us all into trouble."

Therese ignored her completely, opting instead to mimic holding an enormous Bible. She drooped her eyes and somehow took on the persona of Father Johann. "Little girl, have you been snoozing?"

The other girls, with growing fearlessness, giggled, but not Girt. She continued to stare in silent horror.

"Now comes the part where you need to give me your hand. Give me, Girt. Roll up your sleeve."

"Therese! Why are you being so cruel?"

"What, cruel? It's funny. It was funny, wasn't it, girls? You could hear it *swap!* clear to the back of the room, I'll bet. Quite a show our little Käthe put on for everybody, wasn't it?"

I remained rooted to my chair, the heat from the fireplace no match for the heat rising within. It grew and bubbled, the moment of shame rising up again before my very eyes. The smirk on Therese's face obscured any trace of the friend I once knew, and while I might have been too little to defend myself against Father Johann, years of scrapping with my brothers had trained me to identify an assailable foe. With no thought given to the sanctions of the afternoon, I let out a howl that carried every pent-up syllable since the morning prayers. In a flash, I leapt out of my chair and launched myself across the room, screaming foul threats to Therese until the second I was on the girl herself, then over her, raining open slaps against her pretty face.

"Get off! You little—" And, demonstrating her own skill in combat, Therese locked me between her knees, then flipped the both of us. My arms were soon pinned, but not before I grabbed two handfuls of thin blonde hair, bringing forth a loud, sustained yelp.

A chorus of our peers encouraged the violence, and I was searching for an open spot to deliver a wood-shod kick when the room filled with the presence of Sister Odile and the normally unflappable Sister Elisabeth.

"Stop it! Both of you!"

It was Sister Odile's voice that cut through the screeching of the girls but Sister Elisabeth who inserted herself physically into the fight. She wrapped her arms around Therese's shoulders and urged, "There, now. That's enough," holding on until I was safe to scoot myself out from under Therese's weight. When she was near the point of release, though, Therese wrested herself from Sister Elisabeth's grip and, in a last spiteful move, stomped her foot on the hem of my dress. The sound of the ripping fabric pierced the brief silence.

Therese and I, newly peaceful in our conflict, looked at one another, and just as quickly as my heart had been torn, it healed to perfection.

Sister Odile swooped down, taking each of us under an arm. "Look what you did," she said, twisting her body to bring Therese into view of the damaged dress. "For that, *you,* Therese, will spend the afternoon mending Katharina's dress. And, Katharina—" She stopped abruptly, her heightened emotion evident. With little ceremony, she dropped her grip on Therese and went to her knees, bringing herself eye level. "You, little one, have had a difficult day. Have you not?"

I nodded, feeling the saltiness of my lunchtime broth gurgling at the top of my throat—almost like tears.

"Well, then. Why don't you pop into your nightdress and lie down in your bed for the afternoon. Would that be nice?"

"Yes, Sister Odile." I tried not to sound too eager, though already I could feel the cool, welcome comfort of the pillow. The room would be cold, but it would be quiet. A better quiet than the sitting room. An alone quiet.

"And," she said, her voice once again filled with towering authority, "Therese will mend your dress and deliver it to you before supper. Won't you, Therese?"

"Yes, Sister Odile," Therese said in a way that only those who didn't know her would find to be sincere.

Chapter 4

Therese had striped hands in the morning, and a close inspection showed traces of her blood near the perfectly mended patch. I felt a new weight on my shoulders when I put the dress on that morning—not only that of the locket, which I knew to be hiding somewhere in the hem, but the burden of understanding my friend's sacrifice.

"I will be your friend forever," I whispered in her ear as we stood in line for the washbasin. When my turn came, I brought her with me and lifted the pitcher to pour clean, fresh water into the basin for her hands.

"You won't," she said, patting her face dry with the towel.

"What do you mean? Of course I will."

She waited while I washed my own face, then led me away from the line, back to her bunk, where I helped by tying the ribbon at the back of her dress.

"We won't *be* here forever, silly. You're from a noble family. You'll go home eventually, if you decide not to take the vows. You have that choice. I don't."

“What do you mean? They can’t force you to be a nun.”

“No, but I want to be. With all my heart. I have no other family.”

She sat on the bed and I sat behind her, brushing her white-silk hair until it shone before plaiting it. “Neither do I, really.”

Therese risked the pain of tugging to snap her head around. “Ungrateful. Of course you do.”

“Not that really care about me. Why else would I be here?” I held the brush aloft, not resuming until she turned around again.

“Do you know why I’m here, Käthe?”

“Same as any of us, I suppose.” Truthfully, I hadn’t considered anybody having a story much different from mine. Girt, I knew, was here from some sort of family obligation. A donation of land, and the life of a daughter, given to the Church as an offering. I too was an offering, in hopes that my absence from the home would bring God’s blessing upon it. Therese, however, never spoke of her family, which made me think it was as ordinary as the rest of ours. I kept my eyes trained on the pretty nape of her neck, ready to disappear behind her story.

“I’m not like any of you. My family isn’t like any of yours. Not my mother, anyway. She was a prostitute. Not even she knew who my father is. I knew my grandparents, though. Her parents. She used to send me to their house when we didn’t have any money, and I would beg them for food, or a blanket, or anything we could sell."

"Why didn't you live with them?"

"Because I loved my mother. I couldn't leave her alone. Not even after she . . ."

Therese bowed her head, and I let the braid go slack in my hand. "Did she get sick?"

"We were going to go live with my grandparents finally. And have a home and everything, when . . ."

I felt the pain emanating from her shoulders. "You don't have to tell me if you don't want to."

"She died. I was with her, just the two of us in our little room. I was sleeping right next to her, and when I woke up, she was dead."

Our dormitory was emptied of the other girls, eager to get their breakfast. Only Girt remained—Girt, who must have known this story already, because she sat on the other side of Therese, barely touching the girl's striped hand. "Tell her," Girt said. "Tell her about the angel."

"A man came into the room that first night. He put a chair in front of the door and sat on it. I heard men on the other side—Mother's men—pounding and calling her name, but the door didn't budge. And I could somehow hear him speak, but he never said a word."

"Did he have wings?" I asked. By now the brush sat in my lap, forgotten.

Therese shook her head. "No, but he was the

biggest man I'd ever seen. Taller than the door, stronger than the walls. His clothes were ordinary but clean. He touched my skin, and it burned, here." She stretched out her arm, and I saw the faintest pink swipe on her flesh. "I climbed up into his lap and slept for two days. Then he stood up, moved the chair. The landlord pounded on the door, looking for the rent. My grandfather was with him, but the man? He was gone, and even in those moments I started to forget about him. It's like he stayed hidden in my mind until my grandfather brought me here."

"How do you know he was an angel?"

"Because he was handsome. And clean. And no man who ever came through our door was either of those things. And most of all, he didn't frighten me. He didn't try to—" she took a deep, shuddering breath—"do things. To me, like the other men did."

I had no idea what kind of *things* would cause such pain in memory, but I dared not ask.

"My grandparents brought me to their home, but they were too old to raise me. Another nun I knew, Sister Heida, brought me here. I think of myself as an offering to atone for the sins of my mother."

Girt took over the braiding of Therese's hair, tying the end with a scrap of black ribbon, then tucking it up under her cap and tying that, too.

"So, you see—" Therese's great, blue eyes

filled the space between us—"we can never be friends forever, here. Not for our whole lives."

By far, the best hours of every week came at two o'clock, after dinner and outside play time. While all the other girls went to the big classroom to spend an hour in their copybooks, I went for catechism in preparation for my first Holy Communion. This meant time alone, being trusted to walk the long hallway that took me through the school building, across the courtyard, and to the chapel. Even better, I was allowed up a narrow, winding stone staircase, at the top of which a small room nestled in the rafters.

The first time I'd come under the guidance of Sister Gerda, who'd clutched my hand and muttered, "Come on, you! I'm not leading you to any gallows." But who could tell where the blind old nun was going? The sound of my wooden shoes punctuated the particular scraping step of Sister Gerda, who all the while grumbled about taking in such young girls.

"Not even a proper Catholic," she said as her gnarled hand trailed along the wall, measuring. "Too much to ask that they come knowing the sacraments? Why not drop a dozen unbaptized babies at the gate?"

She stopped talking when we came to the staircase, then uttered a perfunctory *watch your step* without implying that she cared one whit whether I made it to the top or tumbled down and down.

Every inch of the fearful trek proved its worth, however, once I ascended the top step and found myself in a cozy attic room. The rafters were bare, the windows low along the slanted roof, and a layer of sweet straw covered the floor. The furnishings consisted of two wooden stools and a small table. It looked for all the world like a bird's nest, and on that first day, Sister Gerda handed me over to Sister Elisabeth, the bird within.

Now allowed to make the journey on my own, I walked with decorum through the school, marching in the great echoing stone hallway that led to the church. I tried to create a rhythm with my shoes as I ascended the steps, kicking my toe against each one—twice—before stepping up to the next. Then, at the top, Sister Elisabeth would be waiting.

Sister Elisabeth wasn't like any of the other sisters at Brehna. For one thing, she was pretty. Soft brown eyes, narrow nose, and a smile that revealed perfect, straight, clean teeth. I knew well the beauty of Sister Elisabeth's teeth because, in a second characteristic that set her apart from the other nuns, she smiled wide, and often, greeting me every day with, "Why, hello, Katharina," as if my arrival were some welcome surprise. Most fascinating, though, were her hands. Beautiful, delicate, with nails that looked like flower petals had floated on a spring breeze and attached themselves to the tips. Surely Sister Elisabeth did her share of labor, washing up and scrubbing down, cooking and sweeping and all the good work of maintaining the house of the Lord, but her hands held the quality of a fair maiden hidden in a turret. On the rare occasions when she appeared outside of our nest, she always moved softly, swiftly, as if a proper gust of wind beneath her habit would send her into swirling flight.

This afternoon, I popped my head into the room to find Sister Elisabeth waiting as usual, perched on her stool. Instead of her usual chipper greeting, however, she remained silent, her welcoming hand stretched out from within its black woolen wing.

"Sweet Katharina," she said, and in the next second, I was folded within that arm, feeling Sister Elisabeth's cool cheek against my own. "Have you quite recovered from your tussle?"

"Yes, Sister Elisabeth."

"And that other? Let me see."

Understanding, I stepped back and raised my sleeve. Two days had passed, but even in the dim light of the attic room, the mark of the priest's touch remained clearly etched in the flesh, surrounded by a bruising yellow cloud.

"He was wrong to have done this."

The sting of shame flared up anew, just as sharp as the pain that was by now, thankfully, nothing more than a memory. Emboldened by the promise of an ally, I fought against the threatening tears.

"You should have seen it right after. You could even see the wrinkles from his fingers."

Sister Elisabeth smiled, salving the lingering hurt. "What a brave girl you are. And so smart, too. I was very proud of you. I just wish I could have done something—"

"I've memorized the Apostles' Creed," I said, wanting to change the subject before my courage disappeared. I pulled myself away and settled on my own wooden stool, trying to match Sister Elisabeth's manner of soft authority. "Shall we start there?"

"Why the rush?" Sister Elisabeth fished behind her, produced a linen napkin, and unfolded it to reveal a small, dark cake. I could smell the spices emanating from it, and my cheeks tingled for the taste. With the cake nestled in her lap, Sister Elisabeth brought forth a small crock pitcher, which she declared to be fresh milk, a treat I hadn't tasted since leaving home. She poured a measure into a pewter cup and set both on the table before me.

"Now we'll begin. Who made the world?"

"God made the world," I said, anticipating the taste of cake.

"And who is God?"

"God is the creator of all things in heaven and on earth."

"And man?"

"Man is a creation of body and soul, brought to life in the image and likeness of God."

Sister Elisabeth smiled, pinched off a corner of the cake, and placed it—still warm—in my open hand.

"Thank you," I said before my mouth filled with nutmeg and cloves. Then a sip of milk, cool in its pewter cup. I wished Father Johann could see me now and felt a secret, sly grin at how incensed he'd be at the picture of this tiny, insolent girl so pampered and privileged at the catechism. Hazarding a glimpse over the top of the cup, I wondered how great a risk Sister Elisabeth had taken in bringing such a delicacy. Moreover, why would she bother? When our eyes met, I had my answer, in all of its simplicity. Sister Elisabeth was kind.

"Shall we continue?"

I wiped my lip with my sleeve and handed back the cup. "Yes, Sister."

"Now, my sparrow. Why did God make you?"

This had been the hardest question of all, the first time I heard it. The others, about God and creation, were easy. Anybody with a soul could answer. But this? Why would God make a little girl with a dead mother and a weak father and mean brothers? Why would he make her if all he intended to do was pick her up and drop her in this place, surrounded by other girls whose lives held no more meaning? I had nothing to offer this world, not even enough to offer my friend Girt, who still sometimes wept late into the night. Katharina von Bora was needless and small, but with Sister Elisabeth's initial prompting, I'd learned the answer.

"God made me to know him. And to love him. And to serve him in this world for as long as I live. And then, when I die, to be happy with him forever in heaven."

I knew I'd recited the correct answer, but I hoped Sister Elisabeth wouldn't give me another piece of cake. It didn't seem right, somehow, to be rewarded for saying a truth that didn't seem *real.* Or at least one that didn't bring with it any sense of joy. Why couldn't the answer be reversed? Why couldn't God have made me to be happy in *this* world, and to serve him in the next? The moment the thought entered, I squelched it, in fear of the next question.

"What must we do to save our souls?"

I took a deep breath. "We must worship God in faith, hope, and charity."

"And what does that mean?" Sister Elisabeth prompted.

"It means to save my soul, I must hope in him. Believe in him. And love him with all of my heart."

I waited for what should surely be the next question, in which Sister Elisabeth would lean forward, stretching her beautiful face beyond the confines of the wimple, and ask, *Do you, Katharina? Do you love God with all of your heart?* But she didn't ask. She never had, perhaps sparing both of us. Yes, I believed in God, if for no other reason than out of the fear of *not* believing, but the thought of loving him brought with it another kind of fear. I loved my own father with all of my heart, and he'd said often enough that, without my love, he'd never live another day. I supposed that all of the people with *truly* saved souls—the priests, the sisters, the saints—simply had no one else to love. But I did. I loved my father, I hoped in my father, but even so, after so many nights of witnessing his soiled clothing and endless weeping, I knew better than to ever believe in him.

Sister Elisabeth interrupted my thoughts. "How shall we know what things to believe?"

I stared down at my hands, picturing the faded bruise beneath the sleeve. "God speaks to us through the teachings of the Church, giving us all things we are to believe."

"And where can the truths of the Church be found?" Sister Elisabeth's voice lilted with excitement.

"In the Apostles' Creed."

"Yes!" She clasped her hands to her chin. "Now. Can you recite it?"

I stood up, as such an occasion called for, and swept the crumbs and wrinkles from my dress. *"I believe in God, the Father Almighty, Creator of heaven and earth, and in Jesus Christ, his only Son, our Lord, who was conceived by the Holy Ghost, born of the Virgin Mary, suffered under Pontius Pilate, was crucified, died, and was buried."*

I continued what was, in my mind, a perfect recitation, picturing Christ's descent into hell and ascension into heaven. I imagined him at that moment, sitting at the right hand of God, on a throne in a place that rivaled the beauty of the greatest cathedral. Not that I'd ever seen a great cathedral. The chapel here at Brehna was drab and worn, no place for Christ to sit. No place for him to judge the living and the dead, but oh, wouldn't I love to see the judgment of Father Johann? Wouldn't I love to see Jesus lick his fingers with fire and strike them down on the priest's deserving flesh?

"I believe in the Holy Ghost, the Holy Catholic Church, the communion of saints, the forgiveness of sins, the resurrection of the body, and the life everlasting."

I stopped, realizing I'd risen to my toes within my wooden shoes. Sister Elisabeth said nothing, only looked on, eyes brimming with pride and a hint of expectation.

"Amen."

"Perfect!" Sister Elisabeth pulled me in for a quick kiss to my cheek. "You may have another bite of cake while we begin the next lesson."

For the balance of the hour Sister Elisabeth offered instruction on the sacraments of baptism, confirmation, and confession, and I listened, consumed and fascinated by the complexities of faith. I couldn't remember my own baptism, of course, but I had witnessed many others, breathless at the moment the tiny soul was sealed to heaven. And I'd even practiced confession, once, with my father. He stood behind the drapery while I confessed that I sometimes hated my brothers. Papa had said, *My child, if you harbor hatred in your heart, you leave no room for love.* For penance, I was told to speak only sweetly to my brothers for the next three days, and to pray for them every evening for the next seven. I followed through, completely, and felt the darkness lift until the day Hans pelted me mercilessly with walnuts as I tried to cross the yard.

When the bell chimed three, Sister Elisabeth wrapped the remainder of the cake in its linen cloth and told me she would save it until our next lesson, two days hence.

"Thank you, Sister Elisabeth," I said, and turned to leave.

"And remember, my girl, during our study here, you are free to ask me questions, as many questions as I ask you." Sister Elisabeth took a pinch of cake. "Don't think I don't notice how far your mind flies when we are studying. Your knowledge is not limited by my knowledge. You have the mind of Christ, endless in what it can pursue."

"But I don't know what I don't know."

Sister Elisabeth laughed—a beautiful sound that reminded me of a dove's call in the morning. "Then we shall continue to discover God's teachings together."

Chapter 5

1509

I stepped into the confessional, closed the door, and breathed in the darkness before the tiny window slid open, revealing the priest's profile on the other side of the thin, intricately carved barrier. Although I knew it was forbidden, I hazarded a look. Since Father Johann's untimely death nearly a year earlier, the confessional and pulpit had been filled by all manner of itinerant priests, those either ascending in rank or nearing their time of pasture. One had to be repeatedly poked by a resident deacon when loud snores were reported by the penitents. This one was young. Smooth skin, round face, and the good manners not to be staring right at me through the lattice.

"Bless me, Father," I said with rote obedience, "for I have sinned. It is one week since my last confession."

"In what way have you sinned, my child?" His voice was tinged with humor, as if knowing the confession of a ten-year-old girl could be harmless at best.

"I harbored evil thoughts about my stepmother."

"What kind of evil thoughts?"

My mind filled with a litany of complaints. For all the time I'd been at Brehna, I hadn't been invited home for the Christmas holidays, and four birthdays had passed without even a letter of recognition or praise. All of this I attributed to Retta, as the two letters I *had* received from Papa were filled with his own rantings against her overbearing nature, saying that if he were a stronger man, he would bring me back home. But he bowed to her wisdom, as she was a woman and thus must know what would be best for a young girl. None of this, however, excused the darkness of my heart.

"I hate her."

"Scriptures tell us that anyone who hates another human being has committed murder in his—or her—heart."

"I know." My hands reached for the necklace hidden in its secret pocket. This was my fourth dress since arriving at this place and had been torn during a rousing game of tag in the courtyard. "She's never come even once to visit me."

"If you hate her, why would you want her to come visit?"

I shrugged, as if the priest could see. "I don't, really. But that means Papa hasn't come either. Because he bows to her. Why should I bother even *having* a stepmother if I'm never going to see her? I wish she'd died instead of my mother, but then she wouldn't be my stepmother, and I'd never know enough to hate her."

When he spoke again, his voice was softer. "After confession, and three times every day until your next confession, you are to ask the Blessed Mother to protect your stepmother. And as you pray, you must promise the Father that you will try very hard to love her. We cannot pray falsehoods to God, and in time, you will love her."

Never. But I said only, "Yes, Father."

"And have you any other sins to confess?"

"Three nights this week I took my supper biscuit out of the dining hall and ate it in my bed."

I thought I heard an exhalation that sounded a bit like laughter. "And this is a sin?"

"It's against the rules."

"And why do you break such a rule so willingly?"

"Because I am hungry, sometimes, late at night, and it's hard to sleep when you're both hungry *and* cold. But if I lay on top of the biscuit for a few minutes, it gets warm, and then it warms my insides, too."

"But doesn't it make you thirsty?" With that question, the priest became a partner in conversation rather than an appointed absolver of my sin.

"A little, but I don't notice much until the morning."

"You know, young lady, they have these rules for a reason. Can you guess the reason?"

There was no hint of condescension in his voice; only an opportunity for me to supply the answer we both knew to be correct. "Because of the rats."

"That's right. Rats. And you wouldn't want to wake up some morning to find a rat nibbling through your blankets in search of the last few crumbs of a forgotten biscuit, would you?"

"No," I said truthfully after weighing the probability.

"Even worse, the rat might give up a quest for crumbs and come nibbling directly at your nose."

Here I giggled, as I was clearly meant to do.

"Child," he said, returning to a tone of kind, spiritual authority, "if you are hungry at night, recall this Scripture: *The bread of God is he which cometh down from heaven, and giveth life unto the world.* And when the followers of Christ asked him to give them this bread so that they could eat it and be full, do you remember what our Savior told them?"

"That he was the bread of life."

"Exactly. *Jesus said unto them, I am the bread of life: he that cometh to me shall never hunger; and he that believeth on me shall never thirst.* You believe in Jesus Christ, do you not?"

"I do." In that moment, I believed a little more.

"Then feast upon him. In those quiet moments, before sleep, when your stomach might be empty, fill your thoughts with the hope of Christ. Think on his goodness and his mercy. Thank him for the fact that, even though you might be hungry in the moment, you know dawn is coming with the promise of porridge."

I giggled again, softer this time, not knowing if I was supposed to. How on earth did he know we had porridge for breakfast every morning?

"And if you are cold," he continued, "fold your body as if kneeling in prayer. Clasp your hands together, and breathe upon them. The Holy Ghost lives within you. Imagine his fire, warming your body through your blood. He may not give you a second blanket, but his strength can double the weight of the one you lie under. Only ask it, and it will be given."

"I will, Father," I said, wishing I could go this very minute to my narrow cot, third from the washstand at the far end of the room.

"Now—" I could see the faint image of his hand moving to make the sign of the cross—"*in nomine Patris, et Filii, et Spiritus Sancti*. Depart in peace and be warmed and filled."

I crossed myself. "In the name of the Father, the Son, and the Holy Ghost. Amen, and thank you, Father."

I exited the confessional, wishing very much

I could linger to see the man behind the voice. But his instructions to pray for my stepmother took me straight to the altar, where I genuflected, saying, "*In nomine Patris*, *et Filii*, *et Spiritus Sancti*," and then knelt, feeling the comforting edge of the locket in the hidden pocket beneath my knee.

"Blessed Mother," I prayed, and then could go no further. The priest had instructed me to ask Holy Mary to protect my stepmother and to promise God the Father that I would love her. In that moment, the entire prayer got tangled up in my head. Which was more important? Which more powerful, less painful? My selfishness couldn't, in all honesty, bring forth a genuine prayer for protection. For all I cared, Retta could fall down a well, or get kicked in the behind by the family's cantankerous mule, or catch her eyebrows on fire bringing burning bread out of the oven. What need did my family have of the woman? For all I knew, my brothers were grown and gone, and I hardly felt in need of anyone's care. The locket was now boring into my knee, but I did not shift my weight.

I should love her.

The priest had told me only to try. To try very hard.

I crossed myself—"*In nomine Patris*, *et Filii*, *et Spiritus Sancti*"—and tried again. "Heavenly Father, God, I ask you and our Blessed Mother, who watches over us in heaven, to watch over Mama Retta at home. I ask that she be well and happy, and for that happiness to make her kind and loving. And I shall try to love her in my head, even if I cannot love her in my heart."

I spoke the prayer loud enough for the priest to hear, had he been so inclined, and remained at the altar with an unreasonable hope that he might reveal himself in approval of my obedience. When he didn't, I stood, knowing the locket had left a dimple in the skin of my knee. Since I was older now, I no longer had to wear wooden shoes, so my steps were nearly silent as I exited the chapel. Nagging curiosity tempted me to remain, silent and still at the door, until he—thinking the room to be empty—might emerge for his own prayer.

Instead, I heard my name. Softly at first, but then again, louder, coming from the back of the sanctuary.

"Kat!"

Therese, of course. Only she called me by that name. I hurried down the aisle and found my friend standing in the shadows, her white skin luminous in the dim light.

"There's a letter for you," she whispered. "Well, not so much for you, but about you. From the abbess at Marienthrone."

"My mother's cousin. Margarete."

Therese waved the detail away. "Sister Odile

was sending Sister Gerda to fetch you, but I'm faster. I wanted to tell you first."

I reached to my friend for strength as my stomach dropped in anticipation of the missive's news. "Do you think they're sending for me, then?"

"What else could it be? I couldn't hear everything, but Sister Odile said something about 'the time has come,' and she told Sister Gerda to say nothing. Only to fetch you to the sisters' common room right away."

As if confirming, the shuffling step of Sister Gerda echoed in the vestibule of the sanctuary, and we dropped our voices to something close to silence.

"Don't let on that you know."

"I won't. But you should go, or Sister Gerda will know for sure you told me."

"Watch; I'll move right past her."

The old nun's small, bent form came into view, her steps guided by the fingertips of the gnarled hand grazing the wall. As promised, Therese moved with swift, noiseless steps against the opposite wall, garnering little more than a sniff of attention.

"Katharina von Bora?" Sister Gerda spoke to the air, repeating the name twice more in different directions before the object of her search responded.

"I'm here, Sister Gerda."

"Sister Odile said you would be in confession."

"I have confessed already, Sister Gerda. And said my prayers."

"Then come with me." She extended an elbow, clearly intended for me to take. "We'll walk together, and you can tell me all about the day."

In the years since I first arrived, I had grown to be a head taller than Sister Gerda, and the fear she once inspired had tempered into a true, reverent affection. I stooped a bit to take the woman's arm and bore the extra weight as I turned us in the opposite direction.

"What would you like me to tell you?"

"I feel the warmth of the afternoon," Sister Gerda said, her words swished with toothlessness, "but shouldn't the sun shine more brightly?"

"We're in the shade now, under that covered walkway."

"I know where we are, girl. I've walked these grounds for more than twice your lifetime."

"Forgive me, Sister. I meant no disrespect."

"It is a gift from our Father, to be so familiar with the sights that have fallen away. I see these walls as clearly as I touch them, and I can count the steps in prayer from one room to the next. I meant only that the light seems dim for the hour."

I studied the courtyard. "I believe you're right, Sister. The sky's not so much cloudy, but dim. More like autumn than summer."

"As I thought."

I waited for further instruction in conversation but then noticed the old woman's lips moving silently. I kept my own shut tight until we came to the antechamber of the common room.

"Come then," Sister Gerda said. "Open the door, child. All is well."

I did as she bid, then stepped back to allow her to enter first before following.

As much as we girls relished our Sunday afternoons in the common room, it was also a place fraught with legend and dread, for behind its doors, girls received punishments for infractions that occurred after school hours. Once, Therese called it the Chamber of Sadness because girls who were summoned here often came out crying with news from home. A dead parent, a summoning home, a fire that burned house and barn and livestock—all bad news delivered within hours after a whispered invitation to this place. So despite Sister Gerda's assurance that all was well and Therese's news about the letter from Marienthrone, I brought my own misgivings with me over the threshold.

"Katharina von Bora," Sister Odile said, greeting me the way she had on every occasion since my arrival. She stood in the center of the room, despite the abundance of furniture on which to sit.

"Good afternoon, Sister Odile." I offered a curtsy and bowed head as I'd been taught.

"I suppose you know already that I have received word from Marienthrone." She cocked an eyebrow, communicating that it would be both useless and unnecessary to lie.

"I don't know the nature of the word, Sister Odile. Is there news from Girt?"

Girt's family, upon receiving word that their daughter would, indeed, take her vows to become a nun, had arranged for her to go to Marienthrone—a more prestigious institution than Brehna, and thus an augmentation to her family's name.

"This letter is from the abbess herself, and it concerns you alone. Shall I read it to you?"

"I can read it for myself, if you'd prefer."

"I will not miss your impudence," Sister Odile said, confirming what I'd hoped to hear.

"So I'm to go?"

"She says she will welcome you, though that may be because she's yet to meet you."

Nothing Sister Odile said could stem my enthusiasm, and before I could think about how a proper young lady would conduct herself, I clapped my hands and let forth a sound of rejoicing. Unlike Girt, I was far from settled on the question of taking the veil, but I had come to the end of what could be called an education here at Brehna. Even though I was only ten, I attended classes with all the older girls and helped them with their Latin and theology studies. Marienthrone offered more, for me and for my friend.

"What did she say about Therese? Can she come too?"

A dependent of the charity of the Church, Therese could not hope to gain entrance into so fine a convent without a sponsor. My family did not have the means to provide for Therese—I doubted they would be able to send me there without the benefit of family connection. The fact remained, though, that we *did* have such a connection, and since the day Therese tore and then mended my dress, I'd been searching for a way to repay her. Christmas the previous year sparked my idea.

I would go to Marienthrone, and I would take Therese with me.

"She, too, is welcome," Sister Odile said, "though it will make me sad to see both of you go."

Nothing in Sister Odile's face indicated sadness. Instead, it was Sister Gerda who sniffed a small sniff before turning her clouded eye to the window.

"We have done our part here," Sister Odile said, her voice deep with reassurance. "God brings us these children, and we raise them to be his bride. What greater honor than to see our hard work come to fruition."

The meaning behind her words was not lost.

She knew I'd made no such commitment, and that if I did, this hovel of a place would receive no credit. But Therese, I knew, longed for the day when she would be old enough to commit her life to the vows of poverty, chastity, and servitude to Christ.

"When do we leave?" I tried to somewhat mask my enthusiasm.

"Two weeks hence," Sister Odile said. "Sister Gerda will accompany you and speak our introduction. Would you like that, Gerda?"

"Oh, I think that's fine. Just fine," she said, looking as if she believed it.

After settling the details of the travel, I walked out of the common room to see Therese waiting in the hall.

"Chamber of Sadness, Kat?"

"Hardly." I took her by the hand and led her off to a quiet place where I could tell her everything. She was, after all, my best friend, and I'd just won my first battle to keep us together.

Chapter 6

I braced my toes against the front of the carriage, holding myself to my seat as it careened down, down into the valley. Stretching, I pulled the curtain aside and looked out the window. The late-afternoon sky was tinged golden, infused with the aura of autumn. That's how I would have described it to Sister Gerda. The woman claimed to see clouds of shadow and color, and not even her blindness would be able to block out the blazing reds and oranges of the underbrush of the forest rolling beside the lumbering coach.

Why she had been chosen to accompany us as chaperone remained a mystery. She could offer neither protection from would-be rogues nor guidance during the short forays when we stopped to rest the horses. Perhaps it was her expendability that had brought her out on Sister Odile's arm, to be unceremoniously handed up to the seat opposite Therese and me. Her sharp ears picked up every word of conversation, no matter how loud the jangling of the chains or the rumble of the wheels. But when she slept, she did so deeply, with snores loud enough to frighten foxes. We had giggled at the first, bringing Sister Gerda sharply awake and incurring her wrath for showing such mirth when we were traveling under the mercy of God's guiding hand. For the next hour, she brought us to clutching terror with stories of all that could go wrong for a heedless girl upon the heathen roads.

"Rip you right out of the doors, they can," she said. "One filthy hand over your mouth to keep you from screaming, the other carrying you off to some godforsaken place. Next thing, your virtue is gone, and you're left, tossed into the ruts."

She spoke with such haunting authority that we fell silent until Therese sang a sweet hymn to soften the old nun's glare. After a time, the woman's head bobbed low, a string of spittle dribbling from the corner of her toothless mouth.

"Come over here," Therese beckoned, and I leaned over to look at the scene unfolding on the other side.

At the foot of a rolling hill, the valley opened up to what looked like an entire miniature town. Smoke rose from chimneys, and a series of single-story buildings were laid out in a precise manner, creating a wall of booths and shops surrounding a large structure at the center.

"That's it. Marienthrone," Therese whispered. "Such an honor. I mean, a girl can't just walk through the doors there. It's only for nuns, and only if you have property to give them."

"Or a name." I squeezed her hand. "What do you think it will be like?"

Therese shrugged. "Only God can see the future."

We rode past farmland fresh from the last harvest and orchards of trees laden with fruit. Up close, I noticed the tradesmen—blacksmith, butcher, potters, and carpenters—none of whom offered more than a passing glance.

"There's everything," I said, my voice tinged with awe. My mind reeled with memories of walking beside Papa around the market back home. How long had it been since I'd heard the iron clash of a blacksmith or smelled the meat from a butcher's smokehouse? This, I knew, would be my only glimpse. A locked gate awaited.

"No different from Brehna." Therese sat back in her seat, arms folded. But she didn't fool me. This was new, bigger, and bustling.

"I was worried. It seemed so far away from home."

"Our Savior is our home," Therese said, quoting the phrase so many sniffling girls heard upon their arrival through the big doors at Brehna.

"Good girl." Sister Gerda's eyes were still closed, but a satisfied smile tugged at the corner of her listless mouth. "Remember, not even the Son of God himself had a place to rest his holy head. If you have warmth and food, you have more than you deserve, being a sinner of this world. There are many who don't have even that."

"Yes, Sister," I said, but I couldn't completely quell the disappointment forming deep within my belly. We turned a corner, and I had to poke my head outside the window to see our approach to a low brick wall topped with latticework and vines. Once through the gate, we drove past gardens being tended by women in spotless white robes. A few left their chore and stood, hands shielding their eyes from the setting sun. "They wear white here."

"Not until they take their vows," Sister Gerda said. "And how they can hope to do God's work in such frivolous attire is beyond understanding."

Therese and I exchanged a furtive, amused look before we took one last, lingering glance out the window, breathing in the sweetness of the garden.

When we finally came to a smooth stop, the driver yelled, "Hello at the gate!" I watched him—a burly man, unwashed in flesh and clothing—descend from his seat and approach the arched door, sounding three heavy drops of the iron knocker. Minutes later, the door of the carriage opened, and a grubby hand, calloused from the reins, took mine, helping me step down to the wooden block and then onto the pebbled ground, where my knees wobbled beneath me.

"Steady," he said but offered no assistance.

Therese and Sister Gerda were similarly aided. Then, with a tip of his hat, the driver ascended to his seat, touched his whip to the horses, and disappeared. No sooner had he rounded the corner than the arched wooden door opened, revealing a nun dressed head to toe in pristine white, a black cross hanging from a thin rope settled squarely at her center. She smiled, bringing pink roses to her cheeks, and motioned for us three to follow her. The gesture was lost on Sister Gerda, who erupted in confusion when I took her arm to guide her.

"What's this? Where—?" Her clouded eyes searched high and low before her nose scrunched in distaste. "That's right. So much silent here. Might as well be deaf and dumb."

The nun in white didn't offer so much as a backward glance. I looped my arm more tightly through Sister Gerda's and kept a respectful distance behind. There was nothing to distract me from our guide. No tapestries on the walls, no painted depictions of saints or the Holy Family. Just brick after brick, haphazardly assembled, doing next to nothing to hold back the chill of the approaching evening. The ground was hard-packed earth up to the point where we crossed a threshold, then became uneven stone as we stood in a cavernous room, empty save for a soot-stained fire pit in its center. The air smelled of ashes, and my eyes stung as if smoke lingered in every crevice. But there was no fire, and judging from the charred wood in the center of the pit, there hadn't been one for quite some time.

"I thought it would be so grand," I whispered.

"There's no need for frivolity in doing the Lord's work," Therese said, though I sensed her disappointment too.

Our host held up a hand, indicating we should stay and wait, then disappeared through one of the dark hallways.

Sister Gerda tugged my sleeve. "Tell me."

I whispered in detail all I'd seen since we descended from the coach, concluding with the fact that the room we now stood in appeared to have more than four walls, with several shallow corners surrounding us on all sides, and the impressive pit at its center.

"Warming room," Sister Gerda said, as if answering a question. "Means the rest of the place will be cold as a killer's heart."

"It's a large enough room," Therese said, her soft voice echoing. "Plenty of space to gather."

"Mark me," Sister Gerda said, pointing her arthritic finger toward the massive chimney, "you'll be lucky to get the dregs of warmth come winter."

The small sound of a clearing throat caught our attention. The nun had returned and gestured again for us to follow. Her white habit provided the only light in the corridor, and had it been any later in the day, it too would have been swallowed up in the darkness. The hallway emptied into a small antechamber, equally as Spartan as any room we'd seen thus far, with a plain cross hung above an open, arched doorway. The nun touched Therese and Sister Gerda lightly on their shoulders, then pointed to a crude wooden bench beside the door.

Therese took custody of Sister Gerda and led her to the bench, whispering, "She wants us to sit and wait here."

"Even Katharina?"

"No," Therese said. "She's taking Katharina with her."

Sister Gerda's faint attempt to protest prompted the nun to take my hand and lead me through the doorway into a room that, while simplistic in its design, was more ornate than any we'd encountered so far. A triptych depicting the Annunciation hung on a wall opposite a high window. The late afternoon offered nothing but dull gray light, making the woman standing in the far corner appear like an image coming clear in the face of a pond.

"Sister Clara, some light, please."

At this soft command, the pink-cheeked nun—Sister Clara—stepped into the antechamber and returned with a stub of burning candle, which she touched to one taper after another in the sconces lining the wall. Within a minute, the room blazed with light.

"There you are," said the woman in the corner. The abbess stood awash in authority. She, too, was dressed in a pristine white habit, but the cross hanging from her neck was held with a chain of fine black iron, and her waist was encircled by a wide red belt. She wore not only the golden band on the third finger of her left hand but a ring set with a large red stone on the one extended in welcome. "Katharina. Come to me, child."

She spoke with the affection of familiarity, and the rush of light took my breath. The face framed by the cascading white wimple held every memory I had of my mother. Eyes the same mix of gray and blue, lashes the color of dark ginger. I imagined Mother wearing such a garment—a robe of righteousness, donned at the moment of her passing. My feet longed to run, my body to be swept up in an embrace, the full sleeves wrapped around me like angels' wings. The abbess, however, offered no such invitation. Only one hand, stretched forward, promising nothing more than an opportunity for me to take it in my own and offer a sweet, swift kiss. The stone of her ring felt cold against my cheek.

"At last, cousin," the abbess—Margarete—said. "I despaired of ever meeting you."

I looked up, still struck speechless.

"And, my, but you look like her. I must have

been about your age the last time I saw her, before I came here. It's like going back in time."

Tears pricked at the corners of my eyes, burning my throat, further stalling my ability to speak.

"Come." Her voice was softer now, but no less authoritative. "Sit here." She indicated an upholstered chair beneath the window. "Our supper time has passed, but I'm sure you must be hungry." She turned to the woman who had all but faded into the darkness of the doorway. "Sister Clara, go to the kitchen. Find bread and milk and cheese and have it taken to the guesthouse."

"There's three of us," I said, finding my voice at last. "My friend Therese and Sister Gerda, who came as chaperone."

Margarete leaned forward to give a gentle pat to my knee. "I know, dear one. They shall be fed too. And given a bed for tonight. All of you will spend tonight in the guesthouse. It's more comfortable."

"Thank you." Inexplicable gratitude kept my voice close to a whisper.

"What is this?" Margarete leaned back in her chair and examined me with exaggerated scrutiny. "Sister Odile told me you were a headstrong girl, outspoken and clattering."

I couldn't help smiling at the word. *"Clattering?"*

"She said your little wooden shoes echoed up one hall and down the other, always running around with your compatriots. One of them, I suppose, being this friend who accompanied you?"

"Yes."

"And who walks in to see me but this mouse of a girl who cannot even give me a proper greeting. You are not just a novice, my little Katharina. You are my family. More than a sister in the eyes of God, a cousin of common blood. I know your father's intentions, sending you to Brehna. So much closer to him and your home, but you have *family* here. True, we don't take the little ones, but he could have waited. Kept you home until now. Honestly, that man. If he ever made a decision, it was a bad one."

I bristled at the criticism of my father. "I loved it there. It was pretty."

Margarete laughed. "True enough. You will find life here very different. We tend to be more frugal with the resources granted us by the Church. Not nearly as frivolous as what you've been accustomed to. In that, though, we are much better suited to your family's means. And given the tightfisted nature of your stepmother, I'm surprised you weren't snatched back to the farm the minute your endowment ran dry."

My face burned with shame as this woman—

this *holy* woman—prattled on about the shortcomings of my family. My father, in particular, and his shortsighted choice of a wife. Still, I held my tongue and fumed silently, keeping my eyes fixed on the heavy cross nestled in white wool.

"But you're here now, aren't you? And from what I've heard from the sisters at Brehna, you're quite advanced in your language and arithmetic. Latin, too? Or a bit, as they've said. Well done, little cousin."

Once again she reached across to pat my knee, only this time, Margarete's ring produced a muffled *click* against the metal of the locket hidden within my skirt.

"What is that?"

I said nothing, only shifted position.

Not fooled, Margarete looked at me from an angle of suspicion. "What have you got in your pocket? I heard something."

I shifted again, this time taking care to knock the back of my shoe against the leg of the chair. "Clattering, as Sister Odile says."

At that, Margarete threw her head back and laughed, deep from her throat. Though I had arrived less than an hour ago, I somehow knew the sound was a rare occurrence and pictured a sea of white robes pouring in, worried that their abbess was under some kind of attack. Then, as abruptly as the laughter burst forth, it stopped, and Margarete's hand gripped my leg, obviously searching for the hidden trinket.

"Hear this, my little cousin. You cannot be expecting any special treatment. We are all equal in the eyes of God, and whatever affection I may have for you must be undetectable by the other sisters here."

"I've never detected it all these years," I said. "Why start now?"

"Oh, now your tongue has been set free, has it? Mind your impudence. You'll find very few opportunities for it, anyway. We take our meals in silence and discourage idle conversation. You are to speak in prayer, and to each other only as much as is necessary to complete your service to God. This time we've had together has been a wasted opportunity for you, I'm afraid. But perhaps another time we can catch up. You can tell me all about your brothers."

Her abrupt change in tone when she spoke again of our family was its own lost opportunity. Her smile stretched like an icy path between us, and I cared not if I cracked it. "You probably know more than I do. You seem to know everything."

The abbess sat back, her eyes narrowed to catlike slits. "I do, don't I? See to it that you remember."

Part II

Marienthrone at Nimbschen

1514 – 1515

Chapter 7

The bell rang at the edge of darkness. Nothing loud enough to awaken the uninitiated, as I learned my first weeks here, when I'd been hauled from my bed by one of my fellow novices. It didn't take long to train myself to sleep with the expectation of the predawn wakening. I slept in my socks and undergarments, not only for the added warmth, but for the swiftness in dressing, to be presentable and complete and in the hall by the time Sister Clara arrived to escort us to the sanctuary for the first of seven services that day.

We girls made our silent way through the dark corridors, though I always managed to jockey for a position beside Therese, and we would offer a squeeze to each other's hand as greeting. Girt, too, would fall in place, always with her headpiece askew and her soft cheeks still creased from her bedding.

Every three to four hours, around and around the clock, we filed into the sanctuary, soundlessly bearing the sharp pain as knees and shins butted into pews. To move with careful, outstretched precision was too slow, bringing with it the risk of a piling from behind. The only light came from the single candle of Sister Clara, who would choose some days to lead and others to follow, depending on her suspicions and implied instruction from Abbess Margarete.

Here at Marienthrone, there was no clock to chime the hour, but I knew. It was three o'clock. The hour squarely in the middle between a sinner's sleeping and waking. The hour when, if left untended, a soul could lose itself in sinful dreams, bringing on lustful thoughts or visions of rebellion. And so we were wakened from narrow slumber and brought out to fix our bleary eyes on the pages of dimly lit prayer books and recite words stored just beneath our conscious knowledge.

This was the first truly cold morning, attested by the slick layer of frost on the floor and the shadowy puffs of breath that wrapped around the spoken prayers. The chapel remained icy for this service, as well as the one following breakfast at seven o'clock and the one just before dinner at eleven. There would be no fire until the evening, and perhaps not even then, as it was early in the month and the monks insisted there was no need for such comfort before November.

By silent agreement, Therese, the thinnest and frailest, nestled between Girt and me. As long as there was no watchful eye, we could stand close enough to touch sleeve to sleeve, pressing in to transfer warmth. This we would do at the next service, even with the revelatory risk from the morning light.

"Like a killer's heart." Girt slipped in during the recitation, bringing to mind a favorite saying of Sister Gerda.

"Sharp," I added. "Like his blade."

"Hush," Therese chastised. "You'll get us all in trouble."

There was no priest to officiate this service, and after a lengthy prayer intoned by the abbess, the congregants were released to go back to our beds. We made the same silent procession down the hall, disappearing into our cells.

Having learned through a series of punishments that there was always an ear at the door, I slipped into bed without exchanging a single noise with the other novices who shared my room. Karla and Liese were dull girls anyway, shuttled here after proving themselves useless to their families. Though they were close to my age, they seemed far younger—silly and inexperienced. Often I wondered if they embraced the hours of silence simply because they had nothing to say. If brought home, they might spend endless silent hours binding wheat or scrubbing pots. Even though they came from different families, they shared common characteristics of narrow-set eyes and sallow skin that shone with fat no matter how dry and crisp the air.

I settled into bed and, following the long-ago

advice of the young priest, folded myself as if in prayer, clasping my hands and breathing upon them.

Holy Mother, keep me warm. And give me sleep until breakfast.

The breakfast porridge was warm, and I hurried to my place as quickly as decorum would allow to ensure that it remained so until it settled into my empty stomach. The only sound was that of pewter spoons scraping against wooden bowls, punctuated by the stifled coughs and sniffles that would last throughout the winter. I gave quick, silent thanks for my food and tucked in. Girt and Therese likewise indulged, signing to each other from across the table.

Are you in the bakery today?

No, drying herbs.

For the kitchen?

Infirmary.

I'm helping with deliveries. Again.

This last came from Girt, who delivered the message with her eyes trained up to the ceiling so that neither of us could make contact and entice her to giggles. Though she'd taken her vows and wore the white robes of a nun, she maintained the physique of any healthy farm girl, despite the limited diet of the convent. When local farmers arrived with bushel baskets of vegetables and fruit, or sacks of grain, Girt was called upon to help bring them down from the wagon and carry them within the gates.

And Hans? I made the sign—two fingers posed like legs, thumb and pinky stretched out like long, strong arms.

Girt turned her eyes heavenward again and quickly touched her fingertips in prayer. *I hope so.*

Abbess Margarete cleared her throat, and we concentrated on our porridge.

It was a sin, of course, to encourage such flirtation between Girt and Hans, and Therese made her displeasure known with the flaring of her nostrils and the thinning of her pretty lips. She, too, had taken her vows only a few weeks before and had changed before our very eyes. Her silence was peaceful, her obedience complete.

After breakfast and the service that followed, I returned to the kitchen, where a square wooden tray waited. It held a small loaf of bread, a wedge of cheese, three baked apples cut into slices, a pewter pitcher of milk, and a pot of tea hot enough to still be steaming.

I stood in front of it, questioning the red-faced sister—*May I take it?*—and was given a wave of permission in response.

Though I'd run all the way from the sanctuary for the privilege, I carefully lifted the tray and walked with measured steps out of the kitchen, across the frost-covered yard, and into the nuns' quarters. Only this act of service permitted me to be in the corridor of those who had already taken their vows, and I allowed myself the most surreptitious of glances into the empty cells, knowing they were occupied by both of my dearest friends and other women whom I barely knew. Soon I would be there too. After the New Year, after my sixteenth birthday, when I would take the vows that would grant me entrance. I knew Girt and Therese did not share a room, which gave me some hope that I might be paired with one of them, but was torn as to which I would prefer. Girt, unchanged since the day I opened my eyes in Brehna, would be an entertaining respite from the silent restrictions of the convent—enough to garner punishment from the abbess, but worth the sacrifice of smaller freedoms.

But Therese—I couldn't deny the fascination I had with my friend's illumination. She glowed the moment she stood newly clothed in the robes of the order, a seamless whiteness that made her luminous blue eyes and faintly pink lips the only touch of color on her being. Perhaps, I thought, if I could be given back to this friend, made equal with her, I could capture some of that righteous inner peace. It might flow from Therese's pillow to mine in the few precious hours of sleep, and seep in.

With my own ceremony still months away, I

felt nothing but restlessness. Not fear, not doubt, but a skittish spirit—something I couldn't share with another soul at Marienthrone. Girt would dismiss; Therese would chastise; the abbess would send me to my knees on the stony-cold chapel floor to repent in prayer. And while his office might grant a priest access to my sin, I had no intentions of sharing my deepest thoughts to a faceless man on the other side of a screen.

The corridor became darker as I passed the final open cell, and more narrow as the walls loomed thicker, closing in for a bit before widening again. Wide enough, at least, to allow the view inside a single small room, closed off by a door made of solid wood, save for a square opening right in its center composed of an ornate lattice. Hidden within the design were two hinges and a latch. Beyond it, a room not much wider than the door itself, lit only by a narrow strip of window stretched from one corner to the next.

I had never stepped foot inside the door and had only peeked in once, years ago, when childish curiosity overcame decorum. Now, I balanced the tray on one hand, reached for the strip of leather attached to a small bell hanging above, and gave it one decisive tug, resulting in a faint *ring!*

I saw the form behind the lattice and moved closer to get a better view.

"I've brought you breakfast."

There was a soft *click* of the latch, and the

window opened. Small and square, it would barely allow enough space to pass the tray, but it was enough to provide a clear view of the woman inside.

"Good morning, Sister Gerda."

A slight, toothless smile came at the sound of my voice. I knew I wasn't supposed to speak at all—none of the other sisters did when they completed this errand. Only Girt, Therese, and I carried the history of having known Sister Gerda before she took on this mantle of solitude.

It had seemed almost cruel at first, taking this small, blind, homely old woman and locking her away in something that seemed like a prison. All darkness and isolation while the rest of us busied about, for there was no idle time at Marienthrone. Gardening, washing, cooking, spinning—always something to fill our hours and occupy our hands when we weren't in a time of prayer or attending Mass. But it was Gerda herself who—not wishing to make the journey back to Brehna alone—had thrown herself on Abbess Margarete's mercy, petitioning to be given the gift of solitude, a hermit within our walls. The abbess agreed, with the understanding that Gerda would be exempt from all work, but also excluded from all fellowship. Only to live out her days with the barest of comfort: a bed, a fire, and food. Her meals were to be delivered each morning and evening. The only words exchanged would be those of the psalmists on the rare occasion she made known a request to have Scripture read through the door.

Sly old fox, we'd thought when first we came to know of the plan, and it seemed to me she'd been gloating ever since.

"The tea is still hot," I said, passing the tray through the window. "So drink it quick."

Carefully, tilting her head to take advantage of what little vision remained, Sister Gerda took the tray and set it on the small table beside the narrow cot. A pewter cup hung from a hook, and she took it down, filled it with the steaming tea, and made shuffling steps to bring it back to me.

"No," I protested. "It's for you."

She held it out again, insisting, and I realized she had no other recourse for hospitality. I took one bracing sip before handing the cup back.

"There. The rest is for you."

Sister Gerda made the sign of the cross and offered up a silent blessing, something I hadn't thought to do, but I knew she did so without pretense. Whatever her motivation had been all those years ago when she first took residence here, her solitude had changed her. Humbled her, even. She took the cup back and drank deeply. As long as I'd known her, she'd had an aversion to the cold.

"There's a frost outside," I said, ignoring—as usual—the imposed silence of Sister Gerda's status. "First of the winter. I should have fetched you a shawl or a second blanket. Are you warm enough? I don't know when I'll be able to come again, but if it's not me, I can ask . . . whoever . . . to make sure you have—"

Sister Gerda held up a quieting hand, and I stopped short before whispering, "If I could—if we could, just for a few minutes?"

The old woman took another sip of tea, then set the cup on the tray. Once returned, she slid the wooden latch, and I stepped back, allowing the door to swing open wide into the hallway. I placed my foot on the threshold, the toe of my soft leather shoe just an inch inside the solitary cell. It was the closest I would have to an invitation.

A small shelf jutted out from the narrow space beside the door, and on it an hourglass, though from legend, I knew it contained far less than an hour's time. Mere minutes, actually, during which Sister Gerda could suspend her silence.

"Wait," I said, catching her gnarled hand before she could tip the glass. "I don't want to waste any time on me. I can talk all I want."

Sister Gerda twisted her face into its familiar scowl, the same I remembered from my days as a very little girl, terrified by the mass of boils.

"What if . . . ?" And there was nothing left. In truth, I didn't see Sister Gerda as a confidante. I doubted she had wisdom to offer or would listen with any ear of compassion. But I had no one else to talk to. No one I could trust with the doubts that drifted like clouds within my spirit.

Sister Gerda shuffled back to the table, picked up her cup, and held it in both hands, just under her nose, looking for all the world as if she didn't care whether I spoke another word or not.

I began again.

"I don't know where to start, or what to say, or who to say it to. I'm so full of questions, and I've prayed—you have to believe me, Sister. I close my eyes and I ask God to show me what he wants, what life he intends for me to follow, but of course when I open my eyes, all I see is . . . *this*. I know I'm not worthy of a vision, and I don't want to seem ungrateful for all he's given to me all my life, how he's provided, but I—"

Sister Gerda picked up a slice of baked apple and gummed it with exaggerated, slurping relish.

I took a deep breath. "I just want to be sure. Even though I might not have a choice, I want to know I'm doing the *right* thing, not just the *only* thing." And then I fell silent.

Sister Gerda wiped her hand on her robe—black, as she'd been permitted to wear—and trailed her fingers along the wall, making her way back to the door. Her bent body stretched as she picked up the glass and held it to me, giving me responsibility for measuring the passing time. I counted a hundred grains before she spoke.

"Do you look very much like your cousin?"

The question was so disconnected to my thoughts, I could hardly process the meaning. I wouldn't waste her time with an answer.

"Everybody says you do. But I don't see it. Of course, I don't see much."

Her words came with a harmless shot of humor, and I offered no comment.

"What say you? Are you a pretty girl, Katharina?"

"I-I don't know. I've never thought about it."

She let out a mirthless laugh. "You haven't thought about it because you don't have to. Do you think I've lived a single minute with the same luxury?"

My heart clenched, and I longed for the sand to pour.

"I know your story. A noble family, grown poor over generations. Your father done nothing to improve your prospects." Sister Gerda's words came just short of mocking, as if offering some soft-syllabled punishment. Her lips too loose to smirk. "He married your mother because he loved her, didn't he? Some grand romance despite her family's protest. The abbess spoke of it, to make clear how she was able to live as God's servant, being spared such ruination."

My face burned, shamed at our legacy and angry at Margarete's betrayal.

"And his second wife, your stepmother, has

proven to be another financial disappointment, hasn't she?"

Among other things.

"Outside of these walls, your story would be no different. A poor boy might love you and mire you in poverty. A noble man might love you but choose to share his life—and his fortune—with a more equal match. Only here, within this house of God, can your value be measured by infinite worth."

I wondered what worth had ever been spoken to a young Gerda. When had her body first begun to twist upon itself? What did her face look like before the first bit of flesh formed into a molten glob? My silence must have been taken for some sort of pity, for she smacked her lips dismissively and waved my unspoken platitudes away.

"I am at peace with my lot. Who's to say I wouldn't be here even if I'd been given a life of some great beauty? There are those, you know. Our little Therese, for one."

"I know." And then frustration took hold. We were wasting time. Any second the sand would run out. Or worse, one of the other nuns would hear our voices and report our conversation. Not the details of it, maybe, but the sin of disobedience. "I don't care about any of that, truly. About myself or my life, or what can or cannot be."

"Then what do you want from me?"

Her question carried hurt, and rightfully so. Nobody, as far as I knew, ever asked Sister Gerda for anything. Even I offered only a pretense of seeking guidance, when all I really wanted was a human wall to hear my voice.

"I want you to listen. Because nobody else can. Not even God, because I cannot voice this, even in prayer."

She smiled wide, like a crescent moon. "You think he will not hear you in this place?"

"I know he can. But he won't give me an answer."

"To what, child? Speak it plain."

I could not, yet. "How old were you, Sister Gerda, when you took the veil?"

"Younger than you. I might have been twelve years old, but there's no record of my birth. No mother, and I was so small."

"And if you had a choice. Is this what you would have wanted?"

"Oh, child. Life is meaningless enough. Imagine how much more it would be if we were given only what we want. I'd have a straight back and a smooth face. And likely nothing else in the world. Think to this time yesterday. What did you want?"

I answered without hesitation, remembering clearly. "A piece of ham."

My answer surprised her, and she laughed with true appreciation. "And this time last week?"

"Probably the same thing." I was always hungry.

"And it might have given you a little comfort at the time, but would it have changed you? Brought you closer to God? Or given strength to your faith?" Her clouded eyes grew wider, and it seemed she was envisioning something far beyond this dark room. "We must take care not to think we have any command of our own fate. Providence rests in the hands of God."

"But my father got to make a choice, didn't he? Sending me here?"

"Human decisions are too often born of weakness. I have always been weak, without a life other than God's provision. Think what I would have been, tossed out into the world. Never would I have lived long enough to know Christ. Here, I will never be hungry. Never without shelter. Never at the mercy of those who would do harm."

"But I'm—"

"Not hideous?" The unaccustomed gentleness in her tone granted forgiveness. "No. Neither are you crippled, nor lacking in any womanly grace. I know you think your cousin is hiding me away here. Or that I'm hiding myself. But I'm not. It's a welcome thing for me, a rest for my weary bones. And escape from the whispers I hear from this side." She turned her head to point to her good ear, and I got a glimpse of her profile.

She might have been quite pretty, once. “It might surprise you to know that I spend my time in prayer. For you.”

“For me?”

“I will pray what you cannot.”

The final grain fell, and her good ear heard it.

Sister Gerda reached out her hands, and following an instinct unprecedented in the ten years I’d known her, I stepped in close and bowed. She pulled me to her and planted a moist, thin-lipped kiss on the top of my head.

God bless you.

I answered with a kiss to her smoother cheek, and then—with a hardening of my stomach—one to the mass of pea-sized cysts on the other. She didn’t breathe, and neither did I. The next sound was that of the wooden latch sliding into place.

Chapter 8

At the turn of the new year, I begged Abbess Margarete to send a letter on my behalf. One page, four lines:

> Dearest Papa,
>
> I shall be taking my vows thirty days past my birthday.
>
> With love and appreciation for your sacrifice.
>
> Katharina

It had been sealed with the imprint of the Cistercian order and, as far as I knew, delivered to its intended recipient without mishap. But there had been no reply, and no one from my family arrived on the appointed day to witness the ceremony.

In my confession that morning, I voiced none of the fear or doubt I'd spoken of so boldly with Sister Gerda. Instead, I shared the resentment I felt that not only had my father failed to acknowledge my every birthday, but he would also not be here to see his daughter pursue the life he'd so clearly intended.

For this I was told to pray for my father to be blessed.

I confessed to complaining about the cold.

For this I was told to pray, giving thanks for the walls and the warmth God provided.

After that, I confessed no more.

My prayers complete, I was taken by the hand and led to the first empty cell in the sisters' corridor, where Therese and Girt waited with expressions solemn enough for the occasion. Together, they took away my novice clothing and helped me don the clean, new white tunic. They tied a plain white kerchief over my hair, and each touched my cheeks with a holy kiss.

"Serve God long and well, Sister," Therese said, her voice with the timbre worthy of an abbess.

Girt said only, "God bless you, Sister," as she riffled through the fabric, looking for the hidden pocket. Finding it, she withdrew the locket and handed it to me.

"What shall I—?"

"I'll keep it safe for you," Girt said. "Until you have a place."

The night before, I'd slept with the treasure so tightly clasped in my hand, the filigree had worn itself into the skin of my palm. Even now, hours later, I could see the faint outlines of the pattern and thought briefly of the time the discipline of the priest had been recorded on my flesh.

"Do you think I still need to hide it?"

"You can't ever hide anything from the eyes of God," Therese said, ever the spiritual authority.

"God would not take a child's greatest treasure," I replied. "He took a child's lunch once, and multiplied it to feed thousands. But he'd never take away the one thing—"

In the next breath, Girt dropped the chain around my neck and pulled the tunic far enough from my flesh to arrange the locket's concealment. Therese gasped, but the combined glare from Girt and me held her silent.

"So your mother can be with you," Girt said. "As she should."

Together we walked to the chapel, and for just a moment I longed for the lighter heart of our childhood, when we would run—*clattering*—holding giggles tight behind our hands. It was enough that we held a secret.

The abbess met me at the altar, where all the sisters of Marienthrone gathered, forming a semicircle of white. Though silent at my arrival, they soon joined voices in prayer, their words mingling in clouds of steam above their bowed heads.

In the name of God, our Holy Father,
And his Son, Jesus Christ,
And the Holy Ghost . . .

The air rustled as they made the sign of the

cross in a single fluid motion, their white sleeves sounding like the ascent of so many doves. Why had I never noticed this before?

"May the Most Holy Virgin . . ."

May the Most Holy Virgin

Look down upon this servant

And clothe her in virtue,

As we clothe her in the humble garment.

As you have instructed us to bind ourselves with the belt of truth,

So do we bind her.

Here, one of the nuns—Sister Clara, she who had first greeted me here—approached with a wide white sash, which she wrapped around my waist, capturing the loose fabric of the tunic and bringing it close to my body. She tied it in a decisive knot and gave it a testing tug before returning to her place as Margarete continued the prayer.

We clothe her with a breastplate of righteousness,

That she might be mindful of the righteousness born within her.

Therese emerged next with the scapular. I could only guess she had been given the responsibility because she was one of the few sisters tall enough to lift the garment high enough over my head to let it fall gently to my shoulders. A plain cross was stitched in gold thread, and instinctively I knew it was the handiwork of Therese. She who had stitched my first secret pocket had undertaken the task to stitch the identity I would wear over my heart.

We protect her with the helmet of salvation. A sign to all that she is sanctified to you, submissive to your service.

And the wimple, placed atop the simple kerchief. It covered my ears, immediately magnifying the sound of my own breath. The rest of the prayer sounded like it came through a drum.

And the veil, which she now takes, a covering over all. Let it protect her from the onslaught of Satan, whom we renounce in the name of the Father, and of the Son, and of the Holy Ghost.

The weight of the veil, as it sat upon my head and fell to my shoulders, brought me immediately to a stooping posture, but I stood straight soon enough and stared directly into the eyes of the woman who placed it.

"Are you ready to speak your vows?" Margarete asked, and for a fleeting moment, she looked upon me with the affection of family rather than austere spiritual authority.

"I am."

I was. Though if pressed to answer *why,* I'd be struck silent. I knew only that I'd left Sister Gerda's cell with a lingering vision—a long, dark tunnel of all the years ahead. A young woman, a woman, an old woman, with no idea how to live a life outside of a wall of women. Here was my family. God, my Father. This, my life.

These, the words that would usher it in.

"In nomine Patris, et Filii, et Spiritus Sancti. Amen."

"Amen," my sisters echoed.

After that, I could no longer look into the eyes of the abbess, but instead to the cross of Christ hanging from the iron chain around her neck. I felt the weight of my own necklace and pictured the lock of hair within. It had been too long since I'd opened the clasp, worried that it might dislodge and fall away, or the fragile, tiny hinge might break and leave the only token I had of my mother forever exposed.

Is this truly what you would have me do, Mother?

The cross rose and fell with the breath of the abbess, and I had her answer.

"As witnessed here by the Holy Trinity, and by these, my sisters, I make my promise. I will obey the teachings of Christ and the writings of the Holy Apostles. I will live my life in reverence to the teachings of the one true Church. I take on the honor of poverty in a world that boasts of bounty. I embrace a life of chastity, denying the sinful lust of my own flesh. I will discipline my mind with Scripture, my spirit with prayer, and my flesh with mortification that I might be a worthy vessel of God."

I crossed myself and repeated in chorus with my sisters, "*In nomine Patris, et Filii, et Spiritus Sancti. Amen.*"

Margarete lifted the cross to my lips, and I kissed its center. The metal was cold, but my cousin's lips were warm as they immediately followed the embrace.

"Now, Sister Katharina, having taken the veil of the Cistercian order, you have become, in flesh and spirit, a bride of our Savior Jesus Christ, as will be signified with this ring."

Margarete took my left hand and slid a golden band on the third finger. In anticipation of the moment, I said, "*Ego te sponsabo.*"

I will wed thee.

I kissed the ring, then extended it to the abbess to do the same, before kneeling again, my newly adorned hands clasped in prayer. Eyes closed, I heard a rustle of robes and felt the presence of those who would make a vow on my behalf. On one shoulder, I felt the heavy touch of Girt; on the other, the delicate hand of Therese. Finally, the warm heel of Margarete's palm against my forehead.

"Father in heaven, we ask for your daughter to be infused with the purity of heart and strength of body like that of our Holy Mother. Let chastity and constancy ever reign within her, as with all of us. In the name of our Lord, who did expire on the cross for all mankind, may we be willing to so sacrifice our lives to your service. Amen."

Amen.

In the name of the Father, and of the Son, and of the Holy Ghost.

So it was done.

Part III

Marienthrone at Nimbschen

1522 – Easter 1523

Chapter 9

The earth was cool and moist, but the sun warm on my back as I knelt, my small trowel temporarily forgotten in the garden soil. Despite the imposed rule of silence, noises droned all around—the rhythm of my more industrious sisters hewing out fresh furrows, the rumble of carts and the calls from the merchants outside the convent wall. Beside me, Therese hummed, though she surely was not aware, else she would stop abruptly and offer a silent prayer of repentance. It was such a pleasant sound, no one within its hearing would call it to her attention. The notes carried with them the freshness of spring, blending with the birdsong.

Girt should have been with us, but had been absent now for what must be a quarter of an hour, long enough for me to excavate not only my portion of the garden, but hers as well. I harbored no resentment that my friend might be shirking her share of the assigned work, but if she didn't return by the time the bell rang for dinner, the abbess would surely require an explanation for her absence, and any acceptable one would be a lie.

A subtle change came to Therese's tune, alerting me to the idea that it was not, after all, an act of her subconscious. The notes took on a minor quality and increased in volume, thus attracting the attention of our fellow toilers in the garden. Soon, all eyes were on Therese, who feigned a slow realization, raised her head, and made a great, silent show of apology, begging forgiveness of each sister in turn. I, too, participated in the charade, knowing full well it was meant to divert attention from Girt, who was hurrying back to her place.

Are you crazy? I implored with a sidelong glance.

Sorry. Girt's cheeks were flushed, easily attributed to the nearly noon sun. I decided my friend's breathlessness was due to running back from . . . wherever she'd been, and the smile a result of the beauty of God's day. Anything else, I didn't want to know.

At the first ringing of the bell, I stood with the others and wiped the loose dirt from my hands on the green apron I wore over my habit. I took my turn at a bucket filled with warm water and plunged them in, taking care not to stain my sleeves. A casual glance over my shoulder revealed that Girt chose not to follow, possibly because she had done too little work to actually have dirty hands, but I suspected more.

Once inside, my sisters and I filed into the

refectory and to our seats, standing until the abbess took her place at the head table. At her lead, we moved as one, making the sign of the cross, then joined hands as she led us in a lengthy blessing. By the time she reached the conclusion—"For thy bounty, we do give thanks"—I felt the slip of paper in my hand, passed along with a quick squeeze from Girt. I barely had time to secrete it up my own sleeve before joining in the chorus of *amen.*

It would be a trick, to partake of the meal while keeping the note concealed. I sat patiently, allowing another sister to slice the bread, and accepted Girt's silent offer to ladle the soup into my bowl, all the while working the page farther up my sleeve.

This, I noticed right away, was more than the usual fragment of torn parchment Girt had been slipping to me over the past year. Had I not been far more skilled at reading, I might never have been pulled into the circle of these secret missives. By now, though, it was understood. I would wait for the opportune time and place to read, and then—this being the far more elusive aspect—find time to share, word for word, the message.

Across the table, Therese arched one disapproving brow.

I tilted my head, a plea for mercy, if not approval.

Therese returned her attention to her soup.

Dismissed from dinner, and from the service after, we were granted two hours' time for meditation and reflection. Some sisters went to their cells, where soft snores betrayed the state of their prayers. Others would seek the warming room in winter or, as on this day, a stone bench in the sun-filled courtyard. One could work on stitchery, so long as it was nothing frivolous, or even read aloud from the prayer book to a small gathering of sisters. These were hours in which each soul was accountable to Christ for their passing.

"The Lord is in his holy temple," Abbess Margarete would intone before our dismissal. "The Lord's throne is in heaven: his eyes behold; his eyelids try the children of men."

I headed straight for the sanctuary, knowing no other place in the expanse of the convent would offer as much light. I stopped before the altar, knelt, and prayed.

"Blessed be the Father, and the Son, and the Holy Ghost. Grant me wisdom to understand the words I am about to see, and discernment to find your truth within. I pledge to you my heart, unceasing in its devotion to your will. Pray, find my spirit to be obedient, though my flesh may waver."

I offered the same prayer every time I undertook this mission. After, I took my usual place in the center of the fourth pew, hoping to discourage any other sister from sitting right next to me, and opened my prayer book. With one hand I turned its pages, while the other slipped up my sleeve to dislodge the note hidden there. Once it was brought into view, I surmised that it was no note, but a full page—torn from something greater. A book, maybe, or at the very least a pamphlet.

The Freedom of a Christian.

The title alone held no significance, but when I noticed the author, a familiar sense of excitement ignited at my very core.

Martin Luther.

I knew of him, of course. As much as Marienthrone tried to maintain holy sequestration, ideas seeped in. Literally, in this case, handed over bit by bit, written on scraps of parchment and on the back pages of old ledger books. Simple Bible verses at first: *For by grace are ye saved through faith; and that not of yourselves: it is the gift of God: Not of works, lest any man should boast. Ephesians ii, 8-9.* And others from the Gospels and the Psalms—each with a governing message of faith. All given to me from Girt's soft hand, having been delivered to her by another work-worn, stronger one.

"Where did you get this?" I had asked the first time, when a painstakingly copied verse from the Gospel of John was slipped into my palm.

Jesus saith unto him, I am the way, the truth,

and the life: no man cometh unto the Father, but by me.

My eyes had taken in the words, hearing them in Latin, but seeing them in German—the words of my Savior written in my own tongue.

"Hans says that someday Luther will translate the whole of Scripture," Girt had whispered over her shoulder, her voice filled with equal awe for the messenger as the scholar. "Not only that, but have it printed in books, available to everyone."

Mere knowledge of the plan made us all conspirators, and one secret after another passed from Hans to Girt to my own hand. And then, over the course of two years—from my twenty-first birthday until this spring—thin scraps, torn from a single printed page. It took months before the message of the numbered lines came clear. Luther, speaking out against the corruption of the priests. Of the pope, even, in the selling of indulgences—fees paid to the clergy by family members in mourning, hoping to pay a price on earth to purchase an eternity in heaven for loved ones who died without repentance for their sins.

"Like my mother," Therese said that night in the darkness when we three huddled together, reunited in a common cell, the strips carefully laid out in sequence on the floor between us. "He's saying there's nothing to be done, no hope to bring her soul to God?"

"He means her soul can't be *bought,*" I said,

working the complication of the teaching out in my head even as I spoke. "He's saying that all of us—every person—we're responsible for our *own* repentance. If we confess our sins, Christ forgives us. But nobody can confess for us, and once life is ended, the time for confession has ended."

"I can't believe that," Therese said. She took herself to her narrow bed, disturbing the neat assembly of Luther's words in her wake. Ever since, when the occasion came to study some new message, Therese had lain in resolute silence, facing the wall, feigning sleep.

Since then, new chambers of belief were unlocked with each message. Fresh clarity to Scriptures I had heard from infancy, read by the priests, intoned in Latin.

If we confess our sins, he is faithful and just to forgive us our sins, and to cleanse us from all unrighteousness. With a special notation that it is *he*—Christ himself, our Savior—who cleanses us. A truth recorded centuries before the inception of the Church, the ordinance of confession, and the priesthood established to enforce it. Such power in those little slips of paper. Ancient writing forged with new ideas—messages I'd never heard before in a lifetime of sermons and lessons.

And now, something completely new. *The Freedom of a Christian*. I ran my fingers over the creases on the page, bracing myself for the words to follow.

> Christian faith has appeared to many an easy thing. . . .

Easy thing, indeed. The sleeplessness, the silence, the cold floors and sparse meals and endless scrutiny. This was the very first line, and I found myself not simply reading the page, but conversing with the author.

> For it is not possible for any man to write well about it . . .

And yet he did.

> . . . or to understand well what is rightly written. . . .

As I read, I felt a connection to the man who wrote the words. I'd form a question, and he'd answer it in the next line. At times, I had to furrow my brow and beg him to repeat his logic, so he did in the rereading of a sentence. Or two. Other times, his point would be so strong and perfectly clear, I needed to look away from the text and stare out the window at the square frame of blue sky while the new truth took root.

According to his own text, these were the

words of a poor man, vexed by temptations, yet with the assurance to write about matters of faith. He wrote with *elegance* and *solidity* and a proclaimed desire to serve the ignorant. And who could possibly be more ignorant than I?

Then, the final lines on the page:

> A Christian man is the most free lord of all, and subject to none; a Christian man is the most dutiful servant of all, and subject to every one.

Here was something to ponder, and I read it again. And thrice, bringing the paper closer to my face, as if to make the words clearer, before remembering that to do so would put the paper in full view of any other sister choosing to spend her hours of unassigned time in the chapel. A furtive glance revealed five within my eyesight, and I dared not attract attention by turning my head to see who had come in behind.

Most free of all.

The irony caught me unaware, and a bit of a laugh tried to escape before I captured it and tamed it into a more acceptable outburst.

This single sentence presented itself as a puzzle with contradictory interlocking truth. How could one be, simultaneously, in servitude and free? Subject to none, and to all?

It was maddening, this bit of logic. Or illogic.

For the first time, with all my heart I wished I could turn my head and ask this Luther himself, "What do you mean?" But God had given me a mind of my own, and few enough opportunities to challenge it.

Free. Free from the bondage of sin. Free from condemnation, through repentance and confession. But subject to *none?* Only to Christ, and the pope, and the bishops, and the priests, and the abbess, and Therese, who carried with her always the threat of discovery.

Most dutiful servant. To Christ, to the Church, and therefore, I supposed, to all. Carrying their prayers, creating this haven of worship.

Unsettled by the paradox, I took one last sweeping glance at the paper, folded it, and returned it to my sleeve. Moving as silently as possible, I slid out from the pew and kept my head bowed in contemplation as I traversed the courtyard and entered the sisters' sleeping quarters. Open doors revealed nuns kneeling at their bedside in prayer or stretched on their mattresses in sleep. I quickened my pace, turned the corner, and slipped into the narrow hallway, casting a glance to ensure I hadn't been followed.

It was an unusual time to try to visit with Sister Gerda. I knew I was to ask permission, but this could not wait. I went straight to the door and knocked quietly, not knowing if the sound would travel through the thick wood. I peered through the window. The cell was dark, making the small, misshapen woman appear like a specter floating out of the shadows.

"I know this visit must come as a surprise," I whispered, pressing my face into the latticework so that my words would land only within the close, dark walls, "but will you speak to me?"

Sister Gerda shook her head, a motion so quick I questioned the response.

"Only for a moment?"

Followed by a more convincing dismissal.

"But I-I have questions. And there's no one here that I—" I stopped myself short of saying *trust.* I trusted Girt, and Therese to an extent. But they wouldn't understand any more than I did. Sister Gerda's years of silence had surely nurtured a wisdom more pure than anything outside of this dark place.

I pleaded again. "Will you, then, listen? Just for a moment? I only need—"

This interruption came with the sight of Sister Gerda's hand, so white as it emerged from the black sleeve, it seemed disembodied, yet strong enough to halt the wall of words. Behind her splayed fingers, a stern expression discouraged any further sound. I leaned my head against the door, realizing the true reason I trusted this woman.

Silence keeps secrets.

I turned my back to the door, rested against

it, and slid down until I was sitting on the floor. Taking the page from my sleeve, I opened it, found an angle that afforded the most light, and began to read as loud as I dared. I knew she listened on the other side. Her distinct footfall sounded until she stopped, and I imagined her good ear pressed against an open knot in the wood.

Never had I felt such power as in speaking these words aloud, and I fought to keep my whisper intact. To think, a man had penned them, but I could read them. I could speak them. And yet I had no power to make them my own truth.

When I got to the end, I went back to the top and read the page again. Pausing at the end of each sentence, letting the ideas seep through my lips, through the door. But when I began to read it a third time, a sharp rap came from the other side.

Stop.

I obeyed, midsentence.

"Will you keep this for me?" I asked, pressing the paper against the door. "I can't be found with it, but I–I can't destroy it. Please?"

No sound, no protest. I began to slide it under the door but knew I needed to keep a remnant with me. Carefully, I folded a crease just above the confounding last line. Lifting it to my mouth, I gave it a quick swipe along my tongue before tearing it carefully—imagining each woven strand of paper dislodging—until I'd separated it from the larger page. A single narrow strip. Easily concealed. Swallowed, if necessary. I stood, folded the larger page, and dangled it through the lattice.

"I need to know," I said, speaking blindly into the wood, "and you can answer me whenever you can. *However* you can. But I need to know. What does this mean?"

I would have opened my fingers, allowed the words to drift to the floor of the cell, never to know if they'd fall under the gaze of another soul. But then I felt it—a tug as small as the slip itself.

Chapter 10

Did you read it?" Girt asked as her breath rippled across the spoonful of soup. It was a ruse, of course. Rarely was the soup hot enough to need to be cooled, but the gesture masked speech, and the accompanying rattle of cutlery swallowed the sound.

I nodded but did not look up. I balled my hand into a fist and rested it on the table between us, an indication to *stop*. Then I laid my hand flat and left it there, soft, to let them know I wasn't angry, just insistent.

Later.

At the after-supper service we sang hymns, praising God for the creation of the earth and all within it. A song of spring and life. I stood squarely in the midst of my sisters, freely craning my neck to the left and the right and behind. Some sang with their faces lifted toward heaven, joy shining in their eyes. Others stared resolutely at Sister Benedikta, looking for clues to lyric and tempo. Some met my gaze and offered an encouraging one in return, communicating the glory of God across the notes.

When the last note of the hymn died away,

Margarete took her place behind the pulpit, something she obviously relished during those services for which no priest could be bothered.

"In the name of the Father, and of the Son, and of the Holy Ghost—" the sisters crossed themselves with her—"the fifty-fourth psalm. 'Save me, O God, by thy name, and judge me by thy strength.' "

The sisters repeated. *Save me, O God, by thy name, and judge me by thy strength.*

"Hear my prayer, O God; give ear to the words of my mouth."

For strangers are risen up against me, and oppressors seek after my soul: they have not set God before them. Selah.

My mind wandered from the sacred text. Luther was a stranger, wasn't he?

"Behold, God is mine helper: the Lord is with them that uphold my soul."

I will freely sacrifice unto thee: I will praise thy name, O Lord; for it is good.

There was a final verse to the psalm. I heard Margarete's sonorous voice, and the sweet echo of my sisters, but I chose instead to repeat, "I will freely sacrifice unto thee."

And again, "I will freely sacrifice unto thee."

A chorus of *amen,* followed by silence, into which my lone voice spoke again, "I will freely sacrifice unto thee."

A shuffle of soft leather and white robes all

around, and I stood still in its midst, my eyes focused on the figure of Christ on the cross hanging above the altar.

"I will freely sacrifice unto thee."

"Kat!" Therese tugged on my sleeve.

"I'm staying here," I said, my gaze never wavering. "In the chapel. You all go; I'll meet you later."

Girt leaned close. "But what about—?"

"Later!" I couldn't remember the last time anything so harsh had come from my mouth. I only knew that something had happened, something deep inside a part of my spirit I never knew existed. Something that took me to the freedom of a woman. Back to Eve, when a serpent told her she had a choice. Eat? Not eat? She was free, and utterly incapable of knowing the dire consequences of that freedom.

I knew I was the object of suspicion as the pews emptied around me.

"Are you quite all right, Sister Katharina?" Though we were family, Margarete addressed me with the formality of a stranger.

"I am fine, Mother. I simply want to pray here. Alone, if I may."

Margarete descended slowly, her veil motionless as she walked. "Are you ejecting us from the sanctuary?"

I refused to acknowledge the humor, sensing the bite behind it. "Stay or go as you please." I bowed my head, obscuring my face with my veil in an attempt to show humility.

Margarete remained unconvinced. “You’re to be in your room within the hour.”

“I don’t want to go to my room, and I don’t know if I’ll want to go later.” Margarete drew a sharp breath at my defiance, and a soft press against my shoulder inspired an equally softened tone. “Please, may I stay? This once. I want—I *need* to be in prayer. And sometimes, when there are others in the room, even though we’re supposed to be silent . . .”

Margarete exhaled, acquiescing. “Very well. You may stay until the eleven o’clock service. I’ll leave word that you’re not to be disturbed.”

“Thank you, cousin.”

My eyes following her steps, I remained frozen in my place, not falling to my knees until I knew I was alone. But not at the altar. I couldn’t walk that far. I dropped in place, folding my arms on the seat of the bench and resting my head upon them. Even with my eyes open, I saw nothing but darkness, but I closed them anyway, remembering a trick from childhood. If I closed my eyes, closed them *tight,* I could see my thoughts. Spelled out as clearly as words on a page. And when I did, I saw only one word, written over and over.

Freedom. Freedom. Freedom.

Silently, I appealed to the Holy Father God to

forgive my sin. Not the silly, inconsequential confessions I relayed to the priests in order to fulfill an obligation, but the deeper sin of disbelief so newly revealed. Not until this moment had I understood the sacrifice of Christ on the cross to be the source of forgiveness. Not the words priests told me to say, not memorized prayers—identical from one penitent to another. But Jesus Christ, the Son of God himself, with nothing to stand between his pierced side and my broken heart.

My belief cleansed me.

Freedom.

My confession, here, silent and alone, flew to heaven.

Freedom.

And I felt it, as clear and sharp as the first ball of snow dropped down my neck when we played as children. As heavy as the veil first placed upon my head. I had pledged my faith to Christ—alone. Not to the Church, or to the pope, or to any man or woman who would stake a claim on my allegiance. I was subject to God, and to no one else.

All this was fine, here, alone, where I could stay until eleven o'clock. And then . . .

"Oh, my Father in heaven." My breath returned, sweet from the wood. "What have I done?"

Chapter 11

Since my insistence on a solitary prayer vigil in the chapel, the abbess had been especially watchful, instructing other sisters to separate our trio at meals and services. Therese had been removed from garden duty and brought in to help tutor the village children who came to practice their catechism. Girt was brought into the sewing room, where, according to the grumbling of the other nuns, she ripped out as many stitches as she made. Margarete did not, however, make any attempt to change our cell assignment, perhaps trusting that our need for rest would trump any desire for mischief. Both Girt and Therese seemed to have sensed my change in spirit, for even when we were given moments of hidden time, neither pressed me for information. Therese, no doubt, because she opposed all of the implications of disobedience accompanying these missives. Girt, though, knew—or seemed to know—the import. While she offered the occasional inquisitive invitation, she showed compassion and backed away at my gentle rebuffs.

In the first hours after Easter Sunday, once we were newly deposited in our cell after the three o'clock service, I lay on my cot, eyes trained on a strip of moonlight on the ceiling. The hall outside had been silenced of footsteps for a count of five hundred, giving reasonable assurance that each of the sisters was similarly tucked away to embrace the few hours of sleep that waited. Girt sat on the floor, her head sharing my pillow, speaking in a particular form of whisper we had mastered as children, where the vowels all but disappeared, leaving little more than breath between popping consonants. Thus, any eavesdropper might think it only the rustle of straw when Girt drew close to my ear and said, "Hans wants me to come away."

Then there *was* a rustle of straw as Therese came from her bed to huddle on the floor next to Girt.

"What did you say?"

"Hans. I spoke with him last week. And he wants me to leave with him. To marry him."

"How can you . . . ?" Therese crossed herself without finishing her question. "Jesus, protect us from this sin."

"I haven't sinned," Girt said. "I think I just—" she shrugged her shoulders, at a temporary loss—"love him."

I turned my head, sensing rather than seeing my friend's wide, pretty face in the darkness. "Does he love you?"

"He says he does."

"Stop this." Therese emphasized her command

with a fist slammed into the ticking. "Do you hear yourselves? Have you forgotten who you are?"

"I haven't forgotten anything," Girt said. "But I don't think this is what I want to be for the rest of my life."

I knew it. Therese communicated the sentiment with a single click of her tongue. "All of this sneaking. Notes and messages."

Girt's soft hand touched my shoulder. "Can you tell me, now? What it said?"

I closed my eyes, remembering the words on the page. Not the paradoxical statement that lived as a solitary strip in the ticking of my mattress, but the last complete sentence before the passage was interrupted by the tearing of the page. *"Love is by its own nature dutiful and obedient to the beloved object."*

Girt let out a squeal, then buried her face in the ticking to muffle it. When she lifted her head, I obeyed her plea to repeat.

"He is my beloved object," Girt said, rapturously.

"*Christ* is our beloved," Therese insisted. "You've taken a vow to be obedient to him."

"That was before."

"Exactly my point. Our vows are holy. Sacred. And they take precedence over everything. You shouldn't even be *talking* to this boy."

"He's not a boy," Girt said, her voice dangerously close to a true whisper. "And I was just a girl when I took the veil. If I'd known him, I might not—"

"You cannot compare some fleeting romance to a commitment to Christ. Not to mention the Church."

I listened to the exchange, adding to it a third dimension of my own. What if there weren't a promise of love and marriage on the other side of the convent wall? What if one wanted to leave simply because . . . one wanted to leave? To pursue a life free of dictated worship and punitive absolution? To pursue a life of freedom?

"Luther," I interjected at the next opportunity, "says that to be a true Christian is to be subject to both no one and everyone. As our Apostle Paul writes in the book of Romans, *Owe no man any thing, but to love one another*. That is the duty we have. We are subjected to love one another, so that means you two must stop bickering."

"But we owe everything to the Church," Therese said, calmer. "At least I do. The sisters took me in. They cared for me, fed me."

"As they should." I shifted to my side, bringing all of our faces so close we would have blurred in the vision of full light. "Out of obedience to the command to love one another. It should be enough to love a child and care for her without expecting all of . . . *this*."

"Exactly," Girt said, though I figured my friend

embraced the idea for its support of her desire, rather than for her own philosophical conclusion.

"You are taking the word of a man who has been excommunicated from the Church," Therese said. She spoke truth, as the news had been delivered from the bishop last fall, with an air of triumph. "We should only listen to the Word of God and what we read in the Holy Scriptures."

"But that's just it." I focused my words on Therese. "It doesn't seem like everything we do comes from the Holy Scriptures. And how would we know, if we cannot read them for ourselves? If all we can do is what we're told? And why does the Church have the power to tell us, anyway?"

"Blasphemer," Therese said, recoiling.

"No," I insisted. "It would be blasphemous if I spoke against God, but the Church is not God. I want to obey God, but I want to do so freely. *Subject to no one.*"

There. I'd given voice to the nameless, wordless spirit that had been haunting me from the moment I first read the words—longer, to be truthful. And my friends comforted me with a cushion of silence in their wake. Girt's lips brushed my cheek, but Therese made no such gesture as the two of them rose from their places and returned to their own beds. In their vacancy, I crawled out and went to my knees, the floor punishingly hard beneath them.

Forgive me, Father, for any doubt of your sovereignty and protection. Grant me wisdom to discern your voice from the voices of all others.

I dared not even pray the question that settled like lingering leaves of tea at the bottom of my heart. Could I leave? Could I pursue worship more freely in the world outside these convent walls? Whom would I ask? What would I say? Leaving the convent was not unheard of. I knew of women who returned to their villages to live out their days among family, keeping to their vows of chastity and service until the end of their lives. Some, I knew, left in pursuit of total isolation, offering themselves as living sacrifices, with only God himself for both society and sustenance. And of course, Girt's predicament was nothing new. Indeed, it was why the convents insisted always on such extreme precautions to keep the sisters isolated from the roving world outside. Men were known to be heedless of the sanctity of a nun's virginity—beyond that of any other woman. I'd been warned from an early age about the danger of men's pride, their desire to conquer and take not only what wasn't theirs but what clearly belonged to someone else—even if that someone else was God. For all I knew, Hans's years-long pursuit of Girt was nothing more than a quest of his own pride. My friend, a prize.

As the bone-piercing chill of the floor seeped

in, my thoughts grew cold. Had she been, all this time, nothing more than a victim of a young man's seduction? Perhaps if Girt were more literate, I wouldn't be grappling with these questions at all. I'd be aligned with Therese, watching with faint disapproval as my friend made a romantic fool of herself, blushing within her wimple at the attentions of a handsome farm boy.

I concentrated on the pain, accepting it as punishment for the recklessness of thought. My mattress, though thin, offered comfort. My blanket, warmth. My pillow, undeserved luxury.

But I will accept your rod of discipline. Your staff of correction, O Lord.

As should Girt.

With all sensation absent from my feet, I turned and crawled the short expanse to Girt's bed, where my friend's shallow snores belied any troubled thoughts.

"Girt," I whispered, lips close enough to brush her ear.

"Hmmph?" More sleep than sound.

"You need to tell Hans not to bring any more writings from Luther. Do you understand?"

Girt mumbled another syllable.

"I mean it. Tell him, no more. Not another word unless it's Scripture. Are we clear?"

"Leave her alone." Therese's bold whisper held no remnant of sleep. "If you don't have to feel subject to the Church, why should she be subject to you?"

"It's all right," Girt said, clearly awake now. "If you don't want to read my messages, I'll find someone else who will."

If there were any messages at all in the weeks following, I had no knowledge. Girt's affection toward me cooled considerably as she aligned with other sisters, sitting with them at mealtimes, walking with them to and from services. Only during those short hours of darkness, within the confines of our room, did I have unfettered access, and more often than not was treated with bare civility.

"I saw you near the gate today," I said on one occasion. Girt had been standing at the fence when no matter of convent business would have brought her there.

"Did you?" Girt replied. Not coy, as in times past, but dismissive.

"Everyone did." This from Therese, with unmistakable warning. "You're in danger of committing mortal sin. And you'll have to confess it."

"If I do, it won't be to you," Girt hissed. "Either of you."

The next day at breakfast, I gave an extra prayer of thanks for the fresh berries to stir into my porridge, and when I opened my eyes, I noticed a curl of paper rolled up against my bowl. With practiced stealth, I tucked it into my palm and into the hem of my sleeve, specially tailored for such a purpose. My eyes searched the refectory, but Girt was sitting too far down the table from me. To her left sat Sister Gwenneth, to her right, Sister Ave, neither of whom gave any indication of being an accomplice to the act. But who? Had it been delivered during my short time of prayer? Or had I unknowingly set my bowl next to a message intended for someone else?

The berries lost some of their sweetness, and the porridge became sticky in my mouth. Still, I ate, as it would arouse suspicion were I not to, let alone the accusation of ingratitude for the Lord's bounty. Five bites, six, then two more.

I should wait. Excuse myself to go the chapel early to pray and read it in the solitude of an empty pew. Or sneak back to my cell and read it within the coolness of the four dark walls. My stomach churned, now with excitement more than fear, and I realized how much I missed being party to this risk. How my mind had been aching for something—anything new to decipher and ponder.

Almost without realizing intent, my finger worried the hem of my sleeve, extracting the miniature scroll. Keeping my hands hidden below the table, I bowed my head again and closed my eyes—at least halfway, leaving a narrow slit of sight. Then, making no perceptible movement above my wrists, I unrolled the paper.

Stand fast therefore in the liberty wherewith Christ hath made us free, and be not entangled again with the yoke of bondage. Galatians v. 1.

I covered the words with my palm and saw them instead in my mind.

I wanted to stand, but could not, as the meal had not yet ended.

I wanted to ask who had given this verse, but could not, as the message within it would be construed as rebellious.

I wanted to read the verse that would follow, as the passage was unfamiliar, but could not, as I had no Bible of my own, and no assurance that my study would make the language understandable.

Instinctively I knew the bondage from which I had been freed was the bondage of sin, and that with every confession, every act of contrition, I remained free from that bondage. But once free, did any slave ever return—over and over—to his chains? Wasn't freedom conferred once and for all time? And if my soul was truly free, why then subject my body to such punishing confinement?

I felt a burning. Ears first. Then cheeks, my entire face enflamed. My hand clenched into a fist, mangling the Scripture beneath it. Gwenneth's hand came into my field of vision, palm up, beckoning attention.

Are you all right?

Yes.

Gwenneth lowered her hand below the table, tracking it with her eyes, prompting me to do the same. There, the nun splayed her fingers out, then slowly—deliberately—folded all but the first, then closed her hand and took it away. She returned to her porridge, eating as if nothing at all had transpired. Knowing some communication had taken place, even if I didn't fully understand, I folded the slip of paper into a tiny, tight wad. With as surreptitious a movement as I could muster, I slipped the verse into my mouth, feeling the parchment begin to soften immediately. The ink was bitter, but I imagined it dispersing across my tongue, coating it with its message.

Be not entangled again.

Galatians v. 1.

Five. One.

I closed my eyes and revisited the image of Gwenneth's hand under the table. Five, one.

Gwenneth had given me the paper. Gwenneth knew its message and was kindred in my thoughts, despite her present feigned lack of interest.

When the bell rang to dismiss, I gathered my bowl and my cup, dropped each in the bucket near the door, and proceeded into the hallway toward the chapel. Girt sidled up beside me.

I felt the slightest tug on my sleeve and looked down to see Girt's hand splayed. *Five.* And then a single finger. *One.*

Without hesitation, I repeated the gesture before we joined hands and walked together.

Chapter 12

The words—*leave, escape, freedom*—remained little more than silent thought well into the summer. Girt, Gwenneth, I, and a growing host of other sisters made painstakingly new acquaintance of each other, maneuvering the length of the refectory tables, making tentative signs.

Have you any news from outside?

Would you like to work beside me in the garden?

We could have no obvious gathering together, but a membership was soon enough established, with Girt and I acknowledged as its head. Girt because messages continued to be slipped in by the ever-increasingly amorous Hans, while I resumed my role as primary reader and interpreter of meaning. Then whispers, signs. Scraps of paper slipped into sleeves, smuggled in prayer books. Eventually destroyed.

One morning in the final week of June, I was met in the hallway outside the chapel after morning services by Sister Anne, who held a tray with a small loaf of dark bread, a pitcher of water, and two pears. Without any exchange of words,

I knew this was intended for Sister Gerda, and I'd been charged with its delivery. I hadn't seen her since that afternoon when I shared Luther's passage. On the occasions I asked to deliver Sister Gerda's tray, I'd been resolutely refused permission. Twice I'd sat on the ground outside her door, my presence begging an audience, only to leave—ignored.

Now, this.

I took the tray with a brief nod and wound my way through the dormitory to the dark hallway. It was cooler here than anyplace else within the convent walls. Almost pleasantly so, though the damp prevailed. As on previous occasions, I balanced the tray on my hip as I rapped on the door, speaking out, "Good morning, Sister Gerda."

The door opened, and she emerged from the shadows, taking the tray and depositing it on the rough-hewn table beneath the scrap of window. She came back, holding the two pears, offering one up to me.

"I couldn't." Knowing how little the woman ate. But she insisted, going so far as to take my hand and press the fruit into my palm.

What I wanted more than anything was to be invited over the threshold. To sit on the floor or share the narrow cot and take in the wisdom of this sister who devoted so much of her time to prayer and meditation. Still, I should not reject her offer of hospitality, and once my fingers closed around it, I said, "Thank you" before sinking my teeth in for a juice-filled bite, thankful to know it was soft enough for Sister Gerda to enjoy.

For minutes, neither of us spoke. We simply ate together, smiling as we wiped errant juice from our chins. When the fruit was gone, eaten down to a dotting of seeds on our palms, Sister Gerda took the timer from its shelf and turned it to begin the flow of sand.

"I have been praying over the words you left to me."

"Thank you," I said again, wanting to tell the woman what an honor it seemed to be so gravely considered, but not willing to waste a single precious second on my own words.

"You asked me what it means, this idea of being both a subject and free. But I suspect, in the days that have passed, you have come to your own conclusions."

"Yes." Again, no need to speak what was clearly understood.

"And I suspect now, in all your attempts to speak to me, and to have me speak to you, that you are seeking some kind of blessing."

"Truthfully, Sister, I don't know what I want."

"But *you're* beginning to suspect?"

The boldness of Sister Gerda's words did nothing to bolster my strength, and I looked quickly up and down the dark hallway to see that no one else listened. "I–I haven't—"

"Don't try to convince me that it hasn't crossed your mind. Leaving. Don't think you'd be the first woman to take her veil back out into the world. It happens. But there is a difference between leaving a convent and abandoning your vows."

"I made my vows to the Church."

"Not to God?" Her good eye twinkled behind its cloud.

"He wants nothing but my devotion, and I could be just as devoted to him living the life that other good Christian women live."

"Why, then, do you seek me out?"

"Because I need someone to tell me what to do."

"Someone did tell you what to do. Many years ago. All your life, isn't that so? Be truthful to yourself, my Katharina. What you want is for someone to grant you permission to do what is impermissible. You want someone to transcend God's authority over your life."

"I don't—"

Sister Gerda held up her hand. "I have made my choices, even within the narrow confines of this life. No one sentenced me to this cell. No one insisted I take on the severity of my vows. Some—our abbess, for one—consider me locked away, and thankfully so. But others, daily—and you above all know this—beg me to speak. They think that just because I spend so much time with my lips closed, I must be gathering wisdom for those moments when I open them. They see my life as a miracle because I wasn't left to die at birth. Or because I live on, without my sight. Without my face. And because I have so little time—" she glanced at the rapidly emptying glass—"I won't bother with a lie. I have no greater insight to the Father than do you. Or anyone else who seeks him."

She crossed to her table and came back with Luther's words.

"I heard; I understood and remember. Every word." By her tone I knew she'd been wrestling with the concept of freedom every bit as much as I had all this time. "Do not assume I am a prisoner here. I am subject to no man. I decide if, and when, and to whom I will speak. But I am subject to every man—or to every woman here, bound to live according to the expectation of holiness that you set upon me."

"I could never be what you are."

Sister Gerda laughed. Softly, with most of its impact hidden behind her hand. "Nor should you ever want to. Nor could I have the courage to embark on the adventure that awaits you."

The remaining grains of time numbered in the mere hundreds. "There's no adventure."

"You are subject to God, first and foremost,

and to the Church as his embodiment. What a narrow trestle to walk upon. See that you do not stumble, as you are now subject to all who watch, and look to you."

"But I—"

"We'll not speak again, not until it will be time to truly give you the blessing you seek."

Time emptied itself, revealing nothing but the solid planks of the door as it eased shut.

We whispered plans. Veils intertwined, shielding lips and holding words close. Some, bold, stating we must lock arms and stride straight out the front gate, out to the mysterious, waiting world. Others demanded rescue. Gallant men like the knights of legend, each riding in on a swift white horse and tearing out with a virgin clasped to his chest.

"Keep your wits about you," I would hiss, my eyes trained on whatever task gave us an excuse to gather. "Think to yourselves—why have you come here? And now, why must you leave? This isn't a matter of an escapade. It's an escape, and the only safe way to escape *from* a place is to know that you have somewhere to escape *to.*"

"What you need are husbands," Girt said one afternoon in late October. A small gathering of our committed sisters were in the otherwise empty refectory, slathering the tables with oil, meticulously wiping it into the minuscule cracks in the wood. Each moved a square of cloth in ever-widening circles, knowing we had the luxury of two hours to work and whisper until dinner at noon.

"Easy for you to say." Gwenneth rested her pouting face on one hand while the other performed its chore, listlessly. "We don't all have a suitor at the gate."

Girt leaned forward, drawing us in. "I'm not the one who's saying it."

I didn't trust Girt's knowing smirk. "Who is, exactly?"

"Luther." Her gaze circled the table, obviously hoping for a bigger reaction, but most gave little more than a shrug of recognition.

I held myself still. "What part does he have in it?"

"Hans says he's—what's the word? Sympathetic. Yes, sympathetic to our plight. That he understands what it is to leave the Church—"

"We're not leaving the *Church,*" Gwenneth interrupted.

I touched her sleeve to silence her. "I know what he means. He was a monk. He understands. But what does one have to do with the other?"

"Hans says he has friends. *Luther* has friends. And that he thinks he can match us with suitable partners."

Therese wadded up her rag and tossed it to the middle of the table. "That's the end of it."

She spun on the bench and had stormed to the doorway before I caught up to her.

"Wait—"

"No. I won't stay to hear another minute of this talk. It's one thing to walk away from the solemn vow you took in the name of the Holy Trinity. Then, to turn your back on the truest of Christian marriage. But now—to walk yourselves into this . . . this . . ." Therese contorted her face in search of a word for the disgust lurking beneath.

"None of us have committed—"

"Like a *market.* Worse yet, like when I was little, with my mother. And men would come—"

I didn't mean to slap her. I was just as surprised as Therese when I felt the sting of it radiating across my palm. Not since the days of our childhood wrestling had I struck out at a sister, and I fought back my own tears the moment I saw Therese's welling in her blue eyes.

"You shouldn't—" I choked—"you shouldn't say such things about your mother, God rest her soul."

"My mother's soul is not at rest," Therese said. "Not with all the sin she heaped upon it. And if you follow through with this, mark me—yours won't be either. There's still time, you know. To forget it all. To confess and repent."

"I've nothing to repent." My anger boiled even as my palm cooled.

Perhaps the slap hadn't been as sharp as I feared. Therese's cheek bore only the slightest tinge of pink as her expression softened into one of genuine concern. "Be careful, my friend, that your pride doesn't become a source of betrayal."

"Is that a greater danger than being betrayed by *my* friend?"

"I'll say nothing. You have my word. I can't do anything to guard your soul, but I won't purposefully try to get you in trouble here. Do you believe me?"

I had no choice. "I'm sorry I slapped you. Will you forgive me?"

"I do already." And to prove it, Therese bridged the distance between us and rested her pink cheek next to mine, as if placing a kiss.

She left, and I returned to the others.

Girt looked uneasy. "What was that all about?"

"Just a disagreement among sisters." I came back to the table but left the cleaning cloth untouched. "Now, what is it Luther said? About husbands?"

"You told me once you didn't want to hear any more from him. That you only wanted Scripture—"

"Girt!" My hands twitched, no doubt sending a reminder of the violence they'd inflicted, and all the women recoiled at the sight. "There is no longer time or reason for pettiness. If we've set our minds to leaving, as I believe we—and others—have, then from this moment out we have to be in accord. Now, what says he?"

"Only that . . ." She squinched her face, remembering. "I don't know the words exactly. Hans told me a little, but he didn't have time to read them for me." She shifted in her seat and reached to the bottom of her robe, producing a scrap from a pocket in the hem. "Here."

She handed over a now-familiar offering, a scrap from a leaflet, carefully torn, beginning and ending with unfinished text.

. . . if you have a daughter or friend who has fallen into such an estate and you are sincere and faithful, you should help her to get out, even if you have to risk your goods, body, and life for it. . . .

It was from a writing called "Against the So-called Spiritual Estate of the Pope and the Bishops," according to Girt's closed-eyed, careful recitation.

"But we don't all have families out there to help us," Sister Ave said. She was the youngest of us, barely sixteen years old, and as lovely as youth commanded. "Or friends. I don't know a soul outside of here. And my family? I've no doubt my father put me here in the first place to keep me from marrying someone against his approval. Someone who would sully the bloodline."

I smoothed the paper in my lap, tracing a single finger across the words. "I think you're wrong. I think you do have a friend. We all do. And Girt—" I looked up and coaxed a smile—"your friend just happens to be perhaps the most important and special friend of all. Tell him he needs to find a way. Not just for you, and not just for *us,* but for all the sisters who want to leave."

"How many will that be?"

"I don't know yet. Tell him—and I know this will be very hard for both of you—but tell him he has to stay away. For a long while, because sisters have been noticing your conversations, and it's only a matter of time before the abbess bans him completely. Or sends you away. Tell him to stay away until . . ." I calculated. How long would it take to know how many contemplated this same dream of freedom? Moreover, how long would it take to communicate with Luther, if he were really so inclined to give aid? "After Christmas. Well after Christmas—mid-January. And even then, not to come without a plan. Tell him we'll do exactly as he says."

Girt's smile had faded at the mention of Christmas, but I steeled my heart against sympathy.

"It has to be. If God wills, this will be the last Christmas you celebrate apart from each other. The last New Year you won't ring in together. Now, isn't that worth a little sacrifice?"

The sound of approaching footsteps stole any chance to hear Girt's reply as we returned vigorously—and silently—to our abandoned task. I made a point to offer a warm, welcoming smile to each of the six sisters, including Sister Margitta, the oldest of our order who was more often than not spared any taxing daily chores. The soft, wrinkled skin puckered as she eyed me with appreciative curiosity.

"Sister Therese reports that more help is needed in oiling the tables? But it seems to me you have plenty of capable hands."

"Capable, but idle." This from a girl named Anna Marie, a pock-faced novice who had yet to say anything pleasant since her arrival. I ignored her slight.

"We are capable, Sisters, but short one set. The scent from the oil, it seems, is giving Therese a headache this morning. We need only one of you to take her place, and I know we'll get the task completed in plenty of time." I directed my gaze. "Do you think, Sister Margitta, you could stay? I trust your industriousness to make up for our lost time."

"Of course." She had the good sense to understate her agreement. "It's good to know that there are some who will still find good use in these old hands." Those with her wished us blessings on the day before departing.

Immediately, we went to work. For a time there was no conversation, only the *shushing* of the rags on the wood, soon accompanied by the warbling hum of Sister Margitta. Low and comforting, like I imagined the sound of a lullaby. The tune circulated, unfamiliar. Not a hymn, not anything we'd ever heard in chapel, or even from the strains of the evening choir. But it was simple, inviting. Just six notes in the melody. Someone—Gwenneth, most likely—found a harmony. I listened, in awe of the phenomenon of such immediate unity. Then, as if by design, Ave's sweet, clear soprano gave life to a lyric.

The white doves are flying,
The white foxes slipping,
The white rabbits jumping—
Over, and under, and right through the
wall.

The words peeked out from behind the tune, and two rounds later, another sister joined in. Then another. Then Girt.

Finally, me. Seeing myself first as the fox, wily and elusive. The rabbit, swift and smart. Most of all, though, the dove. The same as Noah sent out from the ark, looking for God's promise of home.

Chapter 13

It was, at first, a single word spoken to Girt, relayed to me, and whispered from one sister to another as we stood in a circle around the fire one dark February night.

Easter.

A single word in reply to a dangerously lengthy letter I had composed, signed, and circulated throughout our ranks for signatures of agreement. Twenty-four names in all, and there could have been more had we been more bold. Still, the number frightened me. How could so many be trusted to keep a secret? Some of the names belonged to familiar faces—women I counted as companions as well as sisters. But some were mere strings of letters. Who was Brigitte? Which Ava was this? And I worried, too, that the scrap would be intercepted and our imminent escape exposed. With my name—Katharina von Bora—boldly scrawled beneath the final plea:

We await your wisdom, and pray for our release.

Only Girt had been spared the commitment of a signature, as any sort of writing proved a painful, humiliating exercise. She, of course, had the most important task of all. It was Girt who found a way to slip the letter into Hans's rein-hardened hand. And it was into Girt's ear that the date of our freedom was declared.

Easter.

The details of our escape followed, the exactness of time and place, meted out in snippets of conversation. An empty farmer's cart at midnight. An overnight journey to Torgau for a short stay before continuing on to Wittenberg.

"But not for all of us," I said to Girt as we lingered in the chapel after early-morning Mass. She stood at my back, keeping watch. "Not everyone who signed the letter."

"Why not?"

"In a single cart?"

"It will be empty. We can squeeze ourselves together."

"All of us slipping out? We'll call attention. Noise and number. We'd have to line up at the gate. See here." I sketched a diagram of the grounds and back gate in the frosted glass, knowing the sun and my sleeve would erase the evidence. "We'd make a solid line along the fence. We can take only half the number. Or less."

"And who's going to decide who goes and who stays?"

"I will." My response came without hesitation. "You, of course. Me, and any who heard from their families since the Christmas letters. Those who have a place to go." I made hash marks in the frost as I listed, knowing only a few of the women had received word back with news of a welcoming reception.

"So, you heard nothing?" Girt asked.

"There's no place for me." Indeed, my father's letter had been equally sparse in words.

"Luther is said to have a plan. A place for all of us, eventually."

"Let's worry about how we're going to get into the wagon before worrying about what might be waiting when we get out."

"You're right. Sister Ave?"

"Yes. And Sister Ave . . ."

"Therese?" Girt's mention of our friend sounded more like a challenge. "Will she have a place with us?"

"I'll talk with her."

"I worry that she might—" Girt craned her neck and waited for the distant sound of a footfall to disappear—"that she might say something. Don't you?"

"I said I'll talk with her. Now, we'll be able to take maybe four more."

"How will we choose?"

My previous decisive bravado left me. How could I possibly take a sister's fate in my hand? I closed my eyes in a silent prayer of contrition, then proceeded to wipe our plan from the glass.

"We won't. We'll let the Lord decide. Only he knows what is waiting on the other side. He will fill the right hearts with courage."

I chose the worthy through silent lottery. Who would be brave enough to hold my gaze during our midday meal? Who would join me in humming our tune of escape? Who would form her hands into the shape of a rabbit in silent greeting when we passed in the corridor? As the date grew nearer, so did the need for true courage, and our numbers dropped with every pair of averted eyes.

On the first day of April, I went to the kitchen to beg the favor of bringing Sister Gerda's meal. It was the last she would have, as for years she had insisted on fasting from sunset on Maundy Thursday until breakfast Easter Monday. As such, it was laden with pickled herring, cheese, bread, and stewed turnips. There was also a second pitcher of water, intended to last all four days. All this made the tray heavy, and when I arrived at her door, I could only kick for her attention. When, after a suitable number of seconds, there was no shuffle of footsteps, let alone a turn of the latch, I kicked again.

"Sister Gerda? I've come with your tray. It's heavy. Open the door, and I'll take it to your table."

Nothing.

She must have known. Somebody—Girt, maybe, in her excitement; or Therese in her lingering disapproval—must have told her of our plan.

"Sister?" And another kick.

A month or more before, I might have respected her reproach. Turned and left the tray on the floor for her to retrieve later, in privacy. But this was not her usual amount of provisions, and this was no ordinary day. She would never be able to lift this burden, and I would never forgive myself for not seeing her one last time. So, doubling my strength with one arm, I eased the other over to the latch, turned it, and pushed the door open, apologizing.

"I'm sorry to intrude on your solitude, but I can't carry this all the way back to the kitchen. I'll just—"

The silence inside the tiny, dark room was more profound than any I'd ever experienced.

"Sister Gerda?" But by then I knew better than to expect a response.

Feeling my strength wash away, I crouched down to set the tray on the floor, and three steps later I was at her bedside.

By some miracle, she'd become even smaller, her twisted form taking up half the space of the narrow cot. She slept—*slept,* as I would always remember—with the tumored side of her face buried in the pillow. Now, in perfect peace, she lay smooth and ageless, the kerchief that covered her hair undisturbed.

"Oh, Sister . . ." I knelt beside her, kissing the cold, gnarled hands clutched in a final prayer. Tears poured, and I gritted my teeth to hold back the sobs that wanted to echo throughout the corridor. Once composed, I raised my head and, out of habit, leaned close to her ear—her good ear—and whispered, "You have been made new. What a sweet, pure spirit to give to our eternal Father. And how clever of you to escape before I have the chance to do so."

This, I knew, would have garnered a wry smile, and I kissed her cheek, allowing my lips to linger in a way she would never have allowed in life.

Never before had I felt so alive. Young and strong, and any doubt I might have harbored disappeared, much as I imagined Sister Gerda's final breath. With peace, unbidden, and carried straight to God.

"I will see you again, sweet Sister." A truth I believed more strongly than if I'd spoken it in farewell. "And we will run to each other, clattering on streets of gold. Shouting praise." A final kiss, and I stood, drawing Sister Gerda's gray wool blanket up and over her still form.

The tray had doubled in weight since I set it down, and the journey back to the kitchen grown at least a mile longer. When I arrived, I set the tray down on the wide worktable, calling the attention of the two sisters chopping vegetables for the day's stew. One looked at me quizzically, and for once the rule of silence worked in my favor. There would be no need for lengthy explanations to sully the sweetness of my final moment with Sister Gerda with details of shock and pity. I simply made the sign of the cross upon my breast and said, "Send word to the abbess. Our sister has gone to be with our Father in heaven."

Then I ran, each step a celebration of my life, God's gift of physical vitality. I ran like I did as a child, steps ahead of Sister Gerda's correction, wishing my shoes would make more noise, enough to reach her and summon her to me, released from hermitage, moving freely beside me. I ran to the sewing room, the classroom, the refectory, and the chapel. Then outside, to the courtyard, to the garden, until I saw her—Therese—wielding a hoe against the earth still cold from winter's frost.

I stopped short, ready to shout her name, but my frantic steps had garnered enough attention, and she stood straight, seeing me. Silently I beckoned, and she approached, leaving her tool in the cart at the end of the furrow. As she drew near, I reached out my hands and fought to remain standing when she took them.

"Kat? What is it?"

The pain on my face must have been apparent to have brought her to speak.

Come with me.

My grip gave her no choice but to obey, and I led her past one curious face after another, without pausing for explanation. Even Girt, who made some attempt to follow, was ignored with nothing more than a flick of my wrist to dissuade her. We didn't stop until I'd dragged Therese to our cell, closed the door behind us, and leaned myself against it.

"Kat, for all that is holy, what has happened? Are you—" she lowered her voice—"in trouble? Do they know?"

I shook my head. "I went to see Sister Gerda this morning. For one last time."

"Oh."

"She was dead."

Therese gasped, her eyes wide above the hand brought to her mouth before she crossed herself, saying, "Heavenly Father grant peace to her soul. Amen."

"Amen," I echoed, both the word and the gesture.

"How awful for you, Kat. I know you loved her."

"I did." Tears came again, in concert with Therese's, and we held each other, not caring if the dirt from her apron transferred to the whiteness of my robe. I felt our bodies reach accord in breath as sounds of comfort passed mutually between us.

"I'm glad you're the one who found her," Therese said as we pulled away.

"I am too. What if it had been Anna Marie? She would have been screaming all over the place."

Therese giggled. "You're terrible. But it's true. Why did you come to me?"

"Because you knew her too. Like I did, from before."

"So did Girt."

"Girt will find out soon enough. I'll tell her myself, if word doesn't reach her before dinner. But listen." I gripped her shoulders, keeping her face—beautiful within the wimple—squarely in front of me. "I want you to come with us. With *me*."

Whatever love we'd shared in the previous moments fell behind a hardened mask. "Don't—"

"I don't want that to happen to you. I don't want you to become an old woman, dying alone. Oh, Therese, think about it. To be completely alone. And what if she'd died tonight? It would be days before anyone would know."

She softened in front of me and led me to sit next to her on her bed. "Remember what I told you about my mother?"

"Yes, I know about your mother. And the angel, and the men. But—"

"She was sick."

"Yes, I know. Fevered and ill."

"But more, too. I didn't think much of it at the time. I was so young. And she tried to hide it from me. But she'd been bleeding from—" she looked away—"from her womanhood. And not the way we do, as God intended. But diseased, because of how she had abused her body."

In all our years together, this was a new detail to her story. I always imagined a beautiful, pale sickness, like the fever I'd seen in some of the girls before they went on to heaven.

"I'm glad they found you."

"You see? Sister Gerda isn't the first woman in my life to be found dead, alone in a room. There are far, far worse circumstances."

"Your mother wasn't alone. She had you. And you had . . . *him*."

"When I woke up, my only words were to ask for my mother. And as for *him* . . . Now, I have Christ himself within me." She held a hand to her breast. "The Holy Ghost indwelling. Isn't that so much more powerful than an angel at the door?"

"I only meant . . . Sister Gerda didn't have what you have. She could never have had a life outside the Church. But you—"

"What makes you think I want a life outside the Church?"

"I don't want to leave you behind."

"Well, then, that makes you selfish." A pretty, small smile softened the insult. "And intolerant and cruel. I've done nothing to hinder your endeavor, have I? Even though I think you are misguided and wrong, I've guarded your secret. Why? Because I respect the vows I took enough to know that no woman should live them half-heartedly."

"On that, at least, we agree," I said, feeling for the first time in well over a year that we might have a kindred spirit after all.

"Believe me when I tell you there is nothing out in the world that interests me. I understand now—and I have for a long time—that I cannot do penance for my mother's sins. Your Luther writes about the freedom of a Christian. This is how I choose to live. Please do not beg me to go, and I will not beg you to stay."

"But we might never see each other again."

"Of course we will, silly. I told you long ago that we wouldn't always be best friends in this world. I'll always love you, but I won't be by your side. We'll see each other, just as we'll see Sister Gerda, and you'll see your mother."

We hugged again, an embrace filled with a new form of comfort this time. Not mourning a past, but reconciling a future. I thought back to the morning I met her, when her quick thinking saved me from my first punishment. I knew, come Easter Monday morning, she would stand before the abbess, pummeled with questions about Girt and me and the others. Where we'd gone, and how, and by what power. And I could picture the scene, as if it played out before me on a stage. Therese, silent and resolute. Her hands clasped behind her back. Her features unreadable. Unlike when we were children, she would choose silence over a lie.

In the distance, the bell rang, summoning us to an untimely chapel, certain to be an announcement of Sister Gerda's passing. Therese and I rose together and walked side by side, for the last time in our lives.

Part IV

Torgau
Reichenbach
Household,
Wittenberg

Spring – Summer 1523

Chapter 14

The tarp thrown over the wagon's bed shielded us from any curious onlooker lurking on the side of the road.

"I'd be far more suspicious of the person who found himself spying on humble farm carts in the dead of night," Sister Margitta said, complaining anew of the pain the rough voyage caused her aging hip.

"It won't be long now." My assurance was born of Hans's promise that we would arrive in Torgau by morning's light, and the spaces between the wagon slats had taken on a hopeful shade of gray. We'd passed the night in utter silence—or at least as much silence as a group of women poised at the point of a new life's journey could muster. When the smoothness of the road allowed, we spoke in prayer, claiming Christ Jesus as our protector and the Holy Ghost as our guide. More often, the ruts and rocks made the wheels clatter and the boards creak, and we stifled our outbursts behind our hands.

So many years of silence had trained us well.

We rode in a cart once used to transport barrels of pickled herring and as such was wide and deep enough to allow some measure of comfort. Despite the thick layer of fresh, sweet-smelling straw kindly spread across the bed, my legs were cramped, my feet numb, and the base of my spine a solid ball of pain. Still, I owed a word of thanksgiving with every turn of the wheel. When I opened my eyes, I met the morning light that had found its way through the tarp and the slats, and I was greeted with the shadowy images of my fellow refugees. Twelve of us in all. How serious they all looked, clutching one another's hands or gripping their veils or staring dejectedly into the emerging shadows.

Ignoring every ache in my body, I rose on my haunches, just enough to elevate my head a bit above the others. "Sweet sisters," I said, hoping my voice sounded stronger than I felt, "we have reached the dawn of a new day. Our first day of freedom, to love and serve our Lord Jesus Christ as we wish. Listen—do you hear my voice? Do you realize that here, huddled in this cart, I can speak to you more freely than I ever could within the walls of Marienthrone?"

The wagon slowed; the road became smooth.

"And listen. Do you hear? The sounds of life. People, merchants, farmers."

"Strangers," Sister Ave piped from the corner by the wagon's gate.

"The farmer's wife is our sister as much as we are to each other," Sister Margitta said, her voice as uneven as the road beneath us. "And the men our brothers."

"And what are we to be to them?" This, again, from Ave, making me wonder if she should have been chosen to make this journey at all. She was young enough to cling to childish petulance, and old enough to know the fear of uncertainty.

"God alone knows that," I said. "Our lives are in his hand, and I believe he is to be trusted more than the pope, wouldn't you say?"

This brought a wave of laughter, albeit of a nervous sort, and by the time it died out, the wheels had stopped turning.

"Oh, sisters." Whether by habit or some new sense of fear, I dropped my voice to a whisper and reached out to either side to take the hands of Margitta and Girt. One, withered and delicate with the brittle bones of waning days, the other thick and strong with a lifetime of labor before it. Soon the silence filled with masculine voices in greeting. Small talk about the journey, the weather. That they'd been blessed with a cool night and dry roads. That the woods had indeed been dark, but the path familiar.

"And the women? What about the women?"

Somehow, I knew it was Luther. His voice tinged with impatience, forceful enough to bring all other conversation to a halt.

"Not a peep from them." This, Hans, who seemed amused at his report.

"You speak as though that's a trait to be admired." Luther again, and I found myself biting my tongue to keep back a retort. "Shall we see what all this fuss has been about?"

The next I knew, the tarp rustled above my head, raining down bits of straw and dust, and I looked up into bright morning sky.

"Sisters of Marienthrone—" again, his voice, with exaggerated grandeur—"may I welcome you to Torgau?"

I gripped the top of the wagon and used it to pull myself to my feet. At least, I assumed I was on my feet, as I could feel nothing of a surface below. Peering down, I saw a man dressed in simple, dark garb. His face was broad and kind—nothing even my limited experience would call handsome. But his eyes glistened with authority and triumph.

"You must be *Herr Doktor* Luther," I said, giving no thought to what I would say if, indeed, he wasn't.

"I am," he said, then laughed. "You seem eager to escape the cart."

Pain now sparked in my feet, and I stamped them, encouraging circulation. "I am."

The tailgate had been lowered, and I inched my way along the edge of the cart, hoping to have full feeling in my feet before jumping. Like sheep at the cliff's edge, one after the other, the sisters descended, some on their own power, others—like Sister Margitta—with unconcealed trepidation.

"Not so eager, then?" Luther stood at the gate, hand extended.

"Doesn't Scripture tell us that the first shall be last?"

"You are the first, then?"

"In a sense, I suppose." I bent at my knees, braced my hands on the lowered gate, and—ignoring his gesture of assistance—somehow got myself to the ground with as much grace as possible. My feet wobbled, my legs threatened to buckle, and my wrist took an uncomfortable twist as I tried to hold myself steady.

"Whoops, there," Luther said, stepping forward but stopping short of touching me. "We don't want the first to be fallen."

"I am Katharina von Bora." How strange my name sounded, spoken aloud like that. All alone, stripped of any meaning or connection. Suddenly, I was six years old again, dropped into the home of a stranger, though I was fairly certain I wouldn't spend this evening curled up in Luther's lap. "I signed the letter we sent."

"So you were the first to sign it?"

"I wrote it."

A statement of fact, nothing more. Certainly not worth the rocking back on his heels, or the thin, approving whistle that came through his barely exposed teeth, but his admiration sparked a fuse of pride in me, and I was glad for the wimple that hid the flush I felt.

"Quite eloquent, I must say. You are a woman of words."

"Just a woman. Though I don't suppose we'll be seen as such. Here, away."

"And why not?"

He was challenging me, inviting further discourse, reminding me of the hours spent in catechism with Sister Elisabeth. I looked around at the sea of stained white robes, so unbefitting this environment, and ran my fingers along the edge of my veil.

"I imagine we'll be objects of curiosity for some time. Pity, maybe? Hostility from those who will see us as having betrayed the Church. Sacred vessels. Brides of Christ. Abominations. Faithless, fallen."

Words poured forth, and somewhere midstream I realized this was the longest uninterrupted speech I'd ever had with a man outside of a confessional. Luther, as one familiar with the sacrament, merely listened, his face unchanged, leaving no hint of his approval or disapproval. To my left, the sisters gathered like a cake newly sprung from a pan, holding the huddled shape from the night's journey in the wagon. I alone had stepped free.

"Some of us," I continued, hiding my own anxiety in the collective, "have no recollection of what it means to walk in a marketplace. Some have never handed money to a merchant or purchased cloth. We don't know patterns, or how to even begin to appear—"

"Are you bemoaning your lack of vanity?"

The humor in his voice pierced me—not in any painful way, but in a manner that deflated my worry and afforded enough space for me to take a deep breath before responding.

"It is not vanity, sir, to wish simply to dress in a way that represents our freedom. I should think you would understand, having played such an instrumental role in attaining it for us."

"Remember the words of our Savior, as recorded in Matthew's Gospel. *Take no thought for your life, what ye shall eat, or what ye shall drink; nor yet for your body, what ye shall put on. Is not the life more than meat, and the body than raiment?*"

Not even the quoting of Scripture could tame the smugness from his demeanor. The words of the Gospel rolled off his tongue as easily as the lyrics of tavern singers from my earliest memories with my father.

Frustration ignited within me, its heat no doubt coloring my cheeks. "I'm afraid you have me at quite the disadvantage, sir. I've not been given such unfettered access to the Scriptures. So while I am steadfast in my faith that he will provide all I need, I lack the words to engage in such an argument."

To my surprise, he laughed—a great guffaw that caused the now-entwined sisters to startle.

"Oh, my, Katharina von Bora," he said, chuckling through each syllable of my name. "I have known you for less than a quarter of an hour, and I can say with all honesty that I doubt you have ever—or *will* ever—lack words for any circumstances."

A collective giggle came from the sisters, Girt's loudest among them. I turned my head, expecting to silence them with a glare, but unable to control a smile.

"Well, I find myself in obedience to one part of the Savior's command," I said. "I've taken no thought. Nothing beyond escape. And now . . ." To my horror, my throat stung with the threat of tears, and if Luther doubted anything would render me unable to speak, he hadn't taken into account the weight of all these women. They stared at me, not challenging, but searching. Girt, usually such a bluster of confidence, chewed her bottom lip. Of all, she had the most promising future, with love and marriage on the horizon. But what of pretty Ave, naive and unaware that there could be any darkness in a human soul? Or our oldest, Margitta, bent with age, knowing nothing but a life lived under the weight of a veil?

My eyes scanned the gathering, and I silently named each one.

Sister Girt.

Sister Gwenneth.

Sister Margitta.

Sister Magdalena.

Sister Maria.

Sister Anna.

Sister . . .

The next face became a blur, nothing more than a swath of flesh within the veil's frame.

"Sister—" I spoke out loud, hoping the sound of my voice would bring the features into focus. Though I stared intently, doing so only made each individual woman blur. Nothing but white, a solid mass. And my legs began to tremble.

"Katharina?" It was Margitta's voice, unmistakable in its quaver. "Are you all right?"

Everything disappeared. The sisters folded into a cloud, and the other souls surrounding—the onlookers who had gathered within my periphery—became a single multicolored ribbon wrapped around this tiny bit of earth. At the edge of hearing, men's voices spoke in low, concerned tones. My mind emptied, save for the echo of Luther's words from the moment before.

Take no thought for your life. What you shall eat. What you shall drink.

No, not Luther's words. The words of Jesus Christ. Recorded and written, meant for comfort in just this time. Not unfamiliar at all. At least, not in form. But in meaning—until now they had been something akin to chastisement.

Take no thought of what ye shall eat. What ye shall drink. Because the Church would provide. Just enough to stave off hunger. Except when there wasn't enough, and there'd be no recourse for more.

Or what ye shall wear. For you take on the robe, the wimple, the veil. Identical to your sisters. Set apart from the fickle fashions of the world.

Take no thought. And I hadn't.

A hand steadied me, grasping my arm. A strong hand, a man's hand, and a voice that sounded as distant as it seemed the first time I ever read his words. With his touch, everything—my balance and my thoughts—was restored.

"There, now." Assurance, without patronization. "You all must be quite exhausted. Let's get you something to eat, and to drink."

"And to wear?" I said it without a single thought of its impertinence.

"Even so." He dropped his grip, but hovered close and whispered words for me alone. "I know your fear. I may understand it better than any person alive. I know what it is to lead, and to bear the weight of those who follow. But our God is mighty in strength to take on such a burden. For now, take a moment to feel his pleasure in your obedience."

He leaned away, scanned the crowd, and raised his hand to beckon a stout, red-faced woman from its midst.

"Frau Dunkel," he said by way of introduction. "Take the ladies inside now, get them something to eat, and then show them each to a bed to rest. It's been an arduous journey, as you can well imagine."

"Aye, Doctor Luther," Frau Dunkel said, her gaze and her voice full of reverence for the man. She began a purposeful stride out of the yard, moving as if she were a knight leading a charge rather than a smallish, round woman herding a crowd of weak and frightened nuns. Silently, we followed, nodding our veiled heads to the villagers who parted themselves like the Red Sea of Moses.

She led us into a long, low-ceilinged room lit only by the morning's light streaming through the windows. A dozen rough-hewn tables were set in an orderly pattern, all square with four benches tucked beneath.

"This seems a fine establishment," I said.

"Haven't had a soul in here for days," Frau Dunkel said, every hint of the civility and deference she'd shown with Luther gone. "Got six rooms upstairs been sitting empty, waiting on your lot to arrive. *Sacrifice for Christ*, he calls it. Empty pocket is what I see."

"I am sure your hospitality will not go unrewarded." This from Margitta, whose strength appeared to be waning with each passing moment.

"This life or the next," Frau Dunkel said, unsoftened. "Take yourselves a seat, and I'll have some food brought out directly."

The habit of silence clung to the sisters as we moved throughout the tables, pulled out the benches, and sat—hands folded in our laps, eyes cast down. Within minutes, the room was filled with noise as Frau Dunkel and a trail of girls—each a nesting-doll replica of her mother—burst from the kitchen, carrying trenchers heaped with bread and stacks of precariously balanced wooden bowls. These were the charge of the youngest of the girls, and she maneuvered through the tables with a practiced ease, saying, "Good morning, miss. And welcome," as she placed a bowl in front of each of us. The girl couldn't have been more than eight years old, pink-cheeked and bright-eyed, her hair an unremarkable shade of brown tied messily at her nape with a scrap of ribbon.

She was followed by an older girl, thinner and slightly taller, who carried a steaming crock of stew, which she ladled into each bowl, spilling nary a drop in the process.

“It’s lamb,” she said, responding to the silent question raised when Girt leaned forward to inhale the enticing scent. “Fit for Easter Monday, don’t you think?”

I thought of Sister Gerda, who would have been breaking her fast this morning had she been alive. She would have been delighted at the beauty, poise, and grace of these girls.

Another delivered the bread; two more brought cups to be filled with sweet, fresh water. Frau Dunkel herself carried nothing, only stood at the door and directed her charges in a voice of strident affection.

I, like all the sisters, remained motionless in the midst of the bustling service, and still after each bowl and cup had been filled. I had no memory of ever lifting a spoon without directed instruction. Someone needed to rise up, pray the blessing over the food, and give permission to eat. But who? Margitta, the oldest, seemed the most logical choice, but I could not catch her eye. So this, too, would fall to me. I braced my hands on the table and was about to stand when Frau Dunkel’s voice rang out.

“Lyse! Say the blessing, will you, so these poor women can eat.”

Lyse, it turned out, was the youngest of the Dunkel daughters, but the child seemed undaunted by the responsibility. She took a step forward from the line in which she and her sisters had assembled, made the cross, and bowed her head. An audible rustle of veils followed.

"Our Father in heaven," she began, the echoes of her mother's strength infusing every word, "we thank thee for the safe journey of these women and ask that the food thou hast provided will replenish the strength they've lost and fill them with new strength for a new day. Amen."

We sisters echoed her *amen* and, without further instruction, dipped our spoons into the stew, showing obvious restraint not to gobble it directly from the bowl.

I, however, remained still, in awe of the boldness of this child.

"Psst. Kat!" Girt broke into my reverie. She hefted her spoon, smiled, and dove it back into her nearly empty bowl.

"Go on, then," Frau Dunkel directed to one of the older girls. "Don't let them see the bottoms." Then, louder, addressing all in the room, "And don't you let my bread go stale in front of you. Sweated over the oven on Easter Sunday so's it would be fresh for you. And if you're waiting on a knife for making pretty slices, you'll waste the day here. Tear into it."

Exhilarated at the invitation, Girt reached for the round brown loaf at the center of the table, picked it up, ripped off an end piece for herself, and continued the process until nothing was left on the trencher and each of the women had a chunk balanced on the edge of her bowl.

"And dunk it in," little Lyse said over our shoulders. "Just like that, to get up all the broth."

The room filled with the sounds of slurping and scraping, punctuated by Frau Dunkel's never-ending stream of commands. More water, here. Get another loaf from the kitchen—two, then. And butter? How could we forget the butter, churned fresh on Friday?

Soon after, my sisters found their voices. Small sounds of appreciation at first, comments on the deliciousness of the food, sincere thanks given to Lyse and the other daughters who served with warm graciousness. Then conversation. Multiple conversations, in fact, with occasional bouts of unchecked laughter. Voices rose to combat each other, to be heard above what had become a veritable din.

I engaged too, confessing to Girt that I'd been sick to my stomach for the better part of the month in fearful anticipation of this day.

"No more of that," Girt said, swiping the air between us with a piece of sodden bread. "Nothing more of fear. Or secrets. Ever."

Frau Dunkel instructed the girls to begin clearing the tables, taking away the abandoned, empty bowls and crumb-filled trenchers. For the first time in any memory, my stomach was comfortably full, and a drowsiness threatened to overtake me in this very place. Luther had promised beds, and it took all my strength not to stretch myself out on the table in front of me—or the bench, or the floor; such was my fatigue. From the looks on the faces around me, my fellow refugees felt the same, and I was about to brave Frau Dunkel with my request when a new bustle of activity came with the encore appearance of the Dunkel daughters. Having divested themselves of food and dishes, they reappeared, each carrying a mountain of fabric that threatened to engulf her completely.

"Now," Frau Dunkel spoke above the curious whispers, "I can't tell you that any of these are new. Except for the linen—that's fresh-spun. But the dresses are quality; that I can assure. Our women work hard, and things have to last. You can't very well go around dressed like a flock of doves, now can you? Never going to catch a gentleman's eye like that."

Four tables remained unoccupied at the top of the room, and it was here that the girls dropped their bundles. A single collective sound of awe rose from the sisters.

"So come," Frau Dunkel said, harsh in her encouragement. "Choose what you like. My little Lyse will close the shutters, so there won't be any eyes peeping while you dress."

In an instant, the women pounced on the

clothes, grappling through piles of fabric and colors and patterns.

I remember my mother had a dress in just this color.

Look at these! Tiny flowers stitched right in!

Anything red? I've always wanted a red dress.

I stood back and watched as they laughed and held the gowns out for scrutiny, plastered them against their chests, and turned to one another. They clucked approval, emitted sounds of delight, and fussed over the choices.

Ave was the first to doff her veil, sending it straight to the floor. Her wimple followed, and she stood bareheaded, her hair cropped to her shoulders. She'd pulled one arm from the sleeve of her robe and appeared ready to yank the entire garment off when a burst of indignation made its way through the stupor brought on by the heartiness of the breakfast.

"Stop it." I spoke quietly at first, a volume that had served well all these years, and had even proven dangerous at times. Here, though, the noise made no impact.

"Stop!"

The compliance was not immediate, but by the time I repeated the command a third—and again, softer—time, it was complete.

"We made a vow the day we took the veil, a vow that we've broken. Do none of you remember the anguish? I cannot be the only one who wrestled in prayer, seeking God's guidance through my freedom. No matter how the Church would seek to confine us, these garments were meant to set us apart, to show us to be holy women, consecrated to Christ." Every word of the ceremony spoken as I donned these garments for the first time echoed through my memory as I spoke. "After this moment, you'll have nothing but your character to act as testament to your faith. Can we please treat these with reverence rather than discarding them like nothing more than turnip tops? And think of the women who acted as our first Christian sisters did, giving of what little they had to those who had less. Can we not take even a moment to pause and give thanks to God the Father for his providence? And to the Holy Ghost who moved within the hearts of these strangers to meet our needs?"

Slowly, silently, Girt picked up the coverings she'd discarded and held them to her breast. The others, too, clutched close whatever they held, and all heads bowed—the covered and the uncovered, including Frau Dunkel and her daughters.

"For your provision, heavenly Father, we are truly grateful. Amen."

Such a short prayer, given the length of the speech that preceded it, but I knew those words spoken to my sisters were taken as sacred by the Father. Some of the women—those who'd been surprised by the prayer's abrupt end, or whose hands were too full of overskirts and kirtles—failed to make the sign of the cross upon the prayer's conclusion. This lapse did not go unnoticed, but neither was it unsettling in any way. Imagine—I'd felt a need to pray, voiced the prayer, and now the activity had resumed, but at a more respectable volume. The women did not appear punished, merely prompted, and they followed Girt's example in removing veil and wimple with reverence and care, folding each carefully and setting them on the empty tables.

A tug on my sleeve called my attention to the oldest of the Dunkel daughters, Marina. A lovely, healthy girl who looked to be about eighteen years old.

"Here, Sister." She held up a garment draped over her arm. "Try this one. I think the color would be perfect for you."

I took the dress and held it at arm's length. It was dark green, the color of moss in shadow, with narrow, widely spaced black stripes. At her unspoken insistence, I held it up, just below my chin, and looked for her approval.

"Oh, how it brings out your eyes, Sister. Such a beautiful shade of green they are, too."

"Are they?" My experience with any kind of looking glass had been limited to brief encounters with clean windows and polished tin, and even then not much of an opportunity beyond ensuring that all of my hair was tucked neatly within my wimple.

"There's a mirror in your room. Look for yourself when you go."

My room.

The fatigue that had been allayed returned, grasping at a place between my shoulder blades and threatening to carry me to a nest in the midst of all those donated dresses.

"Oh, but you must be exhausted," Marina said. Perceptive girl. "Let me ask Mother if I can show you to your beds. Quite a luxury that will be, won't it? To sleep through the day?"

I watched her thread her way back to her mother and comprehended the conversation as all five of the girls were summoned and given orders. At Frau Dunkel's command, they were dispatched and assigned—a daughter or two for each handful of sisters. We were given our final opportunity to pick from among the clothing: linen tunics, a vast array of overshirts and skirts and kirtles. Stockings, caps, headscarves, sleeves, belts, petticoats. So much confusion for a group of women who had been denied such choice for most of their lives.

"Listen here," Frau Dunkel said, speaking at a volume that rendered the rest of us silent. "You ladies just let the girls take you to your rooms. Rest up, and I mean it. A good sleep for all of you. And you just leave it to my Marina to have something set out for you to wear when you wake up."

"I know the perfect thing for each of you," Marina said, eyes bright as she scanned the gathering of ramshackle nuns. "Trust me. You'll all be beautiful."

I began to follow suit with the others, returning my green dress to the common pile, but once again she laid an attention-getting hand on my sleeve.

"Oh, no, Sister Katharina. That I've already picked out for you. Take it upstairs. Come, follow me."

She motioned for Girt and Ave and Margitta to follow her specifically, leading us to the narrow staircase at the end of the room.

"You'll have to share beds," she spoke over her shoulder, "so you might want to open the window a bit for a breeze. Cool the room down, as it gets stuffy. But there's a heavy curtain should keep out most of the light."

"I could sleep on a rock in the middle of the market," Girt said, dragging herself up the final step.

"I'll just pretend I'm in morning chapel," Ave piped up from behind. "After breakfast? Never could stay awake."

This prompted a few giggles, but also a chastising sound from Margitta.

Our room—Girt's and mine—was the first

at the top of the stairs. Marina closed the door behind us, wishing us a good rest, and went on with the others to their accommodations. It was small, even in comparison to the cell I'd shared with Girt and Therese, but the bed was covered with a colorful quilt, and the pitcher on the washstand was a bright blue and decorated with a delicate pattern of vines and leaves.

Immediately I crossed to the window and opened it to the bustling life below. The sweet smell of roasting pine nuts wafted up on the spring breeze, overcoming less pleasant odors. I heard laughter and singing, shouts of impatient mothers, wails of vendors, profane exclamations from men—all of it culminating in a singular, profoundly discordant music.

"Life," I said, speaking out loud to all those who wouldn't hear me.

And then, separate from them all, a solitary, familiar figure. Luther, in his black cloak and worn shoes, stopped in the middle of the path. He placed his hands on his hips, as if posing for a portrait, and lifted his face. The near-afternoon sun caused his eyes to narrow, perhaps blinding him, for I could think of no other reason he would be so bold as to stare directly up at my window. At me.

He showed no reaction as I detached my veil, removed it, followed by my wimple. But then, as I emerged, bareheaded, he smiled. My hair, too, was short—shorter than Girt's, barely covering my ears and the nape of my neck. I knew it to be dark. Not black, nothing so dramatic as a raven's wing. But brown. And plain. I brought my fingers up to touch it and found it thick, with the promise of heaviness when allowed to grow, when there would be braids and pins and all those things of which I had no expertise.

"All is well?" Luther inquired, shouting above the din of village life.

"All is well," I said, just loud enough for my voice to carry. Then I stepped back and closed the curtain.

In the meantime, Girt had divested herself of all clothing, save for the new linen chemise provided by Frau Dunkel.

"It's the softest thing," she said, hugging her own body. "Quick, get changed."

Suddenly my habit felt unbearably heavy, and I took off every piece, folding the panel so that the stitched cross appeared smooth on top and making a neat pile on the bench at the foot of the bed.

"Everything," Girt said. "Don't worry. I'll turn around."

And so my undergarments followed, leaving me, for the first time in any memory, completely naked. True to Marina's word, there hung a small looking glass above the nightstand, affording me a view of my bare shoulders and the hollows that made somewhat of a moat around my narrow neck. I dared not look down, never having seen the evidence of flesh that might prove to be the ruinous temptation of a man. So, like a blind woman, arms outstretched, I found the new chemise and dropped it over my head. It settled like a breeze, cool against my skin, stopping just short of my knees. I peeked at my feet and wiggled my toes, amazed that such distant things could be a part of me.

The bed responded with the groan of ropes when Girt lay upon it, and again when I joined her. It was a tight fit for two, but I took instant comfort in the softness of her body beside me.

"We did it," she whispered.

"We did," I whispered back.

"And I hope Marina chooses the most beautiful gown of all for me."

I gave her a gentle nudge with my elbow. "You never struck me as one for vanity."

"Oh, it's not for vanity's sake. It will be my wedding dress. Hans and I are getting married."

The admission came as no surprise, but the word that followed took my breath.

"Tomorrow."

We lay flat on our backs, staring up at the beamed ceiling, hands close enough to clasp, but separate.

"Tomorrow?"

I felt her nod. "It's all arranged. Luther will

perform the ceremony. And there will be a grand reception here, at the inn. Hans's family arranged that, as I don't have any of my own to host. Oh, Kat!" She took in a deep breath, then expelled it as a yawn, triggering my own.

"And you'll stand up with me, won't you?" she asked, once she'd recovered the power of speech.

"Of course I will." I'd seen plenty of weddings before, in our small chapel at Marienthrone. We sisters were kept to the back rows, as if our solemn faces and hidden figures might sour the joy of the nuptials. "But Luther is an excommunicate. Will your marriage be lawful? Not in the Church, I know, but in God's eyes?"

Girt raised herself up on one elbow to look at me. "Yes. See how everything's changed? If we don't need a priest to confess our sins, why would we need one to profess our love?"

"So you love him, then? That much?"

"With all my heart." She collapsed back onto the mattress, causing it to groan anew.

"But that isn't why you chose to leave, is it? Just to marry Hans?"

"I don't know. Everything happened together, so I get it all mixed up. Nothing seemed truly clear until this morning. When I knew it was real. That it could happen. And I have you to thank for it, Kat."

"Me? If I recall, *you* were the one ferrying in all those messages."

“But I brought them to you because I knew you would know what to do. And see? How you’ve led us all. And all of us will be able to find our own happiness, just like Hans and me.”

“Not all of us have husbands waiting beyond the curtain.” I put the thought of Luther away the moment I said it.

“Some have family.” Her voice grew weaker with sleepiness, the words seeping out of the corner of lips that barely moved. “Parents, brothers. They’re here, or coming here. Waiting.”

“And some have nothing.”

Girt did not respond, as her breath was already even and deep, the mouselike whistling snore that had been my lullaby for the last twenty years. Tomorrow night, she would be in a very different bed—one neither of us could begin to fathom. With a man, a husband.

And I would be utterly alone.

Chapter 15

Nothing would identify the place where Girt and Hans married as anything more than an empty cottage. There were no images of Christ himself, only a swag of velvet with a plain-stitched cross draped across the rough-hewn table functioning as an altar at the front of the room. No place to kneel, the benches little more than split timber, the beveled glass in the windows creating its own prismatic, stainless color.

Luther, dressed in the same clothing he wore the day before, presided over the ceremony. No elaborate robe or sash, his dark coat shabbier after one more day's wear.

I, on the other hand, standing little more than an arm's length away, looked like quite the fine lady. Unused to the clothing of the world outside the cloister, I—along with all of my emancipated sisters—had required extensive help from the Dunkel girls. They'd run from room to room, affixing corsets and lacing laces and attaching petticoats. As a result, I stood tall and confined, acutely aware of every inch of my body, unable to stop my hands from running themselves across the textured fabric of my gown, the tiny ridges formed by the stripes. Best of all, having been rescued from its final hiding place, my mother's locket hung around my neck, suspended by a thin ribbon of black silk. The metal was, at first, cold against my skin, but had now grown warm. I'd taken my own vow to never again conceal it.

If I had any doubt that I gave a pleasing appearance, the look on Luther's face when I first walked into this simple chapel dispelled it. It was the first I'd known of a man's appreciation. Nothing lustful, more of what a man might look like having invented some great thing or completed a master work of art. His eyes never left me from the moment I crossed the threshold until the moment he was forced to turn his attention to the bride and groom waiting for his ministerial courtesy.

After, with Girt and Hans irrevocably united, the wedding party and invited guests moved back to the Brummbär Inn, where Frau Dunkel had laid a feast of roasted pork and vegetables, platters of pastries, and beer that seemed to flow endlessly throughout the day. Unused to such excess, I found my place against the wall, close to the stairs so I could make a quick escape once the celebration ran its course. But it seemed unwilling to end. When one pig's carcass was picked clean, a table-length platter of sausage came to take its place. Loaves of bread appeared at the miraculous rate of those that fed the gathered crowds in the Gospels. Each cake was declared sweeter than the one before.

Girt and Hans rarely left their place of honor, sitting at a table on a raised platform along the longest wall. By afternoon, Girt's cheeks were flushed red from so much laughter. Hans proved to be an attentive groom, keeping her hand in his, kissing her fingers in a way that made me glad for the shadows to hide my own blush. Clearly, she presented just as succulent a feast as anything passed on the platters.

And Luther was everywhere. Not once allowing himself to settle at any table, he wandered the place with a shank of meat and a mug of beer, stopping the moment anyone tugged on his sleeve. There were few children in attendance, but those present clearly loved him. They clung to his leg and snuck coppers from his pockets. He indulged them, briefly, but moved on, and in watching him I detected a purposeful pattern. He would engage in conversation with a particular gentleman, leave him laughing, and immediately make his way to speak with one of my Marienthrone sisters. Soon after, a path was created, bringing the sister to the gentleman, after which Luther backed away, appearing discreet to anybody not watching as closely as I.

Apparently, however, I was not alone in my observation. Frau Dunkel sidled up to me, carrying five roasted pigeons on a spit.

"What he's doing there," she said with an unconcealed sneer. "As if we don't have enough women to marry off. Me and my Bart with four big girls of our own, plus the littlest, and scarcely a man worth the price of a wedding breakfast, let alone a feast like this one. Cleared out the rest of the donations, this did."

Before I could ask her to clarify, a burst of cheers rang out from the crowd as an assembly of musicians arrived. Four hearty men worked to move the bride and groom's table to the floor, giving that space to the band. With renewed purpose, Luther himself joined the group, speaking closely with the young man bearing the lute. Whatever his message, it was passed from the lutist to the two players of pipes, the mouth harpist, and finally, the boy with the drum strapped round his neck.

"*Pfui*," Frau Dunkel said, achieving a new level of disgust. "He means to sing." She moved the spear of pigeon aside to cross herself. "He means to make his mark in the hymnal, too. Might want to refill that to make it come across a little easier."

She indicated my mug of beer, still nearly as full as it had been when it was first thrust upon me to be raised in a toast to the health of the bride and groom. My lips had recoiled at the taste, and no further sips had been successful. Still, I raised it in salute to her retreating back, as she'd been summoned to deliver the birds to a ravenous family of farmers.

I watched, fascinated, as the musicians assembled themselves around Luther, keeping their eyes trained on him as beer sloshed over the lip of the mug in his outstretched hand.

"What a joy it is," he said, speaking above the crowd until they eventually hushed themselves, "to see these two committed to the intentions God held at creation. That man and woman would join in marriage, build a home, and create children."

There was a robust cheer at this last statement, which Luther acknowledged with another hoist of his drink. Hans drew Girt close to his side, and her smile peeped from underneath the hands she'd brought up to cover her face.

"Sister Girt," Luther continued, "now *Frau* Bendel. A good woman now avowed to make Hans a better man. I would ask that you—and all of those here to celebrate you—would indulge me in rendering a bit of God's Holy Word as a prologue to your life of worship together."

A smattering of good-natured groans erupted, but Luther ignored them, taking a long draught of his drink before setting it on the closest table and giving the musicians the signal to begin playing.

The tune was solemn, familiar, and by the third note, the crowd settled to match its quality. After a measure, Luther took a deep breath and sang:

That man a godly life might live,
God did these Ten Commandments give
By his true servant Moses, high
Upon the Mount Sinai.
Have mercy, Lord!

We all echoed, *Have mercy, Lord,* and by the end of the second stanza, recognized the choral nature of the line. He went on to sing of each commandment, each meant to target the newly married couple, though he occasionally scanned the room to remind us that none were exempt.

Be faithful to thy marriage vows,
Thy heart give only to thy spouse;
Thy life keep pure, and lest thou sin,
Use temperance and discipline.
Have mercy, Lord!

His voice could best be described as not unpleasant, but Luther sang each line as if he himself had crafted the words—not just the lyrics, but the essence of the commands. I knew the story: Moses ascended the mountain, returning with the Law meant to govern the children of Israel. I knew, too, that Christ had come to offer grace to anyone who lived outside that Law. And now Luther sang with hooded eyes and half a smile, reminding us all of things that should have been long ingrained, the embodiment of the ease of obedience.

> Help us, Lord Jesus Christ, for we
> A mediator have in thee.
> Our works cannot salvation gain;
> They merit but endless pain.
> Have mercy, Lord!

There was a moment of silence during which no one spoke, no one moved. Even the musicians kept their instruments in frozen animation—lips pursed over the pipes, hand suspended above the strings. A silent *amen.* Then, a few in the crowd made the sign of the cross, and Luther stepped down from the stage. He lifted his drink high, saying, *"Let thy fountain be blessed: and rejoice with the wife of thy youth."* A cheer greater than any yet emitted rang out. The band launched into a lively tune, drawing Hans and Girt out from behind the table scraps of their feast. Hans lifted her high, spun her round, and dropped her midstep into the dance.

Where Girt learned to dance, I have no idea. Perhaps as part of creation, God designed our feet to respond to music. As a spider knows instinctively how to weave a web, so did Girt weave herself through the assembled dancers who joined them on the cleared floor. My own toes tapped beneath my skirt, and I studied, imagining a ribbon pulled through one pass to another, hoping to create a pattern of the steps I could follow later, should someone ask me.

So caught up was I in my mental exercise, I failed to see Luther winding his way toward me, and not until he sat on the steps beside me did I notice his arrival.

"It is no accident that Jesus chose to perform his first miracle at a wedding." He spoke as if we had been engaged in a conversation all this time, and I played along, turning in my seat. He touched his cup to mine and took a long drink. "It is a day marked with hope. A time to reflect on the providence that brought the two lovers together and a foretaste of life's joys to come."

"Are all marriages so consumed with joy?" I, too, took a sip, trying not to cringe at the bitterness.

"Sadly, no. But hope never considers the evidence. It is infectious, bringing everyone to mind of embarking on such a journey. Do you see?" He directed my gaze to Sister Margitta. Her head, swathed in a scarf the color of wine, was bent to give ear to a stout, florid-cheeked gentleman. As I watched, she brought her hand up to capture a giggle, making the last decade of her years fall away.

"What are you implying?" I asked, though a stirring deep within me knew.

"Not all marriages are the beginning of a new

family, but one is never too old to begin a new life. He is a gentleman, wife long dead and children grown, in need of a companion. She is . . . Well, you know quite well what she is."

"And you think he will make her an offer of marriage?" The thought of Sister Margitta, who had known nothing but life in a convent for the better part of half a century, suddenly taking on the role of a new bride might have conjured something akin to revulsion, had the gentleman not at that moment taken her hand to lead her in a dance.

"He will make such an offer," Luther said. "He already has, in an agreement given to me. There are several here with husbands waiting, if they will have each other."

"Husbands for all?" I scanned the room, wondering which homespun farmer might be marked for me.

"Not all. Some are returning to their families. I've received correspondence and have arranged transport. Will I be hearing anything from your father soon?"

I set my drink on the table nearby and studied my folded hands. "No, I think not."

"Ah. Have you gotten word, then? Will you be returning home?"

I gave my response in a simple syllable, "No," and would have been content to close the subject with such, but Luther pressed on.

"*No,* you haven't received word? Or, *no,* you won't be returning home?"

"This day is to inspire hope, and I cannot possibly envision any hope for a future there."

"Not even to tend to him in his doting age?"

"He has a wife to tend to him in his doting age. And his sons, too. My brothers, who I'm sure have not given me more than a thought since I left. Our fortune is small enough to split among the three of them. They would hardly welcome a fourth party."

"But surely, in your hometown, you would be more likely to find a suitable match. He could arrange one for you."

I twisted my body to face him more directly. "You must remember, I am from a noble family plagued with poverty. Whatever dowry my father could have afforded would have been laughable to any 'suitable match.' So he gave it—and me—to the church. There's nothing left, nothing in the family coffers for me. I have only my fading youth and questionable beauty to offer."

I cringed at my unintentional rhyme and waited with unbidden eagerness for him to contradict the status of my beauty. He did not.

"Clearly you've an intellect that will make it a challenging task as well. Few men are likely to be eager to share their lives with a woman who will bring both age and wisdom down the aisle."

I drew back, the better to assess if I should feel

insulted or flattered. His face held too maddening a neutrality to know for sure, so I responded in the same vein.

"Perhaps, like you, *Herr* Luther, I can continue my studies. Become an infamous female theologian and hire myself out as an occasional minstrel. My intellect might not reach the depth of yours, but I'd wager our vocal ability is equally matched."

He laughed, drained his cup, and summoned Marina to bring him another.

"And sharp-tongued, too?" He wiped his mouth with his frayed sleeve. "Why, you are a treasure."

"You seem steeped in bachelorhood yourself, I notice. See, there we are equally matched as well."

"I've far less to offer a woman than you to offer a man. Nothing but a small, moldy room. Full of books and paper and ink. And this?" He bent his arm to show me an ill-patched hole in the elbow of his coat. "This is the best of my clothing."

"And those two?" I pointed to Hans and Girt—she sitting on his lap, his head dangerously close to being nestled in her ample bosom. "Do they have much more than that?"

"He has a cottage. And a proper job, plus a bit of land. They'll have chickens and youth and health. What more could they need?"

"She is older than I. Three years, at least."

He had the decency not to appear shocked at

the news. "Perhaps, but she has more of a girlish spirit than I expect you ever had."

Marina arrived with a freshly filled mug for him, and he slipped her a coin for the favor. I was thankful for the distraction from the thread of our discourse. It seemed a perfect opportunity for me to excuse myself. I stood, ran my palms along my skirt to both smooth the fabric and dry the nervous sweat that had accumulated. Because he sat on the stairs, there was nothing to do but to ask him to let me pass.

"I'm still quite exhausted from our journey. I hope you'll excuse me."

"Come now, Sister. You couldn't possibly sleep with this racket going on. Might as well stay and enjoy. If it is my company that tires you, I shall gladly find an audience elsewhere." He stood up and stepped down, bringing our heights equal to each other.

"It is not, I assure you." I put a hand to my temple just in time for a real pain to emerge. "And I shall quite enjoy closing my eyes and listening to the music, carrying the vision of the dancers to my dreams."

Luther stepped back, holding my gaze, and as he did so, all the noise around me muffled, as if I'd wrapped a wimple of wool five layers thick around my head. Some realization slowly dawned upon him, for a smile unfolded, traveling from the center of his lips to the depths of his eyes.

"Rest up," he said, conscripting my idea as his own. "I'm taking you with me tomorrow to Wittenberg."

"Hasn't that always been the plan? To take us to Wittenberg?"

"Yes, but I plan to escort you personally."

"Where? Why?"

"That, we shall see together, Sister—wait. I don't suppose I should call you *Sister* anymore, should I?"

"I suppose not, though I would still like to be counted as your sister in Christ."

"And I, your brother."

He reached for my hand, and I gave it to him, unprepared for what it would feel like to have his thumb brush across the back of my knuckles. Moreover, to have it brought to his lips, to have the back of it kissed once, and then again, as if sealing the first.

"Until we meet again, my Kate."

Chapter 16

I promised Girt I would write. Immediately upon arrival, and then monthly, if possible, thereafter.

"What am I going to do with a letter without you to read it to me?" It was the afternoon after her wedding, and she was giggly. Flushed and distracted.

"It will be an incentive for you to learn. So we can spare Hans the embarrassment of reading all of our salacious details."

"As if I would," she said once her rosy face was permitted to leave the sleeves in which it was buried. "And just what exploits do you have planned in the great town of Wittenberg?"

"Nothing compared to yours, I'm sure. But—" and here I became solemn—"I have prayerful hope that God will provide such happiness for me as he has for you."

"Oh, Kat!" Unable to contain her joy, she reached across the table and clasped my hands. Were we not under the curious gaze of Frau Dunkel, who wielded a broom with ferocious intent, Girt might have leapt across the table. "I could never have imagined such happiness could have been possible. If you'd told me years ago, when we were girls, that someday I would feel this . . . *full.* Like I'm about to burst."

Frau Dunkel clucked her tongue, but I sensed amusement behind her show of disapproval.

"Sweet, sweet Sister," I said, squeezing her fingers, "your happiness brings me the same. I wish Therese—"

"She's found her own peace."

We embraced, each of us shedding hot tears onto the other's shoulder. Then laughing at the ridiculous display. Then crying again. More.

"Silly," Girt said, wiping her nose with the back of her hand. "You'd think we've never said good-bye to anyone before."

I kissed her cheek, promising to keep her in my prayers, and as I did, spied Hans waiting shyly in the doorway.

"Your husband's here," I said, gently turning her toward the door. In that instant, I was forgotten. Her tears dried; her steps quickened away from me. The last I saw of my dear friend Girt, she was hand in hand with the handsome Hans, bathed in the fullest light of day. When he led her out that door, he awakened a fear greater than any I'd experienced in my captivity or escape.

In all my longing for freedom, for choice, I'd shielded myself from the truth that neither would be afforded to a woman alone. How could I be free while dependent on strangers? How could I choose to be a married woman unless someone asked me to be such? All very well for a man like Luther to decide not to marry. As a woman, I'd have that decision made for me, and I had so little to sway attention to my favor.

At the age of twenty-four, I was neither young nor old. While my particular mix of features kept me from claiming true beauty, I could not accept the idea that I was homely enough to inspire pity. Not until I ventured beyond the convent walls did I realize the extent of my opinionative nature, my tendency to verbosity, the quickness of my wit—all of which no doubt made me a less-attractive prospect as a submissive wife. And judging by just the past moment, when Hans stood in the doorway, summoning Girt with little more than a clearing of his throat, I knew men wanted a woman prone to be sweet-natured and compliant.

Little had I known that I was neither.

The next morning, early enough to be closer to night, with a sack full of sausage and biscuits courtesy of Frau Dunkel, I stepped out of the Brummbär Inn and found myself, for the second time in only a week, being hoisted up into a farm cart. This time, however, I was given a seat on a plank affixed across the wagon bed, and instead of the affable Hans, the driver was a soured old man with the hallmark of being a silent traveling companion.

“I’m sorry there wasn’t any money for a proper carriage,” Luther said. He’d been waiting for me in the candlelight when I descended from my room an hour before. Now he remained on the ground, looking up at me—eerily reminiscent of the first time I saw him. “Do you have your things?”

I held up the canvas bag. “I have dinner and the clothes on my back.”

“And this.” He handed me a small purse. I could count the few coins within it through the silk. “More importantly, this.” A single folded sheet of paper, wax sealed. “A letter of introduction, bearing my testimony that you are a fine, upstanding Christian woman, worthy of the noble hospitality.”

A sobering truth dawned. “Are you not coming with me? You said you would escort me personally.”

A guarded look shadowed his face. “I’m afraid I cannot. My life, I’m sorry to say, is not entirely my own. At times it is best that I not be on the open roads.”

I dared not question further, not about his peril. I had enough of my own. “Are they expecting . . . Do they know me?”

“They are a family who gave generously when I asked for funds to bring you and the other women out of Marienthrone. One family of many, and I asked if some would be willing to open their home for a time, for those who would need a place to live."

"And they said yes?"

"Why else would I be packing you away, having only recently become acquainted with your entertaining company?"

I was not sure whether or not to find irony in his words, but I did detect that he had not answered my question, so I posed it again.

"They did not refuse," he said with assurance.

"So what am I to say when my carriage arrives at their door? Should we maybe toss in a couple of pigs? Or some bags of grain so they'll think I'm just part of a delivery?"

"Nonsense," Luther said, refusing to acknowledge my sarcasm. "Then old Hovart here would have to take you round to the back, and you'd get your shoes all muddy walking up to the house. No, better to arrive a perfectly respectable passenger, sent with a perfectly respectable introduction and reference of character. Oh, and one more thing."

He stepped aside to reveal young Marina Dunkel, dressed in the cleanest dress I'd yet seen. Her hair was fashioned in two braids wrapped around her head, soon hidden by the hood of the cloak tied around her shoulders.

"A respectable lady travels with a companion," Luther said. "After such a long time of sorority, I thought you might enjoy a bit of companionship."

My heart swelled with gratitude. I myself hadn't even realized the precipice of loneliness on which I teetered.

Marina offered a curtsy. "Will you have me, miss? I know I've been nothing but a hard worker all my life, but I've seen all sorts of society coming through the inn. I've served their food and changed their beds, sort of disappearing in the shadows, so I know a lot more than I should."

"Of course I'll have you!" To prove my enthusiasm, I stood and moved to the spot directly behind the driver, making a place for her on the board. I offered a quick prayer of contrition for envying the small bag she tossed into the bed, and Luther gave his hand in helping her over the wheel.

"I'll visit you shortly, God willing. When I know it's safe to do so."

I clasped Marina's hand and bowed my head as he prayed for our safe journey, then accepted his blessings. With a halfhearted slap of the reins, Hovart urged the team of workhorses into motion, and Marina and I lurched into each other.

"I'm sorry, miss," she said, straightening herself, then bracing her arms on the plank to prevent another such collision.

"Do not apologize," I said, giving eye to the pinkest of dawn peeking over the treetops. "I have a feeling this is the smoothest road we'll experience all day."

• • •

As it happened, I did not have a full day's journey to endure. At midmorning, we stopped to refresh the horses, allowing them to graze in an open meadow and drink from one of the streams that fed into the Elbe River. Marina and I took advantage of the stop to get down from the wagon and walk a little, though not so far as to ever be out of Hovart's sight. For Marina, I knew, this was no extraordinary activity. But for me, to be thus surrounded by God's creation, I had to stop frequently to close my eyes and allow my ears to take an equal share of the awesome burden. This was a divine silence—no silence at all, really. Leaves that rustled in the breeze. Birdsong. My steps bending the grass.

We traveled one more hour before stopping to share the dinner sent by Frau Dunkel. Added to my simple meal of biscuits and sausage, Marina had cheese and fruit, with a jar of milk to share around, and sweet herbs to chew after. The horses rested here, too, as did Hovart, recovering from his disappointment that we had no beer.

Then it was just a little over an hour before the road took a turn, and the outline of a country estate rose up from the horizon.

"That cannot be," I said, standing in my seat to get a better view. "Turn around; go back. This must be a mistake."

The house was larger than either of the convents

I'd called home. Windows stretched three stories high, and I counted twelve spanning from end to end. Two turrets rose above the slanted roof, with six chimneys interspersed between them.

"Perhaps there's a cottage?" I mused aloud. "And we're to be given shelter there?"

"Just what's Mr. Luther directed," Hovart said, unimpressed. "Taking you right up to the front door."

Marina looked terrified, and I knew I would have to assume some role of protectiveness. I wondered what could possibly be written in the letter of introduction that would make such a family take me in. Still, I resolved in that moment to be worthy of whatever Luther knew of my breeding and character. I sat up straighter in my borrowed clothes, tucked away any wayward strands of hair, and touched the locket nestled at my throat. We were once such a family, living in such a house, generations before my birth. My blood was every bit as noble as that which coursed through the residents of this estate. More than that, Jesus Christ was the great equalizer of all us sinners.

"When we arrive," I said to Marina, already affecting an authoritative lilt to my voice, "I am going to ask that you and I share a room. At the very least one with an antechamber, so that we will not be separated. I'll explain that I depend on you to see to my needs."

"*Ja, Fräulein.*"

And bless her for not asking what those needs might be, as I myself didn't know. Nothing beyond the need of a companion, someone to speak out to in the night. She, however, sat straighter in her seat, her confidence promising an aptitude for fulfilling her duty. The moment our wagon crossed into the drive, a small gathering came out of the front door, presumably ready to greet us.

"That is Herr Philipp Reichenbach and his wife beside him, Elsa. Those wearing the red with the gold brocade."

If she had not identified them by name, I could still have surmised the owners of the estate. Even from this distance, I recognized the fine quality of their clothing and the puffed-up stance that seemed to come with wealth.

"Our hosts."

"The very same. I know for a fact that they are great friends of Herr Luther. They've come into the inn and had supper with him."

"So they are kind."

"They are generous," Marina said, not confirming my assumption.

Before I could ask what she knew about the dozen or so people gathered around them—some most likely servants, but others dressed respectably—a man stepped into the midst. Even if he didn't stand a good head taller than the others, he could not have escaped my attention. Each turn of the wheels—and there were so few left—brought him into sharper focus. Piercing eyes, a strong jaw, well-trimmed beard. All identifiable features, but they came together to introduce an exciting revelation.

Handsome.

Every assembled person, including my generous hosts, disappeared like ripples in a pond. I wanted to ask Marina, *Who is he? Did he ever come to dine with Luther in Torgau?* But by then we were close enough that he might have overheard my question. I allowed myself ten more clomps of the horses' hooves to take in the breadth of his shoulders, the narrowness of his waist, and all the other attributes of a man's figure that I had never before had occasion to consider because I'd never seen one dressed in a fashion so tailored to reveal it.

The wagon came to a stop, and I felt every eye upon me. His, as much as any other. A boy brought a set of rolling steps to the wagon, sparing me the indignity of climbing over its edge, and Herr Reichenbach himself lifted his hand to escort me to the ground.

"Katharina von Bora," he said in a way that blended introduction and announcement. "Welcome to our home, to stay as our guest for as long as you like." He kissed my hand and offered me over to his wife, a woman with a tall frame and sturdy figure. She kissed both of my cheeks and repeated her husband's offer of hospitality.

Thus followed a round of names: Baron and Baroness Achter; Herr Stadtmueller and his wife, Marie; Lucas and Barbara Cranach . . . a host of others. My confusion must have been evident on my face, for at one point Reichenbach laughed and assured me that by the time our visit was over, I would be conversing with all of them as if we had been friends since the time of creation.

"And this," he said with a point of finality, "is our neighbor Jerome Baumgartner, lately of Nuremberg."

I waited, caught in that pause between the introduction of a man and his spouse. Were there any women left whose names I had not heard? Any who were not wearing a white servant's cap and collar?

As if sensing my question, Jerome took my hand, bowed low over it, then looked up, our gazes meeting for the first time in such proximity.

"I am in awe of your sacrifice and courage." His voice had a singular quality, almost like a whisper, but one that echoes from a dark corner. And his words—this compliment—rendered me an empty shell.

"Surely I've done nothing to deserve such regard."

"Not to hear Luther tell it!" This from Reichenbach, with an accompanying clap of his hands, emitting a sound sharp enough to bring Jerome to stand upright. He'd meant it to be some kind of joke, or at least a humorous observation, and his friends rewarded him with a smattering of laughter.

"And this," I said, finally able to perform some act of civility, "is Marina Dunkel. Some of you know her from the Brummbär Inn in Torgau. I hope it was not too presumptuous to ask her to accompany me."

"Of course not," Frau Reichenbach said. "You should have such a young lady to tend to you. Gretl—" she summoned one of the younger servants who had made her way toward the back of the crowd—"show Fräulein von Bora to her room. And the young Marina, too." Then, back to me, "I'll send a boy up with your bags."

I smoothed my travel-worn, borrowed dress, glad to see Jerome now engaged in conversation with the baron. "I'm afraid I don't have any bags. Only this."

She took the letter of introduction but made no move to open it. "Go up with Gretl all the same, and have a lie-down. We've hours left until supper, and by then I shall have found you something suitable."

Suitable.

There'd be no way to enter the house without walking past Jerome, and in the course of those few steps, I couldn't decide if I desired him to look at me or remain focused on his conversation. I kept my attention on Gretl's cap and was almost through the door when that voice summoned me.

"*Fräulein*?"

I stopped. Turned. "Yes?"

"I believe you are quite well suited to our company already."

Chapter 17

One thought prevailed during my stay with the Reichenbachs. One selfish, sinful thought that brought me to confession with my Savior every night in prayer, and it was this: how envious would my stepmother, Retta, be if she could see me here? The attentions of my hosts extended far beyond any reasonable expectation. Yes, I had food—more sumptuous than my imagination could ever have prepared. Every meal ended with platters of uneaten bread and meat and cheese. Even the water was flavored with fruit. And I had a bed and a roof, both beautiful in their function. The mattress was soft, covered in silk, and wide enough to share with four sisters, had it been wedged into my cell at Marienthrone. The ceiling, like the walls, painted with a pastoral scene, so that every morning I awoke to a view of tranquility matched to that of the gardens outside my window.

So, in the sense of food and a roof, yes—I had everything one could expect when given shelter. Even Abbess Margarete, should some traveler have the unfortunate chance to take shelter in her home, would provide as much.

My days began and ended with the modicum of hospitality, but the hours that stretched between bloated my pride. I spent entire afternoons in the garden, sitting in the shade of one tree or another, wandering the stone paths, peering close at the buds that would someday bathe the grounds in color. How sweet it was to offer up my prayers surrounded by God's manicured creation.

I was given all manner of fabric and thread, encouraged to stitch whatever my fancy. In the evenings, musicians played softly in the corner of the dining room, and whether we had four guests or a dozen, the hours after supper were spent dancing. I had my pick of partners—even the married men—each eager to teach me the steps to some of the newest dances coming from Italy. I went to bed every night, my stomach full of food, my lungs depleted from exercise and laughter.

The small, sinful, prideful part of my spirit claimed that this was the life I'd been meant to have. One of comfortable excess. Had my father's family been better stewards of their land and assets, I might have grown up with memories such as these. Of sitting at my father's feet, the way the youngest Reichenbach daughter did, with my eyes closed in sweet sleep. Already in my short stay I'd heard more laughter than in the rest of my twenty-four years combined. More music, too. More sun, more moonlight. More scent.

In my prayers, I remained faithful to praise God for his providence and to thank him for delivering me to such abundance. In my heart, and voiced into the darkness when I knelt at my bedside each night, I gave thanks for Luther—his obedience to God and his orchestration of my escape. I couldn't imagine what art of persuasion he had used to secure me a place in a home as fine as this, for surely I'd done nothing to deserve such favor. Hour by hour I availed myself of creature comforts he would be denied. Any hope I had of sacrificial piety had disappeared the moment one of the household servants knocked on my door with hot, herb-scented towels with which to wash the road dust from my face and hands.

Somehow, though, I knew Luther would be pleased with my pleasure. The way he had entreated me to dance, to drink my beer, to enjoy all the festivities of the wedding party at Brummbär Inn. In just such a way, I knew that part of his plan included my introduction to Jerome Baumgartner.

Both of these men held precedence in my daily, nightly, sometimes *hourly* conversations with God Almighty. Luther, as I have said, enfolded in my gratitude. Jerome brought forth from the shadows in my confession.

I had been a guest of the Reichenbachs for nearly two weeks when it was decided that my portrait should be painted. I say *it was decided* because, left to my own devices, no such idea would ever have been given life. In my mind, portraits were painted of royalty, saints, and great beauties, none of which applied to me. It happened, though, that my host family had extended an invitation to a budding portraitist recently dismissed from the tutelage of the great Albrecht Dürer. Christoph, who also happened to be a cousin to Elsa Reichenbach, was younger than I, a fact made clear by the way his enthusiasm obscured his lack of talent.

"The most important thing," he said as I sat patiently on the stool provided, "is that the canvas be stretched just right across the frame. And treated so that it neither shrinks nor stretches beneath the paint."

"That is the most important thing?" I asked, watching him *tap,* frown, and *tap* along the edges with a tiny hammer. I'd had occasion to see some of his work hanging in the halls of the servants' quarters and doubted his efforts would survive past the damp of winter. "Can I go, then? And leave you to this most important task? I promise to return the moment I'm needed."

He gave a final *tap* and looked up in triumph. "No. Sit, straight up there. Tilt your head a bit . . . a bit less. Bring your arm up, now down. Just so."

After countless of these minute posing manipulations, I was declared "perfect," and Christoph disappeared behind the canvas. He intermittently muttered and hummed to himself while he sketched with charcoal, and I took care to remain perfectly still.

It was morning, not much past the ninth hour, and Christoph had commandeered the breakfast room for his studio, due to its expanse of windows with an eastern exposure. From the corner of my eye I could see the servants still engaged in clearing the dishes and Marina watching from her spot against the wall, making me feel all the more self-conscious of the artist's attention.

"Tilt your chin," Christoph directed. "And look toward the window; bring the light to your face."

I obeyed, and was rewarded with the sight of a man, tall in the saddle of a glorious black horse. Jerome, bringing the beast to a stop in the yard, dismounting almost before the animal had all four hooves on the ground. He gave the reins to the boy who'd run out to greet him, handing over his leather gloves and hat as well. Aside from the afternoon of my arrival, I'd only had occasion to see him within the confines of the house—in the great dining hall, in the dining room, the front hall when it was cleared for dancing. Now, the breeze caught his hair and lifted it, and I realized it was much the same length as mine. For the portrait, Christoph had wanted me to don my discarded veil, but I refused. We had instead agreed on a length of gold silk, now fashioned in a ridiculous turban. I had been denied the opportunity to see myself in a looking glass before the sitting, but I knew the fashion was out of character, a fact confirmed by Jerome's amused reaction when he spied me through the window.

"Don't move!" Christoph scolded. "How else am I going to master the technique of dimension and shadow?" But too late.

"Perhaps in another sitting," I said, distracted as I wrapped the scarf smooth over my head and twisted the length of it to fall over one shoulder.

It was vain, I suppose, to assume Jerome would have an opinion one way or another about the style of the scarf on my head, but Christoph seemed pleased enough with the result and resumed his sketching.

"Yes, yes. Quite becoming. Simplicity suits you."

"It is my accustomed fashion," I said, and Marina stifled a giggle behind her hand.

Though I sat in obedient stillness, bits of me raced within. My heart, for one, pounding so that I worried its palpitations could be seen in the expanse of skin revealed by the cut of my bodice. And my leg, trembling beneath the fabric of my gown. And my thoughts, calculating the distance between the place where Jerome paused in the window and the front door. Would he knock and wait for a servant to greet and grant him entrance?

Or was he familiar enough with the patrons of the estate to make himself welcome? Two minutes had passed, maybe three. Surely he'd had enough time to engage in a polite exchange with Herr Reichenbach about the weather, his horse, some neighborhood gossip. Or pressing business. Such absurdity to think he'd come here to visit me, simply because we'd sat across from each other at five dinners, beside each other at two, danced no fewer than nine times, and walked the perimeters of the grand hall engaged in conversation about . . . Well, I couldn't recall the topic. But I know I must have been witty, because I made him laugh three times.

"Turn a bit, to the left," Christoph instructed, making me realize I had been staring intently at the door.

It might have been the better part of an hour, or perhaps a time more accurately measured in minutes, before I heard him. First, his steps, unhurried and measured. Then a cautionary clearing of his throat, and I knew he'd entered the room.

"Might I interrupt?" He spoke to Christoph directly, as I had not yet turned my head to allow him into my line of sight.

"Of course you may, sir." Christoph's reply carried his deference to both Jerome's age and social standing, though he kept his artistic irritation barely concealed.

"I was hoping to entice Miss Katharina to join me on a walk in the garden today, if you can spare her."

"Well, I've only just started. . . ."

Jerome walked around to where he was looking over Christoph's shoulder and studied the sketch.

"You have a strong start there," he said. "And it must help having so lovely a subject to capture."

"Indeed," Christoph said, though I doubted he shared the opinion of my beauty. It was something one said in a manner of polite flattery, nothing more, and I chose not to acknowledge the compliment.

I stood, a welcome relief to my cramped muscles, and offered a nod in greeting. "What brings you here to visit so early, Herr Baumgartner? Or has time passed so quickly it is nearly time for supper?" The other night Herr Reichenbach had made a quip about Jerome's frequent presence at the table, and I assumed the warmth of the humor held true.

A chuckle rumbled from the depth of Jerome's broad chest, and Christoph returned his stick of charcoal to the tray in defeat.

"Actually," Jerome said, "I had some business to discuss with Philipp and, with it complete, hoped you could accompany me on a stroll through the garden."

"Oh." It was the first time he'd sought my company in particular—the first time for any man to do so—and I found myself flummoxed for an answer. Did I need to ask permission of my host? Could I trust my own counsel?

Unbeknownst to Jerome, Christoph twisted his spotted face into a knowing smirk, and I felt color rise not only to my cheeks, but also to every bit of my exposed skin. A soft clearing of a throat behind me, and I glanced back to Marina. Here, I was glad to have had a lifetime of silent communication with women, because a single glance from her—quick, hooded, away, and back—and I knew what to say. When I again looked at Jerome, he clearly had seen and understood every unspoken word.

"Of course the young Marina will accompany us, as is proper. I would not want any undue speculation about your character."

I fingered the scarf wrapped so artlessly. "I'm afraid I'm not quite—"

Jerome bowed, dismissing my feeble protest. "I'll wait for you. Rather, I'll wait, for a while. I've no pressing errands this morning."

A turn on his heel, and he left.

Christoph slammed down the lid of the flat wooden box that held his paints and brushes, saying, "Might as well go. Looks like clouds are moving in anyway. Losing the light."

I looked to Marina, silently pleading. *Should I go?*

"Come, miss," she said, approaching and

touching the hem of my sleeve. "Let's go up and I'll dress your hair."

Although Marina and I lived under the appearance that she was an attendant of sorts to me, in truth I relied on her for nearly every social move I made. Though she had never lived in a home as fine as the Reichenbachs', she was a quick study of the human spirit and had served people from all echelons at the inn. I trusted her judgment in all things, from what and how to eat the variety of foods presented in the grand dining hall to how to spark polite conversation with the stranger at my elbow.

Now, we walked quickly through the halls, she with a step light as air, and I with a step *above* it. Not until we reached my room—our room—did she face me full-on, her hands full of breathless giggles.

"Oh, miss! Isn't he the most handsome thing!"

"I don't . . . I don't know what to do." Oh, how I envied her youthful mirth. Even were I a decade younger, I don't know that I could ever have been comfortable with such blatant exuberance.

"What to do? Why, miss, what else can there be to do when a handsome man is waiting in the garden on a fine spring morning? Give me that."

Marina took the gold silk wrap from my head, and I could feel my hair lift and stand on end from the friction. After folding the silk and putting it away, she dipped her hands in the water in the basin and ran them through my hair—still shy of meeting my shoulders—smoothing the tresses until they glistened, then fastening them with a tie at the nape of my neck.

All this I watched through my looking glass, and when I asked, "Why would he want to walk with me?" I spoke as much to myself as to Marina. She, however, had an answer.

"You're a lovely woman. Fair of face, and smart to talk to. That would be enough, I imagine, to capture a man's fancy."

"You don't find it suspicious?"

"Suspicious?"

"Or at least odd?"

"He's a man. You're a woman. Everything is exactly as God intended, I think. Adam and Eve met up in a garden too. Now, I've got something special I fashioned just for you."

She left for a moment and came back carrying a cloth bundle, which she placed on the dressing table and unfolded.

"For your hair. To cover and yet not cover."

It was a broad band, made up of pearlescent beads strung together, wide enough to span from my hairline to the tip of my crown. The width tapered to a point just above my ears, and a bit of fine netting stretched from one tip to the other. This, she rolled up, capturing my sad bit of hair within, but a ginger touch to the back confirmed a false sense of volume.

"How very clever," I said. "Like a real woman."

"Now there, miss. You're as real a woman as ever was." She took the lid off a small pot, and I dipped my finger in, taking a bit of the creamy substance and rubbing it into my lips. "And I'll be right there with you. Behind you, so he'll remember you're a real lady, too."

"Stay close enough to listen. So you can tell me later what I said. Let me know if I'm nearly as foolish as I fear I'll be."

I don't know why I was surprised to find Jerome waiting for me in the garden, just as he said he'd be. I had no evidence that he was anything other than an honest, honorable man. I worried that perhaps we'd spent too long dressing my hair, and he'd grown impatient. Or maybe the idea of an hour in my company lost its appeal in the wake of my lackluster response to the invitation.

And yet, there he was, sitting on a stone bench right at the entrance to a path that wound through the manicured hedges of the Reichenbachs' estate. He stood as I arrived, doffed a plumed hat, and bowed, as if we hadn't seen each other not fifteen minutes before.

"I'm glad to see you didn't change your dress," he said after a suitable greeting. "It's quite becoming."

"Thank you." I smoothed the flat-fronted

bodice. It was the second dress with which I'd been gifted. This one, the color of poppies, embellished with black stitching, was given to me by a cousin of Elsa Reichenbach, sent with a message of her prayer that I would wear it in good health and prosperity.

We walked, our steps in sync on the fine-pebbled path. The slightest chill lingered in the air, with a promise of warmth behind it. The hedges grew waist-high, and were I walking alone, I would be skimming my hand along the top, the coarse green tickling my palm. We talked, too. Inconsequential conversation—inane observations about the weather. I would have shared the same sentences and phrases with a man twice his age, and half as handsome. I kept my wit tucked beneath my cap, having no occasion to employ it.

"Do you miss anything about the convent life?" he asked after a few steps of silence.

"What do you imagine I would miss?"

"I couldn't say, never having lived such a life."

"Then how could you benefit from my response?" I heard Marina make a sound, nothing of which Jerome would take account, as he had no experience with silence. I softened my tone. "I suppose, if anything, I miss not having the fear of making conversation with a gentleman."

He laughed. "Is it such a fearsome thing?"

"Not fearsome. Just . . . unfamiliar. I lived all

my life with so few surprises. Now, it seems every day I encounter something new."

"Well, I'm afraid I intend to continue that tradition today. Tonight, actually, as I will be a guest for supper."

"Your presence at the table is hardly surprising." Indeed, it had become something familiar, and I found myself missing him on the few evenings when he was absent.

"Yes, but this evening I have taken it upon myself to bring two other guests besides."

"Why do you feel the need to tell me this? I'm not the cook. Or will your guests call upon me to give up my share of the lamb?"

"I'm bringing my parents."

"Oh."

We'd come to the midpoint of the garden, a wide, circular space laid with smooth pink stone and a fountain at its center. He led me to a bench and, taking my hand, bade me sit with him.

"I'm bringing them specifically to meet you. They're rather curious."

"Are they?" I withdrew my hand. "I knew we'd be the objects of some speculation. The day we arrived, people stared as if they'd never seen a nun before. I expected such ignorant gawking from a certain class of people, but not from anyone I would presume to be as sophisticated—"

"They want to meet *you,* Katharina. The woman whose name has been on their son's tongue for these past weeks. The woman whose bewitching eyes have robbed them of his company at their own supper table."

I felt myself flush with each word, until there could be nothing to separate the hue of my dress from that of my skin. From the corner of my eye, I saw Marina take a discreet step back into hedges, and I felt no compulsion to summon her.

"You shouldn't speak such flattery," I said with what breath I could muster.

He glanced around and, seeming satisfied with our privacy, took my hand. "I assure you, Katharina. It is not flattery." I felt his breath against my knuckles. Then his lips. The kiss burned—a gathering heat, with nothing but the thin layer of my skin to separate his touch from my blood. Somewhere, from the depths of that same skin, came the memory of another burning, that delivered by the priest at the moment he sensed my disobedient spirit. Those bruises had disappeared within a matter of days, but with this—the first touch of a man intent on some declaration of romantic love—I fully expected to find myself forever marked when he at last lifted his head to look into my eyes once again.

"Herr Baumgartner—"

"Jerome." Breath wrapped itself around his name, and I was close enough to feel it.

"Jerome."

Beyond that, I found I had nothing to say.

Chapter 18

"Tell me again what he said."

Marina held the curling tong at a careful distance from my face and looked approvingly as the hair was released.

"He said—" and here she adopted a near perfect imitation of the deep hollow of Jerome's voice—"*They want to meet* you, *Katharina. The woman whose name has been on their son's tongue for these past weeks. The woman whose bewitching eyes have robbed them of his company at their own supper table.*"

I didn't need to hear it again; I'd repeated the phrases to myself in an endless chorus since the minute after he first uttered them.

"Do I really have *bewitching* eyes?"

Marina lifted another section of hair and wrapped it around the tongs. "All that matters is *he* thinks you do. You've bewitched him well enough."

"That doesn't sound like a very Christian thing to do, though, does it?"

"There's nothing more Christian than falling in love, miss." She said it with the deep sigh of youth.

"Do you think it's possible, then? That he loves me?" The only people I'd ever known to be in love were Girt and Hans, and that seemed more of a gradual dawning. Strengthened and deepened after years of stolen glances and secret exchanges, as if wrung through cheesecloth. Jerome and I, on the other hand, had known each other for only a matter of weeks. Mere hours spent in each other's company, and here I'd been caught in this deluge of professed affection.

"I don't know a lot about the ways of men," Marina said, studying the newest curl, "but I've seen the way he regards you. Like something he's never seen before."

"A curiosity?"

"More like a treasure."

She ran her fingers through the new-formed curls, separating them to frame my face. The rest was tucked and pinned at the back of my head, and a soft, rounded headdress adorned the top.

"Speaking of which," she said, stepping back with a critical eye, "I wish you had a bit of jewelry to wear tonight. Something to show you as a woman of quality. Breeding."

I touched my locket. "This is all I need to prove that. I know who I am, Marina. And *what* I am is penniless. Borrowed robes, an indefinite guest. No bauble is going to change any of that. If anything, it will further disguise the truth. If I were to present myself to Jerome's parents in all honesty, it would be in rags."

"Shall we do that then, miss?" As before, she offered me the small pot of color for my lips. "Or we could do something along the lines of Bathsheba—set you a tub of washing water out in the courtyard and time it to Herr Baumgartner's arrival. Make a nice, honest impression on his parents, wouldn't that?"

"Marina!" But I laughed, both at my exaggerated humility and her ostentatious suggestion.

I touched the color to my lips, a bit more than I had earlier in the afternoon, but refused to allow Marina to dust my face with even a trace of powder. If anything, I envied her robust complexion—the healthy, almost golden glow of her skin, the perpetual pinkness of her cheeks. I knew myself to be sallow, unfashionably pale, and every moment spent with my own reflection brought further questions as to what would catch the interest of a man such as Jerome Baumgartner.

Marina walked with me through the corridor and as far as the main hall, where we parted company for the duration of the evening. I remained outside, smoothing my skirt, fingering my curls, shifting from one foot to the other, all in a nerve-driven attempt to stall my entrance.

Just walk in, I told myself. Like any other evening. By now I was more a resident than a guest, my presence no more noteworthy than if I'd been born to the house. But Jerome's words both bundled and exposed me. Nobody had ever spoken such love to me before, making me a different woman than I'd been the last time I strode in to join the family for supper. I had a new standard to live up to, beyond simply appearing as one accustomed to society.

Then I heard Herr Reichenbach's laugh, rich and deep. Welcoming. It meant somebody was in the middle of an amusing tale, and whoever stood gathered around the great stone fireplace would be engaged, distracted from my entrance. I might be in there for a minute or more before my host would say, *Why, Katharina. There you are.*

Another burst of laughter, more mirth to serve as camouflage. Men and women, so Elsa must be in attendance too, as well as Jerome's mother. I expected to see them, glasses of wine in hand, raised in cheer. I did not, however, expect to see Luther. And yet, in the midst of them, the apparent teller of the tale, there he was.

It had been so long since I'd felt the comfort of reunion, if indeed I ever had. For a moment, all others disappeared as Luther stood, pewter mug in hand, and broke free from his central place of unofficial court by the fire to approach me, his arms open and ready to embrace.

"Elsa told me you had blossomed into a woman of noble beauty, but I had a hard time believing you could surpass the comeliness I first beheld at Easter. And yet, here you are, my Kate."

By the time he finished speaking, he stood right before me, his empty hand gripping my sleeve, and—before I could escape or protest—his kiss on my right cheek.

"It is a welcome surprise to see you." I suppose I should have spoken some protest at his compliment, but something very primal within me enjoyed such attention from two different men in the span of an afternoon.

The first, Jerome, had also broken away from the group gathered at the fire, and as I stepped back from Luther's embrace, I stepped into his—far more chaste, merely a touch of his hand to my elbow.

"Fräulein von Bora, allow me to introduce you to my parents."

He turned me, as if recapturing my attention, and I found myself facing a middle-aged couple who displayed none of their son's good looks or charm. His mother, a small, chinless woman, had stuffed her fingers into so many rings, a metallic *click* accompanied her every gesture. And while his father's lack of interest was at first off-putting, I learned over the course of the evening that he maintained such a countenance whether the conversation centered on politics, fashion, or sheep.

Christoph completed our dining party that

evening, sitting to my right as Luther sat to my left, with Jerome between his parents directly across from us. The Reichenbachs, of course, held their places at the head and foot of their table, and compared to other meals taken here, the number seemed almost intimate.

Luther said a lengthy blessing, thanking God for his safe passage and for the opportunity to break bread with those who were like-minded in worship. At this, I was sure I heard a disapproving *sniff* come from the bumpy nose of Frau Baumgartner, but dared not open my eyes to verify. He ended the prayer in the name of Jesus Christ, our Lord and Savior, in whom alone we should place our faith. When I opened my eyes after making the sign of the cross, her dour expression removed any doubt of the earlier sniff.

"And so, you had no troubles on your journey, Luther?" Reichenbach spoke as if picking up the thread of an earlier conversation.

"None that I'm aware. Perhaps I myself have exaggerated my infamy."

All seated at the table chuckled—Jerome's parents out of politeness—as a servant went round filling our wineglasses. By now it was known that I did not indulge, and I was given water instead, a detail that would not escape Luther's notice.

"Not even to celebrate my arrival? How you wound me."

"My father always said that wine transforms to tears, and to drink too much is to shed too many. If I weep at the conclusion of your visit, certainly you would want me to do so from genuine sorrow, would you not?"

Luther glanced to Jerome, then to me. "I have little reason to hope that you will notice my absence any more than you will appreciate my presence."

I, too, looked at Jerome, pleased to find his eyes resting on me. Any clever reply I might have mustered clogged in my throat, and no taste of water could dislodge it.

Frau Baumgartner also slid her eyes between the two of us, finding the path distasteful, if her expression was any clue. When our soup cups were all set before us, she picked hers up and looked at me across its surface. "Tell me, Fräulein, when will you be returning to your own family?"

She pursed her thin lips and blew a cooling stream of air onto her soup, as if my answer to her question mattered nothing at all. It was enough to establish that I didn't belong here.

I touched my fingers to my own cup, but did not trust myself to lift it. Nor did I dare raise my eyes from the murkiness within. My cheeks burned as hot as the surface of the crockery, fueled by the shame of both my poverty and my abandonment.

"The region, I fear, is far too volatile for her

return." This from Luther, once again at my rescue. "Better she should stay here, wrapped in the protective cloak of hospitality, rather than risk bodily harm at the hordes of murderous peasants."

"Why, Luther," said Frau Baumgartner with a baiting insidiousness, "I would think you of all people would support those who are fighting against injustice. Why, isn't that the mind-set that landed our little Katharina bird here among . . . *us?*"

Luther clucked his tongue, and as he did so, I sensed the long history of friendship with the family across the table. Ostensibly, a friendship of geography and convenience, and not necessarily a meeting of the minds. Though Luther sat beside me, I knew I was an object lobbed between them, carrying with me a set of ideals long debated.

"The gospel of Jesus Christ is not a means for social or political gain," Luther said, his words light with confidence. "The peasants are cloaking themselves in the gospel and committing heinous acts in the name of Christ. Jesus himself instructed the Jews to obey the laws of Caesar."

"Just so," conceded Frau Baumgartner, and I exhaled, hoping in vain for a change of subject. "Then, might I ask, Fräulein: Your family—do they fall on the side of the peasants? Or the princes?"

"Mother." Jerome laid his hand on her sleeve.

"Katharina has been separated from her family for many years. Since she was a young girl. This is, perhaps, a painful topic of conversation for her."

"It isn't painful," I said, finding my voice at last. "I'm afraid it simply isn't interesting. I am a guest in this home; thus I hold a high responsibility not to be a dullard at the table. As I have nothing truly entertaining to offer in way of conversation, I think we should allow Luther to entertain us with his wit. And perhaps, after, with a song."

"Cheers to that!" Reichenbach raised his glass.

Frau Baumgartner glared into her cup, and her husband studied the greenery on the table, as if none of the conversation even happened. Between them, Jerome looked at me with an expression I can only classify as approving, and I knew I had said the right thing, and passed my first test. He lifted his soup in lieu of his wine, and I did the same. We sipped, and it occurred to me that he and I were tasting the same flavor, a pleasant, warm broth.

Beside me, Luther leaned close and whispered, "Good girl," which I hope went unheard in the volume of Reichenbach's cheer.

On my other side, Christoph broke his petulant silence, declaring he, too, had interesting stories to tell, and indeed we sat in rapt attention as he spoke of the great ruins of Rome he'd had occasion to visit. Even Herr Baumgartner seemed engaged, and as we were served all manner of sliced cold meats and plates of boiled vegetables, conversation flowed easily between the men. Spates of laughter, moments of fierce argument and advocacy. Luther quoted Scripture, Christoph cited art, Baumgartner asked for clarification, and Reichenbach demanded the wine replenished. Jerome served as complement to all, maintaining an even temper and good humor throughout, his voice a rumbling undercurrent, thrilling me with its depth.

Dictated by our sex and status, Frau Baumgartner and I remained silent, except at times when we were specifically called upon to make a clarification or take a side. At those times, I refused, saying I desired to neither alienate my host nor offend his guest.

Jerome's mother said, simply, nothing.

On more than one occasion, as I turned my head to appreciate a raucous tale boomed from the head of the table, I felt her eyes upon me, thinking me unaware of her study. And while this was unnerving, I dared not catch her in the act, lest the rest of the diners be called into our quarrel. To avoid her glance, however, meant to deny a chance to spy Jerome, who at one point was telling a story of a youthful indiscretion—something about a boy from his schooling days and a prank pulled on a particularly unassuming priest. Luther, more than any of us, had encouraged the tale, and while I allowed my gaze to feast on the storyteller, I could not ignore the intensity of that directed at me. This, then, another battle, but when I shifted my eyes, the shock was more unsettling than I could have imagined. Frau Baumgartner was not looking at me. She was looking at Luther, and she was looking at him with hate.

There was music after supper, but none of our party felt inclined to dance. Christoph elected to sing a mournful ballad, displaying a talent as questionable as his artistic skill, after which Reichenbach gave a coin to each musician and invited them to take their supper in the kitchen before departing.

"I suppose we must be off as well," Herr Baumgartner said, following a massive yawn. "The hour grows late and will only grow later."

"All the more reason to stay." Reichenbach replenished his glass of port. "Dark is dark. It won't be any lighter for the drive home. And we've plenty of room, if two of our bachelors here won't mind sharing."

"I've no objection to staying with the famous Luther," Jerome said.

"And I believe it's best we go home," his mother said, but one look at her husband, now dozing with his head flung back in his chair, indicated that she stood to lose the argument.

Elsa Reichenbach clapped her hands. "Very good! The beds are made up, and I'll let the kitchen know we'll have three more for breakfast."

With the promise of company in the morning, the evening appeared to be at an end. Christoph excused himself first, after wresting from me a promise to follow shortly so to be well rested for my portrait sitting. Luther followed, joking that his old man's bones would be far gone to sleep before Jerome would put the night behind him.

"Watch who you're calling an old man," Elsa said, jabbing him. "If memory serves, you're a year younger than I."

"I speak by comparison only," Luther said. "You, my dear, have remained ageless for as long as I've known you."

"And I say it's a good thing you were a man of the monastery at the time." Reichenbach pulled his wife into his lap and nuzzled her against her laughing protest. "Otherwise she might have fancied you instead of me, and I'd have been doomed to spend *my* life alone."

We all laughed at the saucy display, but I sensed a wistfulness behind Luther's smile. Not for Elsa herself, or any love lost there, but for the fact that his own status had changed so little, despite his breaking free from the monastic life. In this, we held a common plight. Though at least a decade younger, my prospects for marriage were no less unlikely. Or so I'd thought until this day. Hope sparked within me, as tiny as the flecks of fire dispelled upon the hearth. Once Luther took himself away, there were six of us—three men, two wives, and me.

"Come then," Reichenbach said, rolling Elsa from his lap, "let us show you your room, Baumgartner." He repeated the name again, jolting Herr Baumgartner to complete wakefulness. "Let the young ones enjoy the fire."

Jerome's mother drew up, fortifying herself with indignation. "I don't know if that's the best idea."

Jerome made no move to stand. "We are grown adults, Mother."

"My point exactly." She raised her thread-thin eyebrows, giving me a glimpse of how he might have been chastened as a boy.

"Well, *I* don't know that I appreciate the disparaging implications of the behavior of my houseguests." Reichenbach's tone remained jovial, but I sensed the argument coming to an end in his favor. "Besides which, once we're tucked in, there won't be an empty bed in the house. Can I trust you, lad, with this woman's honor? Think of her as a daughter under my roof, the roof of a man likely to crush your throat if I took such a mind."

"Now, *you*." Elsa jabbed him again. Then, to

us, “See to it the fire burns out. And help yourself to what you will. Come on, then.”

The four left, taking two of the remaining tapers with them, plunging the great hall into something little more than darkness. Half of Jerome turned to shadow, firelight displaying his features in intervals. We sat far apart from each other; had we both stretched out our arms there’d remain a dog’s length between our touch. But for a while, the only sound was the crackling of the flames and the subtle movement as servants cleared the last of the supper dishes.

After a time, Jerome picked up the iron poker and nudged the log, splitting it to bring new life.

“Allow me to apologize for my mother’s unforgivable rudeness,” he said. “She’s not entirely in agreement with Luther’s reformation.”

“And she sees me as a product of his work?” Strange how the idea brought such comfort when held up against the idea that she merely disapproved of me as a mate for her son.

Jerome joined me in the delusion. “Yes. And I’ve never known her to bypass an opportunity to speak her full mind.”

“In that I can admire her, having lived so long without the opportunity to do the same.”

“I can’t imagine anything other than kindness coming from your mouth.”

I laughed. “All the more evidence that I’m not yet accustomed to speaking my mind.”

He, deadly serious: “You’re nothing like what I expected you to be.”

Two questions sprang to life. What had he been led to expect? And why had he been led to expect anything? I indulged the first.

“When Luther came to us—all of us, his friends—needing support for the sisters from the convent, all I could picture were the nuns I saw in church. Just this—” he brought his hands to his face, framing it as if wearing a wimple—“so I suppose I never thought of them as *women.*”

“I think that’s the point.”

“And when he told me about you—”

“About *me?*”

“—and that you’d be a guest here. Staying in this home, our neighbors’ home. And that he hoped I’d meet you. And find you . . . pleasing.”

“He spoke of me?”

“Not spoke. A letter. Dashed off quickly, it seemed. Sent by messenger the day before you arrived. Until then he communicated only with my parents. I have no finances of my own, you see.” At this, a shadow not borne of firelight crossed his face. “So, other than my prayer and occasional standing up in a tavern brawl, I’ve had nothing to offer.”

I ran my finger through the grooves of the intricately carved arm of my chair. “And what do you have to offer him now?”

“Him? Nothing. Nothing directly. But you?”

I stared at the scrolling, madly thinking of the artist who had used such patience and control in its creating.

"Fräulein von Bora?"

Varnished to silk. Brought to shine in the firelight.

"Katharina?"

And then, he was in my line of vision, his face looking up into mine. From here, despite the darkness of the room, I could see the individual whiskers at the edge of his beard. I maintained my grip on the chair's arm, but my other hand, listless in my lap, refused to obey. To my horror I saw my fingers, acting in utter rebellion to any other part of me, lift themselves to stroke the soft expanse. Never in my life had I encountered such a texture, and I could make no determination as to whether it was pleasant or painful. What I do know is that Jerome closed his eyes, and I saw the fringe of dark lashes against his cheek, and I wished desperately for the world to end in this moment. Then he captured my hand beneath his and turned his face to kiss the center of my palm, and I thanked God for granting me those few more seconds, not being so foolish as to listen to my previous desire.

He lowered my hand to my lap, never separating it from his own, and opened his eyes.

"We have not known each other long enough to enter into any kind of agreement. But I want you to know of my sincere affection to this point. I have enjoyed our moments together, and look forward to many more."

I sat in a seat wide enough for two, and he took full advantage, rising and sitting beside me, his arm draped across the back. Not touching, but near. I knew I should move away, but the beautiful feat of carpentry offered no escape. He touched a finger to my chin and tipped my face to meet his.

"I've never thought myself a man to be entrusted with so much."

His mouth brushed against mine. Returned to capture my lower lip, and might have come back again had the fire not suddenly become the object of my utter fascination.

"Surely Luther did not intend such a display when he wrote to you."

"Maybe not," he said, "but I hardly think he would object."

"Then I pray he'll not have the opportunity to do so." I stood, amazed at my ability to balance despite the whirlwind within me. "I'll leave you now to tend to the fire."

He stood too. "Leave the servants to the fire. I'll escort you to your room."

"No." I moved away before he could touch me. "This is my home, temporary as it may be. I'll find my way. Good night."

With every step through the empty halls, I

thought of my wooden shoes at Brehna. How they heralded our presence and kept us from any secret missions. I wished for such shoes now, in lieu of the silk slippers that whispered against the stones. I wanted to announce to the house that I was returning to my room, alone. Free from the scandal of the moment. To wake them all to the temptation I'd denied myself. Most of all, to bring weight to my steps, to keep me from flying back to the fire.

Chapter 19

Something's changed," Christoph said, head cocked, giving me a quizzical look. He emerged from behind the canvas and came to stand an arm's length away. Using his finger like a compass point touched to my chin, he walked a semicircle around me, studying my face from all angles.

"It's the hour," I said. "So much earlier than our sitting yesterday morning."

"No, no . . ." He tapped a fingertip to his lips, thinking. "Take the headdress off. It doesn't suit you this morning."

Thankful, I obeyed, and Marina came to my side to help. She took the length of gold silk and draped it across my shoulders. My hair was loose beneath it, and she ran her fingers through, shaping what she could of last night's curls.

"Yes," Christoph said, pleased. "Much better. A juxtaposition of regal bearing and youth. Well, not *youth,* obviously. But a certain level of abandon. And there's color to your cheeks."

"She was out in the sun for a bit yesterday," Marina volunteered.

"I didn't notice it at supper last night. It helps. Gives life to your complexion."

"Thank you," I said. "That sounds almost like a compliment."

He returned to his work, and I to mine, grateful my current responsibility called for nothing more than to stare out the window of the great hall. To think, I was sitting in the same chair I'd occupied the night before, only now I leaned across the expanse of it, my arms folded in false repose.

I'd come downstairs at the earliest civilized hour past dawn, only to find the table littered with abandoned breakfast dishes and the server's announcement that three of our houseguests had already taken their leave. Not a word to me. Not a note, nor any token of what had transpired between us the night before. And so, when Christoph arrived just minutes after, I dispatched Marina to fetch down the gold silk and sent him back to get his paints. Because the morning light is fleeting.

I told Marina nothing of the moments spent with Jerome by the fire, though she was well awake when I fell through the door. As she helped me with my gown, I knew she took my silence for a way to tamp down something of pleasurable significance, but I shared only the cruel things Frau Baumgartner said, and we spent the night side by side, speaking witty retorts to the ceiling.

"Hold for a moment," Christoph said. "There's one thing missing. Something for your hands. To balance them. Right now they look ready to fly away."

"Your suggestion?" Marina asked, nibbling on a tart from the serving table.

"Do you have a ring? Any sort, not even precious."

"You're an artist," Marina insisted. "You can't just paint one on her hand?"

He uttered a condescending scoff. "How can I, not knowing exactly how her hand will look with a ring on its finger? Maybe even a simple strap of leather . . ."

"She has a ring."

I broke my pose completely to confirm the voice. Luther, looking as disheveled as I'd ever seen him, wearing the same road-worn clothing as the night before.

"Good morning, *Herr Doktor*," Marina said, offering a playful curtsey. He smiled at the deference and gave a soft kiss to her cheek.

"And, pray tell, what jewels am I not aware of?" I asked, though I had some idea of his meaning.

"I never said *jewels*. I said *ring*. And I'm certain you know of what I speak." He took a piece of fruit from the bowl at the center of the table, cut into it, and used the knife point to spear the bite into his mouth. All as if he weren't suggesting I take the ring I'd worn as a symbol of my commitment to Christ and wear it as some token accessory to appease an artist with minimal skill.

"I can't wear that again."

"Can't you?" He spoke as if we were debating something as meaningless as the ripeness of the fruit. "By whose authority?"

"By my own."

Ignoring me, he turned his attention to Marina. "Do you know where she keeps it?"

Marina looked to me. She knew—the little white pouch fashioned from my final, hidden pocket.

"Go." If nothing else, I wanted her to fetch it at my behest, not his. "And, Christoph, find Frau Reichenbach. Perhaps she has something more suitable to be immortalized."

"I should have thought of that first," he said, and left, newly inspired.

Luther, meanwhile, took to filling a plate with what he could find on the table. Buns, fruit, even a spoonful of porridge gone so cold it wobbled as an intact mass.

"It is a good thing for you the family leaves the breakfast out so late. Most laze-a-beds need wait for dinner."

"Is that what you think I've been?" He took a seat at the table and gestured that I might join him. I did, only so that we would not have to shout our conversation across the room.

"I suppose I'm just surprised you didn't rise with your bedmate."

"I was asleep before his arrival and rose before the cockcrow. Did he not wonder about my early absence?" Luther was teasing, something I'd grown used to over the course of our conversations. Trying, I knew, to elicit some news of what occurred last night. I confined myself to truth.

"I did not see any of the family this morning. They departed before I stepped a foot outside my door."

He sobered, then quickly feigned objectivity. "Did they? Why, it's not more than an hour's ride to their home. Must have been some pressing business."

"Indeed." I reached for a roll and pinched off a bit of crust. "Do you think it's possible that I might be part of that pressing business?"

"In what way?" That was the moment I knew he would never be able to hide any truth from me.

"What did you tell him, Luther? About me?"

"Only that I thought you suitable for introduction. Well matched in humor, intellect. Age."

"How well matched are we, exactly, in age?"

"A difference that could be measured in months."

"More than a dozen months?"

He squirmed. "Yes."

"In whose favor?"

"Are you forgetting my preface? That you were well matched in intellect? That—*that,* my dear—is a field in which you are favored."

"Because he is still a student?"

"Kate, Kate, Kate . . . aren't we all perpetual students in life?"

I'd picked my roll to pieces, wanting nothing more than to hurl the largest remnant into Luther's face. Sensing my frustration, he moved his food aside and stilled my hand under his.

"Listen, my girl. If you do not find him to your liking, you've no obligation to grant him favor. I thought only to facilitate an introduction."

I felt the stinging prick of tears and looked away. "It's just that . . . it was a shock. Meaning, I would hope his feelings—if there are, indeed, feelings—to be genuine." I withdrew my hand and pressed my fingertips to my forehead, a further attempt to keep my tears at bay.

"One man cannot dictate the heart of another. So tell me—" he hesitated, gathering his thoughts, seeming to weigh whether or not to continue his question—"to the extent that good taste permits: do you find yourselves to each other's liking?"

I bristled. When I thought of the hours, days, now weeks that I'd lived in freedom, I owed him all. And time stretching back, to the ideas he planted in the minds of those who secured my rescue, to the bold message he delivered so that I might be a woman secure in my salvation, a follower of Christ and not a prisoner of the Church. I owed him my life, my breath. But this question, this simple inquiry to my heart . . . I perceived no debt.

"I simply wish, sir, not to be made a fool. There are so many ways in which we are not well matched. And I do not have any worldly experience to measure my response to his advances."

Luther's brows rose at the word *advances,* but I plunged on.

"I haven't the youth or the position for indiscretion. I cannot make a mistake; do you understand? And if you are leading me into a path—not of wickedness, but folly—know this: I will hold you to account."

"Why are you so frightened?"

"Do you honestly believe, given any circumstances other than your direction, a man such as Jerome Baumgartner—" I stopped, not willing to give words to those moments that should stay tucked as dark memories of the heart.

"Is he so much?"

"He is young."

"As are you."

"And his family—"

"No greater claim to nobility than yours."

"And he is . . . handsome."

The pause that followed stretched, like the abandoned canvas across the frame, its expanse filled with my every flaw. My eyes, at once too narrow and closely set. My nose with its peculiar point. My hair, listless without Marina's intervention. All of me so very plain, even a witless artist knew I needed light and weight to capture an image worth painting. I expected Luther to reply with the Scripture meant to give comfort to all women who harbored my insecurity. *Favour is deceitful, and beauty is vain: but a woman that feareth the Lord, she shall be praised.* No woman who had felt the touch, the kiss, the warmth of a man like Jerome wished to capitalize on her fear of the Lord.

Still, he did not speak. Scripture, I'd learned, was always quick to leap to his tongue, so I knew he was searching for his own words. Comfort, encouragement. Condolence, perhaps.

When at last he spoke, he dropped his voice to little more than a whisper, though we still had the great hall to ourselves, and half of it between us and the door, lest anyone stood on the other side to listen.

"Were I to see you . . ." Something caught in his throat, and he began again. "Were I to see you in some marketplace, and be ignorant of your character and wit, I would say to myself, *What a charming girl.* Lovely in face, and enticing in figure."

My breath caught at the word *girl.*

"But," he continued, "I would make no move to speak. Because it stands to reason that, around some corner, in some other shop, there would be a young man better suited to your attentions."

"And then you would forget me?"

"Yes. As I must. As happens with every man and woman we encounter who isn't meant to occupy our days, or proves unworthy to do so. It may be, in time, that our young man is nothing more than one you pass in the marketplace."

"*Our* young man?"

"If the match proves itself out, I'll accept credit as God's instrument."

"And if it doesn't?"

Before he could answer, Marina arrived, carrying the familiar pouch, with Christoph fast on her heels.

"Frau Reichenbach would have you go to her room, if you like. Take your pick from what she has. And I'll gladly accompany you. Help you choose what would be best."

"No," I said, taking the pouch from Marina. "I'm wearing donated clothes, living under a borrowed roof. That must suffice."

I opened the pouch and dropped the ring into my palm. Simple, solid gold. Thin enough to be painted with a single horsehair strand.

"Let me have that," Luther said, and without question I gave it over to him. "Do you know why we wear such a ring, when it is meant to symbolize marriage, on our fourth finger? Because the ancient Greeks believed that, from that finger, an artery flowed directly to the heart. And so—" he turned my palm up and touched the base of my finger—"this point was the shortest distance to the seat of love."

Behind him, Marina sighed. "How romantic."

"So until such time, my Kate, as you find the man who would be worthy of placing such a ring on your finger, I suggest a new home for this one." He took my right hand, then, and slid the band over the knuckle of the first finger. "You are no less a daughter of our heavenly Father, and as a Christian, no less a bride of Christ. But this is a placement of singularity and value."

There, at the Reichenbachs' table, surrounded by the remains of the morning meal, I felt I'd been a participant in a ceremony unsurpassed by any I'd ever seen. Sealed to myself, exalted to my own esteem. Powerful in a way I could never put into words.

"It's just the thing," Christoph said with dramatic reverence. "Quick, the light is perfect."

Back I went to the seat, my body leaning across the expanse, only now instead of folding my arms in casual repose, I rested one arm across that of the chair and extended my right hand, first finger slightly aloft, toward the window.

"You're gazing . . . ," Christoph said as he worked. "You're watching. . . ."

Luther left the next day, determined to ride south, intending to riddle the route with sermons in an effort to restore peace. There was no conflict, he said, that could not be settled by the teachings of Christ and the Holy Word of God. He deemed his leaving to be an action to ensure the safety of the family, since his outspoken support of the aristocracy branded him as a target to those who fueled the uprising.

I teased him a little, as we gathered in the front courtyard to see him off. "Will you come back, then, and entertain us with songs of your exploits?"

"I hope to come back with reports of peace in our land," he said.

"I hope you come back with my horse," Herr Reichenbach said to our amusement. "It's the best I've got."

I worried less about Luther's safety when I realized he would be riding with a company of men, armed and disciplined, as adroit with Scripture as they were with various weaponry. The armor of God, it seemed, would be sufficient to protect their mission, but sword and crossbow might be needed to protect the man. Looking at him atop his horse, with his patched coat and dirty stockings, I didn't think I'd ever seen a man less likely to engage in physical battle. But the danger, I knew, was very real, a fact confirmed by Elsa's grim expression.

I could've admitted to feeling a spot of grimness in myself at Luther's departure and sought distraction where I could. As such, I didn't mind the time spent posing for Christoph's art, not caring a bit about the finished work. My face was not likely one to be known to posterity, and I had little hope of the painting's being displayed anywhere but the attic once Christoph found another master to take him under tutelage.

Such distraction was necessary for the first two days after Luther's departure, as I saw not a hair of and heard not a word from Jerome. I enticed Christoph to continue work on my portrait late into the afternoons just so I would have the chance to stare out the window, watchful of any sign of arrival. Hour after endless hour, my body posed in longing, my mind following suit, I relived the evening by the fire. Heard his words, felt his kiss. I studied my hand, now wearing its ring, and remembered the feel of his face upon it. I wrote an impossible script, giving myself bold and reckless dialogue. In some scenarios, demanding a promise of marriage before allowing any such embrace. In others, abandoning all inhibitions to declare my love.

For it was, indeed, love. I knew it that night, had wrestled with it even during my conversation with Luther, and carried the burden of it for those two days. On the third, with the sound of a rider on the drive, even before he came fully into view, my love burst from the pocket of fear in which I'd kept it contained. Bounding from my pose, ignoring Christoph's displeasure, I took myself through the front door, Marina on my heels. Jerome dismounted before the horse was at a full stop, ran to me—straight to me—and took my hands in his. Brought them to his lips. There I saw my newly donned ring, touched to the softest part of his cheek. His blue eyes, looking like the sky itself shone through them. Sunlight warm upon my face, more so when he smiled.

"I've been away too long."

"Have you?" All of my imaginary recklessness departed the minute he stood in reach of my words.

"I have, occupied by family matters that I won't bore you with."

In my heart, I knew he was protecting me. Without fear of pride, I knew I must have been a topic of some conversation in the Baumgartner home because I was the object of so much unspoken opinion during our evening together here. I'd not be so vain as to say a battle was waged, but his mother laid plain the fact that her view of me differed vastly from that of her son, and while she may have been able to whisk him away in the predawn light, he was here now, in bright midafternoon.

Behind me, Marina said, "Oh! Look who's come to greet you!" Her words carried enough warning for Jerome and me to step away from each other as Herr Reichenbach and Elsa emerged, their voices raised in welcome and greeting.

Reichenbach clapped Jerome on the back. "Will you be staying with us, my boy? Always a place at the table for you."

"For supper," Jerome said, "if you'll have me."

"And the night?" Elsa implored. "You know there's room."

"I think not." Here, he looked at me, and some instinct bade me drop my gaze.

"Very well." Herr Reichenbach took his wife's arm, and they went off in search of the cook, to inform him of the newest guest at table.

"Marina." I worked my voice into a tone of authority, something I rarely used. "Would you go inside, please, and tell Christoph that I won't be sitting anymore today? I'll be—" I looked up at Jerome—"in the garden? Would that be a pleasant place to spend the afternoon?"

Jerome took my arm with all the proprietary confidence Herr Reichenbach had shown taking Elsa's. "I can think of nothing more."

With Marina dispatched, we began a slow stroll around the side of the house, the gravel path crunching beneath our feet.

"What is so funny?" he asked, making me aware that I'd let a giggle escape.

I told him about my childhood days at Brehna and the wooden shoes. "Perhaps that's why the Reichenbachs have such a resounding surface on their garden path," I said, connecting my thoughts. "So that we can hardly wander off undetected. Sister Gerda could follow our steps." Then I had to tell him about Sister Gerda, too.

"Will you always be so concerned with the protection of your honor?" By now we'd turned a corner, and I knew we were out of view from any window in the house. So, too, were we safe from undetected discovery, as any would-be chaperone's steps would sound just as loud.

"Will you always make me feel it needs to be protected?"

His eyes teased, matching my levity. "I hope to."

Chapter 20

In an unlikely turn of events, I found myself playing the part of the muse to Christoph's continued efforts to perfect his skill. After completing my initial portrait, he declared a desire to paint a series of the wives of the patriarchs. For his first endeavor, I was to be Rebekah, and the fountain in the center of the garden would play the role of the well where she was discovered to be Isaac's bride. Wrapped in yards of a fine, gauzy cloth and given a vase to hold upon my shoulder, I spent untold hours staring into the face of the horse groomer chosen to play the part of the servant who held out a handful of jewels. From the story, I knew the prizes to be a bracelet and a gold ring for the young woman's nose.

Christoph instructed me to look the groomer straight in the eye, intended to demonstrate an acknowledgment and acceptance of my fate. I complied, imagining him to be Luther, fulfilling such a divine errand in introducing me to Jerome. He had claimed me just as if he'd put a ring through my nose, leaving me no choice but to see God's purpose. Posing for Christoph afforded me hours of contemplation. When my eyes lost their focus and my shoulder ached under its burden, my mind set loose, composing endless conversations I would never have.

I imagined seeing my father, telling him, with appropriate humility, that I was living just as he always said our family deserved. My temporary home, my peers, my daily life—all of it fitting our family's station. A life I might have enjoyed had I been born two generations earlier. I like to imagine he'd be pleased, selflessly thankful for God's provision for his daughter. And yet, my clearest memory of my father remained his pale, puffy face at the convent gate. And nothing but silence since. When I searched the darker recesses of my heart, I knew my true motivation was to gloat to my stepmother, to let her see how far I'd risen above her expectation and desire. When I caught myself in those thoughts, I closed my eyes for as long as Christoph would allow, praying for God to forgive my pride.

But then, even in the midst of repentance, I'd wonder—was it pride? Was it truly a sin to be happy, and grateful for that happiness? And yet, how could I ever reach back to people I'd left behind and share with them my happiness, when they had done everything in their power to deny me? When I gave my prayers of thanks, as I did to God every morning and every night on bended knees beside my bed, I thanked him for his provision. For this comfortable home, no matter how temporary, and the graciousness of my hosts, no matter how coerced, and all the small comforts I never imagined during my sparse existence at Marienthrone. I thanked him for granting me understanding of the gospel, and for Luther's work in securing that for all. Those and more, my pious thoughts in prayer.

Always, though, while draped in silks, playing the silent role of a woman on the brink of marriage, my mind wandered to Jerome. Not until I met him did I fully understand why the Church kept its consecrated brides of Christ locked behind convent walls. If one as homely as I could be brought to the precipice of sin, what chance would a beauty like Therese have of standing unscathed? Having just a taste of what it meant to be a woman in a man's embrace, to experience the nascent longing that leads to a fulfillment of purpose, I found myself restless and unsatisfied during any moment spent away from Jerome Baumgartner.

The joyous counter to that dilemma was the fact that I had very few moments spent away from him. He joined us nearly every evening for supper, along with a myriad of neighbors. On evenings when musicians entertained us in exchange for a meal, Jerome and I danced until we were breathless. Nights when we had no music, we walked the extent of the gardens in the moonlight. In either case, our bodies moved together in perfect concert. To be polite, of course, I danced with other guests, as did he, but our eyes found each other's between every turn, and when the music was lively enough for a volta, I declined any other partner. Jerome would grasp my waist, lift me up, spin me nearly all around, and those tiny wisps of time passed like moments of pure flight. Sometimes when we walked in the garden, he would hum a tune and do the same, only holding me aloft longer than any proper choreography would allow. From her place in the shadows, Marina would offer sweet applause, and we would separate and bow. In Marina's presence, he would kiss my hand. When I dismissed her to prepare our room, Jerome would pull me to the shadows, take me in his arms, and kiss me until my whole being felt like it was trapped in a volta spin.

Rather than live as the perpetual houseguest on the charity of the Reichenbachs, I was eventually installed as something of a tutor, giving daily instruction in Latin to the children for two hours each afternoon. This was yet another aspect of my life to be arranged by Luther, proposed to the delight of the parents and despair of the children. However, I proved myself a competent teacher and felt I more than earned my keep.

"Do you think the children would object if I were to sit in on their lessons?" Jerome asked one evening. It was the tail end of June, warm and near dark. Inside, a houseful of guests drank and danced, reveling in the summer solstice, mindless of the pagan roots of the celebration. The festivities allowed us to slip away unnoticed, and we'd walked clear to the back wall of the garden. "My Latin is deplorable. Always has been. Since I was a child."

"So long ago as that?"

"Then again, I don't think I would learn anything from you, either. I would be far too distracted."

I stood still, waiting for his kiss. He'd done so often enough in the weeks since the first that I anticipated the act. I marked the change in his voice, the trailing of the final syllable. There'd be a glint in his eye, an angling of his face. And always, a preceding touch. The tips of his fingers to my jaw, guiding my lips to his, as if they couldn't make their way if left to their own devices.

And yet, despite the routine, this kiss—like the first, like every one since—turned me into something like a molten taper, great globs of my resolve dripping away with each bit of his insistence. I sensed a wick, running down the length of me, fashioned from vows and prayer. It diminished with every minute spent in his embrace and now burned double-bright, threatening to drag me into darkness.

"Wait." I took a moment to catch my breath.

His face hovered inches above mine, far enough that I could see its handsome planes, chiseled sharper in the moonlight. Somewhere behind me, a torch glowed, the orange light dancing in his eyes. Every warning I'd ever heard about the evil of men's intent might have proved him to be the devil himself, if he hadn't smiled and doused the flame.

"There's no one here." He gathered me closer, as if those words and that gesture would serve to quell my fear.

I pressed my hands against his doublet and held him off. "No, Jerome."

Looking chagrined, he backed away. "Forgive me, Katharina. For my forward behavior. I didn't realize—"

"Don't apologize." I kept my hand pressed against his coat, aware of the pulse at my wrist, how it beat against his heart. "You've done nothing I haven't . . . permitted."

Relief washed across his face, and I saw for the first time what he might have looked like as a boy, newly released from guilt. I longed to comb the fallen black curls from his brow, but dared not bring any part of my flesh into contact with his, no matter how innocent the touch. I stepped away, allowing the darkness to cool my cheeks. Strains of music and revelry made their way even to this great distance. I forced my breath to match the rhythm and turned toward the laughter, wishing for a moment of lightness to descend between us.

"Shall I walk you back?" When I declined, he led me to sit on the stone bench with only a pinch to my sleeve. He sat at a distance so respectable, the holy book from which the priest read at mass would fit between us.

"Don't be angry with me, Katharina. I couldn't bear it."

"How could I be? Without turning against myself?" The need to soothe him took me by surprise, and I was glad of the expanse of stone, or I might have taken his petulant head to my lap. "It's only . . . I don't think this is what Luther intended when he arranged for us to meet."

"Really?" Jerome wagged his brows mischievously, becoming more and more of a boy. "Then you don't know him as well as I do. He's hardly the saint his followers would have you believe, and well aware of the workings—"

"Stop!" It was the second time this evening—the second time since our acquaintance—that I put my hand up against him, but this time it was a playful slap in attempt to stop his words, and my breath was short from laughter. "You really are such a child."

"Am I?" He grinned, but made it clear he expected an answer.

I sobered. Of course he was a man, every bit

and breath of him. But I couldn't say as much out loud. In that moment, the very word—*man*—carried a weight of sinful thought. I fought for clarity and composure.

"The Apostle Paul," I said, then repeated the name as Jerome appeared to protest, "says that there comes a time when we must put away childish things. And I fear that, these evenings, my actions with you . . . I have been childish."

"No." He leaned forward, but kept himself behind our agreed invisible barrier. "You are a woman."

"Acting like—"

"A woman."

He was close again, filling all the space between us, filling all my senses, and the only defense I had was my voice.

"I haven't been giving thought to the consequences of my actions. What you must think of me. What . . . my sisters. We risked everything, and here I fritter with this dalliance."

"Is that all I am to you, Katharina?"

I'd hurt him, or was close to it. His eyes never left mine, and his lips remained parted after saying my name.

"I don't know. I don't know what you are because I don't know . . . anything. I've never been a young girl, not in the way young girls are out in the world. I've never been silly."

"Do you feel you're being silly now?"

And there he voiced my greatest fear.

"I feel an obligation to Luther."

He broke our gaze, briefly. "As do I."

The summer night took on a chill, not from the perfumed air of the garden, but from my own lungs, filling with winter, forming a fragile, tight frost. "Is that, then, why you've been so liberal with your attentions?"

He laughed, and I felt a tiny crack of warmth. "If anything, it is my fear of him that has kept my *attentions* at bay. He told me he was bringing a young woman here. Someone close to my age, bright. And that he thought we might get on well enough with each other. And I thought it would be enjoyable to have someone new to talk to. To dance with. But then . . ."

Somehow, my hand was in his again, palm up, his thumb against my wrist. His lips against my pulse, and my heart a wild tumult within. The next I knew, he was on his knees, gazing up, and speaking.

"When I was a child, I spake as a child, I understood as a child, I thought as a child: but when I became a man, I put away childish things."

He bowed, touched his head to my knee, and when he looked up—this was new. This man, this touch, this look that turned his eyes to embers.

"Allow me, then, to put away my childish behavior and present myself to you as a man. A worthy man of God, who offers you his hand in marriage."

A new burst of music came from the house, reminding me that I should be feeling joy, yet I wished with all my heart we'd stayed for the dancing.

"You can't mean that, Jerome."

He looked shocked. Ready to protest. "It's what—"

"Luther wants?"

I'd touched a bit of truth, because he sank back, but then resurged. "It's what *I* want."

"Why?"

Back in the house, I knew couples were reeling, and I counted the measures waiting for his answer, wondering which he would choose. He wanted to marry me to be a part of Luther's grand liberation. He wanted to establish himself as a man, independent of his family. We'd been too familiar with each other, and I'd ignited some level of lust that begged for marriage to legitimize it.

"You're trembling, my darling. Why are you so afraid? I thought—I'd hoped—you'd be happy."

"You mean you've thought about it before this minute?"

"Truthfully? No. But now I can see nothing else."

I was melting again. Not with the flame of passion from moments before, but a gentle, loose puddling. What must it be like to come to such rash decisions? All my life, I'd lived without my own will, and the two commitments I'd made—to take the veil, and to leave it—came after months of agonizing thought. Here he could decide on a spur to propose marriage? As if I could respond in like time? My foot tapped to the music. Faster, even.

"Your parents would never approve."

"My parents have no say in whom I love."

Then the music stopped, and I feared his last words would be swept away with the final notes.

"Do you, Jerome?" Before meeting him, I'd never longed for a man to love me. So many mountains loomed ahead, an entire life for which I'd been ill prepared. How could I survive without such a promise?

He answered as I knew he would—as I hoped he would—with a kiss. One that brought him up from his knees to sit beside me, then brought me to my feet, full against him. He trailed the words down the heat of my throat, until no other possible truth remained.

"I love you, Katharina von Bora. I love you."

I said nothing because I could offer nothing but tears and disbelief until finally he pulled away, gripping my arms, holding me in a still, silent dance, and I confessed my own.

Chapter 21

It was my idea to keep our engagement a secret, at least until Luther returned and I could send word to my father.

"I suppose it would be more appropriate for me to ask him for your hand," Jerome said during one of our daily strolls in the garden.

"My father gave up his authority to grant any kind of blessing the day he left me at the gate of Brehna." I winced at the sound of my own bitterness. "Luther's blessing carries a much greater weight. I'll write to Father once that is secured."

Throughout the rest of the summer, the Reichenbachs included me in accepting all sorts of invitations to neighboring homes. During those times, Jerome and I sought to avoid suspicion and graciously conversed with the person seated near us at table. We danced with different partners, holding each other only with our eyes at the turns. Rumors, we knew, spun rampant around us, but we gave no outward cause for suspicion of either his intent or my character.

We kept our plans from his parents, too, more

at my insistence than his. Nothing seemed more fragile than this love, given only sporadic, stolen life. I likened it to a spider's web, the thinnest filament stringing our moments together. Here in the garden, there in the shadows. Dancing and summer suppers. His mother's great, bulging eyes tracked our every move, measuring the distance between us. She counted every word exchanged and visibly twitched at any inadvertent touch.

"Mother has to think that it is her idea." We were standing in the dining hall of his home, listening to poor verse being recited by a poorer poet. Jerome's whispers landed just behind my ear, and it took all my strength to stand upright. "Wait, and she'll see you often enough, in my company. In our home and in the homes of our friends. And she'll think—*well, what a lovely young lady for my Jerome.*"

I bit my lip not to laugh at the idea, and even that subtle of a response earned a withering glare. If anything, Frau Baumgartner was probably trying to decide just who had invited this *lovely young lady* into her home.

During the stretches of days when we did not see each other, Jerome wrote to me. Single pages, folded and set with his distinctive family seal. Elsa had made it clear that no messages were to be given over to anyone in the household without her knowledge, so she knew of the frequent deliveries. She did, however, allow my privacy in the business of opening and reading, which I conducted in the confines of my room.

> My darling Katharina . . .
> My cherished Katharina . . .
> My beloved K . . .

He wrote silly verses and intimate accounts of our time spent together. He posed questions for our next conversation and gave excuses for his prolonged absence, even though our days apart were never more than three in number.

> Family obligations will keep me from darkening your step this evening. . . .
>
> If I must blame a demon for keeping me abed, it is none other than the fourth glass of port our host forced upon me. . . .
>
> Mother is hosting a banquet in Father's honor, and has demanded my presence, along with an apparently select few from our social circle. . . .

This last one prompted the first chilly rift between my host family and me, as they, too, had been denied an invitation to the Baumgartners' dinner. Mid-August, nearing summer's end and Herr Baumgartner's birthday, it was apparently an annual event, much anticipated, and socially imperative. This year, the summer of their remarkable hospitality, was the first in which the Reichenbachs had not attended.

I learned this at dinner, the day I received Jerome's note, after conversationally inquiring what would prompt a banquet in Herr Baumgartner's honor, and why we would just be hearing about it now.

"We've known about it for months," Elsa said, her lips tight with civility. "Since before you arrived."

"Then of course you should go." I skimmed over Jerome's words. "He says, regretfully, that I have not been extended an invitation, but surely you—"

"We've not." Herr Reichenbach ripped the tiny leg from his quail and devoured it. He and Elsa exchanged a look, each warning the other, and then the meal resumed in silence.

After that, I specifically set about to break Elsa's rule about correspondence. Ignoring the ungraciousness of my actions, I instructed Marina to intercept any messenger before he met up with the mistress of the house and to bring directly any letters addressed to me. In turn, I gave all of my responses to her, to be secreted away by any of the household servants sent out on errand. I only hoped that Jerome was taking similar precautions to keep the extent of our communication hidden from his parents.

It occurred to me that I was in quite the same

situation as I'd been in Marienthrone, with whispers and messages and unspoken aspirations. Only Marina knew—with certainty—my love for Jerome and his for me. Others might have guessed and gossiped, but no one ever spoke of it aloud in my presence. In fact, a growing silence began to engulf me. Conversations halted when I entered a room. Evenings fell to long, quiet suppers where guests and travelers once crowded around the table.

Jerome's visits became matters of awkward, unannounced calling. His invitation to supper was no longer unspoken or expected, and when he joined us, the conversation never ascended beyond cordiality. Just so, my own place in the house suffered a similar diminution.

"I'm sure it's just the summer coming to an end," Marina assured me one evening. She was brushing my hair, now grown to rest comfortably on my shoulders, the stroke of the bristles creating a soothing effect. "People have harvests to oversee and houses to prepare for winter. Saw it all the time at the Brummbär. Nothing like the short days and cold nights to make a family want to stay closer to home."

"But that's just it." I failed to keep the petulance out of my reply. "I've been feeling—all this time—like I'm a part of the family. Maybe because I've never had family, but you have."

"Yes, I have." She set the brush down. "I've always felt that way here, too."

"So you've sensed a change?"

"I would hate to seem ungrateful, miss."

Despite the cautionary reply, her meaning was clear. "Do you think it's because they don't approve of my friendship with Herr Baumgartner?"

She was too late to stop the sassy smile at the word *friendship,* but I found myself smiling too, and the glass reflected a flush to my face.

"It's not my place to say anything on that subject." But she was hiding something, as obviously as if she held the unspoken words in her cheeks, which were now as pink as my own.

I twisted in my chair. "What is it, Marina?"

"Oh, miss. I'm not supposed to say anything yet."

"*Yet?* About what?"

The flesh of her bosom was now patchy with red, her face florid. "I don't know what it means, miss. And I've been arguing with myself all day, wondering where to find the greater sin."

"Marina!"

She disappeared into the shadows of the room, beyond the scope of the candlelight, and came back with a folded, sealed paper.

"This came for you today."

"From Jerome?" I snatched it from her hand. "Why are you just now giving it to me?"

"It was given right to my hand from his house's man. And I was told not to give it to you until past ten tonight."

My heart raced at the mixture of excitement and fear in her demeanor, making me all the more anxious to open the letter. Holding it close to the candle's flame, I noticed it lacked address and asked if she knew for sure it was intended for me. All of his other letters carried my name in a bold, clear script.

"It's what the man said. That I was to hold it until ten o'clock tonight, then give it straight to you."

I ran a blade beneath the seal and took comfort in the immediate recognition of his handwriting, though I had to bring my face closer to read the short message. Then, as if my racing pulse stole my power to comprehend, I read it again.

> Meet me tonight, at midnight.
> At the back wall of the garden.
> ~J

"What does it say?" Marina asked, as if she hadn't read every word over my shoulder. If he'd written in Latin, she would have understood just as well, having spent so many afternoons under my tutelage. I ignored the question.

"What time is it?"

"About half past nine, close as I can guess."

"Don't guess. Go, check the clock."

With unspoken enthusiasm and an obvious bounce to her step, she left the room, giving me a few minutes alone while she ran to the front hall and back.

I read the message three more times, holding it close enough to the candle to catch flame at its corner. I pinched it out with my fingers before the words themselves could be engulfed.

What could it mean? And why the extra pains of subterfuge in its delivery? I had more than a dozen missives, all wrapped together and tied with a scrap of ribbon. Why had he not crafted one of his eloquent pages, adding the invitation as a postscript? Surely he knew my privacy had not been violated, that his words always fell to my eyes alone.

These thoughts I pondered while keeping at bay the more obvious, and life-altering, question. Why was he summoning me at midnight? I dared not entertain the most thrilling of suppositions.

"Not quite ten." Marina was breathless upon return from running the length of the house. "I passed Herr Reichenbach in the hall, but he's already five cups in, so I'm sure the house will be abed by midnight."

"As I might be." I folded the letter and touched it again to the flame.

"Oh, now!" Marina snatched it from my hand,

dropped it to the floor, and stomped it to ashes. "Do you mean to say you won't meet him?" My look must have been withering, because she seemed to shrink a bit before my very eyes. "I'm sorry, but I couldn't help but see. Oh, Fräulein. Is it what I think it is?"

"And what do you think it is?"

"An elopement. It has to be."

"Why? Why must it be an elopement?" Although part of me surged with relief that I wasn't the only one to come up with such an interpretation.

"A secret meeting? Middle of the night? The two of you . . ."

"The two of us?"

"In love?"

I couldn't hold on to another shred of austerity. "He has said he wants to marry me."

"Of course he does! Why wouldn't he?"

"But we've never talked about anything like this. Shouldn't I have known? You can't summon a woman to a marriage with a dozen hastily written words."

"Well, maybe he's coming to talk about it tonight. To make the plans with you." Having settled herself on this truth, Marina giggled and bustled, lighting five more tapers to bring new light into the room. "Shall I pack your things?"

"No!" The thought of such a thing took on true

absurdity at the suggestion. "Why would you take such satisfaction in this event—if, indeed, this *is* the event?"

"You don't find it romantic, miss?"

"To a point, I suppose. But there's something lacking, too, isn't there?" I thought about Girt's celebration, the minstrels and the dancing. Even Luther's taking the stage to sing. I wanted such a party, all of my new friends gathered, wishing us well. I'd snuck off in the middle of the night once before, trembling with fear of discovery. Why should a marriage inspire such a secretive response?

"A handsome man, a lovely lady. What could be lacking?"

"God's blessing." I twisted the thin gold band on my finger. "And the presence of friends and family."

She winked. "I'll go with you if you like. Dance all the dances myself with whatever gentlemen are in attendance." To demonstrate, she twirled with my best gown held to her breast. "Oh, I remember well the couples coming into the inn those late nights, all flushed with love. Rustling up a wedding supper in the dead of night. Sometimes nothing more than bread and cheese, but they'd treat it like a feast."

"Still," I said, determined not to get caught up in her fantasy, "there's a mark of shame with the secrecy, isn't there?"

"There can't be any shame in loving someone, miss, so far as you've a right to."

And therein lay the question: did I have a right to love Jerome? Could the status of my name ever truly stand in for the lowliness of my estate?

"Well, I suppose I should stay dressed, at least."

"And take your cloak. What? It's chilly outside. And maybe take a few hours' rest. No worries that I won't wake you."

As if I could sleep, or even keep my eyes closed in prayer. A shaft of guilt shot through me, knowing this should have been my first response to the missive. Not a repeated study of the words, or a girlish conversation, or indulging in a volley of fantasy and doubt.

"Build us up a fire," I said. "A small one, as we'll keep the window open. Sit by it, and stay awake. I'll be at my bedside, in prayer. Please, pray with me?"

"Of course, miss." Already she'd set about to obey. "And to be clear, I'm to wake you? By, say, a quarter of the hour?"

I laughed. "What? You don't think I'll be able to stay awake during my own prayers?"

"Just in case, miss. I'll keep my ears open for the chimes."

I pulled the cushioned kneeling bench from beneath the bed and set myself upon it, my hands clasped before me on the quilted silk.

"Father in heaven, holy is your name," I began aloud, lapsing into silence when I sensed Marina settled into herself by the fire. *Your will, O Lord, is my desire. Above any other notion. If marriage is your will for me, I will gladly enter into it, and if you desire that I pledge my life to Jerome Baumgartner, I will do so happily. Not only in an act of obedience, as you well know, since my heart hides nothing from you.*

Even in prayer I smiled and turned my face so Marina could not see.

And if it is not . . . oh, Father, we've only a few hours—just a speck in your time eternal—for me to have an answer. A sign to know your will. Make it clear, Lord. Speak plain.

My head swam with all the Scripture I'd memorized, but nothing suited. Only the prayer from the gospel of Matthew, with the instructions, *After this manner, therefore, pray ye . . . ,* which I tailored to my need.

Thy will be done on earth, as it is in heaven.

Lead me not into temptation. Deliver me from evil.

Thy will be done.

Thy will be done.

"Miss . . . Miss Katharina. Wake up."

Marina's hand was cool against my face, lifted from the coverlet and warm with sleep.

"Marina?"

She knelt beside me, filling my vision. "The clock just chimed midnight, miss. If you've a mind to go meet Herr Baumgartner, it's time."

I struggled up, my legs and back stiff from the position in which I'd slept. All the thoughts and confusion and prayer from the previous hours washed upon me, and I sat right back down on the bed.

"I need more time."

"Well, there's none to be had. He's here."

My eyes flew toward the door. Marina had extinguished all but one of the tapers, leaving the room dark enough to harbor any number of callers.

"In the garden," she chided softly. "I saw a light at the top of the drive, blown out before I could see the rider. But I don't think we're expecting any other midnight visitors, are we?"

I envied the lightness of her tone, the irrepressible romantic.

"Come with me?"

"Only far enough to hand you over. Then I'll wait here by the fire, so you can tell me everything."

We opted to keep my hair unbound, loose around my face, but that was the only acknowledgment to the lateness of the hour. Otherwise, I was corseted and laced, dressed as fully as I would be were we meeting at high noon instead of midnight.

"And your cape?"

The garment, dangling empty in her hands, seemed presumptuous. Like I'd dressed with the intention of being swept away on the back of his horse.

"I'll be back for it if I need it."

Then we both collapsed into giggles, the likes of which would have brought the nuns storming from their cells. Once we'd reclaimed our senses, Marina took a stub of a taper, and we cast our shadows upon the walls, taking swift, sure steps through the cavernous great hall and the library, where the beveled glass doors opened onto the back courtyard.

"Shall I wait for you here, miss?"

"No, sweet girl." Overcome, I kissed her round, soft cheek. "Go back to our room. Wait by the fire as we planned."

"And if you don't come back?"

"Then wake up Herr Reichenbach, and have him send out the dogs."

Marina squeezed my hand, and I gave her the taper before opening the door to the night.

The moon was full, but stingy with its light, and I thanked God for a summer of strolls that trained my steps. I maneuvered along the winding path, conscious of the fading fragrance. What life would it have in winter, with snow piled on the hedges and crunching underfoot? Would I even be here to leave my tracks?

The back of the garden, he said. Past the fountain, and I wished he'd thought to meet me in a place that wouldn't leave me to traverse the expanse alone. But then, it might be the last I'd ever be alone, and I knew he was waiting.

I turned the final corner and saw the light. Small, pinpointed within the lantern, and Jerome cast in its glow. He wasn't watching for me; he wasn't watching for anything. He stood at the back wall, faced away from the path, head bowed against his fists. In prayer, as I had been an hour before.

Thy will be done.

My steps were not enough, so I made a small sound. His name, whispered, knowing I wouldn't have the courage to repeat it.

He turned, took three steps, and captured my hands, bringing them to his lips, saying, "You came."

"I did."

"Daring, isn't it?" He seemed so pleased with himself, like we were childhood playmates.

"*Alle, alle auch sind frei,*" I said, softly sounding the rallying cry of a game of hide-and-seek, though neither of us were hidden.

"Does anybody know you're here?"

"Only Marina."

"I hope you weren't frightened."

Not until that moment had I thought to assign *fear* to the litany of emotions I experienced since reading his note. "Should I have been?"

"Midnight? In the garden? Alone? What will people think?"

"Right now, I'm more curious what *you* were thinking."

"I was thinking, my love, that it has been too long since I've seen you, and I could not let another day pass without—" He punctuated his words with kisses to my cheeks, my neck, my lips. Tiny bits of starlight, and with each one it mattered less that I'd been lured away from any sense of moral safety.

"What will we say if someone comes?"

"I will spirit you into the bushes, and we will live in the shadows forever."

I backed away, until I'd created enough distance between us that I could think beyond the glorious fantasy of a life lived like Adam and Eve, alone in a garden, hiding our sin. After all, I'd already lived a life in shadows; I'd risked too much to go back.

"Perhaps we should tell them."

"Tell them? What do they not already know?"

"About your proposal?" I hated my uncertainty. "Our engagement."

"Katharina . . ." He brought me to him again and silenced himself with a kiss. For the first time, I sensed something disingenuous in his affection, and when he pulled away, an unforeseen hint of alienation had crept into his eyes.

"Jerome, what's happened?" A multitude of fears bound themselves together in that question. Where was the unfettered joy of the summer? The whirlwind of society and passion?

"Nothing has happened, my darling."

"I don't believe you. Something's changed."

"My feelings haven't changed. I love you, and we'll be married. Just as we planned."

The memory of the laughter shared with Marina rang bitter in my ears, because without saying a word, he made it perfectly clear there would be no elopement that night. Even worse, sprung to life somewhere at my core, the fear that there'd never be one at all.

"But that's just it." I felt myself hanging on, both with my clutching grip on his sleeves, and to the anchoring presence he'd become. "We haven't planned—"

"We will. We'll tell everybody our intention to marry."

Jerome's voice had become such a part of me, I felt every word—those he said and those he didn't. Here, I could tell, his sentence ended abruptly, broken off and fallen into a pit from which neither of us would wish to retrieve it. I knew I should leave the broken edge exposed, but I'd never been one to leave an unanswered question to languish. That I was only a woman, with no right to enforce his promises or demand accountability, never occurred to me. I knew what it meant to live with certainty, and without. Having taken such extreme measures to forge my own path, I could not simply sink beneath yet another veil of passivity.

"When, Jerome?"

"My first visit back."

I stepped away, so that no part of me touched any part of him—not cloth, not flesh. "Back from where, exactly? I wasn't aware that you were leaving."

"I didn't know myself. Not for certain, anyway."

"Not for certain." So somewhere, behind every embrace, every word, every letter, there'd been a possibility.

"I've yet to finish my studies. And while I'm still young enough, my parents—" he had the good graces to acknowledge my wince at the mention of his parents, but spared my dignity and continued as if the reaction was expected—"they, rather *we,* decided it would be best not to put it off for another term."

"So you're returning to Nuremberg?" I remembered the stories he'd told, the camaraderie with his fellow students. The stern dispositions of the instructors. We'd laughed at how ill-suited he was for the world of academia, and how he'd learned more from lurking outside the Reichenbach children's schoolroom than he had from a near lifetime of studying Latin. My question was a silly one, harmlessly rhetorical, until I gave it edge. "Because there is a fine university here. Or is your mother planning to send you out of the country?"

I hated myself immediately, speaking to him like the fabled fishwife, when I had no right to the title of *wife* at all.

"I'm sorry." I allowed the slightest touch of my hand to his. "That was hateful. You don't owe me an explanation."

"Don't you see, darling? If I do this one thing for them, they'll have nothing to hold over my head. I'll be back in December. For all of Christmas, and we'll make our announcement then."

"December. That's four months from now." I knew better than anyone how drastically one's allegiance could change in such a space of time.

"I'll write to you. Faithfully. And you to me. Keep me abreast of all the neighborhood gossip."

"There won't be any gossip once you've left."

He grinned. "There'd better not be."

I allowed him once again to gather me up, my arms folded and crushed between us. Rather than lift my face for his kiss, I buried it in the soft, warm wool of his vest.

"When do you leave?" My lips scratched against the fabric.

"In a fortnight."

"And until . . . will you be a visitor here? Shall I see you, or is this our good-bye?"

He held me closer and I knew my answer. We could hardly sit at a supper table, or walk in the garden, or look across a chessboard, knowing that each day was bringing us closer to the inevitable parting.

"I do love you, Katharina."

"I know."

"Luther might say that he orchestrated our meeting, but I know it was divine."

I looked up, pleased to find his gaze waiting for me. "All things are orchestrated by God. Even those that bring sorrow."

He cupped my face in his hands, forcing me to see him. "Don't let this bring you sorrow, my love."

His words came out with the barest puff of steam, reminding me of his warmth within. I forced a smile, and he touched his lips to my brow, the gesture making me feel like a child.

"Very well," I said, strained with bravado. "No sorrow, then. Only faith. And hope that the time will pass quickly."

"Before we've had a chance to blink."

Part V

Reichenbach Household, Wittenberg

Autumn – Christmas 1523

Chapter 22

In a month's time, I created a life for myself in shadows. Days stretched, seeming endless, despite the shortened daylight hours. The diversion of posing for Christoph disappeared along with the struggling artist, as he packed up his canvases and paints to go to Italy in hopes of studying with one of the maestros there. Before leaving, he made a gift of both my portrait and the Rebekah painting to the Reichenbach household. Elsa allowed me to hang my own portrait in my room, but the other was whisked away before the wheels of Christoph's hired coach touched the end of the drive.

My role as a Latin tutor for the Reichenbach children expanded into something more like a governess, giving instruction in history and literature, and I was grateful for the added responsibility, as it consumed the better part of my day. Otherwise, I was left to my own lonely devices, strolling the garden now bare of blooms or performing some act of stitchery as an excuse to watch through the window, waiting.

"Just like your portrait," Elsa said, coming upon me late one afternoon. The children had been exhaustive with their questions, and I'd dismissed them early to go enjoy the last few hours of sunlight. I couldn't decipher the tone of Elsa's comment—if she meant to mock or flatter or compliment. So I merely smiled, the tight-lipped response I'd perfected since Jerome's leaving, and returned to my stitching.

"It's a shame, really," she continued, "that you weren't given over to someone with better skill."

"All skills take time to develop." I held up my poor piece of work as an example. "And as I'm not likely to be hounded to pose for another portrait, I'll happily accept the one I have. Someday, when I'm a rickety old hag, I'll be glad of the evidence that I was young once."

To say that Elsa and I had not engaged in truly friendly conversation in most of a month was not an exaggeration, yet she selected this moment to come sit opposite, forcing me to choose between ignoring her with my craft or lifting my face in acknowledgment. Aware that, despite my familiarity, I was still very much a guest in this home, I chose the latter, and was taken aback by the sympathy lurking in her countenance.

"You've still heard nothing?"

Immediately, I regretted my decision to engage her. "No," I said, and bent back to my work. While Jerome and I had done a fair job of hiding the secret of our engagement, we'd failed to conceal our attraction to one another. Now, his total abandonment of my affection lived in full display, making me a household object of pity. Even the scullery maid offered me a look of unhidden compassion when we chanced to pass each other.

"It takes time, I'm sure, to settle in. Young men are inconsistent even in the steadiest of circumstances. Why, if I'd let my Philipp out of my sight for even three days' time in our courtship, I'd be mistress of some other house, you can be sure."

Her words may have been spoken in a noble attempt at levity, but they served only to reinforce my gloom.

"It's not so much, really." I worked the thread in and out of the fabric, barely registering the pattern. "I only hope that he is well."

"Would it cheer you up to know that Luther is coming to visit?"

"I don't need cheering up." For this, I allowed a broader smile. "But Herr Luther is always a welcome presence, isn't he?"

"He is."

Elsa's emphasis on the word *he* implied that the presence of some was not as welcome, and as the only remaining summer guest, I could not escape her meaning.

"When is he due to arrive?"

"Day after tomorrow. I was just about to check the holdings in the wine cellar, to make sure we have enough."

To date, I'd never heard Elsa hint that their house could not provide food and drink and entertainment for half the city. I kept my smile frozen and joined her in her subterfuge.

"Does he drink so much?"

She laughed. "There's always a deception with drink, isn't there? Open a cask, and it seems to be endless, and after a time goes by, you find it spoiled."

"That's why I shy away from drink."

"And how proper for you to do so." Elsa reached over and patted my knee. "Not all of us have that choice."

She left me without a response, claiming a need to check that the kitchen larder would support another houseguest. It may be that she was not aware of the unkindness of her words, but they rang on nonetheless. Without clarification, I understood the intention for my shelter here: a woman in need of a home and a husband; an eligible bachelor neighbor nearby. Doubtless Luther had filled the Reichenbachs' heads with visions of a late-summer wedding, hosted here, where the romance took root. I imagined Luther and Elsa good-naturedly vying to claim responsibility for the match, giving only a passing nod to the providence of God himself. Now, in the shadow of Luther's return, there seemed no chance of such celebration.

I'd heard not a word from Jerome. Not a note to

assure me of his safe arrival, nor a message sent off in haste with a promise of a longer missive to come. He'd left me with no token, and I'd given him none. We had nothing but time spent together and time spent apart. And though the time apart spanned half of that spent together, it had aged me to my very core.

Rather than call for a flame to the sconce when the light from the windows grew too dark for work, I took myself to my room, where Marina waited, herself busy with mending.

"Nothing today?"

A waste of a question, because no amount of decorum would have kept me from running into her arms had I evidence of his promise. In truth, though everyone of my acquaintance seemed to guess at the abandoned love affair, only Marina knew the length to which Jerome and I had pledged each other. Only she knew the scope of the future we'd imagined, because rather than spending that last night riding with him on the back of his horse, I'd spent it weeping on her shoulder. So this evening, when I might have been annoyed at the intrusive nature of her question, I remembered the comfort she'd whispered to me and braced myself for another round.

"Nothing."

"And you don't think it's possible that they'd keep something from you?"

The possibility had crossed my mind, more than once, but I felt no right to ask. "That seems cruel. Too cruel for Elsa. His mother? Maybe. But he would know not to go through her."

"I'm sure he's just—"

"Don't. Don't try to excuse him or explain him. It is all in the hands of God, not for us to bend and twist what we see right before our eyes."

"And you won't consider writing to him, miss?"

"I am not the one who made the promise."

Turning, I slipped off my overdress and asked Marina to unlace my bodice. Stripped to my chemise and stockings, I made my way to the bed and lay down upon it.

"Taking a rest before supper, miss?"

"Find Elsa, please, and tell her I won't be down this evening."

"Are you not feeling well?"

"Not feeling hungry."

"Shall I bring up a tray later?"

The mere question conjured memories of Sister Gerda, bent beneath a lifetime without the love of a man, a person of unabashed pity.

"No, sweet girl. Thank you. It is a luxury to take to one's bed at a whim. I feel I'm overdue for such an indulgence."

"Then I shall leave you to it." She came to my side and made a show of fluffing the pillows behind me and lifting the coverlet with enough force that it drifted to settle around me. "I'll take myself downstairs. See what's about."

Marina left, and the room descended into darkness. Six o'clock, according to the chimes coming from the front hall. Too early for sleep, but I couldn't face another meal with Elsa Reichenbach and her unspoken dismissal. Rather, it had been unspoken up until this day. Recalling our conversation of a few hours before, I realized she couldn't have been more clear.

I had to leave. But where was I to go?

And if I left, how would Jerome ever find me?

The only way he knew to contact me was here: Katharina von Bora, House of Philipp Reichenbach, Wittenberg. Were I to go back to my father, or to the Brummbär with Marina, or to some thatch-roofed hut in the forest, I would never know the reason for his silence. Did he fall ill? Did he succumb to the temptations proffered to a young, unattached man? Did his feelings wane so sharply with time and space wedged between us?

My feelings, of course, remained unchanged. If anything, they'd increased in fervor. Perhaps I'd always been the stronger of the two. He'd been led to love me, and so he did. He'd been encouraged to marry me, and so he offered engagement.

Now Jerome, bereft of Luther's encouragement to love me and his parents' encouragement to leave me, had only his own will to spur him to pursuit. Six weeks without word might speak to a lack of strength, rather than a lack of love.

But I lacked no strength. Never had I relied on any person other than Jesus Christ to shape my thought or bend my will. Marina's hint that I should write only gave voice to the thoughts I'd kept buried in silence since Jerome left. I was no stranger to writing a letter. I risked the fire of the Church to write to Luther. To secure my freedom at any cost. Writing to Jerome inspired no fear, other than the loss of dignity. Then again, my rebirth to this life came from the huddled darkness of a herring wagon.

I climbed out of bed, fetched a candle, and—taking care to check that no one was about to see my state of undress—lit it from the torch outside my door. Once I wedged it in the holder attached to the bedpost, I found my writing desk and brought it straight into bed. From underneath the hinged lid, I retrieved paper, ink, and quill.

My dearest Jerome,

And all my passion, all my noble intention, all my eloquence dissolved. So, too, did his name upon the page, the ink running with my tears. I dropped the quill, uncaring of how it might stain my bed, and picked up the page, intending to rip it to ruin, but paused. How could my lover deny such a blatant display of my heart? I blew across the page, drying the ink and my tears together. Satisfied, I returned it to the writing surface, dipped the quill, and wrote a message equal in brevity to the last he ever wrote me.

Write, as I wait in the garden.
KVB

Chapter 23

The next morning I reclaimed my place as an honored guest, bringing to the breakfast table a stomach unhappy with my decision to forgo supper the night before. Newly resolved in love, I heaped my plate with all that was offered and sent one of the waiters at table to fetch sweet cream for my porridge.

"It's how we made it more palatable in the convent," I said, stirring the contents of my bowl. "Not that this isn't delicious as is, but an acquired taste is often difficult to dislodge."

"All kinds of things in this world are difficult to dislodge," Elsa said, earning a disapproving huff from Herr Reichenbach.

"Which is why one should always opt to add sweetness to the taste." I punctuated my retort with a satisfied slurp from my spoon. Marina, who had long been invited to join us at any meal that didn't include other guests, smiled behind her hand. Later, after breakfast, she would be charged with taking my letter to the market to post. I would have done so myself, but my welcome seemed so precarious, I feared the doors might be locked against me upon my return.

"Have you not yet wearied of speaking against your life behind the walls?"

I jumped at the familiar voice, the spoonful of porridge caught in my throat, and made quite a show of forcing it to swallow.

Never one to subscribe to manners, Marina cried out, "Herr Luther!" and leapt from her place to meet him at the door, throwing her arms around his neck in an embrace fit for a daughter to her father newly returned from soldiering afar. For his part, Luther fit such an image. He was thinner than the last time I'd seen him, his complexion ruddy from the voyage on the road. His clothing still bore the dust of travel, and his eyes were red-rimmed from what I supposed to be lack of sleep. Marina had said nothing when she came to our room after supper, so he must have arrived late in the night. The forced bravery I felt at claiming my place at the table became something else with his presence. Something with weight and warmth.

Luther greeted us in turn, waiting graciously until I recovered power of speech. Elsa made a great show of bringing a plate from the sideboard and sending the cold sausages back to the kitchen to be heated through.

"And another plate?" Suddenly, this morning, there seemed a limit to her hospitality. "Is your friend going to join us?"

Again my throat closed at the thought of who

his friend might be. Had Luther taken it upon himself to fetch Jerome back?

"He will not. I'm afraid Nikolaus is a greater slave to the appetite of sleep than the appetite for sustenance."

We all offered a spatter of laughter, and I felt my pulse settle in disappointment.

"We're just happy to see you safely returned," I said, hoping to establish my place.

"Not as happy as I am, I assure you." Luther spoke with a hint of levity, seemingly for the children's sake, as he directed his countenance upon them. "And if Fräulein von Bora will give you leave of your lessons for an hour, I will tell you all of my adventures."

"Can't I listen too?" I said, with mock hurt.

"Of course." He leaned close then, and whispered, "I hear we can share tales of bravery."

"I see you still wear your ring," Luther said. He held my hand, my palm balanced on his fingertips, as if holding some delicate work of art. "I had hoped to find another, more significant in its place upon my return."

"You hoped no more than I did."

We'd come to the chapel built on the far side of the Reichenbachs' property. It had eight benches—four on each side of a narrow aisle—and a small altar. A tapestry depicting the magi offering gifts to the Christ child hung on one wall, while on the other side, four windows bathed the room in cool blue light. I sat on a back bench, Luther in front of me, his body turned to give me full attention.

"I was under the impression he was quite taken with you."

I smiled and took my hand away. "As was I. In fact, it may be that he fooled even himself, until better sense took hold of him."

I said nothing of the letter Marina was posting at this moment, nothing of my resolve to hear from Jerome himself about the current state of his affections.

"I always feared he was a weak-willed boy," Luther said, crumpling his hat in his hand.

"So weak-willed I would be able to convince him to love me?"

"In your presence, dear lady, even the strongest of men could feel tempted to fall."

I pummeled his shoulder, and he feigned great injury. "Well, then, Jerome is obviously a man of prodigious strength, for I did not tempt him in the least."

"So, all the stories dear Elsa told me about your unaccounted-for hours away from the company of the house . . ."

"Are nothing more than gossip. I take great care with my reputation, Luther. And I hold myself accountable to God for my sins. Were you to take back your priesthood and sit on the other side of the confessional screen, I would have nothing to say to you other than the fact that my heart is tainted with dislike for Frau Baumgartner."

"Ah, yes. The young man's mother. Therein is the weakness I feared."

To my utter horror, tears welled, and I turned my eyes to the window, focusing on the pattern in the glass.

"You did love him, then?" His question rang with such tenderness and truth, my ruse fell to pieces.

"I do still."

"And he, you?"

I wiped the betrayal of my sorrow with my sleeve. "He says—said—he did. And he gave me no reason to doubt his sincerity."

"But there was no proposal?"

I gritted my teeth and faced him. "There was, actually. We kept it a secret, of course. Even I thought it was reckless—too soon. But he very forthrightly declared his love and asked me to be his wife. He said we would announce it to our families—his family, I suppose—when he comes back at Christmastime."

Luther brightened. "There is hope, then?"

"He also said he would write to me. And I've heard nothing. Two weeks passed from the last time I saw him until the day he was to leave for Nuremberg. Nothing. For all I know he has spent the last six weeks at his mother's table. Or in her lap."

Luther rumbled with laughter, and I found some relief in the sharpness of my wit. It always seemed such a waste on Jerome.

"What would you have me do for you, my Katie? I know of another family, another home where you would be welcomed with open arms."

"No, not until I hear . . . something. From him."

"Shall I speak to him? Go to him on your behalf and demand he honor his promise? That's what any other father would do."

"Sweet Luther." I rested my hand on his sleeve, physically holding him back from such a rash action. "You are not my father, and I would never want such an action to further impair your friendship with these people. I fear I've done enough damage in that respect already."

"I could write to him and inquire. After all, I was instrumental in the introduction—"

"And then you left." I squeezed his arm to stay his protest. "No, I offer no criticism in that. There are, after all, events unfolding that have much graver consequences than an ill-fated romance. I only mean that you left the two of us to find each other out. To allow our feelings to materialize and grow. As much as I respect you, Luther, you could never convince me to love someone against the workings of my heart. Nor, with all of your indisputable powers of influence, can you force Jerome to own his love for me."

"Of course I can, if he truly does."

"If he truly does, I would hope that he can live up to his love's demands under his own power. And if he does not . . . Well, nothing satisfying can come from a match born of such strong-armed persuasion."

"What, then, do you propose?"

"I will wait."

"For how long?"

"Until he has had a chance to fulfill his promise. That we would announce our engagement at Christmas. Until that has passed, he's broken no vow to me."

"Did he not also promise to write?"

"And implored me to do the same."

Still I kept secret the letter I'd written today, for fear Luther would question the wisdom of it, as I myself did.

"So, you would like to stay *here* until Christmas?"

"If you could arrange it. I know I've long outlasted my welcome. But I've been a good teacher for the children, and I would take no shame in being considered one of the servants rather than a guest. I've tried always not to overstep my boundaries there."

He shifted away, bowed his head for a moment,

and I felt him searching for the right words in the silence.

"As much as it pains me to say it, my Katie, Frau Baumgartner has turned many of the well-wishers against you. She's made you out to be some sort of a ruthless, lowborn—"

"My family is every bit as good as hers. Better, maybe, if we listed our legacies side by side. I come with a good name."

"But no dowry."

"The fact that I come with love and health and chastity means nothing?"

"None of those can be measured, my dear. And Jerome's mother is one to carry a scale as easily as she carries an opinion."

"Knowing this, why did you ever promote such a match?"

"Because I'm used to getting my way."

We both laughed, and were brought to sobriety only by the introduction of a new voice.

"What would people think, hearing such unchecked levity coming from a former priest and a former nun in a chapel? Surely you're not mocking the Church?"

"Surely not, my friend," Luther said, rising. "I've no need to increase the bounty on my life. Let me introduce you to Miss Katharina von Bora."

"At last." The gentleman extended his hand, and I offered mine, accompanied by a small bow, which he returned. "I cannot tell you, Fräulein, how many miles were passed with stories about you. Your bravery, your strength. I half expected you to look like a cross between a bear and a brawler. I am pleasantly surprised."

I suppressed the urge to chide Luther for allowing a portrayal that overlooked any measurement of my beauty. I'd already won the man over with a pleasant face; no need to slice him with the sharpness of my tongue.

"Luther is always too free with his praise," I said. "He tends to overestimate the qualities of his friends and build up impossible expectations."

"Dare I ask, then, what he has told you of me?"

"Not a word, sir. As yet, not even your name."

"Nikolaus von Amsdorf," Luther said, with the merest hint of indulgence. "A longtime friend and traveling companion. And most important, a crack shot. Good for securing food and safety."

"Very nice to meet you, Herr von Amsdorf. And I thank you for Luther's safe return."

He was a handsome man, roughly Luther's age, though he carried a touch more gray in his hair and beard. His manner of dress differed from Luther too, with an overall attention to fashion. His breeches showed no sign of wear; his vest and coat fit impeccably over what appeared to be a fine, athletic form underneath. All of this I studied in the gathering of seconds when his attention turned again to Luther.

"I apologize for interrupting your conversation. The mistress of the house said I would find you here. She's been kind enough to have a meal prepared this late in the morning, and I've been sent to see if you would like to join me."

"I would, indeed," Luther said, as if he hadn't eaten with me less than an hour ago. "If you would allow us a few more minutes."

"Excellent." Herr von Amsdorf offered another nod of his head. "So nice to have met you, Fräulein. I'm looking forward to hearing some of your stories from your own mouth, as our friend here can be prone to exaggeration."

"And I look forward to hearing what he's said."

With that, Herr von Amsdorf left, my eyes following his every step until the heavy arched door closed behind him.

"What a charming man." I spoke at first to myself, then to Luther. "Why did you not think to marry me off to him?"

Luther recoiled at the idea. "He is nearly twice your age. A good year older than me."

"I would never deem you undesirable because of your age." My teasing tone surprised me, and I prayed he wouldn't ask me just what I *would* find undesirable, because I had no ready answer.

"Is your young man so soon forgotten, then?"

"By no means."

"Then what would you have us do?"

"Us?"

"I feel a certain responsibility for your happiness, Katie. Or at least your settlement. I will speak and act on your behalf however you wish, but *only* in accordance with your command."

"Then speak to Elsa and Herr Reichenbach. Elsa, the more pressing. Convince them to let me stay in the way that we discussed. As a governess. Just until after Christmas. Not because of Jerome—rather, she doesn't need to know of Jerome's promise. But because you cannot arrange for a new situation until that time."

"But that's not the truth. I could—"

"Then give her no reason. Jerome's family will take great satisfaction at seeing my position diminished. I'll move into the children's room, if need be. I'll send Marina back home, as a governess has no need for a lady's maid. I simply cannot leave."

My voice rose in the course of my plea, and by its end, tears threatened again. Luther, however, remained utterly impassive, waiting for me to say my piece.

"Very well. It is always best to wait on the Lord, and that we shall do."

"Does that mean you'll wait with me?" The notion hadn't occurred to me until that very moment, but I seized upon it as if it had been my greatest desire all along. "Stay here? So I'll have someone to talk to? Somebody who appreciates my company?"

"You believe I appreciate your company?"

He was teasing now too. "Of course you do. All the more because you've had so little time to experience it. Elsa and Philipp love you."

"And the Baumgartners do not. You'll not further your case with them if I am a constant presence here."

"I do not wish to further my case with *them*. They will accept me or not, as they choose. Their son and I have pledged our love to each other, and promises were made on that pledge. I simply want to see those promises fulfilled."

"And if they are not? My Katie, I want to spare you from hurt, but it is entirely possible that Jerome has taken the young man's cowardly path to disentangle himself from a promise made in haste."

Perhaps Luther forgot the power of his words, how workings of his mind and heart inflamed the Church and put his very life in danger. His words commanded attention and obedience. He changed minds and hearts. His tongue was a tool of inflammatory persuasion, his hands purveyors of unprecedented truth. So when he spoke such a sentence out loud, giving voice to all my silent fears, I swatted him away.

"Don't say such things."

"I only meant—"

"If, indeed, it was a promise made in haste, we should give it balance—a leisurely time for it to be fulfilled or abandoned. And I promise you, by Christmastime, I shall be equally at peace no matter the outcome."

"You owe no promise to me."

"Then I promise to myself. Only, be here with me?"

"It is a comfortable house, good food and warm people. I shall be proud to wrangle an invitation."

Chapter 24

Luther needed only to express his desire to return to his small, mildewed room, and Elsa Reichenbach insisted that he stay.

"Until the last of the summer is out," she said. "And then stay with us to welcome the rest of the harvest. It's so much more festive to celebrate God's bounty with people who labor in his name."

Over a matter of weeks, most of my visionary plan came to fruition. I was, indeed, given full responsibility as governess to the children, a task I found rewarding, as their bright minds seemed eager to learn. Remembering my own childhood education, with the ever-present fear of punishment and abuse, I endeavored to make myself a patient instructor. I patterned my lessons after those I had with my beloved Sister Elisabeth, being quick to reward responses, even those that were more clever than correct. I was also able to fill in some of the gaps left behind from the nuns' religious emphasis, and together we read passages of anatomy and botany, relishing the scientific study of God's perfect creation.

I was not, however, relegated to a bed in

the children's room. Elsa insisted I keep the room I'd learned to call my own, and with the cooling weather, I was even allowed a ration of firewood for my comfort, and a servant assigned to building a fire each morning before I woke. Luther's presence softened her speech toward me, and after a time we resumed the same ease we'd enjoyed during the early days of my visit. Her rediscovered friendliness proved all the more welcome, as Marina returned home to her family, their need for her greatly outweighing mine. She promised, though, to write, and her promise proved true as no more than two weeks ever passed without word from her. It pleased me to see the continuing improvement of her letters and spelling, and I returned correspondence in kind, offering challenging vocabulary where I could.

From Jerome, however, I heard only silence. There'd been no reply to my first letter, nor to my second, which I sent just in case Marina had sought secretly to spare my pride. The third I sent as an apology for the first two, asking him to forgive my brevity and assumption that he knew my feelings were unchanged. The fourth was an assurance that I still kept my residence with the Reichenbachs, even though I did not engage much with them or their friends in social situations. The fifth an acknowledgment that December loomed ever closer, mere weeks until our proposed reunion, and an expression of my hopes that his heart, like mine, had not changed in the intervening time.

I told nobody about these letters. I wrote them at night, the scratching of the quill the only sound in my quiet room. I took them to the post while running other errands for the household. Once, when Luther offered to escort me, I hastily composed a note to mail to Marina, to give the excuse to enter the shop. The pitying look in his eyes made it clear that I hadn't fooled him in the least, but neither of us said a word.

Luther's friend Nikolaus von Amsdorf accepted his invitation to stay on as well and proved to be a masterful addition to the household. For all of our months together, I never saw him at a loss. Literature, theology, philosophy, mathematics—all areas of academia were fields sown with knowledge. He entertained my questions equally with those of the youngest Reichenbach child, and his wisdom encouraged a deeper sophistication in the search for our own. He lacked the charisma of Luther, making it clear why one would bear the title of "reformer" while the other rested in the shadows, but on more than one occasion, I witnessed their heads bowed together, and I could only stand by and marvel at the exchange of ideas.

During the long stretch of evenings, when the house was well dark by the end of supper, we would all gather in the chairs around the fire in the great hall. Here the children would pepper the two for stories about their travels, or answers to the mysteries of creation, or a response to a question of philosophical import. For example, which was the greater danger: to be a frog in a boiling pot of water, or a deer in the sights of a hunter. Luther and von Amsdorf would choose opposing sides, build ridiculous arguments, and present them with practiced flair of brilliance. Here, I liked to lean my head against the back of my chair and let their voices lull me by the firelight. These were the times my mind could be free of its haunting by Jerome. I fixed my thoughts on Luther—his voice, his mind, growing as familiar as my own.

As Elsa Reichenbach began to prepare her home for Christmas, I gave new thanks to God for allowing me to be a part of the household. Truthfully, the idea that Jerome intended to reunite grew dimmer along with each new winter's sky, but I'd never truly celebrated the holiday in such a homey fashion. Fir branches lined the mantel and the windowsills, bringing a fresh, green fragrance into the house. The children and I dipped tapers made of red and green wax to be used at the table for holiday meals. One afternoon, Elsa came into our classroom and told the children it was time to bring out the special decorations. I followed behind, forcing myself not to match their bouncing gait, and met her in the front hall. A large, wooden trunk sat open, straw spilling from its side. One by one, Elsa removed smaller boxes, each of which held a piece of golden fruit. Apples, pears, plums, each perfect in size and color; each reflecting fire. The fruit was arranged on an ornately carved tray and, surrounded by a nest of fir branches, adorned the dining room table. Never had I beheld anything of such beauty, and I took any excuse I could to wander into the dining room just to behold its opulence.

"It is her pride and joy," Luther said. He'd come up behind me after the table had been cleared for the noon meal. "I could live out the rest of my life on its value. The pears alone could sustain me."

Brazenly, I'd removed an apple from the tray, its gold now warm against my palm. "But isn't it nice to have pretty things? To enjoy them for their own sake?"

"Is that your aspiration? To have such things?"

"For me, to have a life where I can hold a *real* apple. Eat it or not, as my choice. That is all I desire."

He plucked the fruit from my hand. "Good answer. Now, go put on your warmest boots and cloak. We have an important chore to do for the mistress of the house."

Luther refused to offer any more information,

only encouraged me to hurry to my room, change, and meet him in the drive at the front of the house.

It was a cold day, mid-December, with a fresh snow on the ground and a hint of more to come in the air. Elsa had handed down a pair of fur-lined boots, which I wore over warm wool stockings. I also donned an extra wool petticoat and a cloak with a hood lined in rabbit fur. This, too, had been a gift from Elsa, as she noted my lack of a cold-weather garment and her newest one was lined with mink. I had no gloves, but the cape had deep, warm pockets. On an impulse, I dropped in a handful of roasted hazelnuts, in the event that our errand lasted until supper.

Luther waited in the front drive, along with Albert, the horse groomer with whom I'd posed for Christoph's portrait of Rebekah at the well. He stood next to one of the larger workhorses, which had been harnessed to an empty travois.

"Would you care to ride, Katie?" Luther offered with a grand gesture. The horse had no saddle, but its back seemed broad enough for comfort. "I'm not sure how long the walk will be."

"Not far," Albert said, attending to the harness.

"I still don't know where we're going. Or what we're doing."

"We'll walk on ahead." Luther directed his words to Albert, then took my arm companionably. "As to the first question, we are going into the uncleared land of Reichenbach's property. A place of deep, dark forest. We are on a hunt."

"A hunt." I bent back to study him further. "And yet we have no weapon."

"Ah, but we do. In the horse's pack, a hatchet and a saw."

"We're hunting a tree?"

"Precisely."

"Do you mean to say that now, to earn our keep, we must fetch and chop wood?"

"Fetch, yes. Chop, no."

We'd come to the edge of the drive, about to step into the road stretched along the dense woodland. I stopped in the mix of snow and mud, churned with the tracks of wagon wheels and hooves, refusing to take another step. "Tell me."

"We are going to get a tree."

"A tree? How does one *get* a tree?"

"One goes into the woods, finds it, and chops it down."

"But they already have trees. All along the front of the house, and in the back garden."

"We need an evergreen."

"There's a solid wall of evergreens along the side."

"This is for *inside.*"

Somehow, we'd started walking again. I didn't even remember taking the first new step, but his response was so odd, I thought surely I'd misheard him, due to the crunch of the snow beneath our feet.

"Inside, where?"

"Inside the house. In the great hall."

The thought of it seemed too ridiculous—and wonderful—for words. I laughed, sending a puff of steam into the air.

"Why is that so funny?"

"Nobody brings a tree inside the house."

"I thought so, too, but apparently it is becoming quite the thing." As he said it, I could hear Elsa's insistence. "We're to decorate it, just as she did the trees in the front of the house. Ribbons and fruit and the like. She wants it in place for the weeks' festivities."

"She is planning a party, then?"

"More than one, I expect. Philipp told me he might have to sell one of the golden fruits just to pay the butcher."

"And do you think . . . people . . . will attend?"

"Christmas is a time of renewal. A celebration of Christ's birth and the fulfillment of the promised Messiah. It is quite something to see how many grudges are forgotten when there is roasted pork and plenty of ale."

I loved him a little bit at that moment, for knowing the exact nature of my question but refusing any precision in his response.

"Well, then," I said, tucking myself closer,

"what an honor it is to be trusted with such a task."

"It is, indeed."

By then we could hear the jangle of the harness behind us, and we picked up our pace. The air was cold and sharp, making conversation uncomfortable. All the more as we left the road and headed into a clearing. Luther went ahead of me, dragging his steps to make somewhat of a path for me to follow.

"Perhaps this is the point where we should have let the horse take the lead," I said, struggling with my skirts.

"And let him get all the credit? I think not." He turned back to Albert and shouted through cupped hands, "Wait there! We'll go in and bring you when we've found it."

Albert, looking unconcerned, lit a pipe and leaned against the long-suffering animal.

Luther and I continued, becoming swallowed by shadows as the forest closed in from all sides.

"You're not worried we'll get lost?" I asked, betraying the fact that my only experience with forests came from childhood tales.

"I think we've left an impressive set of tracks to follow," Luther said, indicating the chaotic rut behind us. "That will make it easier for the man to find the tree we've chosen, at any rate." He indicated a need for one not too tall, as it must stand beneath the ceiling, and not too wide, as it must fit through the door. “Something with character, as it is going to be invited in to dwell among us.”

“Shall it have a name? As must all good pets?”

“That, we will leave up to Elsa. We are only fulfilling her bidding.”

Battling underbrush and wading through snow proved effort enough, so we talked very little as we moved farther in. The air around us was flat and cold, the greenish-gray of old stone, and the few words we did speak traveled only as far as the steam of our breath. Never before had I felt so utterly alone with another human being. Always there were people on the other side of a wall, or down a corridor, or inside the house behind windows aglow with candlelight. Here with Luther I felt secure, as I had in the evenings after Mother died when I sat by the fire in Father’s lap. Here, too, was the same companionship I’d enjoyed with Jerome in all our hours together. If these moments were to stretch to encompass the rest of my years, I would count the time well spent in good company.

He talked, mostly to himself, allowing me the benefit of listening. Everything within reach seemed to bring him such delight. He commented on the purity of the snow, the precision of the rabbit tracks, and the story they told. He stuck his tongue out, tasting the pure snow on the pine needles, declaring it a sweet winter's treat. He hummed parts of tunes, interspersed with lyrics, allowing the song to trail away the moment he became taken with another point of beauty. I followed, listened, learned. It occurred to me that Luther might behave exactly the same whether or not he had me as his audience, or any audience at all. Rather than this making me feel inconsequential, however, I felt like an important, integral part of his life. But Luther was not a father, not a lover. He was, I realized, a friend. The dearest I had.

"I believe this is the one." Luther stood in front of a snow-tipped tree, diminutive compared to its forest brothers, but looming well over his head.

"Are you going to cut it down?"

"Heavens no, girl. I'm not one to shy away from labor, but I'm more adept at reading Scripture than wielding an axe." He took a scrap of cloth from his pocket and tied it to a branch. "So we don't lose sight. I'll go fetch Albert and the horse, now that we can make a straight path for it. Do you want to come with me? Or wait here, save yourself a trek?"

My breathlessness led my answer. "I'll wait here. Are you sure you'll find your way?"

"Our tracks may not be as precise as the rabbits', but they'll do to bring me back."

He wasn't long out of my sight before I regretted my decision. I could have followed our trail the same as he, but with so little experience in the wilds of nature, I dared not venture beyond what Luther instructed. A new silence settled, heavier and more complete than any I'd experienced at Marienthrone. If it had been the aim of the abbess to instill an environment for meditation and reflection, she should have brought us out here. Left us in the deepest forest, where all sounds save for prayer were swallowed in the wet white batting.

I pushed my hands deep into my pockets, encountering the hazelnuts, but opted to save them for later. Irrational fear made me believe that the slightest scent of food would entice some woodland predator my way. Between the weight of my wet skirts and my impaired balance with my arms wrapped tight around me, walking—even a short pace—proved ungainly, so I stood quite still, imagining myself frozen in place. A statue waiting for spring.

My theory of the noiselessness of the forest, that any uttered sound would be trapped beneath the snowy canopy, proved false, once I heard Luther's unmistakable voice threading through the frosty space. An unforgettable tune, and lyrics that told the story of Christ's birth.

He who made the starry skies,
Sleeping in a manger lies,
Ruler of the centuries.

My mother had sung it to me, not only during Advent, but throughout the year, even on hot summer nights, and I pictured two tableaux in my mind—the soft profile of my mother in the darkness and the image of a sweet baby, swaddled and suckling at his mother's breast.

Luther sang it now, and to my surprise, at the end of one phrasing, another voice took up the next line. A deep, throaty bass to Luther's pure tenor, and they came together with still a third, harmonizing on the refrain.

Lully, lully, lully

I felt quite on the edge of a dream, cold from kicking off my covers, trapped in an unfamiliar place, my mother's voice traveling through on a masculine trio. I hadn't thought of this song in years—longer since I'd heard it. I took my hand from my pocket and clutched the icy cold metal of my necklace, bringing the locket to my lips.

"Sweet mother."

A new pang struck as I realized how long it had been since I'd taken time to miss her. It seemed God brought me from one life to another, with barriers built up to keep me from returning. Once given to the Church, I could not go home. Leaving the Church, I could not go back. At that moment, wrapped in snow and cold, fragile as frost, I wondered what new wall he was building.

Luther burst into the small clearing, with him the mysterious second and third voices. One, the less steady, was Albert, carrying axe and saw and rope. The other, the bass, was Nikolaus von Amsdorf, holding an impressively low note. Finally, Herr Reichenbach, silent but looking more jovial than I'd seen since summer.

"Good afternoon, gentlemen," I said, offering applause. "What a lovely trio you make. If I only had a piece of silver to give you."

Von Amsdorf offered a bow, and Albert's face turned as red as his nose.

"You do not sing as well, Herr Reichenbach?"

"Let's get this tree back to the house, and then my wife will let me know if I've anything to sing about."

The men all laughed, while I made weak protest. After, Albert, von Amsdorf, and Herr Reichenbach studied the tree, divining the best way to fell and drag it from this place to the horse and travois waiting at the forest's edge.

"If you don't mind, gentlemen," I said, "I believe my usefulness here is done. I'll take my leave of you now and see to it a hearty batch of mulled cider awaits your return."

"Go with her, Luther," Herr Reichenbach said, distracted by the task at hand. "We don't want to risk the tree falling and breaking that important head of yours."

"Is my head so much less important?" von Amsdorf asked, feigning offense.

"Not less important, just a trickier target, being so much smaller."

Even Albert joined in the laughter at that, with Luther's loudest of all.

We departed, the sound of the axe striking the trunk thudding behind us. A good two hours must have passed since we left the house, and the light had turned to a darker gray. It would be past dark before the other men would return, and when I voiced this concern, Luther assured me they had light and strength enough.

"Well," I ventured, taking a handful of hazelnuts from my pocket, three for me and four for him, "I must say I was happy for your return."

"Did you have any doubt?" He popped the first hazelnut in his mouth and spoke around it. "Did you think I would leave you in the woods? Did you think I lured you there to meet your fate?"

"No." I was smiling by the third question. "But I had reason to be frightened, didn't I? Aren't there wolves?"

"My girl, there are wolves everywhere."

"True enough. Why *did* you bring me?"

"I thought you would enjoy the excursion. While we must be faithful in giving thanks to God for his provision of a roof and fire to protect us from the harshness of winter, we must also take opportunities to walk out among it."

"In short, a distraction?"
"Yes, but a healthy one."
I offered him another hazelnut, which he took but did not eat. Instead, he held it up in scrutiny. "These are roasted, yes?"
"Yes." An odd, shy pride crept into my reply. "These were one of the few treats we had at Marienthrone. We'd sit, silent, the only sound the cracking of the shells. And we'd watch each other so closely, lest one of the sisters try to sneak some away. For all the days of Advent, the kitchen and refectory smelled of roasting hazelnuts, and at Christmas we'd each get a little bag with our supper."
"Did you roast these here yourself?"
"I did. The one contribution I've made in the kitchen. I purchased them myself, too, at the market. Also the spices. But I've been saving them to give at Christmas."
"Not all of them." He ate it and immediately extended his hand for more.
"I'll be sure to give you a double portion. *On Christmas.*"
"Fair enough."
By the time we'd returned to the main road, my pocket was empty of hazelnuts, my toes numb within my boots, and my lungs stinging from so much laughter in the winter evening's air. In a rare lull following a particularly rollicking story, I heard the familiar sound of a horse's hooves up

the road. My first thought was that the men had worked swiftly, indeed, getting the tree strapped to the travois. But then, the horse was traveling at a pace far beyond what the burdened farm animal would be able to keep.

Luther began another story, speaking louder than necessary, and quicker, too, but I found myself paying no heed to his words. Instead, I was fixated on the sound of the hooves. I knew that sound; I'd trained my ears to hear it every day this summer. The pace was in my pulse, and rising up from the disappearing horizon, Jerome's black steed came into view. Like a nightmare, shadow emerging from shadow, the rider thundered past. I recognized his silhouette, the broadness of his shoulders high in the saddle, never mind that his face was obscured by his hood. I should have pulled mine closer to hide my own. Should have looked away, or kept my eyes trained to my steps. I might have done all of those things, if my feet had not turned to lifeless stumps, stopping me in the slush of the road. If I stopped, surely he would stop too. He was coming from the direction of the Reichenbachs' house. Had he been to see me? Had he been told of my errand? Who else, then, could this cloaked woman on Luther's arm be?

He did not stop.

He did not even slow his pace enough to keep

from splattering us with the slush kicked up from the horse's hooves.

Luther had stopped talking.

"Did you know?"

"I suspected."

Tears—born of anger or sorrow, I couldn't say—pricked cold upon my cheek. "And you said nothing?"

"I had no reason to suspect anything good."

I turned my head, watching him disappear. More than disappear. Escape.

Chapter 25

"Our tree," as Luther insisted on calling it, filled the great hall of the Reichenbachs' home with its fragrance and its presence. Red ribbon had been laced through the branches, scraps of fabric fashioned into bundles and tied to the ends of the limbs. Nestled in the branches were small, oval-shaped ornaments—white-washed wood, decorated by the Reichenbachs' children. For each day of Advent, I asked the children to paint a small picture to represent Jesus Christ in every way that we knew him. As a baby, yes, but also a Shepherd, a Light, a Word.

"Someday," I told them, "you will be able to read the words of Jesus in the Gospels as easily as you read your primers. And you'll be able to thank Herr Luther for that."

Later, when I shared this with Luther, including the children's less-than-enthusiastic response at the prospect, he gently reminded me that I must not be so quick to give him praise.

"Better men than I have died in pursuit of the same goal," he said. "If I am to be branded a heretic by the Church, at least I've escaped execution for the sake of it."

In the days after that walk into the woods to find our tree, I'd had very little to say at all—to Luther, to the children, to anyone. Ten days had passed, and with each one the tree grew more festive, and I more despondent. I convinced myself that Jerome hadn't seen me, given the pace of his horse and the element of dusk. I told myself he wanted to see me alone, not with Luther on my arm, or by my side, or anywhere near enough to monitor our conversation. I told myself he'd been waiting here, at the house, pacing the hall, impatient for my return. I attributed the swiftness of his ride to his frustration, and I pictured him waiting, and planning, for the perfect moment to come to me again.

So, of course, I didn't leave the house. Not for another bracing walk in the snow at the invitation of von Amsdorf, not for supper at the nearest neighbor's home, even though I was flattered at the invitation. I went only where I thought Jerome might be. To church on the Sunday before Christmas, where Luther read from the Gospel of Luke in lyrical German—the first I'd ever heard it in my native tongue. And to the market to help Cook with the necessities for our Christmas supper and celebration the Eve before. Here, I thought, Jerome might be on such an errand. Or perhaps, like Luther who tagged along, he'd want to witness the good-natured bustling at the shops and carts that lined the street. All manner of meats roasted on spits, making the very air smell like a king's smokehouse. And there were cakes and breads and sweets like none I'd seen before. This outing nudged my tongue, and I questioned the vendors, learning of all the decadent ingredients of their wares. I was reminded of something Luther said at the beginning of the summer—how, if he saw me in the marketplace, he would think me a fine-looking girl. Somewhere, lurking in the loss and loneliness for Jerome, I wondered if he thought so still.

Jerome's persistent silence and absence made me wonder if he hadn't been a dream. A frozen mirage. But Luther had seen him too. And like a true friend, said nothing of it since.

Whatever social sin the Reichenbachs had committed in hosting me and encouraging my unworthy pursuit was obviously forgiven, if the crowd gathered in their home on Christmas Eve served as any indication. Their summer parties, resplendent with food and music, paled in comparison to the feast offered this evening. Because there were too many guests to sit at the table, all chairs had been removed and lined the walls. We roamed free, sampling from platters, tasting the days of labor from the kitchen. Mugs were dipped into massive vats of mulled wine or tipped to barrels of ale. One set of musicians played in the dining hall, where the floor was cleared for dancing. In the great hall, where the tree stood in its magnificence, guests sang carols with reverence or gusto, depending on the song and the drink at hand. Brightly wrapped candies had been strung on the lower branches, and the children—too many to count—made a great show of sneaking them away.

Welcomed into the celebration as a guest rather than a servant of the house, I found a moment when I became truly lost in the levity. Von Amsdorf proved himself a perfect dance partner, going through the steps with the stamina of a man half his age. Luther was attentive with food and drink, and Elsa tugged at my ear more than once to offer gossipy insight. By ten o'clock, the revelers who weren't red-faced from drink were sated with food, and laughter filled the house with a solid mass of mirth.

Despite the frigid air outside, Herr Reichenbach kept the windows open. Not wide and welcoming, but inches each, to allow a bit of cold to cut through the heat of the blazing fires and cool our faces. Winded from dancing, I went to stand near the breeze, refreshed instantly. The tendrils of hair set free from my complicated, looping braids turned to icy strands against my face, and I gulped the air the way I would water.

All at once, the break in the music filled with the sound of welcoming cheer as a new arrival entered the room. My stance had taken me away from its center, tucking me close to the edge, so at first I could not see the object of the gathered guests' warm reception. I craned my head, finding a path of vision, and grasped the windowsill for support.

Herr Baumgartner, looking as sleepy as he ever did; Frau Baumgartner with her bulging eyes scanning the crowd; and behind them, Jerome. He wore a doublet of black velvet, embossed with ornate gold stitching, and a silk hat with a brim that touched the top of his left cheek. If he'd meant the hat to mask his identity, he'd wasted its purpose. Even from this angle, with half of his face obscured, I could see well the strength of his chin, the bearing of his body. The dark curls full at the nape of his neck. His hands—one resting on an ornamental sword—called my senses to attention, bringing heat again, despite the chill of winter on my skin.

Elsa and Herr Reichenbach made their way to offer greetings, a kiss to each cheek, and I burned watching Jerome bend to Elsa. While Frau Baumgartner continued to survey the room, Jerome looked nowhere but straight ahead. If he'd turned, just a portion of a degree, our eyes would have met. As it was, I had only the fortune of meeting his mother's gaze, and nearly withered in its triumph.

My fingers grew numb, whether from the cold or the strength of their grip on the windowsill,

I couldn't say. Such a feeling of unbalance, one hand nearly turned to ice, the other hot and slick with sweat. With each breath, my corset constricted, like a whalebone prison, but I took some comfort in the fact that I was breathing at all.

See me. See me. See me.

And he turned.

His eyes widened in recognition, and even from this distance, I saw the infinitesimal clenching of his jaw. I gasped, aloud—the sound masked by the striking of the minstrels. A tune familiar to us, one to which we'd danced many an evening in this very room. One that allowed our hands to touch, and I wondered which I would offer—my cold one or my hot. That is, if he asked. If he threaded his way through the crowd, begging pardon of the gentlemen who stood in our path. Touching his cap to the ladies, suffering the children with a tousle of their hair.

I brought my hands together, clasped them against my stomach, hoping to bring them to a neutral warmth, so that if I touched him—*when* I touched him—he would have no need to startle away. Before I could squelch the betrayal, my foot took a step in his direction, then another, my roiling body set to follow. By the third step, he was gone. No tipping of his cap, no begging of pardon. Were I to take another step, I would have to run to catch up, even to get close enough to touch his sleeve. But the music played on, and a circle of dancers formed between us, and I would not disrupt their joy to display my sorrow.

The first measure half gone, it was too late to join the dance, and I feared my proximity to the couples made me appear desperate for a partner, so I backed up to the wall, where the open window brought me to a new realization. Of course Jerome would have no such public reunion with me. All that we ever were to each other had been based on secrecy, even when it was a secret of which everyone was well aware. He would not rush across a crowded room to take me in his arms. He would hold to his promise in our place of commitment. In the garden.

If I took the time to go to my room and fetch my cloak, I risked the chance of being followed, questioned, delayed. Instead, I inched my way along the wall, crossed the room, and gave not another glance to the revelers around me. I inhaled sharply with my first step outside, finding the bite of the air enough to bring me to my senses. A light snow fell, and I raised my face to it, feeling the sting of each flake, promising myself there would be no tears.

I could still hear the music and found myself humming, intending to announce my presence, lest any other guests be out here, enjoying the solitude as Jerome and I once did. The snow was powder-soft beneath my feet, and though the weight of my overdress and skirts proved enough to keep me warm, I did regret my shoes, as the silk became damp, then wet. Regardless, I charged on, taking the familiar path through the hedges, past the fountain, toward the farthermost wall where he had waited that last night. Never mind that I walked a carpet of purest white, no steps preceding mine. With each one, my promise broke. One tear, then another. Tasting salt, I swiped my sleeve across my face—quickly, lest he be watching from somewhere.

The silence in that garden, gripped in the dead of winter, rivaled that of the deepest forest. The music and laughter seemed miles away, drowned out by my own beating heart, my own shallow breath, my own soft whisper.

"Please. Father in heaven."

And then, an answer. A message, as clear to me as that spoken to the shepherds in the field. He wasn't coming. Not tonight, not at all. Not for me. I knew as much the moment he looked at me. I knew it on the path when he thundered by. I knew it in the months without a word, on the night he left. My memories had no substance; every word he'd ever said floated as weightless as the flakes swirling around me. What a fool I'd been to believe them.

Now I faced foolishness of a new kind, knowing I had to walk back into the party, my shoes wet, my hair nothing but a mass of dripping tendrils.

At least I had the cold to blame for my red nose and blotchy face, but no way to explain why I'd taken myself away from the warmth within. *A breath of fresh air,* I'd say. *A moment of quiet contemplation.*

The walk back to the house stretched twice as long, and the sound of voices made me drag my steps even more. Guests, it seemed, had followed my lead, gathering in pockets in the courtyard. Listening to the conversations, I heard delighted chatter about the refreshing night air, the beauty of the drifting snow, the merriment of the party. I took a final swipe at my eyes and nose, preparing to join in and say, *Yes, a bracing walk is just the thing to clear one's head.* Straightening my spine, I put on my bravest face for one man in particular who had ventured out into the night.

Luther.

Upon seeing me, he peeled away from the small group held rapt by whatever story he told and came straight for me, creating a blessed barrier between me and the others.

"For you." He offered me a cup of mulled wine. I took it in both of my hands and prayed my grip was strong enough to hold it, as I had no true feeling in either. The first sip warmed me, both the temperature of the wine and the spices. I left the cup balanced on my lips and looked down into its blurry depth. Three more sips before I felt strong enough to face him.

"Is he still here?" I had no reason to clarify.

"No."

"Are his parents?"

"Yes."

Another sip, this one draining the cup by half.

"Did anyone notice? Are they talking about me?"

He chuckled. "Don't worry. You are not the object of everyone's attention tonight."

"Not his, anyway. Did you speak to him?"

"No. He made his greetings to Philipp and Elsa, deposited his parents, and left. It seems he has another social engagement this evening."

"Of course he does." I finished the cup and was rewarded with a pleasant blurring of my thoughts. Immediately, I wished for more.

"Now, come inside." Luther put his arm across my shoulder, meaning to comfort or guide me. Or both. "More wine, more music. Dance with von Amsdorf. Or just stand by the fire. You're like ice."

"I don't want to go back in there."

"You can't stay out here."

"I can do as I please." My words came out more harshly than I'd intended, as I kept my jaw clenched to prevent my teeth from chattering.

"You can; of course you can. But might I suggest you find a place to lie down? You'll make a much more tragic corpse when they find you in the morning."

"Your wit is no longer welcome." I pushed against his chest, but he did not move. "I'm going up to my room. To bed."

"Let me fetch you more wine, to warm you."

"I don't want more wine." I shouldered past him, lifting my skirts as if doing so would speed my steps. Heedless of the curious eyes that followed, I made my way around to the side of the house, where an obscure door led to a back stairway I could take directly to my room.

"Katharina." He followed, hard on my heels. "Kate!" This, louder, once we'd turned the corner. My feet, encased in sodden silk, felt like pointed spears of pain, and he soon had my arm, gripped at its elbow. "Wait."

"No! I don't have to do what you say. I don't have to speak to you. I don't have to listen to you. I owe you nothing, Luther."

"You're right." He dropped my arm, and his voice took a turn to sarcasm. "I only rescued you from—"

"You rescued me from nothing." The anger I felt for Jerome, the humiliation I'd heaped upon myself—I fashioned it all into arrows and fired them with my words. "You aided an escape. And then you . . . you abandoned me."

"Abandoned you? In this fine home, with hosts who have been nothing but generous and gracious to you. Wouldn't I love to tell my friends that you feel abandoned?"

"That's not what I meant."

"Then use your mind to better choose your words." He'd come to the end of his patience, armed with anger of his own.

The side of the house was lined with a privet hedge, grown up to the second-floor windows and groomed into spires. I stepped within, seeking to hide myself from whatever onlookers might follow the sound of our argument, and to my surprise, Luther followed, enclosing us with stone, and green, and snow.

"Forgive me if I'm not perfectly articulate," I said, clearly without repentance.

"I'm not asking for perfection. Only perspective."

"Meaning?"

"Meaning, don't let this fool of a man destroy what we've accomplished."

"I don't think anyone in there would say that *he* is the fool."

"Hold your head up, my girl. Come inside and lift a glass. Indulge me that much."

"You speak as if I owe you."

"You owe me nothing, Kate."

"Oh, but I do." A false sense of courage infused me, a heat generated to stave off the chill that threatened to freeze me into complacent obedience. "I owe you my heart. It's been ripped out and broken, and I owe that to you. Before you—before your *rescue*—I had no idea such pain existed. I had no idea I could walk and talk and die inside. So I owe you that, Luther. I owe you my pain and my humiliation. I owe you my loneliness and my despair. All of that—all of it—I lay at your feet."

He allowed me to speak, long after I'd given him reason to rise up and stop the ugliness I spewed. When I'd depleted myself of words, I erupted in bottomless tears and slumped against his familiar, worn black coat.

"There, there." He patted my back, soothing my childish rage, wisely saying nothing even in his own defense. I clutched at his sleeves, drawing him closer, hating myself more with each sob. Soon I felt his lips, a soft kiss at the top of my brow, and I burrowed deeper.

"Look up," he said, inching himself away. "See how clear the stars are tonight."

I obeyed, as we both knew I would, and marveled at the sight. It was one of those rare moments, a break in the clouds, when the snow seems to appear without a source. The stars formed a silver tapestry behind the dance of pure white.

"Imagine the faith it took to follow a single star. To look up into that vastness of the heavens and focus on a single point of light. And then, to follow."

"I suppose you are my single point of light?"

He was still holding me, but stepped away.

"Christ is the Light we follow, Katie. Our own understanding will fail us. Always. Think how frightened and alone Mary must have felt on this night."

"But she wasn't alone. She had a husband. And child. I have nothing. I have nobody."

"Mary held the Christ within her arms. You hold him within your soul. How much more is that?"

I knew he wanted me to say that it was enough. That my faith would be enough to sustain me for the rest of my days. But I knew what it meant to love someone, and to be loved—the way God designed a man to love a woman. Even if Jerome's love hadn't proved to be lasting, its hold on me was strong, and an emptiness ached within me to find such love again.

"Have you no words of wisdom for me, then? No comfort from the man who endangers his life for truth?"

He looked away, gathering his thoughts, seeming to go far away, and then returned. "You saw our tree in the great hall?"

Our tree. "Yes, of course. It's beautiful."

"Is it more beautiful than these?" He opened his arm expansively, directing me to see the clump of firs in the side yard, and then the towers of green offering shelter.

"It's more festive," I said, determined to have a say in the argument. "Unique from these."

"Ah, yes. But more beautiful? No. These here, in starlight, with the whiteness of snow adorning the branches—these manifest God's creation. His perfection. And they will for years and years, long after our death, if left alone. We brought our tree into a place of celebration. But we've killed it. It will never be what God intended, and his plan, his design, is always best."

"Jerome is a good man. A godly man. Why couldn't he have been God's design for me?"

Luther looked like he had an answer but discarded it with a breath of steam. "I don't know. It is not for us to know. At least not now, but maybe someday you'll see everything more clearly."

Slowly, a sense of peace settled in drifts around me. "If only I'd been able to see this clearly in June."

"In June there are only stars, no snow. Now is the time for grace. As the prophet Isaiah records, *Come now, and let us reason together, saith the Lord: though your sins be as scarlet, they shall be white as snow; though they be red like crimson, they shall be as wool.*"

"Are you saying it was a sin to love him?"

"To love him? No."

Luther made it clear that there were other aspects of our love that could be interpreted as sin, and for that I bowed my head. "Are you to be my confessor?"

"No, as I owe you no forgiveness."

"Then what are you to me, Luther?"

Again he searched for an answer, scrutinizing my face as if to find it there. "Tonight, I am your friend, hoping to help you find a place to reason with the Lord."

"You've helped mightily." Somehow, my voice was even, my breath steady, my chattering gone. And though I'd long ago come to think of Luther as a true friend, in the washing white of Christmas Eve, I first pondered if he could be anything more.

Part VI

Cranach Household, Wittenberg

Winter 1524 – Spring 1525

Chapter 26

Until I came into the home of Lucas and Barbara Cranach, I only thought I knew how grand a house could be. Theirs dwarfed the Reichenbachs' in every way. Two grand halls, one specifically for dancing. One dining room with a table big enough to seat fifty people, and another more intimate one for the household. There was a ladies' parlor, a gentlemen's library, and a room designated for sitting in the morning sun. All of this, and two floors besides, with sumptuous hallways and spacious rooms. Eighteen on the second floor, with the nursery and servants on the third.

Accompanied by Luther, I arrived on the third of January, having celebrated Christmas and the New Year with those I had come to know as family, yet they put up no protest at my leaving. Rather, they made me a gift of a trunk, its lid covered in rich red leather, its hardware shining brass. I'd come to their home with all my belongings in a single drawstring pouch; I left the owner of three dresses, a hairbrush and mirror, a cloak and boots, two pair of shoes, and a host of undergarments besides. To my greater delight, though, I was also given the small writing desk, complete with paper and ink and quills.

"So you can keep in touch with us, dear," Elsa said. Never mind that the ride from her house to the Cranachs' took less than an hour's time.

Still, when I stepped out of the coach in front of this home and watched as the footman retrieved my trunk, I felt nothing but a sense of belonging. I knew how to greet my hosts, how to incline my head, how to hold out my hand. Though penniless, I was not without breeding, and my time spent with a fine family reintroduced what I'd lost during my years in the convent. By now, I was no longer "one of the twelve." My story had expanded beyond that of a former nun, now set free. I brought with me the tragic tale of a love affair, and the heartbreak that came of it. My new hosts knew me to be a teacher, a governess not out of necessity, but as a natural use for my education. I played no instrument, but had developed an appreciation for music as well as the other arts. The paintings displayed in the entry of the Cranach home were some of the finest I'd ever seen, beginning with an image of the magi visiting the Christ child, painted in a style I recognized.

"Appropriate, isn't it?" Cranach said, noticing my admiration. "Seeing as we will celebrate Epiphany in a few days. It was a gift from the artist."

"Dürer?" I said, daring to touch one finger along its edge, as it was displayed on an ornate easel, therefore at a level to do so. I'd never been in proximity to a work so rich in detail and depth. "Albrecht Dürer?"

"He is a rival, but also a friend."

"Rival?"

Barbara Cranach took her husband's arm. "Lucas and Albrecht are known to compete sometimes, for the commissions of the church."

"And royalty," Cranach added with good nature. "Not that I'm boasting."

"Of course not," Luther said. "That would be unchristian of you."

As they spoke, I realized I had seen this man's work. "You did the altarpiece, then? In the little chapel on the Reichenbachs' property?"

He bowed in assent. "I did."

"Oh." This conversation made me all the more conscious of the final belonging that sat on top of all my others in the ornate trunk. My portrait, painted by Christoph the Unknown, and an embarrassment among the fine works in the house. In that moment, I questioned whether or not to allow the piece to see the light of day.

I had become acquainted with the family over several occasions at the Reichenbachs', but I had not realized the depth of the friendship between Cranach and Luther. I knew him to be an artist, and the owner of a respected and lucrative pharmacy—two pursuits that seemed opposite of each other, yet served to meet the needs of both parts of the man. The first, to ensure posthumous fame; the other, contemporary wealth. Cranach himself was a large man, with a great white beard and a presence that disguised the depth of his intelligence. He seemed always to be on the verge of teaching, impatient to extract or explain a new thought. His wife, Barbara, was a gentle soul, quiet and plain in both speech and appearance. I felt an instant ease with them, not only because I'd become more accustomed to society, but because I sensed an opportunity for intellectual challenge.

"My dear," Barbara said, "I hope you will not be insulted that I have you in an adjoined room, but I think you will appreciate who we have staying on the other side."

"Who?" I looked to Luther, wondering just what he hadn't told me.

"An old friend." As he said it, he and the Cranachs turned, and I followed suit, finding a familiar face indeed poked through the doorway.

"Ave!"

Without thought to decorum, I ran to her, arms outstretched, and she to me. We embraced in a way that would never have been allowed at Marienthrone, and for which we'd had no opportunity since leaving. She was familiar, yes, though we'd never been close. Seeing her at this moment, having been so uprooted, brought forth a wave of unprecedented nostalgia. I hugged her with all my strength, and she returned in kind. When we separated, we both had been moved to tears, but laughter won out.

"How is it you are here?" I asked, as if claiming her as a gift meant just for me.

She inclined her head toward Luther. "He brought me here when my family wouldn't take me back."

"You see?" Luther said. "My own wretched apartment is just a few minutes' walk from this place. I need no means for myself. I have rich friends to extend my hospitality for me."

Cranach laughed, giving no hint of false modesty regarding his wealth. He could not, as it sprawled all around us. "We tried to convince him to marry her, but he would have none of it."

Ave looked at me, blushing.

"She is far too sweet for an old *Geizhals* like myself. I'd have her thoroughly corrupted in a matter of weeks."

They all laughed, making it clear this was an old joke, which might explain why I didn't find it amusing. I managed a smile, though, for the sake of camaraderie, and wondered just how serious a campaign Luther had pursued.

"I am engaged to a physician," Ave said, "by Luther's introduction. You'll meet him at supper tonight."

"You will join us too, I hope?" Barbara directed her question to Luther, who looked far too pleased with himself.

"I will, indeed. As I've yet to be known to turn down such an opportunity. But it is early in the day, and I have affairs to tend to in my much-neglected abode. I shall take my leave of you until this evening."

He bowed to me and to Ave, kissed Barbara on the cheek, and offered his hand to Cranach, who shook it with the particular affection of long-time friendship. Once he left, Barbara walked me to my room, with Ave following close behind, giving a running commentary of the fine hospitality awaiting me.

"God has richly blessed us," Barbara said. "It seems only right to extend his gifts."

Her gift extended to my room, twice the size of that at the Reichenbachs', with a sitting area and a blazing fire. My trunk waited at the foot of the bed, but I declined Barbara's offer to have help unpacking it.

"I've just a few things," I said, thinking foremost of the portrait on top.

"Very well, then. I'll leave the two of you to catch up, and I'll have something to eat brought to you."

"Thank you," I said, clasping her hand. "And I won't be a bother. I promise."

"A bother? What a silly idea. You're a friend

of Luther's, so a friend of ours as well. You are welcome to all that we have."

"And they have a lot," Ave said once we were alone. She was still not much more than a girl, and draped herself into one of the fireside chairs in a dramatic display of exhaustion. "To think, I was so upset when my father tossed me out, and he doesn't have *half* the wealth that Cranach does. Probably because he is so tightfisted with it, don't you think? Doesn't it seem that God rewards those who are generous with their wealth? I'll ask Martin tonight at supper."

"Martin?"

"He lets me call him that. Cute, isn't it? He's a sweet man."

"He is, indeed." I opened my trunk and removed the blanket on top. I'd stitched the center panel myself, and folding it with the design on full display, I laid it across the foot of my bed. The bed itself came nearly to my waist, an expanse of feather-stuffed mattress and pillows. Something told me I'd be grateful to crawl into it tonight. "So, did he really propose?"

She giggled. "A dozen times, at least. But never seriously. He's a bit old, don't you think?"

"Not so much. He's just turned forty."

"Forty!" She spoke the word as if it were a disfiguring curse. "I couldn't imagine being with a man as old as that."

"What about your physician? He can't be too young, if he bears such a title."

"He is twenty-eight. And handsome, and perfect." The cut of Ave's dress revealed the white creaminess of her skin, and I had no doubt her doctor, too, described her as perfect. Her face had not lost its wide-eyed innocence, but a new, healthy glow replaced the pallor from which we'd all suffered. Even I could claim such an enhancement, though I could never possess her beauty.

"I look forward to meeting him. How excited you must be."

"I am. Truly, I am. But I heard that you had your share of happiness, too? A torrid romance?"

"Not so happy, and not so romantic." I took the painting, grateful that it was wrapped in canvas, and leaned it against the wall. "God has other plans for me, I think."

"Like what?"

"That is for him to know, I suppose."

"No doubt they include Martin." She was holding my mirror and gazing at herself in the glass. Not with brazen vanity, but the way one would, I suppose, given such a reflection to study. For my part, I was thankful she was too distracted to see my reaction.

"Why would you say such a thing?"

She looked at me over the frame. "Because he knows everybody—in this town and a dozen others. He probably has someone else in mind right now. I wouldn't be surprised if he brings him to supper."

I exhaled, surprised and doubtful at my relief. "I'm quite content to find my own way, thank you. Luther doesn't have exclusive access to God's ear."

"You're right, of course." She emitted an appreciative sound at the first dress I removed from the trunk before continuing. "Now, tell me all about this Jerome Baumgartner."

For the next hour, I did just that. Barbara Cranach had a tray of bread and cheese sent up, along with a small carafe of wine. Ave and I ate and drank and talked as if we were better friends than I recalled. I unburdened myself about Jerome, leaving any details that might besmirch my character carefully concealed. After all, I had no idea where these tales might go from here. So, by the firelight on that winter's afternoon, Jerome Baumgartner became a better man than I'd known. Noble and courtly, reserved in his affection.

"Not one to give an impassioned promise," I assured. "And so, rumors of our connection have been greatly exaggerated. He is a young, handsome, and eligible bachelor. I think people were entranced with the idea of a man such as him marrying a nun, when he could have his pick of any lady in the county."

"My Basi, too, could have any pick," Ave said, pouting.

"Ah, yes. But in you, he has a prize, doesn't he? The youngest, the prettiest." I spoke without grudging her a bit. "I, on the other hand, land squarely in the realm of ordinary on all counts."

"But you are the smartest. No one would deny that."

"True. And the moment God creates a man who values a woman's intelligence above all else, I shall stand in triumph."

"Well—" Ave's thin eyebrows danced, and her eyes darted quickly to the bed and back—"maybe not *stand*."

"You're terrible." But I laughed, as heartily as she did, and made no plans to repent of the thought.

As it turned out, Luther did bring a guest of his own to dinner that night, but it was only von Amsdorf, as eager as Luther to be a part of such company. It was during this supper conversation that I learned the true scope of my host's talents. A celebrated artist, that I knew, but I could not have guessed at the prolific extent of his work. All the countries, all the courts—the noble subjects and honors bestowed upon him. He himself gave no listing, but Luther and von Amsdorf were free with their information and praise, and his Barbara sat to his right, beaming at her husband's accomplishments.

Young Doctor Basilius, Ave's fiancé, contributed his own bits of knowledge, noting how the understanding of anatomy played such a crucial part in the true representation of a subject.

"That's right," Ave said, patting his arm the way Barbara patted Cranach's, as if studying the art of being the supportive wife.

"Well, no doubt your models give you opportunity enough to study," Luther said before stuffing his mouth with a heap of buttered turnips.

"Martin!" Barbara chastised, but with no real anger.

I looked to Luther, curious, but he only chewed, swallowed, and took another gulp of wine.

"As the Church dies, so will its call for art," Cranach said, calmly drinking from his own cup, as if he had not just spoken of the end of the Church. "All these Madonnas. I need newer subjects, newer life."

"So, you return to ancient mythology?" This from Luther, expert at all.

"I am finding the match between my talent and the market. An artist must grow, or he will die."

"Tell us, Katharina," Ave said, "what was the painting you brought with you?"

All eyes turned to me, and I fought to keep my voice steady. "Painting?"

"I saw you take it out of your trunk, and a bit of the canvas slipped. I meant to ask you when we were upstairs, but we got to talking about so many other things." She lifted her eyes to her doctor, reassuring him that he, indeed, had been the object of our conversation.

"Your portrait?" Luther said, and my face burned.

"Who painted you?" Cranach seemed genuinely offended that such an occurrence had happened within his neighborhood, and without his condoning it.

"It's nothing, I assure you. A student spent the summer at the Reichenbach house, and I volunteered to be his subject."

Cranach studied me through narrowed eyes. "I'm sure it's awful."

Had he reached across the table and slapped me, I couldn't have been more shocked at his response. The rest of the table seemed equally astonished, as the only sound was the click of Ave's doctor's knife against his plate.

Only Barbara dared to speak in my defense. "Lucas, what a terrible thing to say."

"It's nothing about her." His tone remained steady, whether he was remarking upon the fall of the Church, the worth of a woman, or the intricacies of geometry. "Fetch it to me after supper, and we'll decide together."

The rest of the meal passed in relative silence,

interrupted by bits of polite conversation about the length of the sleeves at court and the benefits of sleeping with an open window on a winter night. Once Cranach finished his last bite, he dispelled any hope I had that he'd forgotten his directive.

"Really," I protested, "it's not—"

"Forgive my brashness," Cranach said, though I didn't believe his humility, "but I think I am a better judge than anyone here of what the painting is or isn't."

Being a guest, I could hardly refuse what amounted to a direct order, so I excused myself, took a taper from the table, and hoped I would remember the steps to my room. Once there, I found the painting just as I'd left it and whispered a mild curse at Ave for bringing it up in conversation. I untied the string and removed the canvas, deciding the piece had no right to a dramatic unveiling in front of the company.

I took my time walking back, thinking, if nothing else, the party would have a chance to drink another glass of wine in my absence, leaving them less inclined for proper judgment or clear memory. I found they had departed from the dining room and had gathered in the library, where a fire roared in a hearth nearly as tall as me. One stumbling step, and the atrocity could disappear forever.

"Well?" Cranach said, without a hint of mercy.

Slowly, I turned the canvas, revealing to him the image. Me, reclined and searching. My hand lifted in anticipation, wearing the same ring that now glinted in the firelight.

"As I suspected." Then he looked right at me. "You weren't ready for a portrait."

"You mean the artist wasn't ready," von Amsdorf said, ever the diplomat. "Fräulein looks quite lovely, I think, but the perspective . . . It seems as if the proportions—"

"It's nothing to do with perspective and proportions. Look at her." Cranach turned to me. "Were you happy in this moment? Relaxed?"

"It was more than just a moment, Herr Cranach. It was days—"

"I know it spanned days, but was there a moment, any moment during the course of the painting, when you felt truly content? At ease?"

"I suppose." But Cranach's gaze brought out the truth. "Not really. I hadn't quite . . . settled."

"There are only two types of people who should be painted. The powerful and the innocent. With the first, their confidence overcomes their flaws. The second? They don't know enough to be self-conscious."

"How can you say she's not an innocent?" Ave asked. "She was a nun."

"Innocence has nothing to do with virtue," Cranach said, directing his reassurance to me.

"And so, when you painted Martin all those years ago?" Barbara said, her voice lilting in a show of levity. "Which was he?"

"You painted Luther?" I asked, instinctively looking around for the evidence.

"It hangs in his studio," Luther said. "Until I have a home with walls worthy enough for a Cranach."

Cranach offered no argument. "You were young but powerful. Even then. Even though you were still a monk, you had all the strength you would ever need. You can see it."

"I thought that was due to your skill as an artist," Luther said.

"That's what I want all my subjects to think. But it's not the case."

"Tell me," I said, desperate to end the conversation, "what should I do with this? Shall I make it a gift to you, Luther? Is it sufficiently horrible to earn a space on your poor wall?"

My little joke was rewarded with laughter all around, even mine, though I looked at the painting in a way I never had before. All of my uncertainty was there, revealed in my uneven expression, the strain in my pose. Perhaps Christoph had been underestimated in his artistry.

"Keep it," Luther said. "My ragged rooms are no place for a woman."

"We'll have it framed," Barbara said, "and hang it in the hall outside of your room. I think there's a loveliness to it. Lucas simply cannot bear the thought of competition."

The clock struck ten, and Cranach insisted his guests—Luther, von Amsdorf, and Doctor Basilius—spend the night rather than venture out into the cold.

"Wouldn't want your corpses on my conscience," he said, "though I'd wager you've had enough of my wine to keep you from freezing."

Later—hours later, in fact, well past midnight—I'd stripped to my chemise and sat on the edge of my bed. Having unpinned the braids, I brushed my hair, smoothing the strands against my hand. The sound was soft and rhythmic, so close to my ear that I questioned whether or not I heard a soft knock at my door. Once I held the brush suspended, though, the knock became clear. Quiet, but intentional. Ave, no doubt, as I'd chased her from my room a few minutes before, despite her protest of wanting to stay up and talk about "our men." To send a message that I was ready for bed, I tucked my hair inside my sleeping cap and tied it loosely beneath my chin.

The knocking continued, even as I reached the door's latch, and to my surprise I opened the door to find Luther's hand poised, midair, an inch away from my nose.

"What are you doing here? It's late." I stretched my neck to look up and down the hallway, then attempted to shut the door.

"Wait."

He wedged his shoulder against the jamb, leaving me no choice but to open the door wider and step back. As conscious as I was about the state of my undress, I knew he saw me in mostly darkness, as the fire had burned down to mere embers, the room lit only by a lone taper on the side of my bed.

"This isn't right, you being here."

"Do you think I've come to ravish you?"

I leaned forward, sniffed, and stood back. "I think you're drunk."

"Well, in that, you may be correct. But on a cold winter's night, in the home of a generous host with an endless cellar—"

"And an endless thirst." I leaned against the edge of the door. "What do you want, Luther?"

"To correct a wrong. A grievous insult."

"And what would that be?"

"Your portrait. I wouldn't want you to think, wouldn't want you to misunderstand, that it wouldn't be welcome."

"You've offered no offense."

"Not merely the portrait. I cannot bring a woman—a wife—into my home."

"As far as I know, no one's asked you to."

He relaxed, reached out, and touched the hair that had sprung free from my cap. "It's grown long."

"It has."

He may have wanted to say more, perhaps about the time that had passed since we met, and how it might be measured in weeks or months, or maybe by the dark strands spilled across my shoulder. His eyes held some message never spoken before, and not to be spoken this night, because the moment I sensed its prelude, it disappeared.

"Have you ever noticed, Fräulein von Bora, that you smile off to one side of your face?"

"Why, no, *Herr Doktor* Luther. I have spent very little time in study of my own reflection."

"It's a most curious thing. I wonder, sometimes, if you do not try to take yourself away from confrontation. And thus—" he touched a finger to my lips and traced it to the center of my cheek—"your very mouth is trying to escape."

I moved my face away, exaggerating my sideways smile. "I admit to staying silent when prudence calls for it, but my mouth, sir, has never run from confrontation. When I speak, I speak my mind, and speak it straight."

"Then, perhaps, on occasion, a hand has been brought up to strike your cheek for your mouth's impertinence?"

He spoke with such soft humor, I could not take offense at the hint of violence. I stood straighter, folded my arms, and addressed him in mock challenge. "I assure you, sir, were there such an occasion, the owner of that hand would be gazing up at me from the flat of his back, with the print of my knuckles square on his jaw."

Luther hooted in response, reminding me of his state of inebriation. "It makes me wonder, then, should you be in full conversation, if one were to perfect his timing, he could aim for a chaste kiss to the cheek—" he leaned in as if to do so—"but find himself infinitely more rewarded."

I leaned a little closer too. "That man would suffer the same consequences as he who would wish to strike me."

"Such brutality from a woman so recently quitted from the veil."

"Such flirtation from a man who spent his youth copying Scripture."

We'd come to an impasse of wit, and as I knew his attentions to be evidence of his intoxication, I refrained from any further coquettish display.

"Have you anything else to tell me, Luther?"

"Only this. That Baumgartner is a fool, and I will see to it that you are happy in this life."

"You do me a great honor to take on such a task. Perhaps you'll think better of it after a good night's sleep."

"Perhaps."

He offered a gracious bow and backed away, wishing me pleasant dreams as if I were a child. I closed the door and leaned against it, guarding myself against a sudden return, but knowing I would welcome his company. No matter the drink, no matter the hour, these truths remained: Luther had looked at me with eyes I'd never seen before. He spoke in a voice I'd never heard, and touched me in a way I could never have imagined in all our times together. With tenderness not paternal in nature. With passion not rooted in religion. And here I stood, a new reaction struck within me. My pulse unsteady, my breath shallow, and something like a giant needle stabbed into the base of my spine. Were I Ave, with her youth and vitality, I might ascribe my visceral reaction to that of a woman newly in love.

But this was fear.

Chapter 27

My life had always been constrained into seasons of learning. As a small girl, I learned I was stronger than anyone could have imagined, that my brothers' age and size and ferocity proved no match to my own. In the brief years I knew my mother, I learned to love—fiercely and completely. I don't know that any woman would have been suitable to take her place in my eyes, and certainly not the monster Papa brought into our home. And so, just as I learned to love, I learned to guard myself, to not be taken in and told to love simply because some authority insisted I do so. It was that lesson, that balance of love and antipathy, two scales swinging from my father's shoulders, with which I would determine to love or not love, follow or not follow every person and path in my life to come.

At Brehna I simply learned—to read adequately, and to cipher, and the catechism of our faith. I memorized passages of Scripture, recited the prayers of the Church, unburdened my young soul to a confessor, and paid my penance without complaint. It is also where I became a sneak and a liar—neither of which I would ever claim as sin, not in the confessional or on my knees at night. I lived with hidden pockets and noisy shoes and endless hope that Papa would come and fetch me home. Even with the new mama I hated, even with the brothers who treated me with disregard. Filtered prayers would go unanswered, God's instruction came with pain, and only friends would save me.

At Marienthrone I became a leader, seeking my own salvation and orchestrating the escape of my fellow sisters. To hear Luther tell it, I've been known to blush and downplay my part. But in my heart I've always recognized my role. I might never speak of it aloud, willing to publicly share the accomplishment with Girt, Ave, and the others. Even with Hans and Luther himself. But God gave me a certain spark. I learned to nurture it, let it grow, and let it blaze a path—for all of us, certainly. However, had I been alone, I would have considered my escape no less a victory.

In the Reichenbach home, I learned to be a woman. To dance and eat meals with multiple courses and conversations. I stitched and read poetry and learned to dress in a way that flattered my figure and my complexion and my youth. More than any of this, of course, I learned to love in the way God designed a woman to love. Headstrong, unafraid—leading myself into the trap, clawing myself out with tears, and all with a facade worthy of a game at cards.

None of this, though, made me a complete being. Not until I became a fixture in the Cranach house did I learn what I would need for survival and success. Barbara Cranach ran a complicated household with a large staff, and under her tutelage I learned to do the same—keeping the pantry stocked, drafting the budget, dispensing salaries, and collecting rent from many of their family holdings.

In addition to his commissioned paintings, Cranach made a lucrative business of selling prints from his woodcuts, and I often aided in those transactions—recording orders, negotiating with the printers, and securing delivery. This I liked best because it gave me occasion to venture into Cranach's studio, a cavernous room on the third floor with windows that allowed it to be filled with bright, natural light. I'd pick my way through the unfinished canvases propped against the wall, gingerly peeking at one image behind another. Some abandoned because of Cranach's temperament, others because a client failed to pay a fee. While no one could argue his artistic genius, neither could one ignore the fact that he capitalized on the value of his talent. I thought of poor Christoph, struggling and devoid of skill, living off the generosity of patrons and friends, destined to live out his days in some bedraggled attic.

If I confessed truly to myself, though, I would

have to admit that I took advantage of any excuse to go into Cranach's studio because there hung the portrait of Luther. The man himself had been a rare guest at the house—fewer than one visit a week, and then nothing beyond polite conversation at supper and an exit into the evening. Neither of us ever spoke of his late visit to my room, how he talked about my lips and touched my hair. Part of me hoped he didn't remember; having not experienced true intoxication, I could not say what havoc a night of imbibing would have on a morning's memory. He'd left by the time I came down from my room the next morning, and when next I did see him, he clearly remembered every word. I knew this because he spoke so few, and wouldn't look squarely at me when he did so.

And so, on my visits to Cranach's studio, on whatever trivial excuse I could find to make the journey, I would stand patiently, waiting for his attention, and study the portrait. Though it had been painted just a few years before, it clearly testified to the physical toll of Luther's campaign. The man in the portrait shared Luther's humor, with his full lips poised to upturn in a smile, but there was no hint of the strain that often crept into his countenance. Cranach's thin brush had captured each of Luther's whiskers—an ever-present shadow—and the nuanced brown of his eyes. The cap rendered in oil might be the same ratty one he wore in summer, and the brown curls beneath it had grown longer and lighter.

"Not so handsome a devil, is he?" Cranach said one day, catching me in study.

"No more or less than most other men," I said, surprising us both with my defensiveness.

"Do you think him more handsome here? Or in his living flesh?"

I evaded the directness of the question. "He's younger here."

"It's how I remember my friend, before all of this—" He waved his hand, still clutching a brush, as if clearing the consequences of Luther's actions with a single broad stroke.

I looked back at the painting, closer, since I had no reason to hide my scrutiny. I could see it, the affection, the friendship. Luther's eyes looked away, dreaming at something far off. Christoph had attempted the same such gaze in my portrait—to a far lesser success. But what had been my feigned vision? A feckless lover? Much as I maligned Christoph's skill, my greater shame came from knowing what I'd been thinking, feeling, wanting at the time he touched the paint to the canvas.

But Luther. In his eyes—unfocused and far off as they were—he held his future. His passion and intelligence. The seed of rebellion planted within a field of composure and faith.

• • •

Ave married her doctor in the spring—late May, to be exact, just weeks after marking the first anniversary of our escape from Marienthrone. Luther officiated, looking every bit as comfortable standing at the front of *Stadtkirche* as he ever looked sitting at a supper table, or in front of a fire, or under a snow-filled sky. I stood as a maid of honor, and von Amsdorf as a groomsman—as if we were all lifelong friends and not acquaintances thrown together through the machinations of the minister performing the ceremony.

Barbara Cranach had been giving me a small living allowance, in recompense of my position in the house. I could not afford a new gown for the occasion, but I managed to set aside a portion each week until I'd saved enough to purchase a new forepart to wear with my green gown. It was stitched with the colors of spring, winding vines and roses, and held the distinction of being the first garment I had ever purchased for myself. In the year's time, my hair had grown. Dark and thick, it fell below my shoulders, and I understood for the first time why it was called both a crowning glory and a covering. I wore it braided and pinned, with a simple cap befitting my place.

Though I arrived at the church that morning feeling, for the first time since Jerome's declaration of love, pretty, I was no match for the vision coming down the aisle. Ave, wearing a gown the color of a fresh quince with sleeves that draped to the floor and a train that swept behind her steps, moved like a ray of sun within the high gray walls of the chapel. Her blonde hair had been fashioned into spiraling curls, then pinned with intertwining jewels in a fashion I had never before seen. A gossamer veil draped over it and fell prettily on her shoulders. How cruel it would be to have kept such loveliness confined beneath the white woolen veil of a nun. More so to deny the young man standing opposite me the opportunity to see such a vision and know that he would wrap it in his arms and live with its beauty forever.

I hazarded a glance at Luther, who smiled in a paternal fashion, and another over at von Amsdorf, who seemed appropriately impressed. Ave came up alongside her groom, and they knelt in prayer, reverent to Luther's speech.

"When God spoke life into the first man, Adam, he knew it would not be good for man to be alone. So he created Eve, and designed with his holy hand the gift of marriage."

Luther's voice echoed in the cavernous chapel; he spoke as if each pew were filled with his followers, listening in rapt attention—a common scenario on days he preached from this pulpit. In reality, there were few in attendance. Besides those of us standing at the altar, a smattering of guests looked on. Ave's parents had softened in their displeasure, though her mother wept openly throughout the ceremony, and her father never did unfold his arms. The good doctor was well represented in friends, as evidenced by the gathering of distinguished men sitting off to one side. Finally, to my greatest delight, Girt—enormous with child—and her Hans slipped into the back row. I could feel her joy reach up the entirety of the aisle.

Luther spoke Scripture, the bride and groom spoke vows, and I half-listened, too caught up in my own reverie to take account of the promises spoken. In a little more than a year, I had transformed from a woman who never envisioned this ceremony for herself to one who accepted its invitation to one who recognized it as a fruitless pursuit. I would never be a vision of innocence like Ave, or a woman content with a simple farm life as Girt seemed to be. I longed for society beyond my means and responsibilities beyond my gender. My happiest moments were spent in spirited discourse, a mutual challenging of ideas. How many times had Luther chided me about my tongue, saying no man wanted a woman who could slice him to the quick with little more than a word?

"A continual dropping in a very rainy day and a contentious woman are alike," he'd said,

quoting the proverb. This on one of his rare visits the past winter, late February, when we'd been debating the merits of overt generosity in lieu of prudent saving and investment.

"But why must a difference of opinion be defined as contentious?" I'd asked.

"By its very definition," he'd said, declaring the subject closed.

"But, then, wouldn't a contentious man be equally unbearable?"

"I suppose a contentious woman would say so."

Invariably he compared me to Ave, not on our differences in age and beauty, but comportment and presence.

"Note how she listens to every word the man says," he observed once. Our heads were inclined toward each other's, watching Ave and her fiancé discuss the priorities in furnishing their future home. "How she allows him to speak to the tail end of a sentence before racing in with her own thought."

"Yes," I'd concurred in mock admiration, "and even more delightful is the fact that her own thoughts are mere diminutive versions of his own."

Now, beside me, the bride's and groom's words indeed echoed each other. Vows of fidelity, of strength and protection. And love. Somehow God had brought together two perfect strangers and, in a matter of months, joined their hearts to beat for a single lifetime. In all of creation, I could imagine no greater miracle.

Afterwards, when they were declared man and wife in the eyes of God and all the witnesses, we—von Amsdorf, Luther, and I—followed them down the aisle, though I peeled off before exiting the church to wrap my arms around dear Girt—to the extent that my arms would reach.

“I see you’ve wasted no time.” My chiding was soft and, to her credit, brought no blush to Girt’s cheek.

“We’re hoping for a boy, of course. Hans already has a list of farm chores for him to do.”

I offered a kiss to Hans and issued an invitation that they join us at the Cranachs’ for the reception supper and celebration.

“You don’t think they’ll mind, do you?” I inquired of Luther over my shoulder. “It’s just two more people. There’ll be plenty.”

“The way this one eats, more like four.” Hans attempted to put an affectionate arm around Girt’s shoulder, then laughed when she elbowed him away.

Luther came to the same conclusion, that the Cranach household was one resplendent with hospitality, and the presence of these good people would be welcome at any cost. I instructed them to simply follow the wedding party in its walk to the house, but lingered with Luther at the church door. It was a sight to see, how the celebration continued on the steps and into the street as passersby recognized a wedding party and sang out blessings and well-wishings. They took fruit and bread from their shopping baskets and handed it to the parade of guests—contributions to the wedding feast. Little girls reached tentative hands toward Ave's dress and were allowed to lift the train from off the street and follow her all the way to the Cranachs' house, where they would receive a small cake as a reward. Had I such an opportunity as a child, to touch my hand to such elegance, to participate in a ceremony of such joy, I never would have allowed myself to be given over to a life that would deny its quest. I knew these girls with their grubby hands and silken braids would dream of nothing else but to be a bride. Even I could not escape its allure, though I'd lost an entire year and a portion of my innocence to chase it.

"Shall we?" Luther offered his arm.

I nodded and took it, mindful of how he paused at the door.

"Do you remember that night, still?" I asked, following his gaze to the doors closed behind us, their heavy wood still marked by his nails.

"Such a reckless act."

"Does courage not necessitate a certain heedless temperament? What if you'd waited until morning? What if you'd given it one more night's sleep?"

He didn't answer, as I knew he wouldn't. Luther preferred to communicate in facts, not hypotheticals, but I hadn't posed the question for his benefit. Rather, it served as a residual, haunting regret of my own lost happiness. What if Jerome had stepped away from his parents at the Reichenbachs' Christmas party and fulfilled his promise? What if he'd posted any of the dozens of letters I imagined he wrote, only to discard them in a fit of uncertainty? What if—as Marina hinted—he had taken me away from the garden that night? Such abandon then would mean stability now. My own husband, my own home, perhaps my own child growing within this emptiness.

"Tell me something, Luther." We began our walk to the Cranachs' home, a short distance through streets that were bustling at midmorning. "Do you truly believe what God said—that it was not good for man to be alone?"

"I believe every word of God," he said, his attention divided between my conversation and his acquaintances.

"Do you think it applies to women as well as men?"

"More so. As women are the weaker sex. Their lives can only be enhanced by marriage."

We walked, my hand resting lightly on his arm, and I wondered what people might make of us. Strangers in the street offered me greetings, blessings on my day, and I knew their friendliness had root in my association. Nobody, I'm sure, thought me to be his wife. The marriage of Martin Luther would have been an event to be recognized in every household from pope to pauper. Clearly, though, I was seen as his equal, perhaps in a way I never would if we were bound in any way other than mutual esteem.

"Would you have married him, Kate?" The question came with the ease of conversation, though we hadn't spoken for several steps. And we hadn't spoken of him since Christmas.

"Yes. I would have."

"Because you loved him?"

"What other reason?"

"Oh, you know as well as I that there are other reasons."

"Especially for a woman, I suppose?"

"For a man, too."

And we walked. I had no desire to quarrel today, not on an occasion so joyous. So I made a small sound of agreement.

"Do you want to be married?"

At the moment he asked, I stumbled. Ostensibly because I struck my foot against a stone, but then I might not have done so if I'd had all my senses engaged in my steps. Instead, every part of my body below the ears that heard his question went numb, and I relied on his strength to hold me up, because I could no longer trust my grip on his arm.

"What did you—?"

"Oh, not to me, of course." He laughed, deeming the misunderstanding a trifle. As if in a divided second of time my future hadn't been secure.

"Oh," I said, my composure as unstable as my step. "I only thought—"

"I meant, as a theoretical state. Do you want to be married? Would you want to be someone's wife?"

"God said it is good that I do so."

"Yes, yes." He held my arm tight, still. Guiding my steps closer to his. "But is it what *you* want? Do you think it would make you happy? Would you have been happy with young Baumgartner? Don't you think by now you would have run out of things to say to each other?"

I smiled. "There are many ways for a couple to communicate."

"Saucy girl. Now, answer my question. Is it the desire of your heart to be married?"

"It is." Never before had I been so grateful to be in a public place. We shared the street with a multitude of people, and for all they knew, we were discussing the pattern of the clouds against the sky.

"And do you still harbor feelings for the young man? Or is your heart open to the affections of another?"

"I have no claim to Jerome, and no control of my heart, other than to love God."

"But you've heard nothing from him?"

"From Jerome? Nothing. From God? He speaks to me in *der Krimskrams*. Bits and pieces here and there, telling me to listen. And wait. And trust him to meet all of my needs."

"And you need a husband."

It was a statement, not a question. Whether its truth came from God's command or Luther's sense of duty, I could not tell.

"Someday, maybe," I said. "But for now I am content."

"Are you?" He didn't believe me either.

"I've been working with the gardener, preparing the soil to plant. He's given me my own corner. I also have my own pig to raise, and their cook is teaching me too. More than just roasting hazelnuts. Next time you come for dinner, I'll prepare something for you. I think you'll be impressed."

"So, you're preparing yourself to be a lady of some great house, then?"

I laughed. "Or the wife of a pig farmer."

"Perhaps a great pig farmer."

"If he were kind, and he loved me, I could ask for no more."

We'd arrived at the Cranachs', and I sensed my steps slowing. I didn't want to go in. Despite the feasting that awaited, the music and the dancing and the laughter and games, I knew the minute we walked through the door I'd be pulled away. Or he'd be pulled away. No doubt, a handful of guests among the horde came to celebrate a wedding as an excuse to see the fugitive monk who had called the Church to task. To me, though, he held no celebrity. I'd grown comfortable with his presence beside me. Our conversations and comfortable silence. I wanted a few more minutes, a few more steps. An afternoon, or more. More.

I didn't want to lose him to those less deserving.

I didn't want to lose him at all.

Chapter 28

But I did lose him.

I lost him to the summer, with its long days and mild evenings—time for him to travel to neighboring towns and villages, where emerging Protestants called for his teaching. I lost him to the pulpit and the hours dedicated to preparing the sermons he preached behind it. I lost him to his friends, who called upon him to be the guest in their homes and at their tables, who kept him as a hostage of hospitality for weeks at a time. I lost him to his enemies, those who saw his journeys, his teaching, his fellowship as a threat to not only the Church, but his loyalty to our country. I lost him to the Scriptures and the hours spent toiling in translation.

Most of all, I lost him to himself.

For me, he became a fleeting shadow. Cordial and proper. Almost paternal. Talking to Luther became something like talking to a priest on the other side of the confessional screen. Only, instead of listing my sins, I listed my accomplishments from the time since our last visit. I learned how to coax the sweetness out of berries too tart for strudel. I survived the butchering of my first hog. I completed my reading of the Gospel of Mark and prayed for the time when all who had a desire to read it could do so.

Nothing reached him. He remained passive and polite—frustratingly so—and distant in a way he hadn't been since he first handed me down from the wagon in Torgau.

By autumn, Barbara Cranach and I had become close friends, and I asked her if she'd noticed a change in Luther's demeanor.

"With me, I mean." We were working side by side, bundling herbs to dry. It never ceased to amaze me how a mistress of so fine a house as this dedicated herself to any task at hand.

"He's a mercurial one, that man is," she said, wrapping a bunch of basil with thin brown twine. "Always has been: bold one moment, and then the next—like he's realized just how far afield he's gone. His followers don't like to think he has a weakness of any kind, but he does. He has fears, just as we all do."

I gathered a fresh bunch of the herb and smelled its sweetness. Unable to resist, I pinched off a leaf, put it in my mouth, and bit down, hoping the freshness would flavor my words—conveying my questions while masking my intent.

"Is he afraid of me, do you think?"

"Of you? Why should he be?"

"Not of me, completely, but of what he might . . . *feel* for me?"

It was the first I'd spoken aloud of such a possibility, and if nothing else I owed Barbara Cranach a debt of gratitude for not bursting into laughter at the thought.

"He cares for you a great deal," she said. "I know that."

"I know that too. I've always thought of him as a dear friend."

"And he thinks of you as the same."

"Yes." I took the length of twine she gave me and began twisting it.

"But you wonder if there could ever be more between you?"

"Yes."

"Would you like there to be?"

A pause. "Yes." I swallowed the basil, felt it catch in my throat, making it impossible for me to say anything more in the moment.

"We've all said that he should marry. That he cannot speak out against imposed celibacy on the clergy while he himself abides by it. I can't imagine you wouldn't make as fine a wife as anybody. I can have Lucas speak to him, if you like. Make your case."

"No!" Thankfully, I'd swallowed the herb, or I might have choked on it before stopping her. "I would never want that—to be an obligation. I only wondered if—"

"If he cares for you?" Her kind eyes sparkled with the question, and I knew for a moment what it must feel like to have a mother.

"Something like that, yes."

"Oh, my girl." She set aside her task. "Think of all that is in our Martin's head and heart. His life is a gift to so many people. He doesn't live with the same luxury that we do, finding our own path. He's forging a path for . . . for everybody. Those who will love and follow him, as well as those who won't. Left to his own devices, I wouldn't be surprised if he never marries, only because he cannot justify the time to pursue a woman in courtship. But for you, there'd be no pursuit, would there?"

The grin that accompanied her question was almost wicked, and I felt the color rising on my cheeks.

"I like him," I said, in some attempt to maintain my composure and pride. "That is all. And I suppose I was worried that I'd done something to make him uncomfortable. Because he's seemed ill at ease of late. I wouldn't want to be a distraction."

"Well, if it's any comfort, I don't know that you could be a distraction."

I said nothing, because her words weren't a comfort at all. Only proof of what I suspected: that Luther saw me as nothing more than any other person—man or woman—who supped at his elbow and sat across from him by the fire, listening to his teaching and searching out his wisdom.

"Please," I said, touching my idle hand to her sleeve, "say nothing to him—to anyone—about this conversation? Sometimes the spinster in me gets ideas, and I don't think about the consequences of sharing them. Having spent so many years in silence, I suppose I haven't mastered the art of casual conversation."

She smiled at my little joke, though she was far too intuitive to accept the truth of it. "I shall be like a stone. Your confidence, unbreakable."

It was a crisp, cold night in late October when I first had reason to question Barbara's fealty. Luther arrived, late afternoon, hours before supper and invited to stay—a familiar pattern. I hadn't seen him since voicing to Barbara the truth of my affections, so I well understood the knots in my stomach. My confession to her served as a confession to myself, and seeing him in this new light gave him a glow that made it impossible to look either at him or away.

"Herr Luther." I greeted him with a dip of my head and a dip of my knees. More formal than necessary, but a fitting cover for the imbalance I felt. An excuse to avert my eyes. When I did look up, as I had to, he was glancing away. Equally formal.

"Fräulein." Not *Kate*, and he spoke as if we were being introduced for the first time.

Throughout the evening, he conversed around me, as if obeying some silent instruction to include me. He was kind. And polite. Complimentary of my cooking, but refusing seconds, even though the last time he'd eaten my *Semmelknödel*, he'd challenged von Amsdorf to a duel of Scripture memory for the last one. Von Amsdorf bested him with a recitation of the entire Sermon on the Mount, as recorded in the Gospel of Matthew, and looked about in triumph as he ate the dumpling that had long grown cold during the contest. Luther had moped and made me promise to make the dish again upon his next visit. Shortly after our overly formal greeting, I'd excused myself to the kitchen, doubling my ingredients to fill the shallow bowl that now sat—half full—in front of him.

"Not hungry?" I prodded, looking from the *Semmelknödel* to him.

"Perhaps later." He spoke distractedly, as if it weren't already nine o'clock.

He did, however, avail himself of a third glass of wine, and a fourth; and once, in a brief moment when the glass was not in his hand, we caught ourselves both staring at the dancing reflection of the flames in the cut glass. For me, at least, it seemed like Luther and I were the only ones at the table, consumed in a careful avoidance.

"It's late," I said, pushing my chair from the table.

"Might I speak with you first?" Luther exchanged a look with Cranach and Barbara that assured me there was some secret being kept. The apprehension that had plagued me since his arrival turned into a spark of hope.

"You can speak to me as much as you like." I attempted to make my voice light. "It might make for a nice change to the evening."

He met my quip with silence, then asked if we couldn't go into the front room.

"What could you possibly have to say that you couldn't say in front of our hosts?"

"Not all revelations require an audience." This from Cranach, who displayed no hint of curiosity.

"There's a fire laid," Barbara said, her expression inscrutable, leaving me no closer to knowing if I should feel suspicion or hope.

Luther downed the last of his wine and, perhaps as nothing more than a gesture of goodwill, took a dumpling with his bare fingers and popped it—whole—in his mouth.

Because this house was, by now, as much a home to me as anything, I needed no escort to the front room. I led the way myself, saying nothing until I had occasion to thank him when he invited me to sit in the ornate high-backed chair before the roaring fire.

I spoke first, having grown impatient with his reticence. "Is everything all right?"

"It is, I believe. Or it will be, God willing."

"Don't be cryptic, Luther. I've had enough of secrets in my life."

"Ah, Kate. Forthright as ever." His response was patient, indulgent, and brimming with protection. "That quality gives me hope that you'll forgive me for what I've done."

I turned to ice despite the fire and sat back. Waiting.

"I took it upon myself to bring a certain matter to a close."

"What certain matter?" Though I knew.

"I wrote a letter to your young man."

"I don't have a young man, unless there's something else you're not telling me."

Indulgence, again. "Baumgartner."

"It's been over a year." I fought for calm. "Why would you—?"

"He spoke you a promise. And as far as I know, he's never formally rescinded it. Unless there's something else *you're* not telling *me.*"

"You know I've told you everything. I tell you everything."

"Yes." He spoke the word as if a burden.

"Can I expect the same from you?"

He shifted his weight and stared into the flames. They transformed his face into shadows, their *hiss* and *pop* filling in momentarily for words. "I wrote to him, demanding an answer on your behalf."

"On my behalf." I couldn't look up, couldn't lift my head under the weight of humiliation. Of course I knew Jerome's answer. I'd known it since Christmas. I'd known it, really, since the night he left me in the garden. *Please, God. Let this be the last I suffer this rejection.* I returned to my unanswered question. "Why would you do this?"

"Because I had to know."

A bitter laugh escaped me. "I could have told you."

"I had to know for myself. I told him there might be others—"

My head snapped up to look at him. "Others?"

"One other, I'd say."

I didn't speak. Couldn't speak, for fear the sharpness of my tongue would slice the ribbon of promise wrapped around his words.

"I couldn't very well encourage a suitor—any suitor—to court you if there was a previous understanding. No matter how tremulous."

"Tremulous? Jerome's proposal would need to strengthen itself tenfold to be tremulous. Looking now, it seems . . . silly." But I couldn't delay the inevitable. "Did he respond?"

"He did." Luther took my hand in a warm, dry grip, telling me everything I needed to know.

"Well, then." Unwanted, unwarranted tears

spilled from the corners of my eyes, and I took one hand away to wipe them with the back of my wrist. "Whatever shall I do with my dowry? There's enough to buy a good goat, at least."

"Don't forget, Kate. I asked not only on your behalf, but on behalf of another."

"Ah, yes." My tears stopped. "The other suitors." I gave emphasis to the plural.

"If there were another—just one other, mind you—with whom I feel you would be suited . . . do you think you could open your heart to such a man?"

"My heart is open to the Lord's direction," I said, trying to shrink beneath the formality of his words.

"Even if I warn you this man is no aesthetic match for Baumgartner? He is well beyond youth, and a few degrees from handsome."

"Isn't it possible that you are judging him too harshly?" I wanted to touch him, my palm to his soft face, velvet with whiskers and flushed with wine.

"Time will tell, my Kate. Time will tell."

I could tell you now, I thought. *Ask me.*

But Luther was in the midst of his own thoughts, and despite our earlier conversation, they seemed to exclude me. I joined him in his silence, feeling welcomed to do so, and stole only occasional glances at his face, finding it far more pleasant in its shadows than I had only moments before. After a time Cranach and Barbara joined us, and I had to chastise myself for resenting their company in front of their own fire. They came with glasses of port, which I would normally decline, but everything about me felt so sharp, I needed its softening effect.

"Seems we'll be seeing our first frost of the winter tonight," Barbara said, obviously sensing a need to fill the hearth with conversation. "Are you sure you won't stay the night with us, Martin?"

"Thank you," Luther said, "but no. I've work to tend to. Preparations to make." At this he looked at me rather meaningfully. "Besides, if I were to become too accustomed to your hospitality, I might never be content in my own cold room again."

"I'll send a man ahead with some firewood," Barbara said, and before Luther could protest, she'd jumped up from her seat and gone off to find him.

I knew at the same moment, a servant was in *my* room, laying a fire—a luxury I'd be loath to give up for any circumstance other than my own bed in my own home, preferably shared with a husband. And as of the last hour, the possibility of that husband being the man who sat across from me now. The port settled in my belly, a pooling warmth, bringing with it a contented drowsiness that bade me stare into my glass rather than lift it again to my lips.

"Very generous, and thank you," Luther said to Cranach, who waved off the expression of gratitude as if insulted by its offer.

"Can't have the great Luther frozen in his bed," Cranach said. "Those who thirst for an end to your life would find it far too inauspicious."

"This is hardly a fatal chill. We've been colder, haven't we, Katie?"

The intimacy of the question caught me off guard and ignited heat enough to turn ice to steam upon my skin. But then, we'd shared experiences, hadn't we? Not together, not concurrently, but we both knew what it was to be consecrated to a life devoid of even the most basic of human comforts. To sleep on hard mattresses in cold rooms, with empty stomachs and burdened hearts—all the while thinking it a sin to ask for more.

"Indeed." I took a sip of wine, relishing the taste of luxurious rebellion on my tongue.

"When I was a little boy," Luther said, "and I would complain to my father about being cold in the night, he would tell me to fold my body as if kneeling in prayer. To clasp my hands and breathe upon them . . ."

The Holy Ghost lives within you.

The flames touched a dry pocket in the wood, sending a loud *pop* and shooting of sparks as

Luther's words and my thoughts found each other in perfect unison.

"Imagine his fire," Luther said, somewhat amused at the timing, "warming your body through your very blood. He may not give you a second blanket, but his strength can double the weight of the one you lay under."

Only ask it, and it will be given.

Beyond my power, I'd spoken this last line aloud, garnering Luther's full attention.

"Your father is a wise man," Cranach said, his face buried in his cup, oblivious to the realization coming to life before him.

Luther knew, too. He must. He regarded me in that way he had when puzzling, and I well knew the pieces he was fitting together. Calculating the dates. A child at Brehna. How many years ago? Sixteen? Seventeen? A child with a stepmother. A quick wit and brazen tongue. Defiant of the rules, and—

"So," he said, with a tone acknowledging we'd come to the conclusion together, "we met long ago, did we, Katie?"

"It would seem."

"And did you follow my father's advice?"

"Many nights."

"But not tonight. For tonight, we shall be warm in our beds, thanks to the kindness, hospitality, and generosity of our fine hosts, shall we not?"

Cranach, for his part, didn't seem to care a whit about our secret conversation. Either that or he'd been specifically schooled by Barbara to give wide berth to any sign of tenderness between Luther and me. He stood, bade good night to both of us, and left the room, muttering something about seeking the warmth of his own wife for his own bed.

No sooner did he leave than Luther followed suit. He drained his cup and stood, stretching, like a great, sleepy bear. He shouted a farewell to the house in general before bending low to me, placing a chaste kiss upon my cheek. Withdrawing, he whispered, "Need I warn your hosts about your penchant for sneaking biscuits into bed?"

I shivered, not only at the memory of my long-ago confession, but at the tickling of his breath upon my nape.

"Never fear. I've put away many childish things." I looked up to find him still close—close enough that I could kiss him, with very little effort on my part. Not only because of his physical proximity, but because every word of our conversation invited my advance. Or my acquiescence. I engaged in neither, opting instead to lift my glass for a final, bracing sip.

"Speaking of the wisdom of fathers," Luther said, having taken a step back, "didn't yours once say that a life of drinking wine led to a life of shedding tears? There was a time, my Kate, when you wouldn't touch a drop."

"There was a time, Herr Luther, when I had so many other reasons to shed tears. Now, I believe, I'd be hard-pressed to find a single one."

"You are happy, then?"

"I am."

He smiled, satisfied. It was what he had promised me, after all.

Chapter 29

I don't know why I expected to see him the next day. Perhaps because I spent my night tossing on my feather mattress, wondering if he was warm. The year before, when he'd stayed on as a guest at the Reichenbachs', I'd come to the breakfast table late, having learned his habit to spend the earliest hours in prayer and study. By then I had my own copy of his translated New Testament, and I read it faithfully, marveling at the intertwining of the three: the ancient texts, my own language, and Luther's own hand penning the phrases. On this morning, I opened my testament and ran my hand along its page. To think that, during my final years at Marienthrone, existing from one scrap of paper to the next, he had the luxury of all this knowledge. How could I help but marvel at a God who would join our lives together?

I tilted the Scripture toward the morning light but could not bring my eyes to focus. Rather, I could not bring my *mind* to focus. Every phrase dissolved into a vision of Luther's profile against the firelight. The words of our Savior melted into a single command: *Only ask and it shall be given.*

Could it be that I'd never asked? All those years ago, when the confessor and the little girl spoke for the first time, that had been the answer to a multitude of need. Hunger, cold, loss. How faithful God had been to provide, to meet my needs and fill my life with people who would love me in a way my own family never would. He took me from my cruel brothers and surrounded me with loving sisters—Therese and Girt closest of all. Sister Elisabeth and Sister Gerda were mothers to me, God himself my father. These he gave me, without my asking.

I hadn't asked for Jerome, either. I never prayed for him to love me—I simply assumed he did, and mourned when he did not.

I never prayed for Luther, either. I never asked for him to love me in the way a man loves a woman. I never expected him to be anything more than a voice on the other side of silence.

God gave, without my asking. The same God who kept me safe from a stepmother's punishing spoon brought me to a home where I could live and learn at the guiding hands of a caring woman. Yes, I'd known hunger, but never starvation, and after so many months in this home, my stomach ached from overindulgence more than it ever had from emptiness. My room was often too warm in winter, the fire blazing too hot for one person. My hands had grown softer for lack of labor, my mind sharper with unfettered access to books of all subjects, my soul surrounded by Scripture—open to my own discovery. Beautiful art graced every wall, fine furnishings in every room. My ears rang with laughter and music and conversation.

All of this, because of Luther.

I wanted to tell him that—to share with him my revelation of the morning. To confess, maybe, as I had all those years ago, though I couldn't pinpoint the sin. A passive faith, perhaps, trusting God in hindsight. Allowing Luther to be the agent of God's gifts. Only now, with full clarity, did I see the need to make my desire known to God.

I want a husband, Lord. Not a suitor, not a lover. A man and a home and children. I want . . .

I dared not voice it, not even in the silent space between my mind and my heart. Perhaps such a prayer deserved more than silence.

I closed the precious tome and set it in my lap, my hands folded upon it. Eyes open, staring at the ring glinting gold on my finger, I spoke.

"Martin."

I could articulate no more.

He—Luther—was not at the Cranachs' table for breakfast that morning, and I chided myself for even imagining the possibility. Neither was he there for supper that night. Nor the next. Nor the next. I did not remark upon his absence, having no reason other than the expectations built in my own mind. Still, Barbara noticed my distraction, my startled reaction to each summons to the front door, my suspicious inquiries about the night's supper menu.

"Do you think the goose is large enough? Or shall I go to the market for another?"

"Shall I make dumplings for the stew?"

"Perhaps another bottle of wine from the cellar?"

If she suspected my intent, she said nothing to force a confession. She indulged my ruse, informing me that, no, Luther was not joining us tonight, without ever speaking his name.

Four days passed when the art-covered walls and the comfortable roaring fires and the plush furnishings proved every bit as prisonlike as the sparse, cold surroundings of the convent. I donned my warmest cloak and boots and declared I must step out for a breath of fresh air.

"So late?" Barbara asked, looking up from the ledger she was balancing.

"It's not quite five o'clock."

"That means less than an hour until dark. Wait a moment, and I'll have one of the servants go with you."

"I'll be fine. Just to the pharmacy and back, to see if I can get a tincture. I feel a headache coming on." Which was true—the nascent pain sprouted right behind my eyes. "As much, I think, from the dry air in the house. The walk will probably prove just as fine a remedy as anything."

"Well, if you see my husband at the pharmacy, tell him to close up and come home. And if you don't see him there, pop your head into *Der Rote Bart* and deliver the same message."

Der Rote Bart was a small tavern frequented by Luther and Cranach and their friends. I promised to send Cranach home from whatever the venue, and turned to leave.

"Oh, and Katharina?"

I paused at the door.

"If you run into Martin, send our regards, and tell him we miss him at our table."

Outside, the snow fell in thick, soft flakes, and I turned my face up to it, the way I knew I would do were he at my side. The Cranachs' house was the grandest on the street—the grandest in the city—but before long I was surrounded by much smaller, humbler homes. Here children raced by, enjoying one last run before being called in to supper. Contrarily, I slowed my pace, taking in the smells coming from the kitchens, listening to the sounds of life: the jangle of bells on a harness, far-off chimes ringing the hour. I greeted my neighbors—some by name, others by smile.

I walked until my steps fell not on the hard-packed dirt, but the uneven cobblestones that ran the center of the streets leading into Market

Square. The snow fell harder, and my legs felt the incline, more pronounced with the gathering slickness on the ground. I passed Cranach's pharmacy on the corner and, noticing the windows were dark, took no action to see if Cranach was within. As I suspected, the fresh air and exercise cleared my head as much as any powder might have done.

The booths of Market Square were empty too. Butchers and farmers and others long packed up and home. I could no longer deny even to myself my true destination. To *Stadtkirche* at the top of Castle Square, where, on the intervening lawn, a line of girls made a solemn trek from the chapel to the ramshackle building that was their school. I imagined a frugal supper awaiting, followed by an evening of reading Scripture and then sleep on narrow, inadequate beds. They wore red cloaks pulled full around their faces, but the last little girl happened to turn, and I saw brown-button eyes looking straight at me. I lifted my hand—just bent at the elbow—and offered an imperceptible wave, which she returned in kind. Then I gave a cautionary gesture, warning her to turn her attention to the path at hand, lest she—or I—be found out by the mistress setting a strident pace at the front of the line.

She obeyed.

More than once it had been brought to my attention that I could become an instructress at this school. I was adequately educated, and a capable teacher. Always the suggestion came with the unspoken caveat of *if you do not marry* . . . And so, politely, I'd hummed something agreeable and assured all that my love of children would, indeed, make this an ideal situation. But looking at the column of marching red robes struck a core of familiar sadness. I wanted to teach, yes. My *own* children, in my *own* home. Each passing day, month, year, took that dream further and further from my grasp.

Yet, as the grand doors of the Castle Church loomed large in front of me, I forced myself to remember that no dream, if planted in the heart of one called to God's purpose and spoken in prayer with faithful assurance, ever remained unfulfilled.

It was a midweek evening, no call for the church to be occupied, having been so recently emptied of the girls and boys from the neighboring schools. The windows glowed pale, the doors were shut tight, but still I ascended the steps. I knew the doors were open to those seeking sanctuary, and though I could claim no peril, I saw myself no less deserving, if nothing else to escape the snow that now fell in a solid, swirling curtain. My hand on the latch, I noticed—as I did each time I stood here—the nail marks on the door. Once again I marveled at the man who would take such an action. Moreover, I wondered how I could ever be worthy of his affections. And with the past four days of silence, I couldn't help but doubt them.

What was I thinking? What would I say? Suppose I opened the door, walked in, and found Luther behind his pulpit, scribbling sermon notes. Or more likely, engaged with a congregant, their heads tipped in earnest discourse. And I would bluster in, sodden with snow, to say . . . what?

Where have you been these four days?

No. While I still had pride intact, I dropped my grip of the latch and turned my back to the door. My feet had left a path leading up, which I obscured on my way down, and once to the street, I took a sharp left toward *Der Rote Bart*, legitimizing my presence in the street, alone, at this hour. Just here to fetch the master at the mistress's request.

I could tell from looking through the window that the tavern was crowded, and not surprisingly, given the weather. Inside, I knew university students would be packed like straw in a ticking, steins raised in camaraderie, voices raised in song. It was a respectable establishment, one I'd been in just twice before—once with Herr and Barbara Cranach, and once with Luther, when he invited us all to raise a glass in honor of his birthday.

So dense was the gathering of patrons, I could barely wedge the door open, and I had to squeeze myself through. While the bulkiness of my cloak made for a tighter fit, I was grateful for the garment to protect the brocade stitching on my overskirt. Inside, the air was steamy and warm, the atmosphere amiable. Nobody offered me a second glance, allowing anonymity as I searched the crowd for a familiar face. Cranach, primarily, as was my task, but I hoped for him to be sharing a drink with an old, dear friend.

I wedged between shoulders and dodged elbows and kept my eyes trained from face to face.

Then, a familiar voice in my ear.

"Fräulein?" Louder, "Fräulein von Bora!"

Behind me, Nikolaus von Amsdorf, by far the most distinguished-looking gentleman in the establishment—a fact that held true no matter where he happened to be. Rarely had I seen him without Luther nearby, so once I'd offered suitable greeting, I craned my neck, looking for a second familiar face.

Von Amsdorf, too, appeared to be searching for my escort. "What brings you here?"

"I'm here to fetch Herr Cranach. Is he about?"

"Frau Cranach sent you out in this weather?" The dear man looked genuinely concerned, as if ready to bring the woman to task on my behalf.

I leapt to her defense. "Not at all. I love the first real snow and wanted to walk out in it. She only asked if I would stop by."

"Did she?"

Von Amsdorf's suspicion was infectious, and my own doubts surfaced. Never would she risk her husband's pride by having a guest beckon him home—not when he might be thrice in his cups with his peers. She, like me, gifted with a woman's aptitude for ruse, intended me to follow through just as I had. A convenient search for Luther.

"I don't see him," I said, rather than perpetuate the falsehood. "So I'll be on my way." I didn't see Luther, either.

"It's cold out. Would you not like something bracing before heading back?"

"No, thank you, Herr von Amsdorf. I would not want to be late for supper."

"Wait, then. Let me settle up and I'll walk you back. It's growing dark."

"Really, there's no need—"

"Don't worry." He leaned close. "I won't try to wrangle an invitation to supper. I have plans to dine with a friend."

"With Luther?" The question flew out before I could stop myself.

He reared back, surprised. "Did he not tell you?"

The closeness and the heat of the room began to take their toll, and my throat went dry. Why had I refused a glass of wine? "He's said nothing of import. Is he out of town?"

Von Amsdorf raised a finger. "Wait here."

En route to a table in a back corner of the room, he caught the attention of a serving girl and handed her a generous stack of coins taken from a leather pouch, indicating it was to pay for not only his drink, but those of his tablemates as well. I recognized a few by face, though not by name, and I returned their amiable greeting with a ladylike acknowledgment.

"Shall we?" And von Amsdorf touched his hand to my back in escort.

Outside, the weather had turned into a true winter's night, and I accepted the arm offered to me as we began the walk back to the Cranachs' home.

"It's a heavy snowfall for so early in the season," von Amsdorf said, and I agreed.

"Has Luther flown away to escape it?" I attempted a shot of levity. "To Spain, perhaps, to tackle new Catholics in a more temperate climate?"

"Nothing quite so far, nor so dramatic. Only to visit his parents. He got word two days ago that his father had taken ill, and left straightaway. I'm surprised he didn't leave a message, with Cranach at the very least."

"Why?" My interest piqued. "Why would he tell the Cranachs?"

"Because it's growing cold and Cranach's house is warm, their table full, and the company pleasant."

I exhaled a slow breath of relief, knowing I should inquire about the specifics of his father's health, but not wanting to pass up the opportunity to ferret out some detail of Martin's idea of *pleasant company* at the Cranach house. "I'm sure Luther realized our paths would cross at some point and you'd tell me. Rather, us. At the house. Besides, he owes us no account of his time."

"Still, it's rude. I'll tell him so at the first opportunity. Bring him to task."

"Do you really have that kind of an influence on his behavior?"

"I've known Luther as long as I've known anyone, outside my own family. I can't imagine what I couldn't safely relay."

His words extended like an invitation. The snow fell between us, almost thick enough to act as a confessor's screen.

"Would it be safe to say that Luther sees you as an equal confidant?"

"I'd like to say yes, but I'm not sure I hold that place. Luther confides in the Lord and seeks his counsel above all others. I don't know that any mere mortal could convince him to do—or not to do—anything he didn't perceive to be directed of God."

"So you can speak your opinion, but he can defy you?"

He chuckled. "I've no authority, so it's hardly defiance, but yes."

"In what regard?"

"Well, now you're tempting me to gossip, Fräulein."

"Not at all, Herr von Amsdorf. I simply wonder at your scope of influence."

"In what matters?"

"Matters of safety, for instance. Do you find he is overly bold?"

"In some matters, perhaps. In others, not nearly bold enough."

Our conversation brought to mind evenings when I danced with this man. For all his broad-shouldered athleticism, he was a gifted and sprightly dancer. Here our feet maintained a slow, steady stroll while our words circled around each other, not quite touching directly.

"In matters of theology he seems dauntless," I said.

"Yes, and fearless in the face of the Church. But matters of the heart . . ."

We'd come to the corner of the Cranachs' property, and I stopped, putting myself directly in front of him, lest he seek an escape from both my company and my inevitable query.

"Matters of the heart?"

"Fräulein, you cannot expect me to speak in detail."

"Only this." And I searched my mind for the single best question to satisfy my unsettled spirit. "Do you think he truly cared for young Ave?"

My question was answered with a hearty guffaw. Loud enough to startle me, and I half-expected it to summon curious neighbors. I pouted in defense. “He said as much, you know.”

“Ah, never trust what the man says about women. The Church still has a grip there, I’d say.”

Snow fell on my lashes, as I’d raised my face to look at him. My eyes stung with the cold, and I knew my nose must be red as a beet, my cheeks as well, yet he loomed composed and handsome as the day I met him. Why could I not love him instead?

“So you think there’s a chance he’ll never marry?”

“I hope not.” He gripped my arm, reassuring. “Meaning, I hope he *will* marry. To complete his stand against the Church, if for no other reason.”

“But there are other reasons.” I battled the snow to keep my face upturned, wanting von Amsdorf to see me, framed in white, so the next time he and Luther had this conversation, no matter the circumstances, he might recall this image. Then, without another word on the subject, I wished him good night.

Chapter 30

The tree brought in for the Cranachs' Christmas celebration had surely been a Goliath in the midst of its Black Forest home. Seeing the tree was too large for even the grandest hall inside, Barbara consented to have it on display in the courtyard out front, so that all of the residents on the street could enjoy its beauty. On the evening of the winter solstice, all who wished were welcome to come decorate its branches. By the time the stars shone bright, so did the tree below, festooned with white ribbons and glass bulbs that reflected the light of the dozen surrounding torches. Walnuts were wrapped in imitation gold leaf and affixed to the branches, while the lowest boughs hosted small wooden toys, tucked in by the neighborhood children. Cranach gave each one a coin for their contribution, knowing some gave their greatest treasure, and promised they could reclaim their playthings on Christmas morning.

This, my second Christmas outside of the convent, bore little resemblance to the first. Here I was an accepted part of a family, not a tolerated guest. I participated in planning the festivities and gave orders to the staff with authority equal to those with the Cranach name. I cringed to think of the woman I'd been just a year before, her heart tied to a man who had made it perfectly clear he held no real affection for her. This year, not only was the tree taller and more grand, so too were my own hopes for my future. Luther had written me twice in the five weeks he was home with his ailing father. The first, a belated explanation for his absence and an early assurance that while his father was indeed ill, he showed great signs of a full recovery. The second, addressed to me personally, promising that he would be back in Wittenberg in time to celebrate Christmas. By the twenty-first, in fact, to attend the Cranachs' celebration.

And that he hoped, especially, to see me there.

I read it over and over, counting the words, counting the days, remembering that our friendship began through reading his words. Even a note this brief brought his voice to life and ignited an ache of absence within me.

Gathered with the townsfolk in the courtyard in front of the grand house God had given me as my home, I feigned enthusiasm for all the activity. When a child bolted up against my skirts, I smiled and tousled his hair, all the while scanning the crowd for Luther. The hired minstrels struck their chord, and I hummed along with the hymn, too distracted to remember the lyrics. When I finally saw him, his familiar black cap bobbing above the crowd, it took all of my composure not to elbow my way through our guests in pursuit of a greeting. Instead, I took a deep breath, focused on the expanse of evergreen in front of me, and poured my heart into singing about the Christ child.

Soon, I thought, *he'll be beside me.* I imagined his tenor joining my uncertain alto as it had so many times before. And yet, by the time we concluded with *amen,* a crowd still mingled between us. Which brought me to question—should I approach him? Coyly let him approach me? The prospect of any kind of meeting grew dim, as he seemed determined to keep his head turned in an inconvenient direction, shaking hands and sharing greetings with half a dozen men—notable members of the town council, great supporters of his work and ministry. I nudged myself a bit closer, overstepping the baker's wife and the seamstress who had recently fitted me for a new Christmas dress.

When a light snow began to fall, the musicians begged to go inside. Cranach's voice rose above the crowd, shouting a greeting and farewell to all, wishing blessings for the season, and the crowd divided along unspoken but perfectly understood lines: those who would be invited in to continue the festivities, and those who would fellowship out in the snow for a time before returning to their own homes—or to *Der Rote Bart* for a pint of ale to stave the chill. I, of course, joined the trickle of those headed inside and was pleased to see with a glimpse over my shoulder that Luther would be joining us too. I did not, however, recognize the man who accompanied him. Tall and gaunt, with an untrimmed beard and wearing a coat even shabbier than Luther's, he appeared at ease with the prospect of going inside. If he were an entire stranger to me, though, surely he must be somewhat of a stranger to the family, and I looked on to see if Luther introduced him to anybody in particular. He did not. Instead, as we neared the massive double front doors, Luther—finally—caught my eye, saying, "Fräulein! At last!"

While he didn't specifically instruct me to wait, I did, my arms folded, both in a brace against the cold and a growing sense that I needed a barrier. We were on the front steps, ready to walk inside, and still the stranger lurked.

"*Herr Doktor*."

At my greeting, the two looked at each other conspiratorially. "Which of us do you suppose she addresses?" Luther said, smiling at some private joke. Then, finally, he stepped back and offered an introduction. "Fräulein von Bora, may I present to you Doctor Kaspar Glatz from our parish at Orlamunde? Kaspar, the intrepid Katharina."

Glatz studied me as if I were some new puzzle. He did not extend his hand until he had used it to tug at his beard, having come to some decision. "Our mutual friend has misrepresented you."

"Has he?" I made no attempt to hide my suspicion. "That's no surprise. It is one of his favorite hobbies."

Luther alone laughed, then ushered us across the threshold, acting every bit the host and master of the house. He urged Glatz to go into the dining hall and avail himself of all that surely awaited there, all the while holding the crook of my arm. "I apologize for the delay in introduction," he said, leaning close. "Between my father's illness and a slight crisis of congregation—" at this he looked meaningfully at Glatz before continuing—"it seemed to be one obstacle after another getting the two of you within speaking distance of each other. But here you are."

"Indeed." I had no choice but to respond as if I understood the nature of Luther's statement, as he seemed so jovial. So accomplished.

"And what he said about my *misrepresenting* you? I have no idea. His form of flattery, I suppose. But rest assured I've been nothing but complimentary. That you are lovely of face and quick of wit, and seemingly endless in all that you set out to learn and accomplish. If anything, I have *understated* your vast appeal, so as not to scare the poor man off. You can be quite intimidating, you know, my Katie."

Understanding dawned as he spoke, bringing no comfort with it. I reined every muscle in my *lovely* face to utter stillness, lest the salty burn at the back of my throat betray me. My *quick wit,* the one that I'd assumed was a match for Luther's alone, begged to protest. This? This was the suitor about whom he'd hinted all those months ago by the fire? Every adjective he'd ascribed—older, less handsome, learned—applied to both men equally, and a person with no inclination to the working of the heart might find them interchangeable. But Glatz was *not* Luther. Not my friend, not my confidant, not the voice that had guided me to freedom with Christ, outside the walls of a convent. Just another suitor brought within my grasp. Worse, still, the fact that I, too, deserved so little consideration. Knowing full well the pain I endured at his previous matrimonial effort, Luther showed no hesitation to toss me out again. The entire business just that—a transaction, like a dispute with a butcher over a cut of meat.

Luther prattled on, but I heard nothing as my mind worked to settle which of us had been more blind to the other's intent. At the moment, the only one of our newly constructed trio with any sight appeared to be Glatz, who reappeared with a cup of wine in one hand, a piece of shortbread in the other, and eyes that roved about the room, taking in every detail. Unfavorably.

"It is a very good wine our host has provided," he said, marking the first time I'd ever heard such a statement delivered with a scowl. "Too good for such a crowd."

I rushed to Cranach's defense, smile frozen on my face. "Isn't that a hallmark of good hospitality?"

"I meant only that a good many of these people surely qualify as casual acquaintances at best. Myself included in that number. This seems a wine to be shared with those more intimate."

"I might be able to assure you that Herr Cranach has even finer than this in his cellar. But seeing as you have not thought to bring me—"

"Did I not say?" Luther interrupted, draping a genial arm across my shoulders, its weight unbearable. "A sharp one, she is. But I vouch for the impeccable taste of our host. Allow me to bring you to him and reintroduce you. If I recall, you've met on several occasions."

Luther steered Glatz away, and I felt my body press against my corset in exhalation. Certainly such insufferableness had been on display before. My instincts told me this was not the first glass of wine to be criticized by *Herr Doktor* Glatz, and it would not be the last. As I stood back and watched the two men in conversation, I marveled that they had anything to talk about at all. Yet

Cranach greeted him warmly, as did Barbara, though she sent me a look that only another woman could interpret. She, too, had taken measure of Glatz, and had found him wanting.

By now we had been drawn into the great hall, where the musicians struck up a tune, and the floor cleared for dancing. I stood along the wall, foot tapping, grateful for the servant who came by with warm mulled cider. The mug warmed my hand, and the spices proved pleasant, if for no other reason than the fact that I knew their worth, having purchased and measured them myself. Gazing at the crowd around me, I realized I knew most of them by name. I knew the names of their children and the nature of their businesses. They were worth every poor copper handed over at market and would be served in solid gold cups if such were available.

Luther was soon at my side again. "Did you see the tree? What am I saying, of course you saw it. The whole city can see it."

"That might be a bit of an exaggeration," I said, speaking with disciplined politesse. "But it is lovely, isn't it?"

"Waste of lumber." Glatz had returned. "And all the baubles on the branches? Wasteful and ostentatious."

"Do you dance, *Herr Doktor*?" I determined to find something amiable about the man, for Luther's sake if nothing else.

"I did when I was younger. It is a sport of youth, I find."

I pointed to Herr Cranach and Barbara engaged in a turn. "I don't know that many of the couples would agree."

"Ah, but they have been dancing together for quite some time, have they not?" This, chimed in from Luther.

"I'll have you know I have danced with men of all ages," I said, looking around the room. "Herr von Amsdorf, for example. Is he not here?"

"He is not," Luther said.

"Pity," I said, with my best attempt at coquettishness. "He is my favorite of your friends."

Glatz took no offense at my comment. In fact, I had no evidence that he even heard. He was once again nibbling on a piece of shortbread, clearly annoyed by a young boy who tore through the crowd, brandishing a shiny silver coin. Upon closer study, I realized he was not glaring at the boy, but at our host, who had given it to the lad in return for singing a chorus of the minstrel's song.

"What?" Luther said, clearly understanding the scene as I did. "Do you not think the boy deserves a reward?"

"It seems an excessive amount for so small a task."

"Then you should be well pleased to hear *Herr Doktor* Luther sing," I said. "He often gets no reward at all."

"My, you are sharp," Glatz said, his tone far from complimentary.

"Surprisingly so," Luther said, prompting my apology.

"You've been away too long," I said in way of explanation. "I've been too mired in civility. But I shall temper my words in order to make a good impression on our new friend here."

"Kaspar is an *old* friend of mine," Luther said. "But a new one to you, and I hope the two of you will become well acquainted over the course of the season."

"The season?"

"I'll be staying here until after the New Year, at least." Glatz said. "In a residence at the university."

"How nice." I took a sip of my cider.

"We will both be joining you for Christmas supper," Luther said. "As of yet, that is our only invitation here."

I looked at him over the brim of my cup. Surely I had no power to issue an invitation to supper—or even an afternoon call. Clearly, though, I was expected to do something of the kind. For once, however, I made it my business not to live up to Luther's expectation.

Chapter 31

Two roast pigs, their snouts nearly touching, lay in the center of the table, surrounded by mounds of vegetables, baskets piled high with bread, platters of sausages, and bowls of steaming cabbage. I was seated among the guests with Luther nowhere near enough for conversation. To my right, an unresponsive councilman; across from me, his unpleasant wife, leaving Glatz, conveniently at my left, as the sole person with whom to pass the meal.

"All of it, quite delicious," he said, catching the server's eye for another helping. "I was invited last year but had the duties of my church to tend to. Rest assured, I'll not pass up such an opportunity again."

"They are good, generous people," I said, holding back the observation that the quality of food must finally meet the quality of the guest.

"So measured by the loyalty and praise of their friends."

It was the most complimentary statement I'd heard him make about anybody, and I allowed myself to reflect upon him, thinking that perhaps I'd judged him too harshly upon our first meeting.

No amount of reconsideration would render him higher than Luther in my esteem. I still felt the sting of my misunderstanding, and glad that I hadn't made any kind of rash declaration. Upon a second look, I could concede that Glatz was a handsome man—well preserved in his years. And yet, he lacked any truly distinctive feature. I imagined myself scanning a crowd, looking for him as I so often found myself looking for Luther, and I realized I might pass my eyes right over him without recognition.

As an experiment, I turned to listen to the rantings of the councilman on my right—something about the rising cost of maintaining the university, and how it should shoulder a greater share of the budget—and found I'd almost completely forgotten what Glatz looked like. Try as I might, I could not conjure his face, to the point where, when I did turn back to him, I was startled by his appearance. Had he been replaced by some other man, one of the many who passed in and out of Cranach's pharmacy, for example, I'd have been none the wiser.

"Describe him to me," Ave had said when she and her husband appeared in the hour before supper. Having shared Luther's latest attempt to marry me off, under the guise of amusement, I found myself devoid of a single adjective to paint a picture of the candidate.

Only two aspects stood clear. First, the unforgivable state of his dress. I, at the Christmas table, wore a new red gown—new in the sense that it had been given to me by Barbara Cranach, then tailored to my figure and embellished with a rich pattern of gold stitching and a thick stripe of velvet.

Glatz, on the other hand, wore the same shabby outfit he'd worn upon arrival to Wittenberg four days ago. Well I understood the constraints of poverty, and even more the eschewing of fashion in light of ministerial pursuits. Luther, to be sure, wore plain clothes taken from a sparse wardrobe. But when society demanded, they were always clean and mended, and tonight he'd taken special pains to match the magnitude of the celebration. His black coat brushed free of lint, his stockings without mends, his sleeves without stains—and all this I remembered from the few minutes' observation upon his arrival hours before. On the occasion that he leaned forward, bringing his head into my view down the length of the table, I marked how his hair had been newly trimmed, his face shaved clean.

"Tell me, Fräulein," Glatz said, calling my attention back to him completely, "being so established in this household must be quite a change from your life as a nun. Have you acquired a taste for such a lavish lifestyle?"

"A taste for it?" I smiled, emphasizing the coincidental timing of the remark as I speared a chunk of baked yam and popped it into my mouth, chewing throughout the awkward silence that followed. "I wouldn't say a *taste* so much as an appreciation for the prodigious amount of work that makes such a household possible."

"Work?"

"With great wealth comes great responsibility."

He looked like he wanted to reply, but chose instead to take another slice of pork from a passing platter. An odd thing to do, as his plate sat full before him; then I noticed his new serving didn't go onto his plate at all, but into a large, square napkin, which he folded and knotted and slipped into his coat pocket. Too late, I averted my eyes from his action.

"Don't bother yourself being embarrassed for me, Fräulein. I assure you I am not so much poor as practical."

I smiled politely, as if nary a disparaging thought had entered my mind. "When I was a little girl, I used to take biscuits from our dinner and sneak them into bed. I confessed my sin to the priest, and he chastised me, warning me that rats could come in the night to nibble it away."

"Perhaps I risk a greater danger of being followed home by a neighborhood dog?"

It was the first I'd heard him attempt a joke, and I rewarded his effort with a chuckle and a promise that I, too, would be sneaking a sweet from the table to my room.

“So, we are not so different after all, Fräulein?”

He said it with such a sense of sweet conviction, I had not the heart to disagree.

Shortly after Christmas, it became clear to all who knew me that Glatz had in his mind to be my suitor, and that he did so with Luther’s encouragement and insistence. Both men came to call nearly daily, and after a time, Glatz came alone, bringing with him opportunities for long, awkward stretches of silence, leaving Barbara to fill the void with neighborhood news. We graduated to taking walks together, when the temperature allowed.

“I would like to show you my home,” he said one evening. It was the first week of March, with a distant hint of spring in the air. My mind was preoccupied with thoughts of the garden, what I might plant in the corner over which I’d been given full stewardship. Peas, perhaps. Or some other legume. The household did not observe strict meatlessness on Fridays, but I enjoyed cultivating new recipes, soups especially, with a thicker, more substantial broth—

“Fräulein?”

He’d been speaking, for quite some time if his frustration was any measure, and I apologized for my absence of mind. “You were saying?”

“Only that I would like to take you to my home, to let you see where I live, even temporarily.”

"*Herr Doktor* Glatz—" I feigned blushing offense—"I don't know if that would be proper without a chaperone."

He laughed, a not-entirely unpleasant sound, and assured me no one would give a second thought.

Bereft of excuses, I agreed and tucked my hands deeper in the woolen muff, though the late-afternoon sun made it almost too warm.

"Can I ask you where you were, just those few minutes ago? What were you thinking?"

It was the most intimate question he had asked, and I felt I owed him honesty.

"My garden—the section I oversee at the Cranachs'. I was thinking of what I might plant."

He seemed satisfied and asked no more.

We arrived at the small home, built with the sprawling university and *Stadtkirche* in plain view behind it. I glanced up, wondering if Luther might be inside, working on notes for an upcoming sermon, or writing some correspondence. I hesitated long enough on Glatz's threshold to cause him again to ask for my thoughts, but this time I said nothing close to the truth, only that I wondered where I should scrape the mud from my boots.

"No worries about that," he said, but I made a show of wiping the soles of my boots on the stones in front of the door.

Though the outside of the house made no secret

of its humble nature, the interior was monastic in design. A small, square table, two high-backed wooden chairs. A measly pile of wood scattered in the metal box beside the cold, dark fireplace. A closed door must have led to a bedchamber, and before I could stop myself, I pictured a thin, narrow bed within.

"Modest, I know," Glatz said, making no move to ask me to sit on either of his two chairs. "But clean."

"Very much so." I had to take his word, as there was not enough light to confirm. It was colder in this room than it was outside, the windows small and high, limiting the light. "Though it's small enough that it wouldn't offer much of a challenge to a charwoman."

He waved off my words. "The parsonage in Orlamunde came with a small staff, but not here. I do my own cleaning, actually. And have learned to make a few simple meals on my own."

I'd been witness to his *simple meals.* More than one had been pilfered and pocketed beneath my very nose.

"But why not hire a woman?"

"Because it would fall to me to pay her wages."

He spoke without discernible pride, only a blatantly stated fact that I could not help but take as a challenge.

"Don't you see that you are preventing some woman from earning an honest wage?"

"Good women do not seek to earn a wage. They seek marriage."

I said nothing, not wanting to engage in this topic of conversation. Obviously, I was a woman with neither a wage nor a husband. Only a minute within these walls, and I knew well what Kaspar Glatz would be willing to offer.

"Might be best," I said, "seeing that this is a temporary home for you. How long will you be in Wittenberg?"

He accepted my evasion with surprising grace, and I felt my first twinge of pity. "I've not yet decided. Rather, it hasn't been decided for me. Where and when the Lord would have me go."

"Isn't that the case for us all?"

"I suppose it is."

Silence, then the scraping of a chair, and Glatz's offer for me to sit.

"A glass of wine?" he asked when I was comfortably at table. "It was a Christmas gift from Cranach. One of his best, I'd say."

"Thank you, but no." I had no desire to have anything but a clear, sharp head. "In fact, I should get back soon. I'm expected for supper." And I prayed he would not take such as an invitation.

"Very well." He returned the bottle to its cupboard, unopened. "But before you leave, I want to make one thing clear to you."

"You've nothing to make clear—"

"This is not all I have. I have cash enough

for a fine home. A farm, even, should I choose. Nothing like what you have now—"

"Please." I was desperate to stop him. "I have nothing of my own. Nothing other than my character and my conscience. Nothing to bring—"

"I am not a young man, clearly. Neither are you a particularly young woman. In that, at least, we are matched."

"You can't . . ." I stood and took a purposeful step toward the door. "You mustn't—"

"Fräulein, please." He nearly barked the words with the type of unpleasant authority that begged both obedience and contempt. "I've no intentions of molesting your person."

"I didn't believe you would, sir." I would not insult him with laughter, though somewhere in my darkest recesses, amusement took hold. "I simply cannot encourage this conversation further. I must leave."

"My only wish," he continued as if I hadn't spoken a word, "is some sort of companionship. As I am getting older, and my eyes fail ever more, I find I can hardly read."

The little laughter that followed simply could not be helped. "Read?"

"I've thought, lately, it might do to have someone who can read to me. And Martin told me what a bright mind you have, though I've yet to see much of it displayed. I can trust that you are literate? Even in Latin?"

"You cannot mean—"

"I am sure we can find a mode of living suitable to both of our tastes. Less lavish, of course, than what you currently enjoy. But I can concede—"

"Concede nothing." This time it was I who gave weight to my words, and he fell silent. I steeled myself against pity, as he had the decency to look embarrassed for his display. "This is neither the time nor the place for this conversation. We've been acquainted a mere matter of months, and I can truthfully say that I have not spent the time since our acquaintance in contemplation of any such arrangement."

"But Martin assured me—"

I made a dismissive sound. "This wouldn't be the first time *Herr Doktor* Luther overstepped his bounds in an attempt to secure my future."

"But he said you had no prospects. No future. That yours was a desperate situation, and perhaps my opportunity to benefit from a certain kindness and—" he gulped the word—"generosity."

Stunned, I took in the details of the room, my eyes now adjusted to the dim light. The thin layer of grime on the table, the dirt crusted on the window. If I recalled correctly, my chair had been both imbalanced and uncomfortable, and there was only one other to be had. Unless there was a chair in the bedroom. Next to the bed.

The last time a man proposed marriage to me,

my body had burned with such passion, I would have found all other furniture superfluous to our happiness. How, then, had I become—over the course of only a year—a woman who would be considered content as nothing more than a cook and a companion to an old man? How could my passion for learning be reduced to an ability to read? Here, in the gray frigidity of this room, I could clearly recall every moment Luther made me feel like a woman afire, even as my feckless heart burned for Jerome. Going back, I suppose, to the first moment I beheld him in the street below my window at the Brummbär Inn. When he slid my ring upon my finger. When he held strands of my hair, like a man in the throes of restraint. I'd held his gaze at dinner, the candlelight no doubt enhancing my features. I knew what it was to see him talk to the bore at his left while his eyes saw nothing but me. I knew none other who could make him laugh with the abandon I cultivated. I'd never seen him in silence so profound as the times we sat together by a dying fire. Yet Luther not only disavowed the power I had over him, but implied that I would *generously* apply it to any man of his choosing.

"Is that what he said?"

Glatz had the goodness, at least, to be chagrined. "Not in so many words."

"But in spirit."

"If you recall, upon our introduction, I said he had been misleading."

"You did." I gathered my skirts, preparing to leave. "So if nothing else, we should both have come to the conclusion not to believe a word that comes out of the man's mouth."

He drew up. "How dare you speak of the man that way."

"I dare, because I know him. Better than you do, for all you might claim. Now, I'll take my leave, and I'll ask you not to call on me again. If you are a guest of the Cranachs, I cannot refuse your company. But our intent toward each other has been made, I believe, perfectly clear. And we have no mutual understanding."

Glatz paid me the highest honor by making no move to hinder my exit. He said not a word, even as I struggled with the swollen door, and I gave no glance over my shoulder to see if he stood within its frame. I would not turn around, *could* not turn around, because the stinging shame of my tears would have presented such a weakness of my sex as to give credence to Luther's claim: that I was weak, desperate.

Half his age, and he said I was not a young woman.

Able to speak in circles around him, and he said I am not bright.

There would be no glance at *Stadtkirche* as I stormed away, caring not a whit where Luther might be, or what he might be doing. The pace of my walk stirred my blood hot enough to match my anger, and I could feel my face flush, then cool as the breeze blew against my tears. I must have been a frightful sight, a fact confirmed by the curious glances of those I passed. Some, familiar, offered a cautious greeting, which I curtly returned. Others *tsk*ed and turned their heads, unsympathetic to my distress.

I slushed through the semi-melted snow, careless of the muddy and wet consequences to my skirt. This wasn't my best gown, by far. My oldest, actually, given as my first encounter with charity only hours after climbing down from the wagon in Torgau. My new, best red gown I kept away, pressed and ready for a visit from Luther, as he'd remarked on the color it brought to my cheeks.

I wished—truly, for the first time since leaving Marienthrone—for the comfort of my sisters. A childish longing for Sister Odile and her generous lap, Sister Elisabeth and her purloined spice cake, Sister Gerda and her insulated wisdom—any of them would be able to tell me, without hesitation, that I had been given the mind of Christ, and that my future would not be held hostage by marriage, to any man. I did not regret my freedom, for I relished every brisk, unfettered step I took, but I had no idea I would become some sort of bartered prize in the hands of the man who orchestrated it.

At Schoenberg Street, I came to the place where a turn to the left would bring me to the Cranachs'; to the right, Market Square, still buzzing with activity. Not ready to face Barbara and her winsome curiosity about my afternoon with Glatz, I turned to the right and felt the welcome return of composure as I wove throughout the booths and shops. My ears rang with the merchants' calling, and I traded a few of the coins in my pocket for a book of poetry. Something frivolous, as I felt I was due, along with a small bag of sweet biscuits and a pot of jam, which I would share with the Cranachs once I'd eaten my fill.

By then I'd taken myself far from the main street and worried I'd lost my way when I turned a corner to see Luther, not ten feet away, coming from a stationer's with a bundle of fresh, clean paper tied with red string.

"Katie!" he called, as if he had some right of affection or authority to summon me so in a public place.

"*Herr Doktor*," I said, once the distance had closed enough between us to allow me to greet him without raising my voice.

He frowned. "You seem displeased for a woman walking so freely with her purchases on an afternoon in nearly spring."

"Well, then, I must be, as you are the expert in all avenues of my emotions."

"What's this?" Then he took on a pitying look I had come to hate. "Ah, Katie. You must have heard the news."

From the look on his face, the news was nothing good. "What news?"

"It's Baumgartner."

"Jerome?" It was all I could do to speak his name as a certain dread closed around my throat. "Has something happened to him? Is he ill?"

Luther's expression grew more grave. "Worse, I'm afraid. He's engaged."

He allowed the ruse to continue for a second longer before bursting into his mischievous grin as I traveled a reactionary journey from relief to irritation to something bottomless within me that defied anything I'd ever felt before.

"That's a terrible joke, Luther."

"I'm sorry. I meant only to lighten the moment."

That's when I noticed he clutched my arm, as I must have appeared faint. I shook off his grip.

"I'm a grown woman, capable of handling the truth, especially when it is a truth that doesn't affect me in the least."

"Doesn't it?"

"No."

"Because your affections have been claimed by another?"

There was no way to answer truthfully. "No, Luther. They haven't."

"I see." He rocked back on his heels and tucked his package under his arm. "And you don't foresee any change of heart?"

"Not mine."

My answer seemed to settle the discussion, even if not to his satisfaction, and I allowed him to declare the matter closed with a final, decisive sound. "May I see you home?"

Minutes before I'd been angry enough to wish never to see Luther again. But he'd been estranged, of late, and even this conversation served to cleanse my palate from the unpleasantness that defined any moment spent with Kaspar Glatz. I must have taken too long to respond because he assured me he had no intentions of keeping me from either my new book or my new pastries.

"I shall abandon you at the door upon arrival," he said, offering me his free arm. Rather than take it, I clutched at my bundle, my muff slid up to the elbow, and fell into an easy, familiar step beside him.

"You told me once," I said, "that you would not speak to me if you saw me in the market."

"I was speaking hypothetically, in conjecture of a world in which I did not know you."

I did not bring up all the other things he had said, about how he would think me to be a *charming girl. Lovely in face and enticing in figure.* In fact, our walk was accompanied entirely by unspoken words. He did not ask about Glatz; I did not tell him. Yet the matter was settled between us. The whole matter of Glatz had lived and died through suggestion and innuendo; why dredge up details now? I asked nothing about Jerome's engagement, not the name or nature of his fiancée, knowing gossip would reveal all details soon enough. And I did not—would not—share my feelings for him, having had two such devastating truths revealed to me. First, that he saw me in such a despairing light. Second, that in the cold, hard light of such knowledge, I loved him still.

Chapter 32

When I came inside after my walk home that afternoon, I forgot about my new book of poetry. Instead, I went immediately to Barbara Cranach, pulled her away from the kitchen, where she was giving the cook final instructions for supper, and insisted that she listen to the entirety of my tale. My love and loss of Jerome, my contempt for Glatz and the clumsiness of his confession, and the depths of my feelings for Luther. She listened to it all without a hint of surprise and offered no comment beyond a broad, soft bosom on which to rest my sob-wracked head.

"And so," I said when the power of speech returned, "I cannot see him again."

"But that hardly seems best. Let me talk—"

"No. I don't want to add embellishment to that image he already has. That I need someone to be cajoled into having me. The last squab on the platter, growing colder and less appetizing with each passing moment."

She chuckled. "You're hardly a squab."

"You're right. I don't know that I merit even that distinction."

"You *will* see him again, in the same capacity in which you always have. He is a friend of our family, a welcome guest in our home, a member of our community, and the leader of our church. What? Did you think you would simply lock yourself away in your room every time he comes to dinner?"

"No." I swallowed, bracing myself to voice my actual thought. "I thought it might be time that I leave this place."

"*Leave?* Our home? Your home? Where would you go?"

"I'm a qualified governess. Or teacher—maybe even at the girls' school here. I could find a room—"

"You have a room. Here."

"But surely when I arrived here, you had not thought for me to stay forever."

"Truthfully? No. I hoped not, because I knew Luther wanted to find a husband for you. He still wants that, I'm sure."

I tried to smile. "So did I, until today. But I want to love the man I marry, and I want to marry the man I love."

"As you should. In the meantime, you'll stay on here, just as you have been, without argument, and without sulking. There's no shame in caring for a man, and I won't have you hiding away as if there were."

And so, I did not. Her words prompted a new

surge of strength. I allowed my prayers to take on a new confidence, praying not for Luther's love, but for his safety, and the continued efforts to bring people into the same freedom I now knew. I worshiped under his leadership, singing hymns penned by his hand. I sat under his instruction on those Sundays he taught from behind the pulpit. Each time my heart wandered into longing, I took it captive and turned to Scripture to find a more fitting object of desire. To learn, to read, to study in a manner befitting the risk I took with my very life.

Still, though, in all of this, I allowed myself to embrace what it meant to be a woman of my age and standing. With my second year of freedom coming to a close, I embarked on a quest to embrace all forms of vanity so long denied during my years beneath the veil. I could not turn back the years, could not wake up in the morning as a dewy-faced girl of nineteen, but neither did I need to comport myself as a fitting mate for a nearsighted man in need of a reading companion.

With Barbara's help, I adopted a new hairstyle, winding my braids in a crown at the back of my head, with the front left in long, loose curls that fell to my shoulders. My ears were pierced, and I took to wearing a pair of earrings given to Cranach as payment for a portrait.

"But on condition," he said, "that you sit for me for your own portrait."

"Do you think I am ready?" It was one of those rare evenings when only the three of us supped in the family dining room.

He considered me for a time. "Not yet."

In a sense, I did hide from Luther in that I was always before him, but always out of reach. Any evening he came to the Cranach home for supper, I sat myself beside him but spoke only as much as good manners required. If I found myself in another's home, at another table, I maneuvered to sit as far away as possible and made great sport of catching his eye. I wore my red dress with more than fashionable frequency and sought two more gowns in equally flattering colors, collecting them from Barbara Cranach's generous friends, then altering them with my own brocade and stitchery to make them unrecognizable from their original style.

The previous spring, I'd been too preoccupied with Ave and the preparations for her wedding to take full advantage of all the social opportunities in the small town of Wittenberg, but this year I would not make the same mistake. Once released from the somber observance of Lent, the town embarked on a season of celebrations. Grand houses, like the Cranachs', hosted banquets and balls, with music and dancing that lasted well into the morning. When there was no home to host, the community hall opened wide its doors to men and women of all society faced off in long lines of dancing. Here I was held aloft in the strong arms of a blacksmith, touched hands to the butcher, and locked elbows with the man who had sold me my favorite book of poems.

Luther was here, too, as was Glatz, marking his final evening before returning to Orlamunde. I danced with neither. Not with Glatz, of course, because he never indulged, and not with Luther because we had a long-held understanding that we did not dance with each other. On any other occasion, however, he would be at my elbow, in my ear, commenting on the couples, pointing out the next best prospect for a turn. On this night, I kept myself on the other side of the room, knowing with the musicians' every flourish, my face flushed a little more, my breath came with an attractive heaving, and my eyes shone bright enough to catch his. I offered no smile, no wave, not so much as an acknowledging crook of my finger. But his eyes, I knew, never left me. In fact, I felt every eye on me, knowing I was the whisper of the town—the former nun, the last to be unmarried, shamelessly on display.

While I may have exaggerated my status in the eyes of Wittenberg, I did not imagine one particular set trained upon me as I drained my cup of the delicious, fruity concoction dipped from the large bowl at the back table. They were as distinct as the evening I first saw them, just as bulbous and unforgiving. Frau Baumgartner, her face both round and pinched, coming to a point with her ever-disapprovingly pursed lips.

Startled, I turned my back to Jerome's mother to hide the straightening of my dress, the patting of the sweat from my brow, and the deep, bracing breath I would need to face her.

"Fräulein von Bora?" Her voice dripped with empty friendship. "It is still *Fräulein*, is it not?"

I ran my hands the length of my bodice and offered an equally forced smile. "Frau Baumgartner. What a surprise to see you here."

"I would have hardly known it was you. You've—" she made an obvious search for the word—"changed."

I dipped my cup again, my eyes scanning the crowd over the brim, thinking there must be someone who could rescue me, when I saw Nikolaus von Amsdorf making his way toward me.

Escape.

"If you'll—"

"Surprisingly enough," she continued, "we do have some family in this city, so we've come to introduce Jerome's fiancée. Have you had an opportunity to meet her yet?"

"I have not. Ah, Herr von Amsdorf." I could hardly stand up under the relief. "I believe you had the next dance, did you not?"

"I did." He offered his arm, nodded to Frau

Baumgartner, and took the cup from my hand, setting it on the table. He led me away, steadying me as I stumbled against his step.

The musicians were mid-tune in a complicated dance of intertwining couples, nothing we could immediately join, making me doubly grateful for his participation in our ruse.

"Where are you taking me?" I asked, as we were clearly not joining the dance.

"Outside," he answered genially. "You need some air."

I tugged myself back. "I don't have to leave. I belong here as much as anyone." My belligerence surprised me, as did the very sound of my words, thick within my mouth, and rounder than they should be.

"You're a little *beschwipst*."

"Drunk? I haven't touched the wine."

"The punch, Fräulein. Just as dangerous."

"Oh." I glanced over my shoulder to see if Luther was watching, wondering what he might think of such a display; instead, I saw a face equally familiar.

Though it had been months, I reacted to the sight of Jerome Baumgartner as if I'd seen him just yesterday. The same thick, dark hair, the same shadow of a beard on his face, the same dark lashes that would fan across the top of his cheeks when he closed his eyes. His eyes were not closed, however. They caught mine and held in a steady gaze, causing me to grip von Amsdorf's arm all the harder.

I tucked my face into the crook of von Amsdorf's neck and whispered loud enough to be heard above the music. "Is that his fiancée?"

"It is. Fräulein *Geldsack*," von Amsdorf said wryly.

The young lady in question may have been blessed with wealth, as von Amsdorf's unflattering nickname alleged, but she was a homely girl, with sallow cheeks and a dreary expression. She clutched Jerome's arm like a farmer's wife with a wayward goat. Though her dress was the height of fashion and made from material finer than I'd ever know, she seemed little more than a form within its frame. It seemed to touch no part of her body, unlike the lank hair that escaped from her cap and lay in spears against her neck.

"Sweet Saint Paul, von Amsdorf. How rich is she?" My own question brought me to a fit of laughter, undaunted by the cupping of my hand against my mouth, and he speeded our progress through the crowd and out into the courtyard, where a ring of torches gave light and warmth against the chilly spring night.

Once we were safely outside, von Amsdorf informed me that she was from a very important family.

"Ah, yes." I stood on my own. "Well I know the

importance of a good family to the Baumgartners. But I repeat: how rich is she?"

He smiled, creating handsome planes in the torchlight. "Very."

"And how young?" He looked uncomfortable, and I continued. "It's a fair question. The girl still has pimples on her face."

"Fourteen," he said, and I made him repeat it.

"So." The ground was spinning again, and I backed into a stone bench and sat down. "I've been thrown over for an ugly child?"

"We've always said Baumgartner was a fool." He sat next to me. "Unworthy of you."

"We?"

"Luther. Me. Anyone who knows the tale."

"Except Frau Baumgartner."

"Yes, except her. Luther isn't happy with the match at all."

"I don't give a fig what Luther is and isn't happy about." Again my words surprised me, but I knew they rang true—not a product of too much punch. "I believe he has grown too fond of his own opinion."

"You know he holds you in high regard."

"So high that he would foist me onto a man like Kaspar Glatz?"

Von Amsdorf said nothing, but his silence conceded my point.

"Am I so undesirable?"

"You know better than that, Fräulein. If

anything Martin would be hard-pressed to find anybody he deemed good enough for you."

"Then why not him? Or you?" I laughed, a sound far too bitter, considering the lingering sweetness in my mouth. "I declare in this moment I will consider only two men *worthy* of me. You, because you are handsome, and a fine dancer, and have the physique and—I assume—the vigor of a man half your age."

He laughed but did not disagree.

"Or Luther. Because I love him."

There was enough of a reaction on his part to assure me of the sharpness of my senses and the fact that I had confirmed a suspicion he'd long held.

"Have you told him this?"

"Not in so many words, no. And I'm asking you, as a friend, not to tell him either. I don't know why I said anything—and no, it is not because I am, as you say, *beschwipst*. It is a truth I have carried longer than I can say."

"You have my word," he said, and I utterly trusted him.

Inside, the crowd applauded the end of the song, and von Amsdorf held out his hand. "Shall we?"

I shook my head. "I can't go back in there. I can't face him."

Had von Amsdorf asked me if, by *him,* I meant Jerome, Luther, or even Glatz, I would not have been able to say. Thankfully, he did not ask. He simply took my hand and brought it to his lips, placing a lingering kiss that made me wish I could open my heart to him.

"Do you want to know why I think Luther never considered a marriage between you and me?" he asked, looking up over the back of my own hand.

"Yes."

"Because I am one of his closest friends. We will always be in each other's lives. And I don't think he could bear it."

Whether or not they were true, von Amsdorf's words healed me in a way no priestly absolution ever had, and I brought his hand to my lips to kiss. "Will you go inside and find the Cranachs? Tell them I've gone home?"

"Of course. Wait here, and I'll escort you."

"No, please. I don't want to infringe on your evening. They've a coach here, and a driver."

"A coach? On such a fine night, for such a short walk?" He inhaled, expanding his strong, broad shoulders. "Nonsense. I'll send word in to Lucas, and then I'm walking you home, so you can tell me every word you said to that skinflint Glatz."

Chapter 33

I chopped the spade into the earth, creating dark, orderly furrows. Barbara had tried to convince me to give this chore over to the gardener, sparing myself the labor, but as the sun beat warm on my back and the ground moved cool beneath my hands, I was glad to have taken it on for myself. Even though I might come away with blisters on my palms and an ache between my shoulders, in the moment I felt alive. Healthy and strong. Birdsong and soil filled my senses, and I hummed as I worked, a tune no one else in the household would recognize. Eventually the words joined me in my toil:

The white doves are flying,
The white foxes slipping,
The white rabbits jumping—
Over, and under, and right through the wall.

Intermittently I hummed and I sang, trying to remember just what I thought I would find on the other side. Here, too, I lived behind a wall. My own choosing of late, as I hadn't accepted a single social invitation since the *Frühlingstanz* where I'd seen Jerome. Then again, none had been extended. Still, the boundaries had fallen unto me in pleasant places, as the psalmist wrote, and if I lived my life with my comfortable room and a generous garden, it would be enough. My Savior promised me an eternal inheritance; I lived as his daughter in this world.

I began humming again, thinking of those creatures bent on escape. I was the dove, sent out first and living with the promise of God's provision. I was the fox, wily and quick, slipping into the houses of great, important families, stealing all I needed. And the rabbit—quick to avoid the snare.

"That is an unfamiliar tune," said a familiar voice behind me. I straightened and turned to see Luther at the garden gate. He picked up the melody where I'd left it and hummed it to perfection as he walked toward me.

"It is of my own invention," I said, resuming my task.

"Is there a lyric? I am always searching for new hymns for the congregation."

I smiled slyly, even though he couldn't see my face. "I don't think this is a song you would want your parishioners to sing."

"Not bawdy, I hope?"

"Not at all. Merely subversive."

I hacked at the earth, imagining each strike of the spade's edge to be a sharp word said against him. Challenging his characterization of me as a weak, desperate woman. *See? How strong I am. See? How capable.* He, however, chipped into my anger with every note of my tune. He'd gone from humming it to expressing each syllable—*"Da-da-da-da-di-dum"*—as if he knew the words and chose not to sing them. After a time, I wished to join him, to lay down my tool and tell him the story and share with him the wonder of how such a sweet, simple image had turned into new life for so many women. Marriages, children—new families born of our doves and foxes and rabbits.

Stubbornly, though, I held my lips shut and increased my efforts, until Luther, his voice choked with frustration, said, "For the sake of sanity, Katie. Put that down and talk to me."

I stood straight again, leaving the tool lodged in the dirt, but did not turn. "What have I to say to you?"

"Plenty, from what I've heard. Now, come."

I felt his hand close around mine and tried to snatch it away. "You'll get dirty."

"I don't care."

Luther kept his grip, leading me to a long, rough-hewn bench along the garden wall. He let go as I sat down and took to pacing the length of it in front of me while I made a valiant attempt to tuck my stray hair behind the plain gray kerchief tied around my head and dust the lingering grains of soil from the apron I wore over my dress.

"Kaspar Glatz has left town," he said, then paused for my reaction. I gave him none. "And he told me before he left that you said you would not have him for a husband."

"*I* told you that day at the market that I would not have him."

"No, you told me that you had no affection for him."

"That is the second side to the same coin."

"Hardly." He stopped directly in my sight and stood, hands clasped behind his back like an expectant schoolteacher. "One need not have affection in order to embark on a marriage."

"You are correct about that, *Herr Doktor*." I dared not look up at him.

"Von Amsdorf says I was a fool to even suggest such a match. His opinion of my friend is surprisingly unfavorable."

"Which friend?" I asked. "Herr Glatz or me?"

"Ah, my girl, you know he is unreasonably fond of you. And ever since I first proposed to mediate an introduction between you and Kaspar, Nikolaus has been vocally opposed. On more than one occasion he has said that you are far too fine a woman to have such a skinflint foisted upon her."

I cringed at the familiarity of the insult. "You must believe me when I tell you that I never used such a phrase to disparage Glatz's person."

"But do you now object? I see not. So it was

not merely a matter of Nikolaus leaping to be your champion."

He spoke it not as a question, so I offered no commentary. Yet the specificity of his words assured me that the two had discussed more than Glatz's parsimony.

"What else did Herr von Amsdorf tell you?"

In response, Luther began pacing again. "Despite what he thinks—or you, or any of the hundreds of people so willing to advise me on matters that are little of their concern—I am not some great, sexless log."

Before I could stop myself, I tasted garden dirt on my tongue as I clapped a hand over my mouth to stifle a laugh. "No one has ever said—"

"I may lack the youth of that fool Baumgartner, but I assure you, if given the opportunity, I shall show myself more than capable of marital vigor."

Then I did laugh, right out loud and lustily, though I knew a more timid maiden would blush at the implication. Luther, I could tell, appreciated my laughter, rewarding me with an approving gaze that lapped at my indignation.

"And I," he said, "unlike Kaspar Glatz, do not live in a state of poverty by choice. I have nothing, Katharina, to offer a woman. He has money enough to buy a home for each season, and I maintain a single room, cold in the winter and insufferable in the summer. Never mind luxury. I can scarcely offer comfort."

"I seek none of that." I spoke softly, not directly to him, as he had yet to offer me the little he had.

He came to sit beside me and touched his knuckle to my chin, lifting my face, forcing my gaze. "I gave my life to Jesus Christ the moment I left the priesthood."

"As did I, even before I left—"

"But unlike you, I live in a certain danger because of my decision. My actions. Always. A price on my head, a threat on my life. Dear friends of mine have been lost to this conflict with the Church. So to say that I would offer a woman—that I would offer *you*—my life . . . I have not even that to give. Daily I live only by Christ's protection and grace. How can I give what is not mine?"

"I ask you for nothing, Luther. You say you have no wealth; I ask for no wealth. You say you have no life? I ask for nothing more than . . ." I stopped and turned away, humiliated at the onset of tears and devastated at his gentleness as he untied the kerchief, setting free my hair, and handed it to me to dry them.

"Nothing more than . . ."

"Nothing more than what was promised. Freedom to pursue the life of my choosing. Not just a husband. I didn't forsake my vows simply to gain favor in marriage. You didn't either. But couldn't it be that our freedom released us to find each other?"

I remained still as a rabbit in the field, waiting upon his response.

Finally, with a voice too soft to startle, he spoke. "It is my greatest joy, Kate, to find you. When we are apart, I hear your voice. It echoes without words, pleasant as the tune that beckoned me today. I long for your opinions, silly as they might be at times. I anticipate your face, and when I know I am to see you after some long absence, my steps quicken to find your company. My eyes do not rest until they fall upon your countenance. You are dearer to me than any friend."

My heart soared as he spoke, like the dove over the wall, but faltered at his conclusion, for he unequivocally defined me as a friend, and I knew after this conversation, I would have to be so much more. Or nothing at all.

I took his hand, opened it, and laid my own within. I stared down, mesmerized by the sight of our flesh intertwined. "Do you know when I first heard your voice? Not from the confessional, and not that day in Torgau, when you asked about *the women.* Not the sound you make when you speak, but your *voice?* It was months before. Years, even, when I held a scrap of paper with your writing. 'The Freedom of a Christian.' "

"I remember sending that to you."

"Not to me directly, I know. But I was the

first to read it, and somehow, I heard it in your voice. God whispered it to me, calling forth such a longing to understand. I wanted nothing more than to talk to you. And as I questioned, I felt you answer. Your letters, your messages, your translations spoke to me. Oh, my darling." Slowly, I lifted my gaze to find him waiting. "From the moment I held your words, you have been my home."

I watched, intently, looking for any change in his countenance. Relief, consternation, enlightenment—anything but this mask of control. When he spoke, I sank at the familiar refrain.

"I have no worldly goods to give you."

"In that, we are equal."

"And—" he held my hand tighter—"I will not mislead you in the matter of love. For I cannot say even now that I offer you the entirety of my heart."

"I know that." And I did. I always had.

He traced his finger along the thin gold band I wore. "I shall have to buy you a new ring one day. But until then, Fräulein von Bora, would you be content to simply take my hand?"

"In what way do you mean?" I would not suffer another bout of misunderstanding. I deserved a true proposal in the midst of such indirection. A sweet breeze came, blowing cool against my neck and lifting my hair to bring it—a mass of tangled strands—in a veil to obscure my vision.

Gently, Luther—Martin—smoothed it from my face, and there I found him changed.

"As my wife, in every way that God intended."

In response, I took his hand and laid it to my breast. "You have my heart, Martin. Fully and completely. And for now, I am content to share yours."

He stood, drawing me to my feet, then closer still, into an embrace, and kissed me. Sweetly at first, fraught with trepidation. Finding no resistance on my part, he pulled me closer, his fingers tangled in my hair, my hands—their dirt long forgotten—touched to his cheeks. When he pulled away, I marked his transformation complete.

"You shall have everything that is mine to give, my Kate." I could not mistake the dimension of his meaning. Our kiss had awakened something he feared had lain dormant too long. Age—his or mine—had not tempered desire. "All I shall ask you to share is my joy, and my sorrow."

"That may be said of any marriage. I want more. I want to share in your thoughts. Your conversation." I could see he intended to kiss me again, and I braced against him. "I want to know that my mind will hold a place in our home equal to any other part of my body."

"I assure you, I should like nothing more than to begin and end each day hearing your voice in prayer."

"What about those times when I am not in prayer?"

"Well, then—" he kissed my brow—"I can think of no other sound more pleasing to punctuate the hours of our solitude."

I closed my eyes, content in his embrace. With him I could foresee no solitude at all.

Author's Note

Dear Reader,

It is just occurring to me now, at this minute, as I type this late in the evening and days past deadline, that I am going to meet Katharina von Bora Luther someday. She has been dwelling in the back corner of my mind since that summer night in 2014 when, frankly, I first heard her name. In the shorthand of my writing, I have always called this project *Luther*. But it's never been about him. It's never been about *them.* It's been about her. And the day will come when I will meet her in glorified perfection.

What is not glorified perfection, however, is this work of fiction. While I have tried to be true to the history and the biographical facts of the characters involved, I have taken some license with others to smooth the story.

A few points of note:

For me, the story fell together with this excerpt from Martin Luther to Jerome Baumgartner, dated October 1524, in which he writes: *If you want your Katie von Bora, you had best act quickly, before she is given to someone else who wants her. She has not yet conquered her love for you. I would gladly see you married to each other.*

Throughout the portion of the story when Katharina is considering the essence of her salvation and her life as a nun, I bring her into contact with Luther's writings. I tried to strike a balance between those writings that would best suit the story and those that would be true to the narrative chronology. If I failed on that part, I offer apologies to the Luther scholars and hope they will allow themselves to be swept up in the romance and forgive me.

For all of Katharina's days in the convent, I relied on research not for her specific order, but for the details of cloistered life for the surrounding centuries. I have included book titles at the end of this note. The ritual and dialogue for the ceremony in which Katharina takes the veil are born completely from my imagination.

One purposeful omission for the sake of narrative is the fact that Katharina had another relative at Marienthrone. In addition to her cousin, the abbess, she had an aunt (some sources liken her to more of a cousin as well), named Magdalene (Magdalena), who was one of the twelve nuns who escaped that Easter night. Because the escape occurs about one-third into the story and my research gave up no real details about an ongoing relationship after, I opted to excise Magdalene from the story to better focus on Katharina. Now I'm thinking how really awkward that heavenly reunion might be. . . .

Every time a finished book falls into an author's hand, we think of a million things we would have done differently. Better words, other scenes, different structure, stronger sequence. Given that this book was first nothing but a whisper followed by months of doubt, years of fear, and a constant undertow of anxiety and inadequacy, I'm looking at the final manuscript with a sweet sense of satisfaction. I plan to enjoy that until the book falls into readers' hands, and then I truly hope to hear that you've become as taken with Katie as I am.

Your Sister,
Allison Pittman
October 31—Reformation Day—2016

The Habit by Elizabeth Kuhns
Virgins of Venice: Broken Vows and Cloistered Lives in the Renaissance Convent by Mary Laven
Convents Confront Reformation: Catholic and Protestant Nuns in Germany by Merry Wiesner-Hanks, translated by Joan Skocir and Merry Wiesner-Hanks
Nuns: A History of Convent Life by Sylvia Evangelisti
In Her Words: Women's Writings in the

History of Christian Thought edited by Amy Oden

Katharina von Bora: A Reformation Life by Rudolph Markwald

About the Author

Allison Pittman is the author of more than a dozen critically acclaimed novels and a three-time Christy Award finalist—twice for her Sister Wife series and once for *All for a Story* from her take on the Roaring Twenties. She lives in San Antonio, Texas, blissfully sharing an empty nest with her husband, Mike. Connect with her on Facebook (Allison Pittman Author), Twitter (@allisonkpittman), or her website: allisonkpittman.com.

Discussion Questions

1. What kind of faith examples does Katharina receive from the authority figures in her younger years—Sister Odile, Sister Gerda, Father Johann, Sister Elisabeth, Abbess Margarete? Who had a formative influence on your own early experiences with faith—for better or worse?

2. Young Katharina wonders, "Why would God make a little girl with a dead mother and a weak father and mean brothers? Why would he make her if all he intended to do was pick her up and drop her in this place, surrounded by other girls whose lives held no more meaning? . . . Why couldn't God have made me to be happy in *this* world, and to serve him in the next?" How would you answer her questions?

3. When she reads Luther's work "*The Freedom of a Christian*," Katharina especially puzzles over this line: *"A Christian man is the most free lord of all, and subject to none; a Christian man is the most dutiful servant*

of all, and subject to every one." What do you think it means for a Christian to be both subject to all and to no one?

4. Girt, Therese, and Katharina all grow up together under the same restrictions and circumstances. How does each respond when faced with an opportunity for escape? How do you imagine you might have responded in their place?

5. Outside the convent, Katharina takes pleasure in the abundance of the Reichenbach household—the material comforts she's suddenly surrounded by. How can we enjoy the comforts of our lives and homes without developing a materialistic focus?

6. Do you believe Jerome Baumgartner truly loved Katharina? Did Katharina handle her side of their romance as she should have?

7. Lucas Cranach claims Katharina wasn't ready to have her portrait painted, arguing that only the powerful and the innocent should be thus portrayed. What does he mean by this? Do you agree? It is interesting to note that, in real life, Cranach did paint the best-known portrait of Katharina von

Bora. At what point in her life do you think the fictional Cranach would have deemed her "ready"?

8. Katharina realizes how many of her needs have been met without asking God for them, and that she's never voiced to God the deepest desire of her heart. Have you ever been guilty of "a passive faith, trusting God in hindsight"? Do you struggle, as Katharina did, to lay your desires before God?

9. As she is portrayed in the novel, what character traits does Katharina possess that would make her a successful woman today?

10. What did you think of this story's portrayal of Martin Luther? In what ways did it align with how you might have imagined him? What surprised you?

11. Though each had a great deal of admiration and respect for the other, the marriage of Martin Luther and Katharina von Bora was probably not inspired by our concepts of romantic love. Luther's decision stemmed from more of a religious obligation; for Katharina, it was a necessity. Where do you think the idea of marriage falls today?

What do you think is better about the way marriage is viewed now? Where might we gain wisdom from the models of the past?

12. While not addressed in the novel, Martin and Katharina Luther went on to have a long and loving marriage. What aspect of their unusual courtship do you think is most responsible for setting up a successful marriage?

Books are produced in the United States using U.S.-based materials

Books are printed using a revolutionary new process called THINKtech™ that lowers energy usage by 70% and increases overall quality

Books are durable and flexible because of smythe-sewing

Paper is sourced using environmentally responsible foresting methods and the paper is acid-free

Center Point Large Print
600 Brooks Road / PO Box 1
Thorndike, ME 04986-0001 USA

(207) 568-3717

US & Canada:
1 800 929-9108
www.centerpointlargeprint.com